DARWIN'S BASTARDS

SELECTED &
EDITED BY
ZSUZSI
GARTNER

ASTOUNDING TALES *from* TOMORROW

DARWIN'S BASTARDS

Douglas & McIntyre
D&M PUBLISHERS INC.
Vancouver/Toronto/Berkeley

© 2010 D&M Publishers Inc.

Introduction © 2010 Zsuzsi Gartner

Stories © 2010 Adam Lewis Schroeder, Lee Henderson, Douglas Coupland, Stephen Marche, Yann Martel, Timothy Taylor, Mark Anthony Jarman, Jessica Grant, Elyse Friedman, Annabel Lyon, Anosh Irani, William Gibson, Buffy Cram, Paul Carlucci, Sheila Heti, Heather O'Neill, Oliver Kellhammer, Laura Trunkey, David Whitton, Pasha Malla, Neil Smith, Jay Brown, Matthew J. Trafford.

10 11 12 13 14   5 4 3 2 1

Douglas & McIntyre
An imprint of D&M Publishers Inc.
2323 Quebec Street, Suite 201
Vancouver BC Canada V5T 4S7
www.douglas-mcintyre.com

Library and Archives Canada Cataloguing in Publication
Darwin's bastards : astounding tales from tomorrow /
selected & edited by Zsuzsi Gartner.

ISBN 978-1-55365-492-6

1. Short stories, Canadian (English). 2. Canadian fiction (English)—21st century.
I. Gartner, Zsuzsi
PS8329.1D37 2010   C813'.6   C2009-907194-0

Cover and interior design, lettering, and illustrations by Peter Cocking
Printed and bound in Canada by Friesens
Printed on paper that comes from sustainable forests
managed under the Forest Stewardship Council
Distributed in the U.S. by Publishers Group West

Mixed Sources
Cert no. SW-COC-001271
© 1996 FSC
FSC

We gratefully acknowledge the financial support of the Canada Council for the Arts, the British Columbia Arts Council, the Province of British Columbia through the Book Publishing Tax Credit and the Government of Canada through the Canada Book Fund.

Some of these stories have been previously published in various journals in different forms: "Survivor" by Douglas Coupland in *McSweeney's*; "Personasts" by Stephen Marche in *Conjunctions*; "We Ate the Children Last" by Yann Martel in *Grain*; "Remote Control" by Annabel Lyon in *Geist*; "There is No Time in Waterloo" by Sheila Heti in *McSweeney's*; "Crush" by Oliver Kellhammer in *Vancouver Review*; and "Fire from Heaven" by Laura Trunkey in *Vancouver Review*.

CONTENTS

A FEW HUNDRED WORDS
FROM THE EDITOR

on EVOLUTION, PROPHETS (false & otherwise),
GODS & MONSTERS, HISTORY, the Possibilities
of LOVE (or something like it), the FUTURE,
MORAL IMAGINATION, DYSTOPIAS & UTOPIAS,
my idea of FUN, the concept of –ISH, and,
of course, DARWIN & BASTARDS.

JUST THIS MORNING my son said to me, "You know how some mutations are successful and some aren't?" Honestly, these are the kinds of things I wake up to, the sleep not yet out of my eyes. "In the world of the book you're reading, or in our world?" I asked him. I didn't say "in the *real* world" because we both know the world of a story is a real world too. It turns out he meant both, and followed up with a nine-year-old's rapid textbook synopsis of evolution and adaptation that would have had your average proponent of Intelligent Design sticking her fingers in her ears and humming I *can't hear you!*

But in the world (or rather, *worlds*) of the book my son is reading[1] it turns out that with each successful mutation of a species the world splits off into another frequency where things evolve differently—so there are multiples of our Earth, same year AD, but with no road not taken. In one of these frequencies there exists a being that looks like a giant, purple, five-armed baby, a fish-head with tentacles and the lower body of an eel

---

1   *Ignatius MacFarland: Frequenaut!* by Paul Feig (also the writer of an adult memoir called *Superstud*).

("feels," they're called), and big spiky trees with thorns for bark. And a cat-*ish* creature, and a dog-*ish* creature.

Ish. Bear with me.

I adore Charles (Chuck, Chas) Darwin. Not because he's the go-to guy on natural selection,[2] but because he was a man of faith whose belief was sorely tested when a daughter died young, and I'm convinced he retained threads of that faith, like a vestigial limb, long after his *On the Origin of Species* challenged the orthodoxy of the day; because of his lifelong, childlike curiosity; because for a man of science he was riddled with unscientific contradictions;[3] because in his writings he uses exclamation marks as liberally as a fourteen-year-old girl; and because at sixteen he wrote in a letter from Cambridge to a cousin: "*My Dear Fox, I am dying by inches, from not having any body to talk to about insects—*"

What would Darwin make of what has become of natural selection with humankind's aspirations to godlike dominion over all of creation? The wolf indeed dwells with the lamb: in an emboldened new world of pharmaceutical and technological wonders, of changes wrought by environmental degradation, aren't we all Darwin's bastard children?

---

2 The theory of evolution would eventually have come into being whether Darwin had existed or not. It was present in *l'air du temps*. For instance, the naturalist Alfred Russel Wallace sent a paper outlining his own version of natural selection to Darwin in 1858, and the two men quickly published a joint paper on the subject, a year prior to the latter's groundbreaking book.

3 Desperate for respite from his ceaseless intestinal and other ailments, Darwin (who may have suffered from a) hypochondria, b) panic disorder, c) Lupus, d) lactose intolerance, or e) all of the above) allowed himself to be subjected to hydrotherapy, electrical stimulation of his abdomen with a "shocking belt," and other quackeries of his time.

Genetic engineering, cosmetic pharmacology, avatar sex, Google-brains, melting ice caps, and everything virtual, nothing private. 1984 came and went and Big Brother doesn't scare us anymore because we're either auditioning for the TV show or one of its freak offspring, or else playing our own Big Brothers with blogs and webcams. And I don't know about you, but the term "recombinant DNA" fills me with as much dread these days as the words "global warming," if not more.

"For the first time," wrote the editors of *Nature* magazine in 2007 in a simpatico commentary on synthetic biology, "God has competition." And so does Darwin. The chief proponent of the technology, a Stanford professor who is also co-founder of the BioBricks Foundation,[4] told a *New Yorker* reporter this fall: "What if we could liberate ourselves from the tyranny of evolution by being able to design our own offspring?"

Are we witnessing the final evolution—or implosion—of our species? (Of all species? Speaking of scary, millions of sockeye salmon vanished from the west coast of North America this year—just like that. The grizzlies are more concerned than the humans.) Is there any doubt that the future is *now*? Will our descendants be human—or human-*ish*?

Ah, but we're writers here, *imaginative* writers, as the late master of dystopian landscapes and sensibilities J.G. Ballard called those who explored worlds other than our own (always leaving silently dangling the implication of what other writers were)[5]— not scientists or seers. Our business is to ask *What If?*

---

4 Drew Endy, former Lego fanatic and modern-day Dr. Frankenstein, and president of the non-profit foundation (which makes available the components of DNA in a kind of on-line catalogue), prefers to say he's "constructing" rather than "creating."

5 He did tell an interviewer back in 1988, "I think realistic fiction has shot its bolt—it just doesn't describe the world we live in anymore."

What if someone decoded the DNA of the Tasmanian tiger, an animal believed to have been extinct for over seventy years?—oops, that's been done. But, what if someone resurrected the DNA of Jesus Christ? What if ♀ (a.k.a. Prince) was the last man on Earth? What if celebrity became a crime? What if marauding gangs of over-educated, deeply philosophical homeless people invaded your suburban neighbourhood? What if private golf clubs were the new nation-states? What if your BlackBerry could be programmed to function like the Oracle of Delphi?

What if, just what if, someone fished the last star from the sky?

This is the part where I'm supposed to extol the far-reaching significance of these stories, of this entire enterprise; how it will profoundly change the way you perceive the world, our world, the *real* world, as well as chasten you to further reduce your carbon footprint, pour your little blue pills into the garbage, go off-line, barricade your doors against both the wolves and the sheep (and the wolf-*ish* and the sheep-*ish*), plant heirloom tomatoes and join hands and sing "Kumbaya" one more time before it's too late.

You can get all egg-heady about it, too, if you like. I could tell you that because most of these writers didn't grow up in the shadow of the Cold War, the overall spectre is not that of nuclear annihilation or forced egalitarianism, not a paralyzing (dis)order, but the chaos of capitalism run amuck, modern terrorism, collapsing ecosystems, and death by anomie and ennui. I could tell you that these writers are unafraid of engaging with pop culture, and that although most of their stories are set in the near-future[6] or in a version of our ever-changing present,

---

6 Liberally interpreted by the authors as anything from an alternate Year 2000, to a cozily close 2015, to the early 24th century.

the past haunts many of them much the way that the history of our species (and of every species) haunts our own bodies at the cellular level.

I could also wax Latinate about utopias vs. dystopias vs. the apocalyptic. In fact, I can go one better and simply quote William Gibson from "Dougal Discarnate," his meta-fictive ode to the Vancouver neighbourhood of Kitsilano: "One person's raging dystopia is another's hot immigration opportunity." How true. In Lee Henderson's "The Aurochs," a beleaguered curator of post-industrial antiquities is dying to retire from a tired Earth to luxe Mars; whereas Mark Anthony Jarman's lovesick space cowboy in "The December Astronauts" waits longingly on a colonized moon to be reassigned to Earth.

But what if I told you that this book is supposed to be fun? My idea of fun[7]—entertaining and provocative, punch-drunk on language, fizzing with ideas. And that's what I got when I asked Canadian short-fiction writers not normally known for an exploration of future times[8] for their social satire, fabulist tales, and irreverent dystopian visions of the day after tomorrow. The one stipulation: the stories could not already have been published in book form, as *Darwin's Bastards* is not meant so much to be an "anthology" as a collection of original fiction— an album of new, unheard music, not greatest hits. The response was so enthusiastic that the book you hold in your hands is almost twice as fat as originally intended, the majority of its pages seen here in print for the first time.

---

7 Also the name of a novel by British writer Will Self, author of some of the most freakishly good dystopian fictions of the past decade or so, and who could be viewed as Ballard's bastard literary offspring.

8 With the exception of Gibson (who publishes his first short story since 1997 in this collection) and Douglas Coupland, whose latest novel, *Generation A*, traces implications of a world without bees.

Surprises? Only one. That so many of these stories are about the possibility of love. Sure, there are survivors, outliers,[9] and warriors, too. But a lot of the survivors are lovers as well. And some of the lovers, warriors. All of the warriors, outliers. And the outliers do their damnedest to survive.

Regrets? Only two. There are no talking animals in these pages (at least of the non-human variety) and no giant, purple, five-armed babies.[10]

But there are the stories—kinetic, idiosyncratic, disturbing, hilarious and heartbreaking, rife with moral imagination, and deeply human. Nothing –ish about it.

ZSUZSI GARTNER
Vancouver, October 17, 2009

---

9 Before that smarty pants Malcolm Gladwell co-opted it for his 2008 book on success, *Outliers*, the term connoted "a result differing greatly from others in the same sample," and that is the spirit I use it in.

10 Adam Lewis Schroeder's talking vacuum cleaners in "This is Not the End My Friend" are pretty fine consolation, though.

SURVIVORS

ADAM LEWIS SCHROEDER

THIS IS NOT THE END MY FRIEND

Dear reader every kilometre is the farthest I have been from the ocean in my whole life story. When Carla cracks her window the air is like a sandblaster scouring mould off so she shuts it again.

"What is that?" I say

"A dead deer," says Oldy Oldster

"Composter will pick it up," says Uncle Chad. "Nothing we can do to help it, girls."

So this is where the land mammals come to die.

ONCE UPON A TIME PEOPLE ATE MEAT, writes Carla

AND PUKED IN THEIR SLEEP, I type with my thumbs. Uncle Chad and Carla and I are driving Oldy Oldster from the dock at Hope to a little town hours and hours away so he can talk to a ROCKSTAR

WHAT IS THE PLACE CALLED AGAIN? I type into my phone

Dear reader you cannot imagine how many times I have had to fix my mistakes. Uncle Chad said that before the talker software got good enough they used to TYPE everything so I am typing these words on one of their old phones he gave Carla and I so we could TEXT each other across the back seat. Half a metre to my right Carla writes into her phone it is called SUMMERLAND

I type SUMMERLAND SOUNDS LIKE A CONDOVILLE WHERE THE OLYMPIANS SOAK IN WINDEX.

THAT WAS LOATHING she types. DOES WINDEX TURN YOUR HAIR BLONDE? and she is right. I thought it was loathing too. Carla is bored now so bites her cuticles. Earrings like helicopters.

Uncle Chad says Oldy Oldster is an ethno-music-ologist called Dr. Bryant Cuban who was friends with the parents of Aunt Miriam before Aunt Miriam and her parents died in the flood. They did not die the same DAY as our parents but the same WEEK. We have had other bad weeks since then like the capsize for example but once Uncle Chad said that that one was THE WORST WEEK and he would call the story of his life THE WORST WEEK and he petted the cat so its tail twisted up his sleeve and he laughed. Like a life story is a joke and nobody would actually want to read THE CONFESSIONS OF ZRBZTZ2I or MY LIFE SO FAR BY A3B03392 but I sure would and so would the girls from the pigsty up the hill. So I am writing a life story every minute. It will start when the dike around Vancouver got a hole in it even tho I was a baby

My thumbs are so sore. Carla says her thumbs are tough from ping-pong that is why she is sending a message every two seconds about the birds flying over the trees while it takes me forever. But she does not know I found a NOTES section in the thing so I am writing the good stuff the pants stuff in the NOTES section but every five minutes I write her a message and say THIS WINCES because I cannot find the symbol to make an abbreviation so I have to write the entire word every time so I am talking like the vacuum. SORRY TO BRUISE MISS YUKON, the robot vacuum says, BUT I THOUGHT THE LEG OF YOUR SLACKS WAS THE HAT RACK. Uncle Chad said before vacuums got sentient the houses were messy but you did not have to watch for them creeping up behind you all the time. And he says MISS YUKON is funny as stink and I ought to wear my tiara more often

DR. CUBAN

Whirring east between the pines, tucked as I am behind the wheel of the rental car as Chad nods half-asleep against his seat-belt and the two girls smirk behind me, I keep having to shake my head to keep from thinking it's twenty-odd years before. The trees are so much alike, you see. In '37 I drove my colleagues to Moncton for the academic conference that would ultimately elect to preserve Alan Lomax's field recordings—rescued the previous month, you may recall, before the Smithsonian was devoured in flame—by launching them into space. But our car was stopped by an Olympian roadblock outside Rivière-du-Loup. I shut the ignition off and sat gazing at their blinking cameras, AK-47s and boom microphones, but my colleagues had evidently watched the American feeds more closely than I and so knew what these "people" were capable of, and there-fore panicked and ran for the woods. When the Olympians approached the car afterwards they actually asked for my ID—hard to believe, I know, but those were early days—and, stranger still, one of them recognized the Forces Veteran Discount stamp on the back of my driver's licence and hurried it over to their leader, a dog-collared girl of twelve. I remembered her as the Bible-quoting stepdaughter on some short-lived sitcom, and that brief celebrity must have earned her sergeant's stripes with the Olympians. With a toothy, blood-spattered grin she returned the cards and waved me under the steel hawsers, and that night, in a Moncton motel room, I watched loops of my colleagues being summarily gutted outside Rivière-du-Loup via a rebroadcast feed sponsored by Kissinger's Tooth-Whitening & Ass-Tightening Spray, while down the hall the Archival Redistribution Chair blared Lomax's record of Ervin Webb singing, "I'm goin' home, oh, YES!"

That was a new experience for me—but encountering things I'd never seen or done was far more common then. Almost two decades of stagnation ever since. These two girls in the back of the rental would scarce believe that U.S. feeds *ever* came into Canada, or that we ever made a distinction between sub-human Olympians and the tax-paying, lawn-mowing Americans of legend. Because nowadays they're all Olympians.

UNCLE CHAD

I'm dreaming I'm darning Min's turquoise sweater until Cuban says, "You asked what my interview subjects knew about all this."

I rub my eyes.

"Well," he drones, "I put my abstract in the seat pocket there. The very same draft I sent the old girl. Just look that first page over and see whether it's clear as mud."

He shifts his white-haired knuckles on the steering wheel then glances into the rearview mirror at the girls, but they're too busy texting to pay him any attention.

"All right back there?" I ask.

Carla glances outside long enough to make sure we aren't about to crash but Yukon just keeps typing, her copper hair in her eyes. I'll take the memory sticks out of the phones when we get back. This is the girl who stapled finger paintings to the condo fence; it wouldn't be like her to sit on material. Cuban taps the read-out folder with his square yellow fingernail.

"Might give you a fresh perspective," he says.

Undisclosed ID (Cuban Bryant, MA, PhD)
Chrétien University. Public © 2055 pending review.

To Fade Away?
Foreword.

Personal fame, as humanity had come to understand it, was outlawed in 2038 by 89 per cent of Earth's governments after dominant figures in the international community realized that no one was paying attention to the world going to hell—the ice caps melted to the size of tennis shoes, a single wildfire raged from Alberta to Ecuador, the world's precious stock of frozen vegetables tainted with Ebola—and that the world was going to hell because no one was paying attention. Indeed, in that year citizens of more-stable nations increased their view time on celebrity-gossip feeds to a daily average of nineteen hours, while the United States, a markedly less-stable nation, was in the throes of what could only be described as societal meltdown. The only functioning sector of the U.S. economy, in fact, remains the celebrity feeds themselves, with the most popular streaming-homicide addresses apparently commanding $1 billion monthly for marginal advertising space, though following the collapse of the U.S. banking system it remains to be seen who could afford such fees or what form payment might take. Individual U.S. communities now *secure their own fuel and food supplies, reportedly by the most violent means possible.*

Dry as toast in August. Just because he was Min's godfather doesn't mean he's going to smell like flowers or even be interesting, I guess—anyway, if the government thought enough of him to have put him on a flight from Ottawa, I shouldn't drop anchor on him. That's what I told *my* office, anyway, and they signed me off for the week—I mean, would the average claimant in our pen have any notion that they've waited a year *plus a week* for their immigration interview? Cuban paid for the car, secured travel licences, and the girls *should* see the country sometime. "The country." I showed them Min's map where the Hudson Sea is still Hudson Bay and Calgary is nowhere near the coast and their eyes just about popped, then Yukon went straight to her room to commemorate the experience of having her eyes just about pop. Which is a worry. What's she going to do with all that writing?

"Feed says forty-five degrees outside," Cuban says. "Is that normal?"

Apparently he wants us to keep him company, and I suppose it could get dangerous for an old guy heading east through British Columbia. Though I can't imagine how.

"For March? That's probably average," I say. "How is it in Ottawa?"

"Cooler than it used to be. Wind off the lakes."

The U.S. government was the only non-autocracy in '38 to refrain from enacting celebrity-secrecy legislation in any form, thus allowing its citizens' violent glory-hound agendas to continue to chart the national course. Better To Burn Out Than It Is To Rust became the "Olympians'" motto—inscribed on the smattering of currency issued in the past seventeen years, and succinctly (though

*no doubt accidentally) describing humanity's dilemma to this day,
caught as we are between high surface temperatures and even
higher water.*

"I meant to ask if you've got family out there," I say. To keep
myself awake.

The road's shoulders go out three or four metres into the
pine trees to make room for the compost trucks. Honestly, I
haven't been on Highway 3 since the '30's.

"No, no," Cuban says quietly. "Not since the vegetables. And
thankfully we never had children in the first place."

"What, the Ebola?"

"My grown niece was pregnant at the time. That was the
worst of it."

He keeps one hand on the wheel, plucks a wiry hair from his
neck and rolls it between thumb and forefinger.

*Accordingly, in '38 the Canadian federal government outlawed
any and all communication with the United States, began construction on a five-metre-high barrier along the two nations'
6400-kilometre primary border—a floating barrier where it
bisects the Great Lake—and passed its stringent Universal Privacy Act. Canadian actors and musicians were purportedly shut
up in safe houses between performances to remove them from
public scrutiny, but in practice these individuals were exiled to
isolated communities. (Of course, thanks to rising seas—Hudson
Bay's eradication of both Manitoba and Saskatchewan being the
most glaring example—what community does not seem isolated
these days?) The enactment of the UPA fell short of full-blown
Stalinism only in that the artists and intellectuals of our era were
not, to the best of our knowledge, murdered outright. In '42 any
creator deemed able to contribute anonymously to the "cultural
dialogue" (which in my opinion is simply the commitment to not*

say anything) was issued a Public ID and allowed to produce some form of work for distribution via federally subsidized broadcast feeds. Any existing cultural material deemed "distractingly popular" was eradicated via digital virus, though in the case of artists too well entrenched in the public consciousness—Stan Lee, Eli Roth, Franklin W. Dixon—the eight provinces' Ministries of Education now insist these individuals were merely figureheads for bland corporations.

Lord, couldn't he have been a professor of poker strategy?

YUKON

Chad said an ethnomusicologist studies what old music means to a country and its people and I said LIKE ROCKSTARS? and Uncle Chad said EXACTLY and touched the point of his nose. He can remember when everyone knew who the famous people WERE. Dear reader that would have winced. It is better to be secret. For example I SOMETIMES THINK ZRBZTZ2I IS A MAN WITH A BEARD and sometimes I imagine it is a seven-year-old girl sitting in her room talking to the software but I do not care who it is. I just like every one of their songs. Plus it is dangerous if it is not secret because then all the work for the world would be undone for example gpm36c spent 21 hours every day reading about MS CHILDISH O TOOLE then after everything went secret gpm36c invented the OZONE SPIT VALVE. In school we learned Vv3bV was just as distracted as gpm36c before Vv3bV ever thought to sink congeal-pods under the Arctic Circle

I actually typed SOMETIMES I THINK IT IS A MAN WITH A BEAR before, dear reader, so I went back and fixed it but I ought to have left it because that is pants, that is so good

UNCLE CHAD

We're a hundred clicks from Princeton but hydrogen is down to 18 per cent according to the windshield feed. Which wouldn't be such a cramp if Cuban's breath wasn't a mash-up of herring and garburator.

> *None of the far-flung politicians who enacted similar legislation in '38 have been seen publicly since, and though text-only candidates have purportedly been running and winning in elections for the past seventeen years, the public has no way of knowing whether Cameron Miller, for example, hasn't remained as Canadian prime minister to this day.*

"Specifically," I say, "Miller's brain in a jar."

"Some people will tell you that," says Cuban, eyes glued to the road.

> *All this is public knowledge, of course, but I feel it necessary to establish a rhetorical framework in which to construct the arguments that follow, more often than not from the perspective of the artists themselves. I will recommend changes to federal policy that will never be implemented. I will ask what we've lost of our souls.*

"But more likely," I grin, "it's his cat that's been running the show. A brain in a jar wouldn't have lost its mind over those über-protectionist tariffs."

"Maybe you ought to drive," he says.

He pulls onto the shoulder and I get rattled by the gravel thunking against the chassis. I'm used to the boat. Over my shoulder the girls straighten up in case they have to dive out the windows.

"Now how will the university get it published?" I whisper. "I understood the Equanimity people didn't want any policy out in the—"

"Oh, speak *up*, Chad! It's a rental car—they'd hear if we played charades!" Cuban jerks up the anchor brake. "Even if the book never comes out, at least *someone* at Equanimity will read it." His eyebrows climb his forehead, to increase his earnestness. "Maybe the interview this afternoon will make them think. I want to see a *show* again, you understand, even if it's in a parking lot and the singer's wearing a blindfold and a ball-gag— 'Here at last is a new experience,' my brain wants to say, 'the show's about to begin.'"

I give him my best-of-luck-with-that-but-it's-out-of-my-hands look I give every immigration claimant and put his folder in the pocket.

"It does give a fresh perspective," I say. "At our office, I know, they saw it as nothing but a refugee problem. All those horrors down south might not have been happening."

"That's the wonder of history," he says, and his seatbelt flies up like a seagull. "Everyone sees it differently."

YUKON

There are trees growing on the bank right up through the dead ones. Instead of the car I wish we were in the boat where you can feel the spray on your hands or you can lie in the bottom with the enamel on your cheek and pretend every bump and whoosh is the sperm whales underneath us talking. Uncle Chad says his family used to DRIVE A VAN from North Vancouver to Hope or from North Vancouver into Washington State—that would wince so much! Do they even have roads? I saw an old map where that highway was called 1-5. I coo that. I will submit 1-5 for my PUBLIC NAME because it is so pants. Hit single from 1-5 streaming 24 hours continuous

Oldy Oldster should not have had that hamburger because he keeps foiling and he pretends he has not foiled but I know a foil when I smell one who

Oops, Carla was supposed to read that. Forgot to get out of notes. I will work harder and that way we will get there eventually.

Oldster wants to talk to all of the ROCKSTARS that are still alive because their voices might still carry weight. And I like that phrase but how can it be true since no one even knows or cares if the ROCKSTARS are alive or dead? And what could be more useless than dead people?

"Quick-sotic," Oldy Oldster says. Out of the blue. KIKS-OTIC? I will check the spelling before I send this, tho Chad said besides Carla there is no one to send to. Thinking about ROCKSTARS makes everything wince. I ask out loud who the ROCKSTAR in Summerland is just in case it is a3b03392 and his bear

Oldster says, "Before publics her name was Leslie Feist. She is eighty-one years old."

They said at school that anyone who does not drown trapped in their attic in a wash of foam can live to be 110. Carla asks out loud "Is that like a feisty serve in ping-pong?" and Dr. Cuban says "Why, yes" and tug-jobs a white hair out of the side of his neck.

I ask, "What is her public name now?"

Oldy Oldster laughs like that was loathing and says,
"Well girls we cannot know both names at any one time
can we?" He is a wad

DOES YOUR PHONE SAY THIS? writes Carla

She holds hers up and there is a whirly design in the
middle. Mine shows that too, and then

SUBSCRIBERS IN RANGE: 195 016. NETWORK PRES-
ENTLY: UNMONITORED

UNCLE CHAD

"A kid in school asked a funny thing," Yukon says from the back.

"What'd he ask?" I get a better grip on the steering wheel
than just my thumbs.

"He asked what 'unmonitored' meant."

"'Unmonitored'?" Cuban winks beside me. "Haven't heard
that in fifteen years!"

I manage to find Yukon's eyes in the rearview mirror—the
zipper-cut has its charms, but being able to see where you're
going can't be one of them.

"It *used* to mean," I say, "that whatever you said on your
phone, the government couldn't hear that network. Equanimity
arrested people for being unmonitored. But your phones don't
even have transmitters anymore, in the meantime everything's
gone satellite, and implants are even easier to monitor, so…
yeah."

Yukon goes back to playing with my late wife's phone and
I remember the texts I sent Min describing my elaborate plans
to go down on her—were those archived? Those elaborate
plans may have been my last words on Earth to her. Nothing
can ever happen so suddenly again. And what'll be the *absolute*

last words I say? "Implants are easier to monitor"? That'd be one for the books.

"But then how are we reaching each other right now?" asks Carla.

"That's the walkie-talkie function," I say.

"What *do* they teach in school?" Cuban asks, in a tone Yukon is going to eat with a fork and spoon.

"Pod dynamics of sperm whales," says Carla.

"Oh, yeah?" I say, like the girls are still small and describing the underwater hotel they're going to build us.

"For one thing," says Yukon, "every time one whale sends out sonar to find out whether a giant squid or a coral reef is ahead of them, the sonar bounces back for the whole pod to hear and everybody knows what everybody else knows so it's like they're reading each other's minds and don't even think as individuals. They're just the group."

"Like us!" says Carla.

"And what do they teach regarding the Universal Privacy Act?" asks Cuban.

I turn the music up.

"*J'espère voir un ours*," says Carla.

"What was that?" asks Cuban.

"She means we go to Chinese school," says Yukon. "We only learn about China."

Maybe this is just what kids are like, but it seems to me the more the world's difficulties have found solutions the more they talk gibberish. In our country, anyway. I don't know what it's like in places like Japan where a half-dozen first-person-streaming celebrities apparently still captivate the population's waking hours—and sleeping hours too, Jesus Almighty, because what else do they have to dream about?—and everything's so gone-to-shit you can see the carbon smear from space. The

Pacific isn't wide enough. Just like we're planting mines along the New Brunswick border—no joke, the things I hear in the bathroom at work could give a person vertigo. But that's Canada; we may not be famous but they're still battering down the door to get in.

"What have you learned about the wall?" Cuban asks over his shoulder. The brown between his teeth must be another hit with the girls.

"Goes right across Canada," says Yukon.

"Cause Olympians are so crazy," says Carla.

Which is such a vast understatement I push a laugh out my nose—they were too young, thank God. It had looked like Hitler and the Khmer Rouge competing for the lead-off slot on *Entertainment Tonight*. The last glimpse of the U.S. I ever had was of their final stubborn fingernail of government, only nine years ago when the girls had been—what, five and six? During lunch hour at work I watched the Classified Federal: the gang-rapes, initially, of Oregon Vice-Auditor Burton and his family via live feed from the Gubernatorial Mansion, and as the Olympians took their turns they pulled their spangled wigs off to shout their feed addresses and hometowns into the camera. Not until they beheaded the wife did the Classified Federal go dead, never to return, and to explain my expression as I came through the door I had to tell Yukon and Carla that I'd seen a porpoise get hit by a ferry on the way home, and they really did sympathize because that was honestly the worst thing they could imagine.

"Don't suppose they've even *heard* of Cameron Miller."

"That's out of the curriculum," I say as a westbound composter flies past, tubes flapping. "It's all concepts now with the individuals taken out. Kids were so starved for celebrity they dressed up as John A. Macdonald and got drunk at their desks."

"What school did *you* go to?" Yukon shouts.

"Me?" asks Cuban. "At your age I was already at Upper Canada Military College. There was such a thing as peacekeeping abroad in those days—here, what's this we're listening to? That sitar sample's remarkable. Look, goosebumps!"

"I heard it streaming in line at the food dump," I say. "They're called MF33p."

"Was that from the Prince song 'Housequake'?"

"What songs did Feisty sing?" asks Carla.

"Hundreds!" says Cuban. "Her last public single was called 'This Is Not the End My Friend.' Had a lovely moog organ."

"Is she the one with the singing cats?" asks Yukon.

"You're thinking of Lionel Richie," I tell them.

YUKON

CHAD SHOULD LOSE THE EYEBROWS, writes Carla, REALLY

These things are so pants. Hers shakes when the message comes in and mine plays the song from that pelican show

HE LOOKS LOATHING SINCE HE SHAVED OUT THE MIDDLE OF HIS BEARD

She types WE ARE ONLY FIFTY KMS FROM THE OLYMPIAN BORDER RIGHT NOW THAT WINCES. THEY ARE NOT EVEN PEOPLE ANYMORE THEY

I type ZRBZTZ2I IS A MAN WITH A BEAR.

DR. CUBAN

I wake up coughing and look down at the Okanagan Valley. Despite what I've heard I still expect the same desolation as anywhere, pipelines shining and a refrigerated town, but my hands go soft on the dash when I see this valley hasn't been changed by the last thirty years—vineyards still on the bluffs, groves of olive between the houses. The old pines are gone, of course, but heat-resistant saplings cover the hills. In actual *fertile fields* beside the road, people in overalls pull weeds and children run alongside us, kicking up the dirt—nobody waves, of course, because if we'd ever been famous that would be a contravention of the UPA. The girls shade their eyes in the back of the car.

"Where's the carbon haze?" asks the smart-mouth.

"Is that really the town?" asks the other one. "Where are the coils?"

"Looking like wagon wheels buried by the Titans of old," I say.

"What?" asks Chad.

"No need for filtration," I slur. Instead of sleeping I should've been swallowing water pills. "The Federals know, they know if word got out about a location this habitable, a million people would ruin it by the weekend. I've seen pockets like this east *and* west—this is where the old famous people wind up. Remember how at Hope they wanted the *exact* time we'd be back? To debrief us! Insist we forget! Pin us to our pyjamas." I run a fingertip down the glass. "In the Laurentians, you know, Miriam's mom and dad and I were high every day for a year."

"This is a rental," Chad reminds me. "Somebody just wrote that down."

"I'm too dehydrated. I was like this when I found Alanis Morissette and thought her cat was singing 'Hand in My Pocket' at the top of its lungs."

Then I sit back, helpless, my mouth hanging open.

"He foiled," the smart-mouth whispers. "He foiled for the nine hundredth time."

"Can we bring the windows down now?" asks Carla.

"We sure can," says Chad.

UNCLE CHAD

At the Hydrogen Camp we feed him a bagel, some of their local-grown coffee and a banana right off the tree. Cuban's leaning over the counter trying to explain to the owner how the cash register works, but when I give him the banana he shuffles after me to the car. Maybe he's speculating how a year in the Laurentians might've been improved by bananas off the tree. I put an ice cube in his coffee to cool it as his jaws work over the bagel. The girls are whirling sticks down the hill towards the water far below—the lake looks bigger than when I was a kid.

"This is no good," rasps Cuban. "I need to re-hydrate!"

"Get all that in you and I'll buy you some gel."

"Show this to the guy and ask. She probably doesn't use her public name *or* her secret name, and I never got the address. Don't think she has one."

It's a picture of a slender woman with dark brown hair, the bangs nearly in her eyes—like Yukon's, really.

"I thought the rock star was supposed to be eighty."

"So tell him the hair's turned white. Or maybe she's bald!"

He clutches the banana to his cheek and laughs.

I buy the gel-tubes and the owner goes back to polishing his nozzles. The shop vacuum follows me around like it thinks I'm leaking fluid.

"I wonder if you can help me—we came to meet this woman but don't know where she lives exactly. You know her? It's an old picture apparently."

"Huh," he says. "Leslie! Doesn't look any different, either. Say, you got the papers to be asking after her?"

"My friend does."

"That's okay. Come to the window here—don't mind him, he's like that with everybody. His bag needs changing. See the road above those houses? That keeps going into those trees and up and up. You'll see her sooner or later."

"What's the house number?"

"Lives in a bus up there. Gardens under the tarps. You work for her broadcaster?"

"No—I mean, we're sanctioned, just not in that way. My friend's an ethnomusicologist."

"That's okay. You come up Highway 3 from the coast?"

"We did."

My fingers dip into my shirt pocket for the travel licences.

"You lose anybody during the bad week?" he asks.

"Did I—? Oh. Yeah." My fingers come out. "Those are my nieces outside. They're about all I have left."

I don't get the knot in my gut like I used to. It's just information now, like telling somebody which boat I ride to work. The owner lines up his nozzles on the counter.

"I was down there too," he says. "I lost my four kids and Audrey. I came up here—you remember how long ago that was? I can."

"Fourteen years," I say.

"Look at this." He pulls his wallet out of his back pocket and flips it open on the counter, fishes out a slip of grey paper. "A year after I came up here I found this."

He moves his thumb down the slip. A lot of names.

"Shopping list," he finally says, "for Christmas. I looked at it and realized every person on it had passed away. I'd cared enough about each one of them to pick them out a Christmas gift. You remember what month that was?"

Outside the window Yukon piggy-backs Carla. They stagger around the parking lot, hair in their eyes, skinny elbows everywhere. My whole family.

"The wall broke in September," I say.

"Exactly—three *months* before Christmas. See? I was organized. Now you look around this place and it looks like hell. Bobby, come away from there!"

The vacuum slinks behind the counter.

YUKON

Carla is a wad with the dogs so Uncle Chad wants her
to go mild and let them sniff her fingers. It is not pants
to watch her cry so I wander into this sort of meadow
with a drop and the lake a mile below that. Dear NOTES
section. Oldy disappeared inside this Greyhound bus
buried up to its axles. I will sidle up. Nine out of ten he is
not even a QUICK-SOTIC ethnomusicologist and came
up here for a tug-job from a robot houseplant-waterer
with a housecoat tied around its head. If they were sperm
whales they would know I was here but the kitchen
window is open a crack and here is a folding chair

DR. CUBAN

While the dogs outside bark at Chad and the girls, I set up
microphones on either end of the bus so that Leslie Feist can
walk around if she wants to, though she claims she's not too
mobile. The green lights come on. She reads the verification and
lets it waft onto the coffee table while I describe what I've written so far, then before I can ask her to recite the alphabet so I'll
know the talker's working she puts her feet up on the couch and
starts in. She has wonderful teeth for her age.

"You won't get an argument from me—I had *so* many American friends, *great* American friends, who I assume are dead now.
Do you want lemonade? No? That's the crazy thing, isn't it, just
when we cut off our imports we—and I really am sorry your
friends can't come in but yours is the only name on the certifi-
cate and there are Equanimity people up here all the time just in
case I've fallen out of a tree and broken my hip. 'Ethnomusicologist.' That must make me as old as Sara Carter."

"Don't worry about them," I tell her. "Pressed for time as it is.
I thought you *finished* at two—thinking of your stream in Eastern time."

"So, what do we miss without live shows? Oh, daddy. First off, in my situation it might be a mistake to live on a bus. I look past the steering wheel and imagine I'm on my way somewhere. I only lived at gigs, that was real. People brought their bodies there, now we're all a thousand miles apart. Maybe that plays into whatever thesis you're working on."

"Certainly it does."

"But, see, when your career's going well the touring wears you out, and you meet so many people that three or four are bound to be assholes, they just are, and part of me loves it that I've finally been settled so long in one place, but in hindsight, being famous, I mean, if I *was* famous—"

"Certainly you were."

"But then I'm biased as far as the before-and-after, because to be famous and then have it snatched away, I can only remember it as the greatest part of my life. I can't imagine a better life than what I had. You write a song while you're playing ping-pong with your drummer and six months later, five *years* later, people are singing the chorus louder than you can sing it yourself. Imagine you write this book, and six months later people are screaming out the introduction at the top of their lungs."

"That's difficult to imagine."

"It's amazing my name's going to be in it. To be a person who exists—look at me, I'm misty! Don't put that in, 'She got weepy just at the thought.' Okay. I'm fine. How much more do you want? I start streaming in five minutes and after that I go to bed."

"Let's discuss that. Three times a week you stream for two hours, so obviously going secret has not diminished your capacity to make music or to reach people."

She stretches, squeezes her eyes shut, and for a moment I'm not sure she's heard.

"I'm not sure if I reach *anyone*," she mutters, "but as long as the broadcaster pays me, I assume there are three or four listening. The opiate of the masses, that's why the government funds us, and if pap's what they want, well, half the time that's what I give them. But, okay, for your question, I think that not knowing who a song is by, and for it to be illegal to *try* to find out, I think then the song loses a facet of its narrative."

"Now, do you imagine that any listeners recognize your public ID as you, and if so might they achieve any catharsis from that? Keep in mind, I'm trying to compare the experience of a live show with that of a streaming feed."

"Um. I run songs through the filters but there might be one every hour where I turn those off, just to mix it up, and if there's anybody listening from the old days the voice might be strangely familiar. Or they might assume it's some big hairy guy running his voice through a Feist filter! Shit, I have to start tuning."

"I'd like to talk briefly about the events of seventeen years ago, when the prime minister shut down the border and blocked transmissions out of the U.S. on every present and future frequency so that—"

"Was that *seventeen* years ago?"

"At that time, did you feel it was an appropriate culmination of your career when you were the second artist in all of Canada to be removed to a safe house on Prime Minister Mitchell's order?"

"Do you mean was I *flattered* to be flown up to Fort Chipewyan with a bag tied over my head, waiting for the bullet in my neck? Of course, yeah. Exactly like when a dreamy boy has a crush on—wait, did you say I was the *second* one seized?"

"Did you not know that? They didn't sequester artists based on their feed traffic, either, Mitchell just listed his favourites on a napkin—Belinda Flutter, Rock Hard Cocks, Junior Spirit, it went right across the board."

"So who was number one?"

"Neil Young. Luckily for them he was in Toronto. And yes, I asked him the same question and *yes*, he gave me an earful."

"Holy God, you talked to him? How old is *he*?"

"He is 109. Hasn't changed a hair in forty years."

"I used to think women didn't go deaf unless they wanted to. Does that even sound like the same note? These strings buzz like freakin' honeybees and I only get new ones when I—hey, did *you* happen to bring guitar strings?"

"I'm sorry. I was told to bring green beans and a humidifier."

"I can't *believe* you brought beans! Are they modified?"

She sets the guitar down and reads the back of the bag of green beans. I count fifteen tambourines on the wall. Now she's looking at my abstract.

"But what about the argument," she asks, "that we'd reached a point where only assholes and serial killers were famous?"

"Well, that was the America model, yes. My aim is to collect evidence to demonstrate that Canadians were harder working and generally more civic-minded when they at least had you and Sam Roberts and the Barenaked Ladies to emulate. Of course with those examples I date myself by fifty years."

"But how do you quantify civic-mindedness? If you try to make a point with Equanimity they'll want numbers, that's been my experience. And if you ask me there've been more variables than constants in the last seventeen years, between the floods and this heat and the bor—"

"Whether or not my findings are encouraging, the ministry will be happy to have them. They strive constantly to improve public perception, and—"

"Don't fuck with me!" She jerks up, white hair like a bursting dandelion. "Look at our head of state!"

I've been talking into my chest, I realize, folded up in the armchair in the compliant academic pose I've aped for so long it's become my default posture. I straighten up like I'm back on the rail before that last drop into Turkmenistan.

"You refer to the head in a jar," I say.

She gazes out the wall of windows. From my angle I can't see what she sees, but the dogs have stopped barking. She collects her cane from the arm of the sofa and makes her way up to the work table behind the driver's seat. She punches switches. A console like an old-time jukebox lights up.

"I go live in twenty seconds. You can't be in here while I broadcast but it's been nice meeting you, and I hope my tale of woe helps make your point with whoever it is—the cat with cybernetic thumbs."

I don't argue, though Choclair and Buck 65 both insisted that a talking rhesus monkey dictates policy. As I get up I'm so stiff that I might need a cane of my own.

"I can quantify *anything*," I say. "I'll have you back in arenas in six months."

"If they rebuild them." She slips on a pair of headphones resplendent in duct tape. "Stay for the first song. I'll turn a blind eye."

She presses a driver-emergency button above her head and a voice booms from the speaker beside the kitchen sink.

"This has been Gm3b. I've enjoyed the broadcast to you today!" It sounds like a four-year-old girl. "Now here's zrbztz21!"

Feist clears her throat and, like a boxing announcer, pulls a microphone down from the ceiling. I have to grab the back of the folding chair. This is something I have no right to see. This is a live performance. This is something I'd given up any hope of ever seeing, and even if I'm unable to present my arguments to Equanimity due to my litany of legal shortcomings, even if no future eighteen year olds are ever able to have their lives changed as mine was when I saw The Tragically Hip perform "Grace, Too," which then resonated through my brain even as I shook the chute loose and did a dive-roll into Turkmenistan, even if it's a silent jail for me after this, it will be worth it. She holds a pedal down with her cane and grips that microphone. I might retch.

"Head in a jar," she says.

It loops out of the speaker and, presumably, into the world. For four repetitions it's clearly her, but then she taps away at the console so that it's a man with a Newfie accent, then a young-ish-sounding Japanese boy, then she ups the tempo and for the next dozen times it's an old man, it might even be me though I could never talk that fast, then she repeats the whole series but adjusts the pitch so each phrase goes higher at the end.

"Head in a jar? Head in a jar? Head in a jar? Head in a jar? Head in a jar?"

YUKON

My public name will be 1-5, I hope, and I will call all of this THE BEST WEEK because I have found the last famous person on Earth or in Canada, we have no way to know which one, and she has always been my favourite. 3:00 on Saturdays. The girls from the pigsty come down the hill to hear zrbztz21 and we make brownies and drink lemon gin and say IF I TOLD YOU RIGHT NOW I WAS ZRBZTZ21 WOULD YOU SCREAM? My thumbs are going so fast they will burst and IF we had talker software my thumbs would NOT BURST!

WHY ARE YOU GIGGLING? Carla types from across the seat

I do not write her back. I see now as YOU dear reader see that there are SEND/SEND ALL options at the top and after all the hours in the wincing car it is perfect I see this NOW when I finally have something to SAY to the 195 016 users—who are they all? you may wonder. We are not so far from the border so it may be an Olympian network. And unwince that it is unmonitored when I finally have something to SAY.

COO! COO! SECRET FAMOUS ROCKSTAR PERSON NEWS!

Oldy Oldster is typing on his folder up front but whatever he is going to say he is too slow! Carla holds her hands up and mouths what? without saying it

ROCKSTAR ZRBZTZ2I WHO IS JUST SO PANTS, SO LOATHING IN REALITY IS CALLED LESLIE FEIST AND LIVES IN A BUS IN A TOWN CALLED SUMMERLAND ON THE HILL IN CANADA. THERE ARE NOT EVEN COILS! YOU TAKE HWY 3 AT FIRST WE ARE 50 KMS FROM THE OLYMPIAN BORDER. DID YOU HEAR HEAD IN A JAR? ZRBZTZ2I IS CALLED LESLIE FEIST

Then my thumb creeps the wheel back and forth between SEND and SEND ALL until I finally hit SEND ALL to get it over with.

WHAT DID HE JUST SAY? Carla types, because Uncle Chad just told us he is going to drive down 97 but not too close to the border before we turn onto 3

BOTH FINE NUMBERS I write.

And he says if we can find a motel we will sleep in Princeton and go fishing in the morning and he will teach us to tie flies if there is a fly store in Princeton. It is still bright afternoon outside but I might sleep now, dear reader

"Now I remember that song!" Carla says out loud and she sings, "This is not the end my frie-end, this is not-the-end"

"And then the moog comes in!" yells Oldy

All of a sudden my phone plays the song from the pelican show even tho Carla has been singing, not typing, it says

RESPONSE FROM LADY GLORYHOLE. OKAY?

Which is too stupid to be a public ID or a real name, it is really a wad somewhere pretending to be an Olympian so for fun I hit OKAY and the message says

EXPECT LIBERATION

Which makes my stomach feel like the wash behind a ferry. I turn off the phone.

The girls from the pigsty said that when the Olympians liberated Rachel McAdams from her nursing home and flew their sleds home from Timmins to the Floating City of Buffalo they killed 4000 random people on the way. Girls from the pigsty say that but who knows?

Carla hums until she puts her head back and cracks her knuckles which is what she always does before she goes to sleep. Dear reader

UNCLE CHAD

"Seriously," I tell Cuban, "there may still be trout in these streams."

But he just pages through his read-out. Which is exactly what Powter in the corner office does whenever I ask him a question, the same posture and everything, and I wish Cuban wouldn't remind me of work in the middle of what's turning into a pretty nice vacation. The girls fast asleep.

"So," I try again, "what was the old lady like?"

"Hm? Oh, sprightly, certainly."

"Feisty?"

"Yes."

"And was that, like, her last interview on the face of this earth?"

"Very likely." He scratches his neck with his pinkie and makes himself smile. "Unless I can be superhumanly persuasive on the other side of the country."

"So what are her last words on record?"

"Transcriber's just finished . . . let me see. All this useless code."

He monkeys around. The road curves away from the river and goes straight on through the trees. But there's a *pud-pud-pud* noise somewhere. Above us? I'm so used to the boat and the waves constantly thudding against its hull that I can't get used to hearing things from inside the car. It's unnerving.

"Can you hear that?" I ask.

DR. CUBAN

I was not expressly given consent by the administration of Chrétien University to undertake this trip; indeed, all documents required by federal and provincial bodies in order for the final leg of the project to proceed—requiring, in this case, no less than thirteen signatures by nine individuals—were forged by myself. On the occasion of the obligatory video conference

between Deputy Equanimity Minister Q3mv4 and my immediate superior, Dean Cherry, I artfully arranged for local law
enforcement to tow Cherry's car from his driveway that morning and successfully impersonated him simply by wearing a pair
of false teeth over my own, which was only fair considering that
Q3mv4 wore a voice modulator and blackface. The certification
with which I presented Ms. Feist ought to have been embossed
by the Equanimity Ministry and by failing to inspect the document thoroughly she implicated herself under no less than
seven sections of the Universal Privacy Act. Mr. Chad Campbell
and his wards can be charged as accessories under three sections of the Act as they abetted my crimes but held no secrets,
as far as Equanimity is concerned, worth revealing. At any rate
Mr. Chad Campbell is now dead at my side and I can't imagine
the girls in the back are much better off. Leaflets drop from the
sky like someone's opened a bale of them, and one drifts down
through where the windshield used to be and lands in my lap.
Friendly little thing. *Dead or wounded? Keep my tally accurate! Live-
feed.stone.cold.*

The car went out of control, of course, after the Olympians'
grenade blew out the left-hand tires—a classic example of the
murderous precision and absolute randomness that was so
typical of them in the old days—and our impact with the trees
killed Chad rather neatly. Or *quickly*, rather. "Neatly" is not accurate at all. The first thing I do once I'm out in the road is wipe
the blood off my glasses.

The smell from the chewed-up pine trees is rather wonderful.

The trail of the Olympians' exhaust makes a U-turn out over
the forest; they must be steering back to scalp us, but they're
too low now for me to see just where they've gone. What are
those sleds burning, diesel? I hear the rumble but there are
too many echoes to be able to pinpoint them. And what in hell
brought them over the border? It's unheard of since the Gosling,

Jr. Incident in '49. Ah, the smart-mouth girl peers out at me. The way her seat's twisted backwards she must not see the others. Is the quiet one still alive back there?

"There's been an accident," I tell Smart-mouth through the oddly unbroken window. "I need tools. Pop the trunk."

She doesn't blink. She might be in shock. Good Lord, how long does she have? I once saw an entire Central Asian village die from shock. Finally a hand comes up to push the hair out of her eyes.

"Where's the switch?" she asks.

"Beside the emergency brake. Feel behind you with your left hand."

"Where's Carla?"

"Pop it open so I can get the tools."

I crunch over the glass to the back of the car and right away I hear it pop, bless her, even over the roar of them coming, but the trunk can't open because the frame's buckled. I wedge a branch into the gap and force it. My suitcase. I crane my head around to watch the treetops as I feel inside for the gun. From my peace-keeping days. I can't feel it, must be tangled with the recording equipment, so I haul the suitcase out and what, of all things, is under it?

The buckle-proof hydrogen tank. Which was at 93 per cent before the dashboard feed went.

I screw down the shut-offs with one hand and unclamp the brackets with the other, gun already in the back of my belt, and out of the corner of my eye I see Smart-mouth slide out onto the pavement. And the cumulative roar of their sleds is honestly no different, but I know they're upon us because now there's a buzz in the back of my skull, the same manner in which a sperm whale might come to realize that those eternally glamorous Olympians were all of fifty feet away. Had we talked about sperm whales at one point, or was that the dehydration?

In the middle of the road Smart-mouth freezes like a monument to flippancy, hands bunched under her throat, shredded tires scattered around her. I complete my task and turn to see the first Olympian buzz up from behind me, a brute so big his sled lurches under him. Tanned muscles, blond hair, white smile and immodest bathing suit. A feed address is tattooed across his chest—*skull.fucker.gov*—and he's screaming, neck veins bulging, eyes on the girl. How could snapping her back make him any more famous? I'll never understand Americans, I suppose. What makes us Canadian.

I swing the suitcase 270 degrees then let go as he flies past. It hits him in the ribs, not the head like I'd planned, but he's knocked off regardless, crashing through the underbrush on the far side of the road, and his sled cuts a gouge up the asphalt until it stops three feet from the girl. She stares at it and makes a noise like a kicked dog, the same noise Alanis Morissette made when she tripped over her coffee table, though she didn't even bruise. Nimble from yoga.

Now I see how the brute would've commemorated his glory; the rest of the pack, with sequins and mascot dogs, circles the treetops, cameras dangling. Arranging another volunteer to come down after us. Like an old lawnmower the untenanted sled starts with a simple pull-cord, and as a string twangs in my shoulder it clamours to life with one tug. I see myself reflected on the monitor, wearing Dean Cherry's so-called teeth. What great dignity. By the time Cherry sees the documentation I will likely be dead. I strap the hydrogen tank onto the sled with the belts the brute neglected to use and let the sled idle as I pull its nose up. Diesel gusts in my face. The Olympians are in a cluster now, heading west, but after that they'll circle south. I put the thing in drive and as the sled lunges upwards I let go of the handles. The girl's crouched behind me with her hands over her ears.

"Get to the car!" I say. I slide the gun out of my belt."Get inside!"

The Olympians turn south. The sun gleams off their teeth. They talk with their hands. They don't even watch us because they believe it's enough—*more* than enough—to have us on their feeds. I don't lift the gun yet because if my arms get tired they'll shake too much to aim.

The sled's above the trees now, sunlight flashing off the hydrogen tank, and before the Olympians deign to notice I lift the gun and fire.

I might not have had the brains to stay in my disinfected office but I have the brains to not stand gawking. As a new sun opens for business a hundred feet above us I dive-roll towards the open car door, but now I'm lying on my face because my brain has been struck by lightning from my left hip. Broken, of course. Everything goes as black as gouged asphalt, even with the heat melting the hairs on the back of my neck, but now I feel her little hands around my wrists, dragging me. Steel engines clank onto the highway one after another—the aluminum frames must have melted instantaneously. I would explain this to Smart-mouth if I weren't in shock.

She tilts me back in the passenger seat and from there she must see that Mr Chad Campbell is horribly dead. She feeds me six aspirin and I wash them down with gel.

"Carla's all right, though, hey?" Smart-mouth whispers. "Say something, Carla?"

"Who's got a lug-wrench?" asks a small voice in the back.

Smart-mouth smiles.

"Coo that," she says.

She wraps me in a blanket for the shock—something worthwhile is taught in the schools. Every tree in sight is burning; one falls across the road in front of us.

"What happened to the brute down here?" I ask.

"Haven't seen him," says Smart-mouth.

"Me neither," says Carla. "Dr. Cuban, is that right what she said that Chad's hurt?"

"That's true, child. I'm sorry. I'm sorry but he didn't make it."

After a moment I hear disembodied sobs. Lord knows what sort of shape she's in back there. I feel better already, lucid. Is that possible? Was six aspirin too many? I clutch the blanket to my chin.

"Satellites'll see the fire by now, right?" Carla asks between deep breaths. "Then the constables come?"

"They need to come cover him up," Smart-mouth says. "He can't sit looking like that. I can't keep mild much longer. He has to get me to the oboe recital!"

"What's your name again?" I ask her.

She moves her hair aside and gives me a hard look.

"Yukon," she says.

"Yukon?" Suddenly I'm not lucid, my hip can't decide if it's numb or in agony, and all its point-counterpoint is going to make me vomit. "Really, 'Yukon'?"

Why am I speaking such inanities while lodgepole pines collapse against each other and flame roars on all sides? Pine needles curl on the hood of the car. Everything incinerated by that business with the hydrogen tank, my masterstroke of senile grandstanding.

"We should all get out of here," says Carla in the back. "This is all on fire. Hey, look up there! Helicopter."

I blink up through where the windshield used to be and sure enough three of them approach in a triangle—three long-tailed MacKenzies that look like dragonflies. I assume they're constables, but what if they're production assistants for *skull.fucker.gov*? I am numb below the navel and my tongue is a hairbrush. I am incapable of defending these girls beyond the three bullets in the gun now in Yukon's hand, so if it comes to—no, no, not to worry. I can see the maple leaves painted on them. Thank Christ. If they open their storage bay and wheel out the head in a jar I will kiss it on the lips.

Yukon stands in the road, waving her skinny arms as the smoke gusts around her. She kneels beside me.

"After they get Carla out, they'll cover him up and take us all home, all right?"

"Please," says Carla in the back.

"I can't keep looking at him!" blurts her sister. "How long's he going to keep dripping?"

"The helicopters mean it's military now," I say. "They'll take custody of him."

"He won't come with us?" asks Yukon. "He's not useless, you know, he's Uncle Chad!"

"He won't come today," I say.

The point of the triangle is landing. The other two stay aloft.

"I'm going to sing to him then," says Carla from the back.

"Go," says Yukon.

And so she begins to sing. There in the car. A reedy voice, but strong enough. The MacKenzie's crew is disembarking, scuttling towards us, but my attention is elsewhere.

We've been through the hard ti-imes
Come upon some pain
Take my hand and these rhy-ymes
Here comes my refrain

It is a show, though there's no blindfold or ball-gag or parking lot.

This is not the end my frie-end
This is not the end

Yukon kneels on the pavement, clutching my good leg, wetting the seam of my trousers with her snot and tears. Here at last is a new experience and I can't think what to do next. My hands feel like they've spent a year in ice water, but I put one on her shoulder. Carla is projecting more now; she wants her uncle to enjoy the number.

This is not the end my frie-end

She stops there. Yukon looks up, wipes her nose on her wrist and swallows hard.

"That was so pants," she says.

LEE HENDERSON

THE AUROCHS

Beware of the scribes, which desire to walk in long robes, and love greetings in the markets, and the highest seats in the synagogues, and the chief rooms at feasts; LUKE 20:46

VERONA RUPES

I'm known as Verona Rupes. With tons of determination and over many years, never mind how many, I spent my entire life, and mine and not a few other men's fortunes in pursuit of the Aurochs. How I became Director of the Sony-Smithsonian Museum of Extinction in New Hope, Virginia, and commandeered enough respect and trust in my industry to own one, is the story of my life. The Aurochs was more than a giant cow. It was a Polish-made sports utility vehicle. First rolled off the Daewoo Motors assembly line in May 1999 days before the sudden seizure of the nation's economy following a dispute with Russia over oil transfer credits. I searched for one of these SUVs my entire career. I was obsessed, yes. For a few years here and there I can recall being distracted by the happiness of marriage or a mistress or the sale of some trifle, a fleeting success. My most recent wife Polli was a brave blonde meds trafficker with her own skytaxi and looked a ninth my age. But that ended over a decade ago now, and the truth is, all my other endeavours and adventures in the field of antiquities were swings around the light poles in my lifelong hunt for the 1999 Daewoo Aurochs. I swear this car has been stuck in my mind's eye like a fleck of gold I can't rub off. It's because of the Aurochs that my first love is post-Industrial antiquity.

When I was at Sotheby's Primary School where I received formal training—that's when I first saw footage of the Aurochs. I was a preemie born with a heart defect to parents living in the hospice. No one expected me to survive long after my mother died when I was a mere two and a half, but by and by a couple dozen kilos of malleable boyhood formed itself. Harbouring a limp from my malnourishment in infancy, I was teased and ignored at Sotheby's, and my asthma wounded me when I ran and played with other chilteens. My astigmatism surfaced by the age of two and my eyesight has been deteriorating ever since—I'd be blind without my contraband contacts. Imagine me, little Vee Rupes, in 2223, one of a billion orphans aged seven enrolled in a trade school of some kind, and I'm squinting through my blotted vision to find angles where I can see clearly the suv pictured in an old catalogue from Fall 2188—I can practically remember the lot numbers—of nearly priceless antiques from the post-Indies. A hot purple model and the first to surface on the secondary market in more than a century. It belonged to a gravity-transportation czar with a new residence on Mars. It looked to me like the most daunting and indestructible vehicle ever bought or sold. Below the image I read that this was only *one of two* Aurochs left in the universe. Other kids built toy airhorses and were obsessed with learning about our first voyage to Mars in 2110. I studied the dark age before then, with all the gasoline-fuelled cars and drive-thrus and hospitals. I marvelled at the simple smalless of the number two.

BOVINE ORIGINS

The aurochs the vehicle's named after was a massive prehistoric bovine that was swept away in the early tides of the Holocene Extinction Event. The aurochs had no Noah to save it. An aurochs was like a great shaggy bull mastiff with extremely long, sharp horns and blown up to nearly the size of an elephant, way longer horns than an elephant's tusks, which must have been very threatening to people. It was hunted down and killed and skinned and eaten and sacrificed like every other massive predatory animal that lived in herds. Ever-dwindling herds of aurochs were chased by ever-growing human populations. Driven north by insatiable spear-and-bow hunters up from the Indian subcontinent, the aurochs was last seen on Earth in 1627 when two potbellied poachers with muskets took down a young female rutting against a tree in the dense, bleak, smoggy forests of Jaktorow, Poland. The poachers skinned and left the carcass near where Daewoo Motors set up the Aurochs factory nearly four hundred years later in complex tribute.

The Aurochs suv had the most epic hood ornament. Incredible. Award-winning. Dash computer operates on an unfathomably small half gig of memory. Adjustable everything. Seats nine comfortably. Slavic luxury vehicle. The Euro didn't even exist yet to pay for this behemoth with. It was another century before the Euro and dollar merged to become our ears. The Aurochs cost over a million American dollars in Poland, a perestroika nation still teething on democracy, using a nonsense currency a hundredth the value of the American dollar. To ship one to another country required political grease and plenty of muscle—apparently no one in Poland was officially responsible for vehicle exports. The factory was shuttered. The Aurochs became an absurd jewel among automobiles, more of a rumour or myth than transportation. It was too late arriving on the scene to be of much use to people. I must confess I sometimes compare myself to the Aurochs. Even as a child I felt extinct, or approaching so—in any event, lost. The tender, school-age version of myself was as disenchanted a human being as I am today, with nothing in common with anyone, even myself.

The big wagon's value among collectors is hard for an outsider to fathom. The hood ornament is one reason. An aurochs fixed right at the lip there extending out beyond the front of the SUV. A brute bull in his prime with hind legs bent nearly seated on the vehicle, neither rear hoof is flat on the hood, haunch muscles taut and flexed and ripped in the moment before the bull's about to leap forward, his long slightly curved horns tapering to a thin hypodermic vanishing point facing the road ahead, a huge ornament, three kilos of solid steel designed by prominent animalier of the time Stücka Heck, in the clean, unfussy style of Bohumil Kafka. Some auto historians speculate Heck was inspired by the cave paintings in Lascaux, France, and it's quite possible, but tell me, what artist isn't? But no Neanderthal ever came up with the details you see on this ornament, flesh rumpling, fierce, seething nostrils, grumped brow—and a detail you don't notice immediately: a scorpion lying on the hood underneath the aurochs, clamped to its testicles. The scorpion's got the balls securely pinched in its front claws and is about to pierce the aurochs' belly with the tip of its venomous tail. All solid steel. You have to imagine the scale of this ornament, in 1999— any other car's fibreglass hood would buckle under the weight. The Aurochs was one of the three largest vehicles on Earth.

GROTESQUE IN NATURE

The Aurochs was made for an age when people believed human beings were a separate spectacle of the grotesque, practically unrelated to nature. They also thought a shopping frenzy was outside nature, or overspending in a jewellery store or auto mall an irrational and vulnerable mindset, or the gut instinct that drives franchise obesity or bulldozing or ghettos or congested sinuses—none of this seemed natural to our ancestors. Doctors, medicine, hospitals, these were all legal. Because they were shook by the face of death. This was an age of unfetteredness, freedom heaped upon freedom, vice upon vice, and, shook to the core, they *watched their health*. The closer they came to neutralizing cancer and dementia the less they smoked—now we encourage smoking and criminalize synthetic treatments. Thirty-six billion people on earth and we're proud of a billion or more dying a year—there's too many of us! I've seen many go, we all have, until the ordeal of living becomes unbearable. I get shook by death, too, but like a late-twentieth century Boomer. I don't run towards it, I defend myself against it. I know where to buy antibiotics when I need them. Chemos got me through the bouts, without them I'd be dead, too.

As I said, I was never naturally healthy. I failed to mention that along with asthma and astigmatism, my hair went prematurely white when I was three. I chipped a tooth on a banana around this time and was almost willing to believe my own rep, *weak at the soul* the nannies used to call me around Sotheby's daycare, and the label stuck. I give off this deathly pall apparently, even though I live and everyone around me dies. My cheeks, my eye sockets, how sunken are they? As I grew older I hoped the grey made me look like my father before his death, and I used my hair to get me the respect granted an adult before I gained some confidence in my voice. I never said a word in protest when I stood by and watched my mother wave *so long* and leave the planet without me, not so much as a, *No, Mama!* I said nothing at my father's death, either, not a year later, and my memories of their funerals are as fresh and lurid as if they both happened yesterday when I rewatched the footage. Mother waving her hand from there inside the silk interior of the coffin and a smile of such contented self-satisfaction as she lay her palm back on top of the white bow on her chest. They both seemed so proud to be leaving me, last of the Rupes, as they did their duty for the planet. I remember my mother's last words to me: See you soon.

I'm divorced twice and a widower four times over. My parents raised me briefly, between smoke therapy and vomits, and then left me with nothing besides a scholarship to an auction school. My siblings and relatives all took their lives or caught a similar plague trend. The few dear friends I once had have all passed. My last wife Polaris sold black-market chemos and antibiotics out of her skytaxi until she was murdered by twelve members of a drug cartellite. Of the nine, all but one of my children are gone, and my frail son Melvin's on his way out soon, too, I fear. I'm the only one left. I raised a devout family. I spent my life among the devout. I acted devout. I acted natural through every pandemic, disease outbreak, and infection. They died. I didn't. I never explained myself. But among those who ignore the natural health law there is an unspoken oath, and that's never snitch on a doctor. We take our medicines and have the surgeries but not even my dying child learns the name of my GP. If you're caught, the police are merciless and the law is unforgiving.

Had I not learned to conceal from myself the dark sorrow I should have felt over my parents' deaths, I'm sure I would be dead, too. Everyone at Sotheby's expected me to follow my parents at any moment. The Aurochs was how I pulled through; it's how I've always pulled through.

Mars has known the name Verona Rupes since I was a grad student. As intern auctioneer I was notorious for driving up prices for neglected masterpieces of the post-Industrial market.

I was in my thesis year at Sotheby's—on the post-Indies—first in my class, and even had the strongest chin, like a cliff, and weakest temper, like a cave where my heart was meant to be. There was nothing I could do about my temperament. But in my field, self-centredness is an asset. Bidders bought into the arrogance and vanity I exuded. Ever since I was in school I've regularly visited surgery parlours—they're in every city, it's the first thing I need to know about a new place—where's the doctor's den. I've justified breaking the law in the name of historical research and as a sentimental attachment to the manners of post-Indies. I have a strong survival instinct. Say if another student auctioneer outsold me on a Tuesday, I found a way to ruin his confidence. For example, I'd say something like, Hey, Burke, I watched you at last evening's Ikea auctions. Oh, is that so, Rupes, I didn't see you. And I'd say, I thought your descriptions of the objects sounded like greeting-card free verse and wondered if by your tone of voice you meant to infantilise my field of expertise? And this combined with your misguided précis in the catalogue made the evening go from ambient to kinda suffocating. Then I'd watch as the auctioneer would sweat furiously, sure to go home gnawing over my comments, spend a sleepless night in bed shouting at me, and draw hardly a single sale on Wednesday. By Thursday I'd have ostracized the nuisance Burke from his and my colleagues, exposing him as a dilettante and memorizer, regaining my leadership and top ranking.

MODIFIED AUROCHS

A second Aurochs did go on the block in Spring 2255. I was two years fresh on the job as director and couldn't raise the ears. I couldn't sleep until I saw it though. I flew around the clock to see the thing where it was stashed in a suburb of Xamar,

Usaomalia. It turned out to be a phoney third, or not a phoney, but a viciously superficial restoration job. A collector had
found it on bricks being used as a shelter for a family of seven
in the Adabiyat jungles of Qaraqalpaqstan. Father of the family sold it for a tune, and the new owner went looking for cans
of a 1999 brand of Calcutta latex paint to match the period-
accurate gunmetal-grey used on this Aurochs, which was
stripped bare to the foam shell in places. Couldn't find paint,
couldn't find parts or repairman willing to work for him. So
besides reconstructing the entire interior with stem-cell leather,
a great deal of fake restoration was done to the chassis, which
was bullet-riddled. And the original overhead cam engine was
half-missing. What was left of the parts the slum family had
rigged into an ingenious indoor plumbing system. So the restoration team used parts from a mass-produced engine of a
Chrysler Dynasty from the period, easy enough to come across.
Like patching up a shattered Ming vase with scraps from your
grandmother's mugs-of-America collection.

The auctioneer for the event was Burke Nkubra, whose
oily moustache I'd known since school days. For this event he
was also boasting a virulent tumour on his neck the size of a
gavel-head and in his opening remarks he justified this whole
charade with some gak about how the restorers wanted to sell
a roadworthy vehicle and so on. I loathed this funky Aurochs
and I found Burke a tedious auctioneer, and I couldn't afford
it, I couldn't afford the thing that wasn't even close to what
I really wanted, so I decided to poison its sale, deflate the bids,
kill the buzz. I still had what looked like my same white hairstyle from when I was a kid, except now I was a man. I went
before the cameras with my lens-corrected eyes and enhanced
lips and albedo-like chin and argued vehemently that whatever
the outcome of the auction this was not a legitimate Aurochs,
nor, I added, was its sale representative of any market price for

genuine post-Industrial antiques, and being well regarded and having spoken first on the subject naturally the majority of the hamsters in my field agreed with me. In the end the sale went to a race-car junkie for a little under six-and-a-half-billion ears, and that was fifty-nine years ago.

I walked away from that phoney auction with a weird hunch. I'm flying home to meet my kids and Coleco, my third wife, for dinner, and slapping my proverbial forehead the whole time thinking why hadn't it occurred to me sooner: There must be more Aurochs out there. Two mint and a third refurbished? Is that really all? If there's thirty-plus billion people on the planet, can't there be someone out there like me, an educated man with a full head of hair-grafts who beat bone marrow cancer, colon cancer, and childhood leukemia, and an abiding love for the tangible beauties of bygone days, but this alter-ego of mine is doing business on the *other* side of the fence from the institution, so to speak, and all he wants is to highway-drive an Aurochs, and day by day he's stockpiling parts as they come on the block or whispering in parallel shadow markets, all to eventually mickeymouse a roadworthy model of his own. A man might want *one* Aurochs for the secret ex-airport hangar showroom and one Aurochs to take out on private ranch raceways.

Occasionally someone like Burke would auction a piece, some cracked crankshaft might surface in a dig—a rusty fan belt or a muffler—that I refused to go near. They all sold for astronomical sums, of course. I only wanted my name associated with perfection. This is also our natural way, though, and I couldn't blame the buyers for having a bricoleur's mentality—just as I wasn't surprised by the public's reaction when the suggestion of jettisoning all our garbage into space was put to referendum. Because I was born in the dump I know what a lot of people were thinking when they cast their vote, What if there's *something valuable in there* I could *use or sell*? Many people have Noah's instincts to build an Ark of their own, someplace to put all the precious things they come across for safety, stow them away in sets of two from the uncertain tides of oblivion.

CASHMERE MOUNTAINS

I found the museum its male and female aurochs specimens on an expedition thirty years ago, into what was then a war zone. Or rather, the animals were found on protected land, frozen in time, and I shipped them out. When I was Director of the Extinction Museum I'd thought if I acquired an aurochs, an actual skeleton of one of these mammoth oxen, for the museum, then I could position it centre stage, as it were, and begin to push the aurochs forward as *the narrative* for the museum, and inch myself closer to a budget for *the vehicle*. I think I was quoted at the time as saying it was the great hand of fortune that helped me to find those two enormous aurochs specimens. After all they weren't skeletons, these were beasts on ice. It was all well publicized—we filmed the entire visit to the remote Cashmere Mountains Resorts where the world's multi-billionaires own millions of acres of private property behind giant electrified walls that protect them from tour guides and insurgents while their names rise on the waitlist for homes on Mars.

My aurochs discovery was all thanks to a couple of bony-necked and bucktoothed young hermaphrodites interning for Extinction.com who skyped me one night from seven thousand metres above sea level, where they'd found the two frozen inside a big bobbing ice cube they'd watched roll down a serac and go floating out into the glacial meltwater lakes in the Gasbroom Valley. I tracked their coordinates and promised to buy the specimens from them at a boner of a price and grant them staggering promotions to VPs of .com—with their promise of strict confidentiality and exclusivity. The interns were to wait at the nearest private resort until I came and met them. I told them I wanted to see the beasts on ice for myself. Unfortunately, when I arrived the two .com interns were nowhere around, and I learned from the security guards they had disappeared shortly before I arrived—likely kidnapped and tortured by the so-called Bermuda Shortstroopers, the guards guessed. The region's tourists claimed the land as a traditional site of attraction and were at war with the local security guards and megawealthy residents over the right to vacation in Cashmere; so no easy place to remove giant frozen oxen from, and shaggy and sharp extinct animals don't just slip under your anorak. But knowing the right people helps, and after another six months of negotiations with agents and lawyers and producers I was able to extract the aurochs-on-ice with my own museum team and a documentary crew and a publishing deal in place. The aurochs were sent to our lab to be plastinated, and a year later I installed them as the main attraction.

BURKE NKUBRA

Thirteen years ago, on a bright winter day, I was walking to work. I remember the air tasted distinctly of aluminum, a cleansing chill off the ashy sea. Just as I pulled into my office I got a call with a Martian area code. It was the representatives of a prominent financial backer to the museum saying it was time I retired as director. I insisted I had to stay; my work was incomplete. I was told to quietly step aside and welcome our new director, Burke Nkubra, who was already in place, yes, as I learned like everyone else when I read it in the newsfeed the moment I hung up from the meeting with the representatives and walked out my office door into the press conference. That's how quickly I was swatted out of the way, like *that*. Burke had somehow lived long enough to replace me; the once-oily moustache now dandered, the pink grapefruit hanging on his neck had been a benign pulp this whole time, more of an affectation than any kind of life-threatening risk. Only day of my life I wanted to die, really wanted to.

Without the overwhelming distraction of my directorship and all my daily bullying around the halls to preoccupy me, left to my own devices, I found myself easily bored, anxious, and, on a good day, prone to really childish, bestial rages. I pursued the Aurochs with an even greater zeal; perhaps now, looking back, I could say it was *irresponsible* zeal—but not reckless. It was a depressive zeal. That is, I pursued the car all the more anxiously while developing an even greater sense of stealth in my approach. My self-discipline over myself was punishing. In public I showed absolutely no interest in the aurochs or the Aurochs now that I was out of the museum. So far as I was concerned, publicly, the aurochs was their business. Secrecy was my only way of knowing that the dream couldn't be taken away from me. Knowing that my love for the Aurochs was a secret was all that kept me from disintegrating. Otherwise I was a leper. I felt pulled apart. I was nothing without the directorship. I was falling apart one limb at a time, a cheek in bed, an eyelid over the phone, a toe floated to the surface of the bathwater. I left my fingers behind at a restaurant.

A couple of years after my retirement—by force, from a position I'd held for most of my life, a handful of profitable decades, nothing more—I was wallowing in the black market while sucking up to narcopharmaceutical gangs, and that's when I met Polli, my most recent wife. Thanks to her, I found the spunk to forge ahead and forget the past. I downloaded a new hairstyle. Enough with my white hair from childhood, I didn't want to be an old man a minute longer. I got a completely new cut, dyed an all-natural purple wow by essence of jacaranda. I designed myself a whole new wardrobe to coordinate with my colourful new wife, new hair, and new career—importer-exporter—even switched my irises, and immediately began brokering sales of antiques and offering my consulting services to large estates needing expert evaluation of holdings before going to an auction house or institution.

And I had better black market opportunities now that I was with Polaris, who was in league with health criminals and corrupt Martians of all variety. I encouraged her and through her I met at least twenty-three dead-serious *parts* collectors on Mars. They didn't know each other. All bidding was by proxy. But I knew them all, and how much they all hated the thought of each other and had suspicions about who was who.

To start with I was careful to only sell small things in large quantities when I was buying and trading objects on the black market, like Aztec gold medallions, ostrich eggs, or once in a while swap a sea serpent for something worth a little more, like Hitler's brain, the Bagram ivories. These bargains earned me trust among the agents and proxies. Along the way I discovered underground hospitals and learned who fronted as convenience stores or public relations firms, and who could put me in contact with the owners of famous Caravaggios stolen five hundred and fifty years ago, Tupac verses thought to be destroyed, lost religious knowledge, coercion technologies no one is aware exist but are still being used today. I traded it all, as well as live animals thought to be long extinct, like the polar bear. Lazarus Taxa, it's called.

POLARIS FROM DURBAN

When I met Polaris she was a young idealistic soldier strapped for cash—but very aggressive. She drove an armoured skytaxi over Durban that doubled as a travelling pharmacy and made deliveries. I was going through another bout of the C— and needed a lift. I called a number and she arrived. Meds up, she said, and walked in to my place and took a seat. I loved her fiercely from the moment I saw her, how confident she was in her long tousled wig, sunken eyes and cheeks, thin spotty torso, and a taxi-driver's fidgety legs. Narrower shoulders than even an old bone-rack like me. What ails you? she asked, jingling with pockets full of pills. I told her my condition, the smoke-like frailty of my existence. She let me peruse among her specialties, she was selling pure chocolate, homemade chemo drugs, and whatever was fresh from the Alzheimer's labs. I wanted a little of everything. She said I couldn't just take pills, I'd also need the pricey twice-daily intravenous injections into the tailbone and monthly blood transfusions to cure me. After a few sessions with the needles, and getting a chance to talk and touch veins, I could tell Polli saw past my wiki-gen16 to the real me. She asked me what I did for a living now that I'd been fired, and I said that I too survived in a secondary market. I said that whereas her business was in medicine trafficking, mine was the memory market. The antiquities game. That keening in the heart for the thing, I told her. The special thing. The must-have. If enough people are keen, the thing itself begins to glow or beat. Consumer aura determines price.

Who buys this junk? she said, while helping me with my transfusion.

I said, People on Mars, for the most part.

Then she said to me, Martians take what they like and leave us to die like hogs.

I agreed with her, they *are* greedy up there. But there's no use complaining, I thought, because that's where I'm headed.

Those epically rich island townships they call dubais that speckle the crystal oceans of Mars, that's where I want to live. This after years of ignoring the importance of Mars to my status on Earth, and knowing that Martians are responsible for the conditions we endure. It's the money they inject into our economy through nostalgia purchases that's made it possible for me to take advantage of their monopoly over our lives.

I always had a thing for women who peddled drugs, and having always married within a conveniently devout circle, I felt liberated knowing that I could talk to Polli about my health. She also had close contacts among the mafias who operate the Lagrange tollbooths along the interplanetary gravity tunnels between here and Mars. Before her grisly murder I was able enough to engage with some of these militant fellows who profit from the bright stars in our sky. The big orbiting mallships we can even see in broad daylight, they all lease space from the drug cartellites, and they are the ones who really own the gravity junctions between here and Mars.

We married in April that year, and spent eleven months together that I'll never regret. I've had the cancer fourteen times. I've had five very natural wives. Before Polli, none of my wives knew of my criminal double life, and if they suspected, we never spoke of it. No one at the Extinction Museum knew a thing; once you're past a certain age suspicion is inevitable anyway; what's the saying, Don't trust anyone over sixty? As director there were things I had wanted to accomplish for the institution, and I had a staff of over eight thousand to ride. I'd been the public face representing an institutional pillar of our social contract to remain part of the natural cycle of life and death. I'm not ashamed anymore but at the time I thought my fear of death and the lengths I went to stay alive contradicted everything I stood for in my social and business life.

LAZARUS TAXA

The twenty-three Aurochs collectors are all from Mars. Since I was retired from the museum I've worked exclusively with

Martians. Nostalgia for Earth up there is fervent. Mars wor-
ships nostalgia. That lethargic, blue-hued and misty-eyed sense
of lost time is a Martian's most holy feeling, whole Martian culture guided by nostalgia for Earth. Ridiculous, you say—who
cares? Up there they give each other Earth gifts for everything,
for birthdays, for name days, for Venus Day, any occasion. They
spend more on gifts up there for each other to show off at tri-
fling parties than the averagely educated man earns in a year
down here on Earth.

Shortly after Polli's murder I was hired to do an evaluation of the holdings from the early twenty-second century for
a deceased banana-peel energy oligarch named Omidyar, and
that's where I found my Aurochs. The Omidyar family owned
two of every automobile ever made, hidden a kilometre under
the city of Kitimat. His elegant, satin-skinned daughter told me
her father estimated that the family owned enough cars—they
weren't certain how many because all the records were on decades
worth of hard drives—and easily 30-billion ears' worth of cars—
oh, yes, yes, I assured the family (rubbing my chin thoughtfully
when really it was to conceal my drool), the sales would easily be enough money to get your children to Mars; the dreary
part of my job was to update and confirm the collection in the
database. In the will, the Omidyar patriarch stipulated that the
automobiles be auctioned in separate lots, that is, even go so far
as to split the pairs and sell each individually for greater profit
to share among the living relatives. An excellent idea, I told the
grieving eldest daughter, one of six blood relations with rights
to the Omidyar clan's fortune. I was all alone for miles in every
direction with some shah of shah's complete car collection. And
there behind a concrete wall, hidden in its own garage at the far
end of the bunker, an off-the-line 1999 Daewoo Aurochs in pristine condition. There it was. For a moment I didn't even want

to recognize it, my mind wouldn't let me believe it; besides, the light was dim, the surface of the thing was soft from dust, and too pristine to be true. Then I felt it in my heart, soon the feeling was in every vein, that all my life's work was worth it, worth every crime; oh, boy, that perfectly thermophallic shell, the muscular hips, period-accurate chrome spinner rims, five per cent tint on the windows, big smiling chrome grille, those bright-black rubber-tree tires, to say nothing of the hood ornament—God, it all made it so unbeatably terrestrial, so loaded down, a volcano with a burning, lava-red chassis.

Species vanish and then are discovered alive after decades or centuries with no signs; I wrote a popular post on the phenomenon. The Lazarus Taxa is central to the philosophy of Extinctionism. My Lazarus Taxa was cherry red. Blood-red interior leather. Cherry wood wheel. I mean I was sobbing. I was on my knees. I pressed my slobbering face against the hood and even after centuries that bus still tasted like gasoline. I cried and cried and it echoed in the vast underground bunker. The Omidyar family owned two of every automobile ever made. Two of everything, but they only owned one Aurochs.

When I scanned and rescanned the databases, the Aurochs wasn't there. No, I thought, I'm wrong, denying my impossible good fortune. I feared there might have been a paper copy made of the collection from generations ago—and indeed there was a small office inside the Kitimat bunker, and in it I found a rusted metal file cabinet and a janky ring binder with a handwritten list of six thousand cars dated to 2101. I came to the page where I saw the Aurochs. Written in pencil, my god, pencil, very faint graphite shale on the legal pad. I simply dusted over the page and the letters 1999 Daewoo Auroch vanished, leaving no trace whatsoever. Not satisfied, I crushed the entire pad of paper as if it had been a clump of ash lying in a fireplace.

THE EVAGINATION OF MY LAZARUS TAXA

I decided I would not keep the Aurochs. I decided I would not sell it either. Thinking about Polli's murder helped me decide what to do. My anguish, my loss. And my wife Coleco, and Melvin, my siblings, and everyone dying from easy things we used to cure with a poke or a pill two hundred years ago. Instead of cherishing the thing whole I set about disassembling the SUV for greater profit. At first I could barely touch it, all my faculties resisted, and yet over a period of some months—still in mourning—I dissected the beauty. I pulled it apart entirely. I took my time. And lay every last piece separately on the floor. Then, quietly and carefully and biting my knuckles, so to speak, I sent them off to the market like the faces of lovers. The first piece I sold was the four-wheel drive. It fetched me a great deal. I sweated and stressed and I pawed tearfully over the exhaust manifold before giving it up. Kissed and fondled each baby-like airbag.

During the past decade I've put the four-wheel drive on the block, then the oil pan, and the A/C condenser, but not the hood ornament, not yet, I can't put that to auction yet. I told colleagues I found pieces over the years on my obsessive flea market hunts throughout the junk cities and had been keeping them for my retirement fund. No one would dare investigate those sepulchrous alleys where I said I made my finds. And selling two or three parts every year, so discreet, on the black market, to keep that line open. The hand-milled steel turbo unit had to go, finally, to bribe a Martian minister of real estate. The odometer: seven kilometres. Fetched me enough ears to feed a billion. Even the little oxygen sensor fetched an impressive price. Passenger-side seatbelt. Not the hood ornament, not yet.

Why did I do it—pluck to death this rare SUV? I asked myself that every day and still I tore the car apart. I dithered and wept and fought my instincts. Then I ratcheted out another bolt. I remembered the words in the will of the man I stole the Aurochs from, never for a moment did I forget who rightly owned the SUV, and how Omidyar advised his heirs. I counted myself one of his heirs. What I took was on par with a gallerist's fee—fifty per cent. One Aurochs was worth as much as all those thousands of other vehicles, if you took it apart. Sell in separate lots, split the pairs, and auction off the collection one by one for the greatest profit. The words in the will rang in my head. And tearing the Aurochs apart like I did, I felt Omidyar's spirit on my conscience, practically speaking, his will being done through me. I got a chilly, lonely-but-triumphant pleasure in having seen through my greatest self-deception and finally giving in to my addiction to life. Perhaps memories of my anaemic childhood got woven up in my mind with the story of the rare and exquisite Aurochs SUV. How else could I find strength to debone the angel I'd used to guide me until that day if I hadn't realized that my life meant more than it? How else could I afford Mars? Mars: with health care, I can go on.

Butchering the Aurochs was no easy task. I was constantly telling myself, This Tiptronic keeps me alive, this dual climate control keeps me alive, these chrome nudge bars keep me alive. When I take the hood ornament to Sotheby's, I can only imagine what that great silver aurochs dashing to his feet will inspire in collectors, with the scorpion pinching its balls and about to strike the soft flesh of the belly, as if to remind buyers to *step on it*, act fast or be overbid. I estimate the sale of the ornament alone will buy me a seat among the elite—the healthiest, most aspirant, most discerning Martian class. I am near the top on a waitlist for a unit in a Cape Verde high-rise overlooking the general hospital of the Victoria Lake dubai. So, keeping all this in mind, I cut apart that ox car like a pomegranate and sold every last red pebble. I remember Omidyar's testament, written in the spirit of the age of the Aurochs.

DOUGLAS COUPLAND
SURVIVOR

FUCKING FUCK, THERE is no place worse than the port side of
the Luxurious CBS Yacht. Each morning I'm greeted by sauna-
like humidity and the perpetual odour of tuna sandwiches, plus,
believe it or not, the sound of CBS executives playing racquet-
ball. Their court is on the other side of my headboard's wall.
Thank you, British divorce laws, for handing me this sack-of-
shit career move. We're in the middle of fucking nowhere and
sleep doesn't even provide me with dreams, just an escape from
those snivelling American shits I now have to shadow all day.
Could these people have found a place on Earth more remote?
Excuse me, but were the Kerguelen Islands all booked up? Did
Pitcairn Island shut down for an extended religious holiday? I
tried Google-mapping this place: Fucking fuckity *fuck*.

. . .

The Republic of Kiribati is an island nation located in the central Pacific Ocean. It comprises thirty-two atolls and one raised
coral island, and is spread over 1.4 million square miles. Kiribati
straddles the equator and, on its east side, borders the International Date Line. Its former colonial name was the Gilbert and

63

Ellice Islands. The capital and largest city is South Tarawa.

Official languages: English, Gilbertese
Population: 105,000
GDP: $206 million
Internet Top-Level Domain (TLD): .ki
International calling code: +686

. . .

Our ludicrous contestants had to choose names for their "tribes" today. I suggested Swallowers versus Spitters and got pursed lips all around. Fucking Americans: no sense of humour. Doubtless they all own *Forrest Gump* on Blu-ray and have already asked each other what they want to be when they grow up. They are monsters.

. . .

Kiribati has few natural resources. Commercially viable phosphate deposits were exhausted at the time of its 1979 independence. Copra (dried coconut kernels) and fish now represent the bulk of production and exports. Tourism provides more than one-fifth of the country's GDP.

. . .

I have eight fellow cameramen, five of them veteran crew members of this wretched show. They divide contestants into two categories: Fuckable and Unfuckable. They treat the latter like Molokai lepers. As far as I can see, our biggest technical issue is ensuring that our shadows not appear on the sand—very hard to do around sunrise and sunset.

. . .

Survivor is a popular reality-TV game show, versions of which have been produced in many different countries. In the show, contestants are isolated in the wilderness and compete for cash and other prizes. The show uses a progressive elimination, allowing the contestants to vote off tribe members until only one remains and wins the title of "Sole Survivor."

The initial U.S. series was a huge ratings success in 2000 and triggered a reality-TV revolution.

. . .

Last night I got saddled with infrared nightshift filming. Ray, another screwed-by-life cameraman from Leeds, told me it's too early in the season for the contestants to truly fuck around, and I was prepared for eight hours of drying paint when a storm came out of nowhere and blasted away the pathetic huts they'd made as shelters. Talk about snivelling! So much fun to see them get what they deserve. The Spitters also inadvertently spilled their rice canister. When they picked it all up, it had become a big white lump filled with dead sand flies. It looked like raisin-bread dough. They are going to starve and it's going to be very funny.

Ray tells me that it usually takes about three storms before the contestants discreetly offer blowjobs in return for chocolate bars, bug repellant, and anti-fungal sprays. Perhaps there is light at the end of this tunnel.

Am feeling a bit ill. Too much sun is getting to me, I think.

. . .

TRAVELLER'S ALERT
Lymphatic filariasis
Dengue-4 virus
Soil-transmitted helminths
Parastrongylus cantonensis
Plas modium berghei
Trypanosoma cruzi

Leishmaniasis
Schistosomiasis
Multidrug-resistant *falciparum*
Simulium (Gomphostilbia) palauense

.   .   .

Tomorrow is my day off—a whole day on the Luxurious CBS Yacht, alone and getting shitfaced! Please, dear God, let me slit my wrists now.

There is a chance I may get to chopper in to the main town on the big island—which actually sounds interesting in a let's-go-whoring kind of way. Ray tells me the Kiribatese women all weigh five hundred pounds and have multiple diabetic amputations, but I find that hard to believe.

.   .   .

South Tarawa is the official capital of the Republic of Kiribati. The South Tarawa population centre consists of the small islets between Kiribatese (on the east). The once-separate islets are joined by causeways, forming one long islet along the southern side of the Tarawa Lagoon. The Parliament meets on Ambo islet; various ministries are scattered between South Tarawa, Betio, and Christmas Island.

.   .   .

My trip to Tarawa? A disaster. The plump, churchy Kiribati girls are apparently immune to my considerable northern-hemispheric charms. I didn't expect a clusterfuck on the high street, but I certainly wasn't expecting dead, frosty stares in return for a flirty goosing here and there. Fucking church. It'll be wanking for me tonight.

I spent the time I'd allotted for whoring walking around enjoying a litter-festooned pseudo-paradise. Its only charms for the casual visitor are the wide array of luncheon meats available in the general store, and nonradioactivity. I'm told this is one of the few atolls around here that didn't get fried by the Americans or the French back in the sixties and seventies.

.   .   .

Pacific Proving Grounds was the name used to describe a number of sites in the Marshall Islands which were used by the United States to conduct nuclear tests between 1946 and 1962. Sixty-seven atmospheric tests were conducted there, many of which were of extremely high yield. The largest test was the fifteen-megaton Castle Bravo shot of 1954, which spread considerable nuclear fallout on many of the islands.

.   .   .

Tuna Schnitzel
Tuna steak in breadcrumbs,
served with potato chips
and cucumber slices.

Tuna Salad
Raw tuna fish with onions in a spicy sauce.
Served with crusty bread.

Tuna Tartare
Raw tuna fish minced together
with hot spices,
spread onto garlic bread.

.   .   .

Vomited up lunch on the side of the grandly named Dai-Nippon Causeway (it's just a road) and was nearly run over by a rusted-out 1982 Chrysler LeBaron driven by some tubby local whose future is doomed by a diet based almost solely on tropical oils and the absence of any form of education.

.   .   .

There was a delay with the chopper back to the Luxurious CBS Yacht: apparently the price of gas tripled last night. The marine fuel pumps were guarded by three morbidly obese thugs in purple T-shirts toting rifles. Not something you see every day. Fucking OPEC. I've never felt this far away from civilization in my life. And what awaits me on the Yacht but booze, body lotion, a hand towel, and my right hand—or my left hand, if I want to make it seem like it's someone else.

.   .   .

We're down to eleven contestants now. They are:
1. Blonde slut.
2. Other blonde slut.
3. Third blonde slut, inside whose chest exist two proud examples of Nena's drifting *neun-und-neunzig luftballons*.
4. Brunette slut.
5. Black guy.
6. Gay guy.
7. Waste-of-space nerd.
8. Scary, well-nourished upper-middle-class woman who would really be better off concealing her wattles beneath a Katharine Hepburn–style beekeeper's hat (and preferably also being on some other show).
9. Worthy black woman who will be eaten alive by a clique of young white people.
10. Dumb hunk.
11. Noble hunk (FDNY).

.   .   .

I just found out from an assistant that when we choppered in yesterday afternoon, we flew too low over a breeding colony of endangered red-tipped auks, and most of them ate their chicks in response. By Jove, nature is majestic.

. . .

Dumb Hunk and Brunette Slut were about to get it on in a plumeria glade when Ray and I got a transmission to come back to the Luxurious CBS Yacht, with the addendum that all shooting for the day was over. Ray, a veteran of eight seasons, said that something like this had never before happened.

Once onboard, we learned that all transmissions to the outside world had stopped at 9:31 PM London time. As well, satellite links to the airport in Kiribati were down. We tried any other number of links, but nothing.

. . .

Southern Cross Cables to NZ, Hawaii, Fiji, and U.S. mainland
Australia–Japan Cable
Indonesian Sea-Me-We3 and Jasuraus links
Papua New Guinea APNG2 link
PPC-1 and Sanchar Nigam links into Guam
Hawaiian Telestra links
Gondwana link from New Caledonia to Australia
Intelsat
Inmarsat
SingTel Optus Earth stations

. . .

Went back to my wretched portside bedsit for a vodka hit. I tried going online, but of course the Internet was out. So I lay back on my bed and attempted to ignore the smell of tuna sandwiches while staring at a map of Southeast Asia. For the first time ever, I looked at the Philippines. I looked at the word over and over.

Philippines
Philippines
Philippines
Philippines
Who the fuck was Philipp?

. . .

Went back upstairs to the bar at the stern of the Luxurious CBS Yacht and everybody was getting hammered. At sunset the tech guy received a weak signal from somewhere and apparently the American air-force base in Guam was nuked by we-know-not-who. Nukes all over the place, like Chinese New Year. Even meek little Auckland, New Zealand got whacked. Nuking New Zealand is like nuking Narnia—and not at all sporting of whoever launched the bombs.

Debate raged as to whether or not we should tell the contestants about world events; we decided, in the absence of anything else constructive to do, to continue shooting. For the night we agreed to leave the contestants unobserved and incommunicado. They're so used to having their every whine recorded that the absence of cameras will be very disorienting indeed. Let them sweat it out, for once.

I returned to bed, passed-out drunk.

. . .

Woke up with acrid vomit rising up my throat and into my sinus cavities. Right, I'd bought six Ambiens from Jerry, the guy with Asperger's down in the editing suite. I'd forgotten the most important maxim of life in the media: booze + pills + full stomach + sleep = rock-star death. Cliché or not, I really thought

I was going to accidentally drown in my own vomit there on my cabin floor, but was able to gargle and sneeze and get everything out just in time. This made me happy not only because I continue to be alive, but also because it was Bug-Eating Contest Day, when contestants eat technically nontoxic but nonetheless motherfucker local insects. Whoever eats the most in two minutes wins a saccharine DVD of friends and family members rooting for them back home. Fucking Americans. Family this, family that, Tell Mom I love her, I love you all so much—they're like children. Maybe we should show them a satellite clip of Auckland, New Zealand roasting in a landscape of radioactive magma instead.

To get us all in the right mood, Autistic Jerry showed us some YouTube clips he'd saved on his hard drive of people at home using their blenders to make insect smoothies.

. . .

http://www.youtube.com/watch?v=SWIBpoIrXEE
http://www.youtube.com/watch?v=1AzYmJiVDqU
http://www.youtube.com/watch?v=__srsDMKo9k

. . .

Hi Lisa!

How are you, Sweetie? We miss you here back home, but we know you're down there being the best Survivor ever. Are you eating enough? Are you outwitting, outsmarting, and outlasting everybody? Have you had the bug-eating contest yet? Bleccch! How can you people do stuff like that? Well, anything to win! Not much to report. Schooner here really misses you, right Schooner? Looks like Schooner's not in a talkative mood today. *Where's Lisa? Where's Lisa? Talk to Lisa!* Just go on winning your game, sweetheart, and know how much we love you and miss you—and if you don't win the million-dollar prize, we'll still love you, right Schooner?

Bye Sweetie
Love you

.　.　.

Our bug-eating shoot was interrupted when I tripped over a root and got an avocado branch javelined directly into my right calf. I took the chopper into Tarawa along with three CBS execs intent on flying home, which, given that the northern hemisphere is most likely a glowing charcoal briquette at the moment, didn't seem to be too swift a decision on their part. But as it turned out their choice to flee was moot. When we arrived at the airport, even a cretin could see that nobody was going anywhere; planes were strewn all over the tarmac like children's toys on a playroom floor. It had just rained, and the tarmac didn't look wet so much as it did like a big dog had pissed on it.

We landed over by a huge mesh fence at the airport's western edge. A passing Air Pacific flight attendant, the luscious "Teehee," just in from a long haul from Singapore and a bit frazzled—hair sticking out in all directions—told us to stay near the helicopter, and this did make intuitive sense, as on the other side of the mesh were maybe a hundred tourists with duffle bags and hastily packed luggage pleading to get into the airport and onto any flight they could.

I stayed in the chopper, injecting myself with morphine; my Spidey senses were tingling and I wasn't planning on going anywhere I didn't have to. The CBS execs, on the other hand, made the mistake of going into one of the corrugated zinc Quonset buildings that turned out to be the customs and immigration shed; they weren't allowed back out. Our pilot, Alan, had been smoking a cigarette out on the tarmac when the execs started screaming. He sprinted back to the chopper, and within thirty seconds we were airborne. "There's no way you want to be down in that rat's nest, mate," he said to me. "And if you ask me, there's not going to be many flights to Brisbane for the next hundred years. Be a mate and reach into that bag over there and get my bottle of cognac. I could use a little lift right now."

As I looked down I saw a quartet of Air Nauru flight attendants throwing conch shells at the angry mob on the other side of the fence, the shells shattering as they hit the fence's metal weave, turning to chalk.

.   .   .

Is there ever such thing as a mob that isn't angry? Or would one simply call that a "crowd"? Is an angry crowd de facto a mob?

.   .   .

FLIGHT 311: NAURU–HONIARA–BRISBANE

Departs Nauru:	06:45	Delayed
Arrives Honiara:	07:30	Delayed
Departs Honiara:	08:15	Delayed
Arrives Brisbane:	10:30	Delayed

.   .   .

In my absence, the Luxurious CBS Yacht polarized into two factions: fuckfest upstairs, gloom and tears and snivelling downstairs. Needless to say, as soon as I got back I was upstairs gorging on a feast of muscle relaxants and pity sex. Thank you, avocado branch, for rendering me fuckable in the eyes of comely production assistants.

The only bad news was Dan "The Danimal," our L.A.-based cameraman, hanged himself from the beams of a ridiculous bamboo contraption designed for tomorrow's archery rewards challenge. Battle scars or not, tomorrow I'm on day-camera duty.

· · ·

HOW TO CALCULATE YOUR TOTAL DAILY CALORIE NEEDS

STEP 1: Multiply your current weight in pounds by ten if you're a woman, or by eleven if you're a man. This number represents your basic calorie needs.

STEP 2: Multiply your basic calorie needs by your activity level— 20 per cent (or 0.2) if you sit or lie still for most of the day, with little or no exercise; 30 per cent if you walk less than two miles per day; 40 per cent if you are somewhat active, doing activities such as dancing, doing a lot of work in the house or garden, or taking exercise classes; and 50 per cent if you're actively involved in a sport or you have a job that requires a great deal of physical labour, such as construction work. The resulting number reflects your activity-based calorie needs.

STEP 3: Add your basic calorie needs from steps 1 and 2, then multiply this sum by 0.1—these are the calories you need for digestion.

STEP 4: Combine the results from steps 1, 2, and 3. This is your total daily calorie need to maintain your weight!

· · ·

Well, here we are. The contestants found out about whatever it is, nuclear war or what have you, and our resulting inability to communicate with the rest of the world. To their credit, they figured it out by noticing a change in crew behavior (pasty over-boozed poker faces; an amplified air of not giving a shit) and the fact that there were fewer of us (B-camera crew, set-dec, and props department, plus half the sound staff on a two-day mini-holiday, all incinerated in the Guam Hotel Nikko).

There were the eleven of them and eight or nine of us standing at the edge of a glorious sapphire lagoon when it came out. The contestants looked like they'd been clubbed.

Then there was this eerie minute where nobody spoke, which lasted until the two chickens that had escaped from the previous week's reward challenge began taunting us with their cackles and shrieks from up in the palmetto scrub.

Couldn't wait to return to the Luxurious CBSY.

· · ·

The LCBSY is gone. Ray and I got into our Zodiac near sunset, having talked down a slim majority of the contestants, then circled the island to where the yacht ought to have been only to find that it was not there. We could have gone searching for it, but when the sun goes down in the Pacific it's like an off switch.

We ended up overnighting on one of the tinier islands, both of us starving. Upon waking, five yacht bodies had washed ashore in the night: Asperger's Jerry, two production assistants, the chef, and the lone CBS executive who'd stayed behind. Things are not going to get better here.

· · ·

There's a part of me that loves the prospect of lawlessness, I have to admit.

· · ·

Kiribati is a constitutional multiparty republic, and the Kiribati government works to respect the civil and human rights of its citizens. There are only a few areas in which problems remain, but in general, Kiribati's laws provide effective means of addressing individual complaints, although there have been some reports of extrajudicial communal justice.

· · ·

We were going to bury our fellow TV comrades but then decided, why the fuck bother? The sand crabs and the gulls will give the corpses a swift and environmentally friendly end.

Food for Ray and me is a different thing. We spent a few hours trying to decide whether we should go to the Swallowers' campsite, where we'd left the gang of twenty—or if we should avoid them altogether. As far as we can estimate, there's zero food on any of our surrounding islands (islets, really) unless one of the sound technicians has a granola bar tucked into his knapsack. The nearest inhabited island is a good hour away by boat, and going there would eat up all the gas in our Zodiac. And with gas currently being the most precious local commodity, it's doubtful any of the Kiribatese will be coming to visit or pillage our sad little society here. We are, pardon my French, *totalement fuckés*.

In the end Ray and I decided it would be fun to do a quick cruise past the inhabited island just to remind them that we have a Zodiac and gasoline, whereas they have nothing—certainly no survival skills. I think one or two of them know how to light a fire, but that's it.

So anyway, after our deeply satisfying strafing of Loser's Island, Ray and I discussed that old TV show *Gilligan's Island*, where six essentially clueless people plus one intelligent professor assembled a reasonable facsimile of civilization from palm fronds and whatever drifted into their lagoon. Surely all of them should have succumbed to rape, buggery, murder, cannibalism, and suicide long before they cobbled together a small Club Med-ish village.

Fucking TV.

·   ·   ·

It's now three foodless days later, and the skin surrounding the interim stitches on my calf is starting to turn all purple and yellow. There's some bloatiness happening. Worst of all, I can't muster the energy or sense of purpose to wank. Before nuclear war my thinking used to be along the lines of, "Sure, right now I'm wanking, but this is just a pale substitute for some genuine bonking I hope to do in the near future." But with no possible bonking available in the near—or distant—term, the sterility and pointlessness of wanking is all too apparent.

And did I mention boredom on top of the starvation and wanklessness? Half-jokingly Ray suggested we Zodiac to the International Date Line and go back and forth across it and hence go back and forth in time.

.   .   .

On January 1, 1995, the Republic of Kiribati introduced a change of date for its eastern half, from time zones −11 and −10 to +13 and +14. Before this, the country was divided by the date line. A consequence of this revision was that Kiribati, by virtue of its easternmost possession, the uninhabited Caroline Atoll at 150°25 west, started the year 2000 before any other country on Earth, a feature the Kiribati government capitalized upon as a potential tourist draw. The international time-keeping community, however, has not taken this date-line adjustment seriously, noting that most world atlases ignore the new Kiribati date-line shift.

.   .   .

One more body washed up (or the remains of one)—Lee-Anne, the makeup woman whom we were able to identify only because the sea creatures who'd nibbled away most of her didn't like the taste of her hippie chunky wood necklace.

. . .

QUESTION: What is "grave wax"?

ANSWER: Grave wax is a crumbly, white, waxy substance that
accumulates on those parts of the body that contain fat—
the cheeks, breasts, abdomen, and buttocks. It is the product
of a chemical reaction in which fats react with water and
hydrogen in the presence of bacterial enzymes, breaking
down into fatty acids and soaps. Grave wax is resistant to
bacteria and can protect a corpse, slowing further decompo-
sition. Grave wax starts to form within a month after death
and has been recorded on bodies that have been exhumed
after one hundred years. If a body is readily accessible to
insects, grave wax is unlikely to form.

. . .

During last night's storm (which we spent beneath the up-
turned Zodiac, thank you) Ray and I were jokingly discussing
who among those left on Loser's Island would be the most delicious to eat, and then suddenly the discussion turned serious,
which was frightening. My kidneys have shrivelled into little
raisins, and my calf is beginning to resemble beef jerky. Our
one conclusion is that we wouldn't touch Third Blonde with
Implants—something just too unappetizing about those two
silicone blancmanges.

So tomorrow we go.

. . .

We woke up to a spooky sight: a U.S. battleship drifting past
the island, the USS *Ronald Reagan*. At first we thought we were
rescued, but after some waving and halloo-ing we dug out
our binoculars and saw that there was nobody on deck. And

then it got caught in a swell and, over the course of a half hour, turned 180 degrees, and we saw that its starboard side had been scorched or melted or something-or-othered by a nuclear blast. Anybody onboard would have been irradiated to pieces on the spot.

And then . . . and then it drifted away, off towards Antarctica.

· · ·

USS RONALD REAGAN

Aircraft carried: Ninety fixed-wing and helicopters
Motto: "Peace Through Strength"
Nickname: "Gipper"
Displacement: 101,000 to 104,000 tons full load
Length—overall: 1,092 ft (333 m)
Length—waterline: 1,040 ft (317 m)
Propulsion: 2 × Westinghouse A4W nuclear reactors
         4 × steam turbines
         4 × shafts 260,000 shp (194 MW)
Speed: 30+ knots (56+ km/h)
Range: Essentially unlimited
Complement: Ship's company: 3,200
Air wing: 2,480

· · ·

The next reward challenge was to have been something involving archery; if nothing else, the citizens of Loser's Island are armed. And yes, I'd prefer not to be shot or have the Zodiac's neoprene skin be compromised. So yes, we were wary as we neared.

Through binoculars we could see from a quarter mile away that there was nobody visible near the main camp. We circled the island 90 degrees, cut the engine, and scrutinized not just the beaches but the shrubbery and the trees. Nobody. Ray said they all must have passed the point where they were awaiting rescue and moved inland, and I said he was a simpleton, my point being that there's nothing in the middle of these islands but nasty scrub, tarantulas, and spiky plants. Our ultimate conclusion was that even if the Losers were lying in wait with their bows and arrows, they'd keep us alive to see if we had any news.

. . .

The presence of insects in a corpse is critical in estimating the time of death over longer time periods. Flies quickly find bodies, and as their life cycles are predictable, a corpse's time of death can be calculated by counting back the days from the state of development of insects within said corpse. Weather conditions can sometimes vary results, and identification of specific maggot species can be difficult.

Here is an example: If a body is found in an air-conditioned building (68°F) with second-instar larvae of Lucilia sericata feeding on the corpse, we can calculate that those larvae had moulted from their first instar in the previous twelve hours. Because the eggs take eighteen hours to hatch and the first instar takes twenty hours to develop, the most recent time the eggs could have been laid would be thirty-eight hours earlier, if the larvae had just moulted. If they were old larvae, about to moult into their third instar, the most recent time of death would be fifty hours prior to the discovery of the body.

. . .

Remember Jonestown? I certainly do, and I imagine the initial investigators on the scene must have felt something akin to what we did upon beaching on Loser's Cove. From five hundred feet away? Paradise. But once you're on land and walking towards the encampment? Carnage. To be specific, carnage mixed with camera and sound equipment. And unlike Jonestown, where bodies were kind enough to array themselves in neat rows, here everybody seems to have simply died wherever, like puppets when the hand is removed. And also, unlike Jonestown, the sixteen bodies at the camp seem to have been murdered. Some by strangulation, some by machete—although it's hard to tell if they were killed here, or if the bodies were dragged over. The rains have washed away that sort of evidence.

By using sticks in the sand, we tried to determine if there were any others still out there. In our minds it had always been twenty of them here, cast and crew, but on close inspection the number was actually seventeen. Which meant there was still one survivor. By laborious deduction we determined it to be Michelle, the Brunette Slut, who at that moment might well have been within an arrow's reach of us.

I said, "Ray, maybe it's best we nab some of this camera equipment and take it to a different island. I'd bet the footage has stories to tell us."

"Righty-O," he said.

The presence of footage offered, if nothing else, the prospect of relief from the crushing boredom of island living, although I did wish the camp had had some food to pillage.

To look on the bright side of things, God bless the Zodiac crew for leaving both morphine and powerful sedatives in the first-aid kit, and, for no reason I can think of, a twelve-pack of Durex Ramses Thins. The last thing our depleted population base needs right now is spermlessness.

.   .   .

RISPERDAL (RISPERIDONE)
Identifiers

CAS *number*: 106266-06-2
ATC *code*: N05AX08
PubChem: 5073
DrugBank: aprd00187
Formula: $C_{23}H_{27}FN_4O_2$
MOL *mass*: 410.485 g/mol
Bioavailability: 70% oral
Metabolism: Hepatic (CYP2D6-mediated)
Half-life: 3–20 hours
Excretion: Urinary

. . .

Fucking *fuck*. While we were bent over gathering cameras, Brunette Slut took the Zodiac. But to where? At this point she has enough gas to get halfway to one of the populated islands—if that. Ray offered the astute observation that, "It's always the brunette who stays under the radar for most of the game who wins these things, isn't it?"

So now it's me and him. On the steadicams we got to witness footage of what went down, *Blair Witch*–style: who killed whom and how. But that's another story, not mine.

In a nook in the rocks, I discovered six cans of Chinese tinned ham (or ham-like) product. Yes, it looked like pâté made from Jeffrey Dahmer's boyfriends, but to me it was a Sunday roast-beef lunch. I haven't shown Ray.

. . .

Maybe two hours after the Zodiac was pilfered, a fourteen-foot aluminum boat with Korean markings beached on the sand a few hundred yards down from us. Its sole passenger was a Korean fisherman. We're debating whether he has any food-stuffs onboard. Well, should he be unwilling to share, our flare guns and some heavy chunks of coral ought to be enough to do him in.

.   .   .

Here's the thing about survival: survival is merely survival. It's nothing else. It's not a work of art. It's only that you survived and someone else didn't. Outwit, outplay, and outlast: and if someone wins this thing, it's fucking well going to be *me*.

STEPHEN MARCHE

THE PERSONASTS

*My Journeys Through Soft
Evenings and Famous Secrets*

IT HAD BEEN two years since my last soft evening and I arrived forty-five minutes late to Madeleine Reid's sprawling neocolonial in the Tuscan Hills subdivision an hour and a half outside San Diego. In the living room, a young Asian woman had already covered herself in Dressdown's rags and dung-smeared leaves and sat in the empty space at the centre of the room scratching her arms and chest, muttering low profanities. A magnificent collection of throws covered the twelve-piece beige sectional, and the other six guests were either watching or dressing. Somebody had already taken the throw of Ninja and was hiding behind the curtain of the nearest window. The young man nearest to me began putting on Mitzi. Mitzi is simple: a gingham dress with a crinoline and a pack of Lucky Strikes. Mitzi smokes and walks barefoot. A friend of mine who regularly becomes her describes Mitzi as a seventy-year-old woman who wakes up in a twenty-two-year-old's body. Even though she never exposes herself and would never dare touch a man, she considers herself very risqué indeed, old-fashioned in her sluttiness.

A fiftyish woman with close-cropped hair had just put an unlit cigar in her mouth. She was Monopoly. Sponge-bag trousers, silk top hat, and morning coat are the other elements of Monopoly's throw. Because of the ludicrous vocabulary and the fact that he's constantly comparing himself to Winston Churchill, I had assumed for years that Monopoly was based on Conrad Black, and I was only convinced otherwise when another personast told me she had seen Monopoly spun in a Dallas suburb in the early seventies. The name, combined with the throw, is probably a tipoff. Americans assume he's a version of the plutocrat character from the game Monopoly. It does explain the name and the top hat but not the sour mood. Perhaps Monopoly is a combination of the two, or perhaps neither. The origin of any highway is never better than vague.

Suddenly Dressdown screamed out: "My back crunches like candy in a six-year-old's baby teeth. Pain candy. Positronic confibulators! Pain candy! Why won't any of you help me?" To me the greatest pleasures of Personism are such expected surprises. In *Melodies of Self*, published in 1999, Columbia sociologist and practising personast Carol Reinhardt described soft evenings as "living tension between posing and becoming, a tension so unstable that it vibrates into a kind of bell tone. It's a tension between posing and being, but it's also a relief of that tension, a relief into noisy silence." Ninja somersaulted through the centre of the room into a low, crouching warrior's pose. His eyes shifted back and forth for a moment. Then he rolled back to the periphery.

I remember almost nothing from the rest of the soft evening because I soon entered myself for a spin as Nick Charles. The others followed quickly afterwards, as The Old Gunfighter, Seagull, and Mr. Clean. Madeleine, our host, entered last, as Joan. We spun a lot of highways that night: Violent B, The Mercy Man, Rufus Wainwright, Sammy Sexy as Shit, Oliver Twist, Mary Magdalene, Scaramouche. Two highways I had never encountered before came—Tramontate and Gumper. The former reminded me vaguely of Luciano Pavarotti, the latter of a beautiful teenage girl's teddy bear. My other memories of the evening are nothing more really than a series of cool, glittering, ephemeral impressions. This was the softness I had craved in my return to Personism, the softness of the highways and, afterwards, the security of the quiet rooms. Lost in the suburbs, I was home again.

Soft evenings always end with quiet rooms. Before the spins every door in the house is left open, until one by one the members leave the highways for privacy. Madeleine was kind enough to provide each room with noise-cancellation headgear and I relished the smooth letdown—like a hot shower after the big game—for perhaps too long. When I emerged, I was again the last one to the party.

The throws had all been tucked away. Madeleine introduced me to the group, a fairly typical assortment for a soft evening. Maxwell Cho, architect, and his stay-at-home wife, Geraldine, had just moved from San Francisco. The other married couple, Quincy and Khadija, were both copyright lawyers—the box-ticking, world-builder types. The lesbians, Marcie and Sammy, looked like young Grandma Moseses. Together they owned a sex shop catering exclusively to women. We had the typical conversations: models of cars, babysitters, cleaning ladies, vacations, mortgages, renovations, gas prices and, above all, real estate. Intimate abandon doesn't end the need for small talk.

"Are you new?" Marcie or Sammy asked me. For a moment I worried that I had misperformed my spin along the highway, that they thought I was a newbie. Then I remembered I had arrived late. She was asking me if I was new to the city.

"No, I'm just getting back into the highways," I replied.

"You took a break?"

"Two years."

"Like Björk."

The Icelandic pop star is the celebrity most open about her Personism. In a recent article in *Rolling Stone*, she discussed falling into and out of the practice. It was the same article that had made such controversial claims about the blindings in Evanston, Illinois being motivated by Personism. Marcie or Sammy and I changed the subject. We were making the rest of the room uncomfortable. Personasts do not talk about Personism at soft evenings; in playgroups and parking lots and soccer practices, yes, but not at soft evenings. The latest "revelations" about Personism in the press have made these silences even more necessary.

Accurate figures on the rise of Personism are difficult to come by. The census keeps no record of Personism because it is not considered a religion. The sociologists who have tried to establish its scope arrive at wildly different conclusions. Estimates for the U.S. and Canada begin at 700,000 and reach as high as several million. Everyone agrees, however, that Personism is spreading. "Every suburb now has its nightly session, and where the suburbs go, Personism follows," writes Carol Reinhardt. "It was a major force by 1982. In the past twenty-five years, Personism has doubled and redoubled countless times." Due to the casual nature of attendance probably no definite answer as to the exact number of personasts is possible. Other questions are more haunting and urgent to outsiders: what is the source of the power in this movement that has no institutions and no leaders? What emotion transports the personasts into their whirligig of shifting identities? What insanity makes them perform the "famous secrets," branding themselves, releasing wild animals onto city streets, burning money?

My own off-and-on relationship with Personism is more or less typical. When I was seventeen, a girlfriend brought me to my first session. At university, I dropped the soft evenings because I had other things to explore. Then I started work at the Quality Assurance department of a multinational legal publishing company in Scarborough, Ontario, and began attending soft evenings at least once a week. My favourite group was over an hour and a half away, deep in an industrial park on the other side of town. My spins with them lasted over two years, my longest uninterrupted stint on the highways.

Manny Seligman, in his 1993 book *The Gods Beyond the Wall: A Field Guide to Spiritual Sprawl*, identifies over three thousand different highways. Many highways are simply well-known historical personalities: Jesus, Buddha, JFK, Malcolm X, Byron, Lorca, Mao, Hitler, Bob Dylan, and so on. Local variations are common. In Canada, I've seen Pierre Trudeau; in California, Ron Howard. Celebrity highways have a tendency to appear and disappear violently. At the time of writing, Paris Hilton appears nightly all over the continent but in six months to a year she will have vanished completely. Purist personasts tend to look down on celebrity spins because they're so shallow.

Highways from literature are rare but often deeply felt and are more or less permanent: Oliver Twist, Bruce Lee, and King Lear will always have a place at good soft evenings. Commercials produce highways: The Michelin Man, Mr. Clean, and Harpy the Happy Housewife. Other highways represent not people so much as ways of speaking. The highway called Confucius utters aphorisms, but these aphorisms are not limited to Confucian sayings. I have heard Confucius quote Marcus Aurelius, Zen koans, and Led Zeppelin lyrics. The Homer highway would not be recognizably Homeric to a Classics scholar. He just speaks with extended, overblown metaphors.

The vast majority of highways present no clear origin and don't fit any category. The most common are Lili, Dressdown,

The Baron, The Swinger, Violent B, Scarface, Dick, The Craving, Mr. Bibbly Burton, Trampoline, Vocallisimus, and The Seagull. To complicate the system even further, many highways seem to stand between categories. Often these in-between highways are feminine. Joan, for example, is a combination of Joan of Arc and Joan Baez dressed in flapper clothes. Barbra and Simone similarly fuse celebrity (Barbra Streisand and Simone de Beauvoir) with fictions (Barbra is a visitor from outer space and Simone is a cynical gardener).

Any explanation for the mass appeal of Personism has to be found in the experience of the soft evening. The soft evening is soft because it is careless, forgetful, the easiest liberation. In the softest evenings, the exquisite loss of the highways stretches into a feeling of distance, a crack that is also a chasm between oneself and everything that matters. After a very soft evening I sometimes feel like I can see into the spirit of strangers in their cars or on their lawns or at their windows. But soft evenings are also profoundly silly. They are childish pranks, larks.

To understand Personism, however, one also has to recognize the power and beauty of the "famous secrets," which, because they are so poorly understood, tend to be the aspect of personast practice most frightening to outsiders, the basis of the wildest rumours. If soft evenings are the downtown core of Personism, then the famous secrets are the suburban sprawl. They are the ceremonies for the loyal few, for those who experience Personism as a part of life rather than an escape from it.

Waste is a big theme in the famous secret ceremonies. A mortgage-burning party is the most common famous secret. Burning piles of one-dollar bills is common as well, and pouring bottles of champagne or vodka into sewers. Other famous secrets seem designed to leave minute marks on other people: giving large sums of money, like twenty thousand dollars, to mentally ill homeless men, or buying the clothes off their backs or paying them to clean up messes of caviar. Other famous secrets focus on the body: deep tanning, excessive exercise, fasting, tattoos or brands (generally of a small grey cloverleaf or red octagon). Sometimes personast ceremonies integrate easily into religious life. The release of doves at weddings began as a famous secret. Other ceremonies act as replacements for religious rituals. A personast funeral involves placing the deceased's ashes into a simple clay pot, hiking into a silent place, walking a hundred yards from the path, and leaving the pot behind.

My own experiences with famous secrets have been rare but powerful. In my sessions at the legal publishers, I once witnessed a friend, with a salary of $27,000 a year, burn a small pile of hundreds amounting to nearly seven thousand dollars. The power of the gesture made me sick to my stomach. I dream about it frequently. The sole personast funeral I attended, in the San Bernardino National Forest, was an overpowering encounter with mortality. But I have always fantasized about trying one famous secret in particular: the liberation of animals. As a celebration of my return to Personism, a pilgrimage of sorts, I decided to try it at last. It would also be a chance to explore the world of organized Personism, which had expanded during my hiatus from a handful of semi-professional outfits into a real growth industry. Every personast I knew wanted to set me up with a company he or she had used. In the end, I went with Jed Cushing's Cloverleaf Tours based out of Canmore, Alberta, in the heart of the Canadian Rockies.

Jed is a friendly man but reserved, as might be expected from a professional personast. His business is famous secrets, and he has the perfected tan and wiry strength of a man whose work is outdoor leisure. The offices of Cloverleaf Tours, where we met to plan my trip, were in a cool basement off Canmore's

main street. Every surface was cluttered with personast paraphernalia. The walls were covered with photographs from his
adventures. Our initial meeting was comically brief. I introduced myself. He suggested a package of silence and release, at a
cost of five hundred dollars. I agreed. He showed me the door. I
wasn't offended by the brevity of the meeting though. Some of
the famous secrets can be shared only by strangers.

I awoke the next morning to the polite antiseptic bleating of
my alarm clock at 3:30. I listened for a while to the buzzing of
the power lines outside my window and made sure to clean my
ears thoroughly after a shower.

Jed was waiting for me in the lobby, his Audi parked outside.
The faint murmuring of the Muzak was painful to him, I could
tell. We didn't even say hello. By the time we arrived at Sunshine Mountain half an hour later, dawn was just beginning to
play on the far faces. The hill was more or less abandoned for the
summer but past the deserted chalet a phantom ski lift continued lifting nobody to nowhere. We loaded ourselves onto a seat
and immediately I was aware of the sound of the breeze. What I
assumed was a perfectly still day was fragile and ragged twenty
feet up.

The view was sublime—the shifting penumbras of the rising
sun against the mountains, deer passing below, flocks of birds.
I concentrated on the sound—the minute tick-tick-ticking of
the chair on the wire, the vast, vital cling-clang as the chair-hook
caught the rotor of the pole, and always the wind.

At the top of the hill Jed led me along a small path through
stands of evergreens. The meaty crunch of our boots on
the crushed gravel was deafening. As we crossed an alpine
meadow, even the squelch of our socks in boots and our boots
on the grass were over-loud. I noticed the sound of my boots
more than the colours of the hundreds of wildflowers. We
descended beyond a small tarn, through a steep valley filled

with galumphing boulders. The valley ended in something like a pile of these boulders, which resembled a cyclopean stairway. Jed stopped me with his hand. He pointed down.

I had to go down alone into the rocks.

There I found silence.

All ambient noise was blocked by the alignment of the stones, all wind too. My own heart's noise grew into a syncopated cash register. It took me a few minutes—or it felt like a few minutes despite my loss of all sense of time—to remember the expected practice for this famous secret. I brought my heart rate down as low as possible. I listened consciously to the silences before and after my heartbeat, paying attention with effort to their encompassing non-sounds.

Soon I was dwelling in true silence. It's no exaggeration to say it was the greatest alleviation of my life.

I dwelt in the silence until a stray host of sparrows overhead passed and wrecked it.

The walk down to the Sunshine Mountain parking lot was so depressing I nearly wept. Others had warned me but their warnings hadn't prepared me. I felt caged in my senses. I craved an end to the sun, to the razorback edges of the mountains, the ruby poppies, my own skin, and above all to the noise. You can't shut your ears, that's the cruellest fact of anatomy, I remember thinking.

It was mid-afternoon by the time we arrived back at Jed's Audi. He popped the trunk and brought out a cage of Boreal chickadees. And once I released the birds from the cage, the feeling of self-loathing, of loathing at having a body, vanished with them into the mountain air. The genius of the famous secret entered my spirit with all its smoothness and coolness.

Jed was chatty as we drove back to Canmore. "We had perfect weather. When it rains or it's really windy, I don't bother.

Sometimes the clouds change in the upper levels and I have to come back with the customers. Four, sometimes five times, until they find the silence."

"How did you discover that location?" I asked.

"I was a hiker before I became a personast and I used to love that hollow. I used to hike up there all the time to visit. I didn't know why."

I asked if his hiking had flowed into Personism naturally. "Not at all. It's like the opposite of loving nature or environmentalism. It's waste. Oblivion."

His sudden friendliness was a relief to me. I was going to spend the night in Canmore and I asked him if he could set me up with a soft evening. He demurred apologetically, claiming he didn't spin on the highways anymore. "I get my fill up here on the mountain during the day." Jed has been on over a hundred famous secrets in foreign countries, in places as distant as Antarctica and Kyrgyzstan. He owns the most expensive noise cancellation technology currently available. "Fifteen grand," he said tapping the small black ball on the dashboard, which explained why the car was so utterly quiet. His basement holds two sensory deprivation tanks.

"How many trips a week do you take?"

"In the summer as many as three or four. That's all kinds of famous secrets though. Not just silence and release."

Canmore is a perfect spot for a business like Cloverleaf Tours. Not only is there enormous traffic from the United States and increasing numbers of European personasts who have bought property in the Canadian Rockies, but the suburban growth in nearby Calgary, an oil town in boom, offers a handy domestic market. "Every week they plant a new bed of roses and I'm the one with the bouquets," Jed said.

I asked what he thought attracted so many people to Personism.

"Have you seen the trees in those Calgary suburbs? Five-foot trees in the middle of the horizon. City ordinances say you got to have them. That's the only reason they're there. You can live in Pine Lake Hills or in Pine Hill Lake. You get lost. 'Oh, no, you're on Riverview Drive in Pleasant Mount View. You want the Riverview Drive in Pleasant Mountain View. It's a very easy mistake to make.' And like that. Which is why I'm here."

The next morning I happened to drive through those suburbs on my way to the airport. The overpasses and cloverleafs in their sublime curves twisted counterintuitively around the never-ending subdivisions, the cathedral-like malls, the walls soundproofing life from the roads, the otiose, mocking patches of grass and sidewalk. This landscape shaped Personism as surely as the Arabian desert shaped Islam or the cool lake of Galilee shaped Christianity. It is also the landscape that shaped me.

In the 1995 case, Reno v. Whittaker, the United States Supreme Court denied tax-exempt status for Personism on the grounds that it didn't qualify as a religion. According to the court, personast activities lack an articulate set of beliefs. Jews, Christians, Muslims, Buddhists, Hindus and atheists all participate at soft evenings without any sense of contradiction. The term "cult" also doesn't apply. No institution benefits from the soft evenings and leading a session doesn't offer financial or status advantages.

Nonetheless sociologists and journalists generally treat Personism as a new religion for lack of a better approach. Brett Groundsman, author of *Bless This House: How New Religions Are Shaping Suburban and Exurban American Life*, justified his inclusion of Personism with the claim that its ritual contains "a complete vision of life and the place of the self in the universe." Groundsman has to find this "vision" in peripheral famous secrets surrounding birth and death, ignoring the fact that the majority of personasts have never heard of these famous secrets and it's hard to see what vision of life, other than ephemerality, one can find in soft evenings.

In search of an answer, or at least clearer questions, I attended the seventh annual conference of SIPS (Society of International Personast Studies) held at the Newport Beach Marriott Hotel in Orange County, California, this past November. The conference venue was almost too appropriate. The hotel's wide grid and large rooms meant that we more or less had to commute to the lobby. The building was attached to Fashion Island, an open-air luxury shopping plaza.

At the opening night reception, over three hundred professors from two hundred universities drank Pinot Grigio around the lobby fountain. Mark Grenstein, a professor of Sociology at Duke University and the president of SIPS, introduced himself. He was a tall man, at least six foot six, with a slightly vulture-like stoop, an English formality of dress, and courtly manners. He had heard that I was working on an article about my experiences as a personast. To change the subject, I complimented him on the venue and remarked on its appropriateness to the subject of the conference.

"Yes, Orange County is something of a homecoming. Our first conference, in October 2001, took place in Orange County." He himself had not begun his work on Personism then. A colleague at Duke had attended and reported back on the scope of the movement. It coincided powerfully with his own research on faith and human geography. Around that time too, he had attended his first soft evening.

"That's the funny thing about SIPS," he said. "Ninety-nine per cent of us practise what we preach, which sounds admirable but doesn't offer the greatest deal of objectivity."

I asked him if the lack of distance was that unusual; the

leading scholars of Buddhism tend to be Buddhists, Catholic theologians are Catholic, and so on.

"I'm not saying it's unusual, I'm saying it's problematic. Besides, Personism is not a religion. Above all it's not a religion. Come hear my talk. The entire point of Personism is that it's not a religion."

Professor Grenstein was called away by a SIPS member who wanted to discuss an article in *Rolling Stone*. The whole party was abuzz with the "Rolling-Stone Issue." Six months earlier the magazine had claimed ("White Voodoo," May 2007) that a series of blindings in Evanston, Illinois were the responsibility of "personast cells" in suburban Chicago. Over the course of two months during the summer of 2005, fifteen people, all homeless men and prostitutes, were dropped in front of Glenbrook and Highland Park Hospitals missing their eyes. They had no recollection of how their eyes had disappeared. Most personasts, myself included, found the idea that personasts could blind people absurd. The violence it would take to rip out the eye of a stranger would be opposite in every way to the spirit of relief in soft evenings. It didn't help his credibility that the author, while claiming to be a personast himself, made basic mistakes. Soft evenings are not like orgies. If we were capable of orgies, we wouldn't need Personism. He also included a description of animal slaughter, which could not have been more inaccurate. Silence and release are famous secrets, not holding and killing.

Everyone at the conference agreed that some kind of statement needed to be made and that SIPS was the appropriate body to make that statement, but who was going to make it, and how, were less clear.

Then, at exactly 9:30, the question was abandoned and the hotel lobby emptied. Too late I realized that I had forgotten to make my own arrangements for a soft evening.

Day One of the conference was humming when I managed to navigate the labyrinth of the hotel's hallways to the conference centre. The choice of panels and variety of approaches was baffling. In the morning, I heard a member of the faculty of religious studies at Harvard analyze the latest statistics on Personism. Her analyses were new because they took into account the financial and racial criteria of the participants but her conclusion, as far as I could tell, was that personasts were all members of the middle class. Next, Gary Portsmouth, who chairs the Urban Studies department at Syracuse University, gave a fascinating dissection of the Lili and Mitzi highways, tracing both of them back to a character in Colette's autobiography, *Earthly Paradise*.

As it turned out, I was going to know Gary well by the end of the conference. After lunch, I attended a panel on the rising popularity of Personism on the Upper West Side of Manhattan. One panellist described it as our "Paul Moment"—the moment when experience separates from setting. The man beside me tapped me on the shoulder. It was Gary Portsmouth. "That is quite a misunderstanding, if you are a reporter. A misunderstanding of Paul, of Personism, of the Upper West Side. Allow me to show you."

At SIPS, the soft evenings begin in the middle of the afternoon and end early in the morning. They are different from ordinary soft evenings in their precision and hallucinogenic intensity. The throws, which for most devoted personasts are four or five objects, become entire costumes with makeup and masks at SIPS. At Gary's session a whole suite had been cleared and filled with two dozen coat racks. People stripped naked before they spun into their highways. Improvisations and integrations were flawless. In the course of the next two days, I witnessed and became the greatest highways of my life. Not only did I meet a dozen fresh highways, like Ivy, Samsung, and

Simon Bolivar, but the common ones like Violent B and Sammy Sexy as Shit were illuminated in excruciatingly vivid new ways.

I pulled myself away only to eat and sleep, but did manage to catch the keynote address by Mark Grenstein that wrapped up the conference: "What Do They Dream About in Paradise?" I caught the last five minutes anyway. Fewer than a dozen people were in attendance. The lecture hall could easily have sat five hundred. "They claim that we're ultimately hollow, that we're just a series of resonant hollow gestures," Mark was saying. "Loneliness is the new epidemic. Loneliness kills more people than heart disease." His voice echoed with double meaning through the hall empty of dreamers too busy dreaming to talk about dreaming.

After the lecture, Gary and I drove out of Orange County. We had agreed to meet some fellow personasts at an Olive Garden in the City of Industry. There were closer Olive Gardens but after two straight days of highways, we wanted to talk. If we stayed close to the hotel, conversation would soon develop into a soft evening, we all knew.

"They're all going to be talking about the blindings," Gary said. "That's all they're going to talk about."

"Sensationalism."

"No, It's true. I was in Evanston. The lunatic fringe, but it's there. Soft evenings, then silences, releases, the wastes, the burnings, the self-etchings. You can see. They call it eye-popping. The same with the fetuses in Atlanta."

"Why don't you mention it to the others?" I asked after a moment.

Gary shrugged.

The Olive Garden was harder to find than we expected. I needed to stop at a liquor outlet for a few bottles of peach schnapps just in case a soft evening broke out, and the slight change in plans had thrown us off course. We turned from a freeway onto a jammed three-lane highway. It took us half an hour to find a turn off the highway, and we took it. The sun by this time had nearly set. It took us another half hour to find a highway going the right way, and then Gary accidentally drifted into the exit lane. We found ourselves in a dead-end back alley at the rear of what looked like a refinery. A youth standing out of the shadows on a loading dock cocked himself out the darkness with pure menace, slackening the leash of a furious pit bull.

Gary swiftly executed a three-point turn and accelerated us back the way we came. "That guy would make a good highway," he said, smiling.

YANN MARTEL
WE ATE THE CHILDREN LAST

THE FIRST HUMAN trial was on Patient D, a fifty-six-year-old
male, single and childless, who was suffering from colon cancer. He was a skeletal man with white, bloodless skin. He was
aware that his case was terminal and he waived all rights to legal
redress should the procedure go wrong.

His recovery was astounding. Two days after the operation,
he ate six lunch meals in one sitting. He gained eighteen kilos
in two weeks. His liver, pancreas, and gall bladder, the sources
of greatest worry, evidently adapted very well to the trans-
plant. The only side effect noted at the time concerned his diet.
Patient D began to eat bananas and oranges without peeling
them. A nurse reported that she had come upon him eating the
flowers in his room.

The French medical team felt vindicated. Until that time,
the success rate of full-organ xenografts was zero; all animal
transplants to humans—the hearts, livers and bone marrow
of baboons, the kidneys of chimpanzees—had failed. The only
achievements in the field were the grafting of porcine heart
valves to repair human hearts and, to a lesser extent, of porcine skin onto burn victims. The team decided to examine the

pig more closely. But the process of rendering a pig's organ immunologically inert proved difficult, and few organs were compatible. The potential of the pig's digestive system, despite its biological flexibility, stirred little interest in the scientific community. It was assumed that the organ would be too voluminous and that its high caloric output would induce obesity in a human. The French were certain that their simple solution to the double problem—using the digestive system of a smaller, pot-bellied species of pig—would become the stuff of scientific legend, like Newton's apple. "We have put into this man a source of energy both compact and powerful—a Ferrari engine!" boasted the leader of the medical team.

A visit to Patient D's apartment three months after his release from hospital revealed that his kitchen was empty. He had sold everything in it, including fridge and stove, and his cupboards were bare. When asked what he ate, he confessed that he went out at night and picked at garbage. Nothing pleased him more, he said, than to gorge himself on putrid sausages, rotten fruit, mouldy brie, baguettes gone green, puffy skins and carcasses, and other soured leftovers and kitchen waste. He spent a good part of the night doing this, he admitted, since he no longer felt the need for much sleep and was embarrassed about his diet. The medical team would have been concerned but for the fact that all tests revealed what was plain to the eye: the man was bursting with good health. He was stronger and fitter than he had been in his entire life.

Regulatory approval came swiftly. The procedure replaced chemotherapy as the standard treatment for all cancers of the digestive tract that did not respond to radiotherapy.

Les Bons Samaritains, a lobby group for the poor, thought to apply this wondrous medical solution to a social problem. They suggested the operation be made available to those receiving social assistance. The poor often have unwholesome diets, at a cost both to their health and to the state, which has to spend on their medical care when they become ill. What better, more visionary remedy, they argued, than a procedure that in reducing food budgets to nothing would create paragons of fitness? A cleverly orchestrated campaign of petitions and protests—"*Malnutrition: zéro! Déficit: zéro!*" read the banners— easily overcame the hesitations of the government.

The procedure caught on among the young and the bohemian, the chic and the radical, among all those who wanted a change in their lives. The opprobrium attached to eating garbage vanished completely. In short order the restaurant became a retrograde institution, and the eating of prepared food a sign of attachment to deplorable bourgeois values. A revolution of the gut swept through society. "*Liberté! Liberté!*" was the cry of the operated. The meaning of wealth changed. It was all so heady. The telltale mark of the procedure was a vertical scar along the belly and a slighter one at the base of the throat. It was a badge we wore with honour.

Garbage became a sought-after commodity. Unscrupulous racketeers began selling it. Dumps became dangerous places. Garbage collectors were assaulted. The less fortunate had to resort to eating grass. Little was made at the time of a report by the *Société Protectrice des Animaux* on the surprising drop in the number of stray cats and dogs.

Then old people began vanishing without a trace. Mothers who had turned away momentarily were finding their baby carriages empty. The government reacted swiftly. The army descended upon every one of the operated, without discriminating between the law-abiding and the criminal. The newspaper *Le Cochon Libre* tried to put out a protest issue, but the police raided their offices and only a handful of copies escaped destruction.

There were terrible scenes during the roundup: neighbours denouncing neighbours, children being separated from their families, men, women and children being stripped in public in humiliating searches for scars, summary executions of people trying to escape. Internment camps were set up, always in remote parts of the country.

No provisions were made for food in any of the camps. The story was the same in all of them: first the detainees ate their clothes. Then the weaker men and women disappeared. Then the rest of the women. Then more of the men. Then we ate those we loved most. The last known prisoner was an exceptional brute by the name of Jean Proti. After forty-one days without a morsel of food except his own toes and ears, he died.

I escaped. I still have a good appetite, but there is a moral rot in this country that even I can't digest. Everyone knew what happened, and how and where. To this day everyone knows. But no one talks about it and no one is guilty. I must live with that.

TIMOTHY TAYLOR

SUNSHINE CITY

∞

INFINITY. THE NUMBER beyond the numbers. That one really messed people up. When they found out what I used to do for a living they'd question me. I remember a man asking once if there wasn't a single pattern behind it all. Like a master key.

I had no answer to that. There either was no pattern, or there was but it had no meaning. Or possibly, there was a pattern but it was coded-up inside everyone. Infinity in our bones and minds. Infinity in the fragmentary moment, the glance, the blink of first love or terror. At the doorstep of sleep, in the pixelation of the day, the greying out of senses. At the moment of death, the dawn of the underworld. Perhaps there, infinity spread. Completion and understanding, the torn veil, revelation and apocalypse.

But I couldn't speak it into existence, even if I knew we all longed for it, ached for it, wept for infinity in our private places.

∞

Frick called from Sunshine City. He said: "Happy fortieth. My God Hoss you really are forty years old. Where the hell are you living?"

I'd been sleeping. Once work was gone, life was an avenue of non-events to which I could not bother assigning probabilities. I doubted probabilities. I let the numbers go and slept a great deal. On waking, I smoked weed, which was free by the forest-load in the hills a few hours' drive from my camp, and so was a vice only as much as it was also a virtue.

I told Frick where I was. In the Mojave fringe. And heard him punch up the lat/long on his computer. He liked this kind of thing, Frick did. Sharp coordinates. "Thirty five point two three two," he said. "One seventeen point eight and a smidge. Hot as hell I bet."

Living in the Rough. Sucks for you.

But then he departed from the routine of these birthday calls and took a different tone, voice levelling off. And I felt some long calculation arrive at its privileged Frickian conclusion.

Frick said: "Hoss, I'm no brainiac like you. No numbers gimp, badge-carrying International Actuarial Forensics specialist."

"Former," I said.

"Former even."

I said, "Frick arriving at his point."

"My point being I'm not blind to the numbers," Frick said. "And the ones I'm seeing now are the money you need, and the job I have that only you can do."

College buddies. He was the rich kid. I was scholarship, beneficiary of a fund named after Frick's great-uncle, mother's side. The geek and the rich kid. We gave each other a reciprocal glimpse of what was wanted most. To be on the inside, to be on the outside.

Twenty years later, Frick was still rich only not a kid. Four decades old himself in a world gone pear-shaped and jowly, where everywhere a new and desperate light glinted from the surface of things, the sun changed with age, flinty and unsure of its own original motives. Solar flares, water shortages, brush fires in the hills. Such was the order of the day, even for the rich. Even for the super-rich living in Sunshine City. Even for the Frick-rich, who had inherited and now owned the Sunshine Cities of this less than brave new world.

Frick's fiefdom. Lat 38.3228 by long 123.0369. He once put it to me in precisely those terms, the situation of his office to four decimal places. What that meant could be more simply expressed along these lines: waterfront, thirty-six holes, housing development, office complex, shopping mall. And all Frick's. Every timber, every brick in the super-luxurious executive-style membership cabanas, every introduced bird species and exotic plant. Part of the Tifway Twelve Golf Alliance. Pebble Beach County was maybe more famous. But Sunshine City was more exclusive, with a membership roll including several former international leaders and dozens of once-bigs from the government/judicial/entertainment complex. And notably—another Frick detail this one, I'd thought about it—Sunshine City was also, by a wide margin, compared to other members of the alliance, extravagantly more of a bitch to play.

I came to this conclusion on my own, surfing the satellite images. Airstrips of golden green. 8200 yards from the tips. Wicked approach play. Evil pin and trap placement. With a handicap of 10, I ghosted some numbers and came up with mean average 4.5 lost balls over 18 holes, nine times out of ten with a confidence of 98%. A monster this nasty enslaved membership, that's what it did. Frick knew what he was doing. He handpicked the members just like he handpicked the staff. Caddies and greenskeepers were all former convicts whose pardons Frick had personally purchased from local authorities. Thieves and fraudsters made humble by Frick's benevolence. He knew the algorithm of isolation and loyalty, my long-ago pal. "Gated community," they used to call this kind of place, although *golf republic* described it better. A self-reliant social and economic zone all ensconced within its own borders, with guard huts and golf carts scooting along the barbed wire which was hung with tiny bells and woven into the high hedges. Intruders were rare, although anonymous people did fire rounds in from the sur- rounding hills now and then, just in spite. A .22 shell winging off the fender of a cart. And if a ball were shanked into one of those hedges, then the bells on the hidden barbed wire would tinkle and trigger audio alarms in a hundred embedded earphones, and guards up and down the length of Sunshine City, with their black ball caps, with their zinced-off noses and jackets with patches from defunct private security outfits—Mandrake, Hol- lis & Tucker etc.—they'd sit a little straighter and adjust aviator frames, scratch their necks and look at their phones, always finding there the same faithful data. Eighty-four degrees, sev- enty-five feet above sea level. Barometric pressure steady, zero chance of precipitation. All those subcutaneous GPS-enabled member chips reassuring that the head count was the same as the day before.

Until the day before Frick called me, that is.

Ten in the morning. I was forty years old. A geriatric Mojave Desert sun was baking the blue tarp I'd strung between the Vanagon and a couple of beavertail cacti. I awoke in submarine light, phone buzzing under my pillow. My blood, so recently sat- urated with the tendril ministrations of tetrahydrocannabinol, oozing like glue in my veins while Frick laid out his unprece- dented offer. A job only I could do.

I rolled onto one elbow, reached for my smokes. I got sparked. I spoke through wreaths of grey that sloped off in the direction of the laundry line hanging near the back of the van, underwear and socks, listless in the light. I said: "I don't suppose this is Griegson-related."

Frick repositioned himself in a distant chair, aware—uncomfortably and all at once—that I knew something about what had happened already. Like maybe his drama up there wouldn't already be making the rounds. Sunshine City member down from gunshot wound on the 14th green. I wasn't working in the field anymore. I might have been a gimp on a graphite-titanium compound peg leg. But I still heard the rumours. And based on what I was hearing, Sunshine City was shaping up to be a good one.

Another sniper in the hills? These incidents did occur. They had precedent and a degree of likelihood greater than zero. A distant prick of light, a thin crack in the air and a low whine off the flagstones. A window shattering in the back of the clubhouse. A hole appearing in the drink vending machine at the turn, sprouting a rivulet of cola, just like in the gag in that old movie.

But the shoptalk wasn't tending in that direction this time. Someone had actually died this time. One shot from somewhere with intent. A body in a sand trap and a caddy for once without rejoinder. Oh yes. Early speculation had it going a different direction this time. Early speculation among the pros was that this time Sunshine City had itself an inside job.

The Jerk. That was the movie with the gunshots and the spouting cans. Frick was still talking, but I starting giggling as the scene came back. Steve Martin pointing at the cans of engine oil, racked near the gas pumps.

It's the cans! He hates these cans!

∞

I did Guilt Probability before the crash. I mean the global crash, yes, but the personal one too. The global one, you know about.

The personal one, well, in sports they call what I got the yips. *Focal dystonia*, if you're in a medical frame of mind, a spasmodic response to moments requiring high degrees of coordination and concentration. But the bottom line for those who get the yips is knowledge that you were able to do a particularly difficult thing one day, and not the next. Bernhard Langer forgetting how to putt. Charles Barkley suddenly unable to sink a free throw. They sometimes call the yips the "Steve Blass Disease" after the Pirates pitcher, whose story is a good way to keep yourself awake at night. Try it sometime. Try thinking about winning the World Series in 1972 with an ERA of 2.49, being runner-up for the Cy Young Award, second in the voting for series MVP behind Roberto Clemente. Then suddenly being unable to get the ball over the plate. Walking eighty-four batters in eighty-eight innings. Crashing into the minors, then out. It took Blass three years to go from the top to retirement. My fall took three weeks, but the idea is similar.

But before I lost it, like Blass, like Langer, like all of them, I really did have it. Senior Analyst, International Actuarial Forensics. IAF. People said it like: Eye-Aff. I'd never seen a case of Frick's particular kind, but I knew why he was calling me, coaxing me out of retirement for one last try. I could have told you cold that member-on-member violence was very bad for business in the golf republics. Shaken confidence among the dues payers can't be valued. Then you have the shit-fight between insuring companies that would surely scorch the earth. Frick could see himself caught in the middle. Sunshine City in the liability crosshairs, paying out all directions. Calling me was Frick's smart move. That was Frick being proactive.

IAF. Good times. Powerful times full of morning energy and a sense of purpose. IAF was the biggest and meanest actuarial expert witness consultancy on the planet in its day. We lived in an insured world, payouts crossing the planet daily based on the outcome of every event and sub-event, criminal or civil. All this money flowing in response to probable lines of responsibility. In a court system backlogged with an estimated ninety-seven years of caseload, you could either start cloning judges and lawyers, start building jails on the moon, or you could settle guilt using the magic available. Surrender to the quantum likelihoods that whirred within us all at the particulate level. *Beyond a reasonable doubt.* Well exactly. It had always been about probability. Why had we ever paid for more certainty than the universe found necessary to govern the spin of its googa-guan-deco-magra-peta-pentillion spheres?

So we did the whole guilt/innocence thing a new way. We evolved. Lawyers still had their chance to argue the old-fashioned way. Call it regulation time with sudden death. Then it went to probability penalty shots. And here the IAF specialists unpacked their spreadsheet souls in a thousand courtrooms, unfurled their cold grids of risk data, their seventy-factor pivot tables. We rolled the reality bones. Guilty nine times out of ten, 93% of the time, your honour. End of story. Send them away. We were minor gods, all Brioni and Vuitton. Ruthless well-tailored Shivas.

Frick's proactive idea was bringing in the Guilt Probability geek beforehand. Before there was a hearing, a judicial finding. He was preparing himself. Frick needed odds run. He needed a friendly brain in a hurry. He offered me a wagonload of money. Water. A new van, if I wanted to do it that way.

"Or, the nickel just dropping now for my oldest true friend Hoss," Frick said. "Limited time offering, Sunshine City membership. Scholarship class."

I swallowed. I butted out the reefer.

∞

I drove up. It took three days. Driving the highway, passing the groaning pickup trucks and loaded trailers. One thing about the Rough little appreciated if you weren't in it: everybody was constantly on the move. Finding better spots; looking for water, or work. I passed the caravans of travelling smithies and shoemakers, doctors and fortune tellers. I kept changing my mind about the whole thing and pulling over, smoking and sleeping under the van. I'd wake up thinking about the pensioned life, time remaining measured in boxes of energy bars and garbage bags of pot dragged down from the hills. Then I'd get back on the road again, point the Vanagon northwest. I washed myself up in a Jack in the Box men's room a couple miles down the road from the Sunshine City main gates. I could smell deep-fryer grease and a trace of sea breeze.

After the guard punched me up on screen and talked to someone in a control room somewhere, they drove me in-complex on a golf cart with little aircon nozzles pointing up out of the dash. I felt myself exit the Rough, crossing a lightly perfumed perimeter line from struggle to repose, from rough to fairway. And I thought about the years gone by, watching a transport helicopter trace the ridgeline opposite, inbound to Harry Zitman Airforce Base. The machine transmitted a faint rumble that shook the ground as it rotored and belched off over the hills and disappeared.

They showed me through a lobby and up some stairs, down a teak-lined corridor and into the sitting room outside Frick's office. When he came out the door—insect legs, thin smile, white hands spread wide in false amazement—his first words spoken into shared air in twenty-odd years were: "Hoss, goddamn it. You're lean. You're fit. You look like you still get it regular. Welcome to 38.41 by 123.23 and change. Now stand up and hug me before you say a cynical word."

So I stood, and we hugged. And Frick hummed a tune from college days in my ear while I looked over his shoulder down a long view corridor towards the sea.

Griegson had been lining up a ten-foot birdie. Almost routine, I would have thought. Griegson's top-five ranking on the Sunshine City leaderboard confirmed as much. But then, he had been having a bad day of subtle shades. Seen drinking heavily the night before. More on that later. The worst part of his day was a 7.62mm round that struck him in the C2 vertebra squarely from behind. Bad outcome given he'd just planted a five-iron on the top tier below the hole. Based on handicap and the fact that he was facing away from the rising sun, facing the sea breeze and stroking the ball out of the calm of his own shadow, I'd say that putt was a better than 90% shot. On the 14th hole and assuming no significant variance in play, that implied Griegson was on track to shoot two under over 18 holes. A nice day, if you live.

As it was, he pole-axed into the sand trap. Very little entry wound. Very much exit wound through the front of the throat.

"Body?"

Morgued until the law arrived, as per resort bylaws governing the death of members.

They had a morgue. "You have a morgue?"

Frick traced a swirl pattern on the arm of his chair. He said: "They do die from time to time. Membership mean age is sixty-eight up here. At forty you'd be a low outlier—although there is some layable skirt in the fifty-five- to sixty-year age bracket. Anyway, the cops are backed up like usual. Not due in until the weekend."

"And you'd like me to be waiting for them," I said to Frick. "Ready to give them a story."

"Not a story, *the* story," Frick answered. "In compelling IAF language. Yes I would."

They had no tape of the incident. Frick knew I wouldn't be impressed by this detail. Security cameras down. I stared at my old friend. He raised his eyebrows, held up his hands. The camera server power-cycled once every year, standard memory maintenance. They'd cycled the year before at the same time, to the minute, to the second. That's what happens when something is in the master maintenance schedule run by a computer cluster doing twenty petaflops in a quake-resistant room three stories under the ground.

"So let's just be clear," I went on. "You need *the* story to be about a sniper in the hills."

Frick made a rotational gesture with his head. That meant: *maybe, probably, yes of course.*

"And we start with the odds that a shooter opens up from the hills during the exact five-minute window your cameras are down," I said. "Five minutes over half a million annually. Call it one chance in a hundred thousand. I'm laughing here. Inside."

"You're doubling," Frick said. "Members don't golf in the dark. Five minutes out of a possible 262,500 hours of daylight is one chance in 52,500."

I said: "Frick catching my mistake, having worked things out in advance."

"Hoss," he said, leaning back, tracing a finger along the lip of a bookshelf behind his desk. "Just talk to the witnesses."

He called in his executive assistant, whose nickname Salary Betty had been shortened over years of service to SaBe. Said like a breath of menthol cigarette smoke released to thrum back out over the vocal cords: *Sah-Bay.* And there you had it, the name and the woman. Mid-thirties. Black hair, mint green eyes. Pinstripe suit pants dropping in a long taper to a roll of soft cuff. White blouse open at the base of an olive-toned throat.

SaBe said: "Mr. Frick?"

Frick said: "Meet Hoss." Creaking back in his leather chair and drawing her attention to me with a thin hand, trembling at full extension. "Bet you can't guess how he got that name."

SaBe looked me over. I felt the menthol. She said: "Cow-poke?"

"SaBe," Frick said, moving on. "Hoss is doing look-see on the Griegson incident."

"Police?" SaBe said.

"IAF, retired. This is a friendly." I produced one of my old cards. "Frick says you saw the whole thing from your bedroom window."

SaBe didn't answer right away. She was still looking me over, caught on something. So I looked her over in return. And I saw some things about her. She was single, no kids or possibly one. There was a guy somewhere, ten states away, crossing borders, lines of longitude clicking under his heels. She hadn't thought of him in a while before that moment. But something had triggered, standing there, looking at me. Not because I look like him, you can be sure. I'm an amputee, a one-legger. And you don't have the money to bet the odds on two monopeds in SaBe's life.

"Named Hoss, as in you're very well endowed," SaBe said.

I pegged over and shook her hand. And we were co-conspirators, just like that. I said: "So what exactly did you see?" Then I plunked down onto the leather sectional and patted the cushion next to me. It sighed, taking her weight. And as Frick left the room, I slid without effort into the deep listening phase of things. Which is not unlike addressing the ball, I would imagine. There is a certain value to waggling in place, waiting for things to balance up just right. Waiting for the settle. For the distribution. For the cosmic intake of breath that nods at the arrival, all at once, of powerful form.

SaBe drove me over to the Sunshine City security centre, where they had a six-drawer morgue in the basement. I was thinking about what she'd told me in our short interview. A woman of few words, she got it all out in sequence and without unnecessary adjectives. Standing at the window, she had seen a puff of smoke in the hills. A lick of flame. She was iffy on the exact sound. Like a thump or a crack. But she remembered a phone ringing somewhere. Just before the shot, or whatever in fact it was.

Now we were carting over to the morgue in the brutal light and I was watching her. Wondering about her. Did I know she was withholding some detail? Yeah, I knew. But such was the stuff of hunch and faith. There wasn't a number in it.

"Was Frick with you when you saw the flash?" I asked her.

She breathed out through her nose, a single sharp exhalation. She said: "How could that be, Hoss? That would imply Mr. Frick was in my bedroom."

"You're single?"

She nodded.

"But not always."

SaBe looked back at me, again sharp. She said: "What about you?"

I stammered. I managed: "I haven't been lucky that way."

She turned back to the road. Gave it several seconds, then said: "His name was Scott. He died March 31st seven years ago. He was kidnapped with a couple of other doctors near Mexico City. Shot during a botched rescue. I'm not sleeping with Frick, no."

"Sorry," I said. "Your turn. Go ahead and ask."

"The Rough," she said. "What's it like for you?"

Not Mad Max, I told her. All those stories were overblown. The Rough was poor, that was basically it. The Rough was low on water, but lower on money.

She said: "And the leg?"

So I gave her the golf-cart-en-route-to-the-morgue version. How I'd been in a car accident once, back in college, passenger side in a vehicle driven by my best buddy. How I nearly died, went near the light. Only there was no light. Or not a light that could be understood as a light.

"A presence?" SaBe asked.

I shook my head. There were no words for this one. It remained with me more as a shrouded formula, an algorithm nestled at the heart of universal affairs. I thought perhaps, at some moment of great epiphany, I might suddenly discover a way of expressing this in numbers.

SaBe was looking at me again. The head tilt. The angling of the eyebrows. She said: "So then what?"

Then, I told her, after a period of time had passed that I would only later appreciate to have been three weeks, I returned to the land of the living by my own crazy choice.

"Crazy why, you think?" SaBe asked me.

"Crazy because I could have stayed," I told her.

We were parked in front of the security centre. SaBe didn't say anything, just sat facing forwards, fingers gripping and re-gripping the wheel.

∞

Griegson's skin was mahogany brown even in death. Good-looking man, dumb-luck sucker that he was. Well-known reader for a financial news cable channel. He had some fame in the western longitudes. I understood that Sunshine City was in the grip of a polite and clubby kind of mourning. Griegson's photo was already being framed the size of a Prince of Baghdad for hanging in the clubhouse. People liked the man. But the fact that this micro-seizure of random violence had chosen him, well… that vaulted Griegson upwards. A known face, but one that now could not be recalled without some other augmented feeling. Something along the lines of awe, even love.

I smoked before looking, extracting a joint from a Ziploc and lighting up. I finished it while looking over the morgue sheet hanging in an envelope from the drawer handle. Age, sex, general health. I skimmed. Cause of death: gunshot wound, massive hemorrhage, etc. And when the joint was finished and I was released to a merciful distance from my own senses, I unzipped the body bag the rest of the way down to Griegson's shoes and looked at what there was to see. He lay in pewter morgue light, in the humming chill. I stared as if trying to bring his face into focus. As if that effort were failing.

SaBe waited outside. I went through Griegson's clothes: open-necked polo with a Maybach logo, chinos, argyle socks, white golf shoes with a kiltie tassel. In his hip pocket was a billfold, twenty-four dollars, some plastic, a Sunshine City ID card. In his left front, some change, a key to his cabana. In his right front a score card (1 under at 14) and a business card. Pale blue, thick card stock. An outfit called Destinex. A phone number and a lat/long address in the Rough.

I dialled the number and let it ring fifteen times, hung up. I looked the body over a final time. Felt down the pant legs. Behind the ears. I was just about to slide the drawer home, leave him be. Then I noticed the golf glove. I peeled it off his left hand and found another phone number scribbled in ballpoint pen on his palm. So he was a palm writer. Very particular type those. Last-minute scramblers. Equivocal. Harried.

I dialled that number too. I heard the line open as someone picked up, familiar bird song, the lightest suggestion of breath. Then the person hung up.

I phoned the number again, immediately. No answer of course.

I went outside and found SaBe sitting in the cart, staring off into the hills east of Sunshine City. I had a sense what she was thinking about. The husband gone. The weight of what came afterwards. But I didn't say anything about it, just told her to run me on down to Griegson's cabana. Then on the way down I asked her about Destinex.

She shook her head. "Name of a company?"

"Looks like," I said, nodding. "Probably nothing."

The wind gusted up just then, blew her hair forwards and over her face. She pulled it back with one hand, still steering the cart. Green eyes locked on the path ahead. I checked out the sky: high and blue. An infinity sky. It arched overhead and contained us as we wound our way up between the cedar-sided buildings and the cacti, the lotus blossoms, the miniature palms, the woodchip flower beds, cameras pivoting from the fence posts, winking and blinking in the hard light. In Sunshine City there was an ambient soundtrack. I hadn't noticed that earlier. But in the quiet of the row of cabanas, I heard it piped in from hidden speakers in the greenery. Celtic strings, faint as the ocean.

Griegson lived in cabana 1211, two shingled buildings around a deck that looked down into a narrow ravine. Very private. Two cabanas actually, the living room and bar area, then the bedroom and massive bathroom. They faced each other around a deck with a hot tub and big chairs made out of bent willow branches with plush leather cushions. All of this facing down into the cool of a ravine that sloped through trees and long grass to the 8th fairway of the second course, right at the black-and-white 150-yard marker.

I went inside to shade-cool rooms, wood-slat blinds drawn. The cleaning staff used a particular kind of soap at Sunshine City and I could smell that here. The air alive with lavender and rosemary. I cracked the blinds and judged the room to have been cleaned up. Signs everywhere: bed perfectly made. Persian runners squared up in the corridor. Items on the desktop perfectly aligned. One wall was covered in bookshelves. Novels, biographies, economics textbooks. Spines dusted and in perfect alignment. In the closet there was a rank of ironed pastel polo shirts on one side, and a rustling hedge of silk Brooks Brothers women's blouses on the other. All this order from a man who scribbled phone numbers on his hand.

I picked up Griegson's phone and listened for the click, then the tone. I visualized the disk starting to spin somewhere, a track laid down with a date code and Griegson's name affixed. I wondered why Frick bothered, what arcane insurance clause made recording every call necessary. I imagined the bored staff who handled the data, storing it for a year or two before purging.

I dialled Frick.

He said: "Already? You're as good as they say."

"Why'd they clean the room?" I asked him.

"Griegson was ..." Frick started.

"Normally a mess?" I said.

Sure, Frick agreed. A mess.

"When did the wife die?"

Frick was nodding into the phone. I could tell this because his chin was rasping the mouthpiece as he did so. A distant feline purr. Large breed. He told me Griegson's wife had passed two years prior. Her name was Savionna. From somewhere in Alabama apparently. "But you know how it is," Frick sighed into the phone. "The old guys tend to go after they lose their girls."

"Generally not by gunshot wound on the 14th green."

"Point taken," Frick said. "You been up the hill yet?"

"Up what hill?"

"Hill 231, where SaBe saw the muzzle flash. She can take you up in one of the security quads. Although it would be a bit of a hike on the peg. Nice peg, by the way. Is that new?"

It was pretty nice. My long-ago insurance provided for a replacement every five years, and this latest one was the stuff, tapering away at the bottom like an antelope. With two I might have looked like a satyr. But there was less than no point in talking to Frick about my prosthetic, just as there was less than no point talking to him about Hill 231. Like someone pops off a shot from the ridgeline and leaves his phone number scratched onto a rock. A heart, some initials. I *came all the way to the Sunshine City and all I got was a lousy washed-up sexagenarian newsreader.*

"Send security up," I told him.

I stood in the cool of Griegson's bedroom. Massive king-size bed with golden bolster, 900-thread-count sheets or whatever it was by now. Maybe this was the exact cabana Frick was planning to give to me if I accepted his offer of membership. I could hear water running in pipes somewhere. Geysers of filtered, lead-free water. Lakes of it stored safely in reservoirs, heaving desalinated seas. What would I be here? Would I work in the office? Do accounting for Frick? Would I make book or settle member disputes, rolling my reality bones in a makeshift hearing room set up off the member's hall, Griegson's face looming large over a glass case where somebody had laid out his clubs?

I logged into Griegson's computer using the password taped to the bottom of the keyboard. Emails from here and there. Nothing much. Browser cache empty. There was a spreadsheet file saved to the desktop under the name "Tally of Scores." I double-clicked the file and popped up a password box. I tried "Savionna." I tried "Sunshine City." I tried "1211." After three tries the box closed down and refused further attempts. I could power off the unit and try again, but I knew it wasn't worth the bother. So he was a score tracker. So he kept a running average. So he had trend software running off tables and graphs. I could always look around for a password-cracker program later, if I really got curious about how Griegson's game had evolved over the years. In the meantime, it felt like a red herring to me.

I pushed back from the desk and spun around in his office chair, spinning, spinning. About the third spin, I saw SaBe in the mirror over the headboard, which offered a bounce-back glimpse of the deck outside. She was sitting in one of those faux-cottage chairs, hands on the bent wood, nestled into the leather. She was watching me. I stopped spinning.

She got up and came to the doorway. "IAF tradecraft. The chair spin."

I said to her: "I was hoping you'd come in."

"Why hope. You can ask. You have me under secondment. You can order me around."

"You like being ordered around?"

"Just because it's my job doesn't mean I have to like it."

"Let me ask you."

She waited.

"You live here. You've got some kind of money. Why play Gal Friday to Frick?"

She sighed and shook her head. I really just didn't get something, apparently.

"Well explain it to me," I said.

"Well for starters," SaBe said, staring at me hard. "I hate golf."

I looked up at her and held the stare. Then I nodded. Fine. So she was bored out of her tree. Trapped and yet too fond of the pampered life to dare think about a shot at freedom. *Out there.* "Frick and Griegson," I said, moving on. "Were they close?"

"Not particularly."

I turned back to his computer and pulled up the search inter-
face, punched in Destinex but the name apparently wasn't in
any document on Griegson's system. I punched in the lat/long
address. Got a cluster of nothing.

I rifled the drawers. Staplers, pens. Cigar cutter. A copy of
Don DeLillo's *Underworld*. I picked that up and shook the book
with the pages open. Nothing. I ran my fingers along the spine
and found the shipping tag from a big mail-order book place out
East.

"Griegson was a reader?"

SaBe looked over at the bookshelves. "Seems so."

"How about you? Don DeLillo. Have you read him?"

"Never got through that one, honestly. I preferred *White
Noise*."

She was looking around the room and I took that chance to
steal a long glance at her standing in the slats of light that were
coming in through the wooden blinds. Hard ribs of white and
black that emphasized the shape, the contour, the flow of fabric
on her arms and legs. Her parents had been members, so many
years before. So she was born a Sunshine City member. The first
I'd ever met other than Frick. A legacy. Born in captivity.

∞

My hunch had been right. Griegson's cabana was to be my own
while I stayed. If I stayed. When Frick phoned me to tell me, I
said: "Like you don't think the cops will find it odd I'm sleeping
in your crime scene."

Frick was in the lounge sipping a gin and tonic. I could hear
the music. Hear the clinking of ice cubes. He said: "We did due
diligence. Scanned the place, took photos. Plus Griegson didn't
die there. So, relax."

I didn't relax. My mood darkened. The next morning I woke under the massive gelatinous weight of the dope I'd smoked to help me sleep. A security guard banging on the door. Against his better judgment, the man agreed to escort SaBe and me the sixteen miles northeast to Destinex as I had requested, through roads parched white, beaten by the heat, the sun. Here's me with a bad morning-after: I keep turning my head to catch things and seeing the inside of my skull before it snaps on around and gets centred up. I was behind myself, somehow. Security dude with shoulder badges from Bartinson Private Solutions has picked all this up of course. He has files open on his desktop back in the guard compound. All my marvellous history. He's gotten to wondering. And the odious whiff of skank isn't helping his mood. Neither is my telling him to put away the shotgun, which he might otherwise have kept in his lap the whole way out. When I turned to say it, I saw myself reflected in his mirrored sunglasses, SaBe off to the side, warping into view on the convexity of that judgmental surface.

There was nothing out there. Nada and then more nada. Destinex was a warehouse among warehouses in a place that used to be busy. Auto parts, machine shop, tattoo parlour, diner. All defunct. There was a man living in the carcass of an old car wash, tented in among the crust-dry brushes next to a chipped mural of a naked Latina lying on the hood of a yellow Koenigsegg. Destinex was what? He shook his head. He said: *a prank?* Then laughed. He wore a cap with an embroidered phrase on the front: Don't That Blow?

I gave him a joint for his trouble and peg-legged back out into the sunshine through those long, hanging clear plastic slats that still covered the entry to the wash. Bartinson Private Solutions was waiting in the jeep with SaBe, glowering. He felt his advice being ignored. Not to drive into the warehouse complex.

Not to get out of the vehicle. Definitely not to enter the car wash. It put him in a certain mood.

"You guys ever shoot back?" I asked him, climbing in. "Someone starts pinging away up there. Don't you ever just want to haul out the old 306 and knock him down? You'd have self-defence on solid odds."

He quoted some Sunshine City ordinance at me, looking towards the sea. He seemed sad, all of a sudden. A real bone-weariness coming now through the mirrors.

"What about Hill 231?" I asked him. "Been up?"

Yes, they'd been up. And they had a casing for me too. 7.62mm.

I raised my eyebrows, impressed. Sixty acres of hillside and they found it. Right up there next to the ridgeline where the barbed wire was strung and the motion detectors stood on towers. Whoever Harry Zitman had been, at the airforce base named after him they weren't into visitors. Danger, danger. Do not pass. We were driving now. Quite fast. SaBe had gotten a whiff of something in our conversation and found a suitable response in speed.

And she wasn't alone. There was an animal out in these parts of the half-green Rough, a starved jackrabbit burnt down so skinny that it looked like a praying mantis slightly bulked out with patchy fur. But it held its speed. I saw one bust out of the weeds and make the road, then the field beyond. A streak. A blur. A ragged, spit-flecked bolt of madness. Rodent, insect, bird. Pygmy. Hard to tell.

We made Sunshine City in silence through the beaten, angry sunlight. SaBe dropped the guard at one of the huts. He went in and came back with a clear plastic envelope containing the casing. 7.62, sure enough. Nice touch.

SaBe said thanks and tipped him a fair-sized clip of cash. Driving away I must have made a face, that minor squint, the lip shift to acknowledge new information. She made a sharp hand motion in return. *Yes, we tip. And if you plan to stick around, you'd better learn to do it too.*

We went together down to Griegson's cabana, a few doors over from the pool complex. There was a sign on the gate with information about Griegson's funeral. Printed up on heavy cardstock, colourful borders and ringed with flowers. The caddy was waiting for me on the porch. We went out back and sat next to the silent hot tub. His name was Wes. A baton of a man, a pole with hands. He apparently shot three over and hit the ball a ton. He'd done six years for stealing money from the Episcopalian Fund for Autism Research. He didn't look at SaBe as she passed him. His eyes, strangely, went right through the willowy length of her. I took a moment to consider what eyes, exposed only to Sunshine City's brutal pleasantry, would not alight on SaBe in the moments when the opportunity arose.

But then, Wes was tight generally. Terse. Angry. Distracted. Or actively thinking about something else. I imagined him polishing club heads in his mind as we spoke. Seeing the 4th green from 150 yards out, bad lie. Calculating the players' odds and his avenues to improving the 18th green tip. *Take the three, sir. Punch it out to the top of the rise. You have a nice soft wedge going into an easy pin.*

Information beaten out of Wes in monosyllables over half an hour of questioning: 1) nobody golfed without a caddy; 2) yes, a party of four would therefore have involved eight people on or near the green at the time the shot was fired; 3) no, foursomes weren't necessary; 4) Griegson was not in a foursome.

I was drooping from the heat. SaBe came out of the cabana living room with a glass of lemonade for me.

"Wes is for what?" I asked him.

"Westlake."

"Is that your given or conviction name?"

Wes still nodding. Lips quivering tight.

SaBe said it quietly from behind me. "Staff use conviction names here, Hoss. Mr. Frick's policy."

I said to Wes. "And you were arrested up north…"

"Near Westlake," he spit at me. "You've cracked it, genius."

I sat back and nodded to SaBe. She brought him a glass of water, which Wes didn't touch. I waited for my next idea.

"All right," I said, finally. "Griegson's party, this past Thursday morning."

He said the word as though he hated it. "Twosome."

There was more here, of course. So I waited again. Then, quietly: "And who would the second player have been, Wes?"

"Didn't show." But he hesitated here, knowing the end was near. Glanced at his fingernails where they rested on the edge of the table. Where I could have told him, they remained as dirty as when he'd come in.

"Mr. Frick," Wes said.

∞

I sat at Griegson's desk, irritable, fussed. Smoking, butting it out. Lighting it up again. Meant nothing. Probably meant nothing. Or nothing meant nothing, probably. I phoned the Destinex number again and let it ring twenty times. When I hung up and set the phone down, it rang again almost immediately. Frick.

I said: "I was just thinking about you."

Fricked sighed, far away. He said: "I spoke to Wes. You've upset him."

"Terribly sorry, old man."

"Caddies are delicate business, you know. And we really do rely on them around here."

"Wes and Griegson," I said. "Were they lovers?"

Frick sighed again. "In a situation like Sunshine City, in a life situation of this kind, situated as that situation is within a larger global situation, or even set of situations . . ."

"Hoss losing patience," I said.

"I'm just trying to explain something that you might not appreciate—coming, as you do, from the relative freedom of the Rough."

"Frick comes to his point," I said, voice raised.

Frick held the phone away from his head a retributive moment. Then came back. "There are relationships that develop here that are of utmost importance. And in Sunshine City, in our present situation, the caddy and player is the key."

I lit up again. I said: "Getting on the green in two is that important."

"It's much more than that, Hoss," Frick said. "A member's caddy is like a butler, a fixer, a life partner. The caddy, in turn, needs the sponsorship of a member."

I said: "And who's your caddy, Frick."

Frick said: "All right. Well, you see. This is perhaps a background detail worth nothing. Games go up and down, you shake things up."

"You were in the process of hiring Westlake away from Griegson."

"They can work for more than one member, Hoss," Frick said.

"Not if two members play together. Why was Griegson drunk in the clubhouse Wednesday night?"

Frick laughed. "Just Wednesday?"

"Good drunk. Different drunk."

Frick sighed.

"He was upset," I said.

"Hoss, I won't deny it. Griegson has had better months."

"You were fighting over a caddy, Frick," I said. "Do you hear that as fucked up as normal people hear it?"

"You mean normal like you, Hoss?" Frick said.

"Why not show up to play Thursday morning?"

"Slept in," Frick said. "Honestly, I slept in."

"Off the top of your head, no pause," I said. "Ready?"

"Ready," Frick said.

"Number of times you slept in last year."

"Maybe twelve, fourteen," Frick said. Fast. It was right there waiting, the estimate.

Which was just bullshit, ten times out of ten with a margin of error of 0.0%. Frick forgot that I knew him. Frick didn't carry the old college pal memories around like I did. Frick didn't carry around the pointless memories, like despair itself. So here I was making neither a guess or giving voice to a hunch. This was a data set riding down hard on a fact: Frick hardly slept.

∞

Feelings. Stable and old feelings. IAF feelings, this closing of forms, this development of probabilistic shapes. These ones, admittedly, taking on a ghostly aura. Frick hovering in the event, at some wrong distance from it. Why had he brought me here? Did he think I'd sense him in the weave of things, then exonerate him for old-time's sake? Stupid fuck.

I watched SaBe at the deck rail at Griegson's place. She was looking down towards the fairway and a snip of sand trap. Someone had just lost a ball and two caddies were looking through the undergrowth, swinging ball-retrievers like scythes. Birds flew against the dome of blue overhead. Strafing the fairways and soaring away. The caddies stood, hands on hips now, talking. The members were sitting in the golf cart behind them, one of them smoking a long thin cigar.

"Bet they don't find that ball," I said to her.

She smiled without looking at me. "They never do. They don't look."

I went over to the railing, looking down past her shoulder. "Why not look?"

"Oh God," she said, infinite boredom grabbing her between breaths. A killing boredom. She said: "I don't know. Balls are insured?"

"What about strokes lost, scores taking a hit? That leaderboard counts for something."

She looked over at me with a narrow smirk. "That leaderboard counts for almost everything. But you've heard of cheating."

I watched the caddies carefully. When they split apart from one another again to continue searching, I saw one go sharply to a squat in the long grass, a few feet short of the rough and the fairway beyond that. I couldn't make out the words but he was calling now. Waving an arm. Magic. He'd just found the ball. I could picture what had happened in the invisible detail here. A matching Titleist 9 dribbled out of the low side pocket of his cargo pants. Just propped up nicely now where it could be punched out to the brow of the rise. Buddy with the cigar was going to loft in a sand wedge from there, get stuck on in three with a playable par. Rankings and positions, the whole architecture of club esteem unchallenged, unswayed. So Sunshine City continued to spin in its even grooves. Were they thinking of Griegson down there? The inexplicable thing to me, just at that moment—crows high overhead and the scent of SaBe close at hand—was my certainty that they were in fact thinking of Griegson then. Guy-chortling their way through the morning, they were nevertheless seeing themselves in debt to the misfortune of a single member down. The numbers gimp up there at work in the cabanas would make sure that club life carried on. The fine balance would be maintained. There would be no cloud, no plague from the outside. The seafoam green, the canary yellow, the Cadillac pink, the madras plaid and seersucker, the whole rainbow of politesse and clueless remove would continue.

SaBe said: "Hoss?"

"Sorry," I said. "Thinking."

"What do we have?"

"Okay," I said. "So Griegson is carrying a card for someplace in the Rough. Meaning he's been out there."

SaBe made a doubtful face. Members hardly ever left.

"What about lifetime members," I asked her.

She didn't look at me. Didn't show me her face. But I heard the words. SaBe said: "Some lifetime members are dying to get out there."

"Humour me," I said. "Griegson has this card. If he were going to go out there, he would have needed."

"A map," SaBe said.

We searched Griegson's cabana for maps. For anything map-like. A hand-jot on a napkin. Lat/longs scribbled in the margin of a bank statement. Directions bookmarked in the map browser on his computer. Nothing and nothing. I punched up the Destinex coordinates again and stared at the map of where we'd been, with no indication that Griegson had ever done the same, much less actually gone out there. Which is just the moment I felt her lean in, felt her warmth at my shoulder, her breath at my ear. SaBe, SaBe. She was having her effect.

She said: "How about satellite view?"

I watched the landscape re-compute itself. Destinex down there in the patchwork brown. I tapped the zoom button, once, twice, three times. I could recall the angle of the street. Where the Bartinsons Private Solutions guy had told us to stop. Where

SaBe had actually stopped next to the car wash. I thought I could see our tracks in the dust there, the distinctive double-tread of the quad. I wondered about how often these images were now updated, daily, hourly.

Then I saw the Destinex warehouse itself. The shape of the front awning. I zoomed more. SaBe's breath still right there. Coming out gently. And then, with the final click of zoom, down to where we could see the roof gravel, her breath went in again, a full breath, very quick.

There were letters down there on the roof. Skyward-facing graffiti, might have been fifty feet end-to-end running west to east across the gravel. Oriented as if designed expressly for satellite viewing.

The letters read: Not a single word.

We exited the random and entered the patterned stage of things. It was an intimacy, nothing less than that. A closeness to purpose and meaning, however invisible those both might be. We searched our experience and imagination. But mostly, we tumbled within the pattern. Not a single word. An ending. A closing off.

"A warning," she said.

"Last lines," I said.

"A suicide note?" SaBe offered.

I was pacing, pegging up and down the dark wood of Griegson's living room. "Last line of a song. A poem."

"Or a book," she said. And then we both listened to the sound that idea made in seconds of silence.

Ultramarine blue outside. Sunshine City slept to a Zamfir soundtrack, but SaBe and I worked. We went through those shelves book by book and we found it. Top shelf, far corner. Saul Bellow. Herzog. A little paperback bound in blue. And when she opened to the last page, I saw her hands start to tremble.

"At this time he had no messages for anyone. Nothing," she read. "Not a single word."

I took the book from her and searched the spine with my fingers. Mail order. I shook the pages gently and watched the business card fall free onto the bedspread.

The card read: Fate Systems Incorporated.

No point phoning the phone number. The old man in the car wash had said *prank?* I wondered now. But I still mapped up the Fate Systems address. SaBe and I together now, she was right at my shoulder, her already familiar warmth and smell, we drilled down and down. And out there at a hook in the coastal highway near Bodega, at the listed address—38.3298 by 123.0112—there it was. A low building with abandoned-looking trucks out back.

We zoomed. We zoomed. We found the fifty-foot letters. They read: *People with no soul.*

∞

I woke to my phone buzzing somewhere nearby but missed the call. Mid-morning. Fog rolling around the corners of my memory. I blinked. Then I moved sharply as a single detail simmered up out of the folds of grey. I rolled off the couch where I'd been sleeping and went to the doorway of Griegson's bedroom, cracked the door quietly and looked in, but she was gone. The bed neatly made, a note left to float in the middle of its king-sized emptiness. *Hope you slept all right out there. Call me.*

No number. Which I might have wondered about if my phone hadn't started humming again. If I hadn't lunged back into the front room, tripped on a ceramic lion guarding the perimeter of the ersatz fireplace and gone down headlong. I lay stunned, my phone just then dropping off the arm of the couch and bouncing onto the carpet next to my ear.

I opened it. I said: "Hi, Frick."

We met down at the driving range. I walked over, waving off cart after cart, people stopping to try to help the sweating gimp with the briefcase and the bed-head, one-sticking his way down between the blooming gingers and flowering ornamental banana trees. The gaping, besotted orchids and drunken, sprawling vines.

I found Frick in his cribbed-off corner at the far end of the lower tier of tee-boxes, facing out from under a shade awning into a wide set of hypothetical holes separated by trees and traps, roved over not just by tractors—as I remembered the last driving range I'd been on, over twenty years prior—but by individual ball collectors. Security-checked kids from the Rough, I'd heard. Paid by the day to hand-pick balls out of the spots the tractors couldn't reach, all of them armoured head-to-toe in riot-squad gear that made them look like black samurai out there, lumbering around in their leg- and shoulder-pads, helmets with visors, ball-retrieving tools. Sometimes you'd see one of them take a knee when they were hit in the back, or at the joint at the side of the knee. Then they'd hold up a hand to signal a tractor to come over and shield them while they recovered.

Frick's corner tee-box had white leather benches for visitors and a fridge for sodas and beer. Have a drink, he gestured, but I shook my head and sat, watching him tee up, then stroke out a three wood. He was either hitting draw or just hooking, hard to tell at first. We both watched the ball head out straight then bend left. The ratchet overspin bounce that took it even farther left and out of play. That whole time watching, Frick never moved from the top of his follow-through, frozen in that pretentious awards-night statuette position golfers learn to strike after a shot, absorbing the magnificence of what they've done. Ball mid-flight, heading to the woods half the time. *Shanked it. Scuffed it. Pushed it. Got under it.* There were a dozen such low-syllable mutterings golfers kept loaded up and ready to drop on the moment, as required.

"Came across it," Frick said, uncoiling from his pose.

"Coming across generally makes you fade the ball," I pointed out. "Or slice."

Frick re-enacted the shot with his rear hand, right in his case. Here was another undying habit of the 18-holers. You hold your hand flat and swing through the imaginary plane of the ball, so correcting in a single sweep all previous error. The imaginary ball flying as it should, that is, never deviating from the course as visualized in the will.

Frick stood down from the tee-box and cracked the fridge, took out a type of Italian orange soda I hadn't seen since the IAF years. Heyday soda. Good times soda. He looked over at me and said: "Frick just noticing his buddy Hoss looks like shit."

I said: "Well wait until you hear this next part."

Frick sipped his soda calmly for the first while I spoke. Then he climbed back up onto the tee-box and tipped a wire-mesh bucket of balls over, letting them spill out onto the Astro-turf surface. He started stroking these out with a five-iron. Click, click. He had all the mechanical automation of the long-timer. Didn't over-think each shot. Didn't act like there was much to be improved. But he was still spraying them. I watched the distribution while I told him the story about Griegson's books. And Frick put thirty-five balls down the fairway during this time, about evenly distributed into a zone twenty yards deep and sixty yards across, which only meant to me that over three or four entire games worth of five-iron approach shots, Frick was probably on the green twice. Yet he was number two on the leaderboard with a handicap of three. Welcome to Sunshine City: Cheaterville. Caddies dropping balls, members skipping strokes. Who wouldn't be dying to get out of this place?

When I got to the end of the strange chain of books and business cards and rooftop messages, Frick was almost through the bucket. And he looked down at the bottom of the range to the tractor and the kids scuttling from tree to trap to pond. He shaded his eyes. Then Frick said: "So what you're saying is you find this unusual."

I went to the fridge and found a Mexican beer. I took a wedge of lime from the bowl and pinched it into the neck of the bottle. I said: "Statistically speaking, call it impossible without planning, deliberation, motive, wherewithal. It's a major problem for me to know this about Griegson and still tell the story you're after. Random event. Bullet comes flying in from the hills, my ass. There's a worm in the apple, Frick. There's aspiration at the heart of these affairs. The numbers aren't flowing your direction. They're heading back towards causes in Griegson's sphere. They're flooding back into Sunshine City."

I drank a long pull of the beer and Frick paced. He was going to recap now, I felt it forming: the point-form summary counted off on the gloved fingers of his left hand. So a business card in Griegson's pocket led to an address, which led to a building, on the roof of which there was some graffiti.

"Check," I said. "Which is odd, although not yet freakishly unlikely."

And the graffiti turns out to be the last line of a book Griegson owned.

"A book many people own," I corrected. "Only Griegson had both the business card and the book. So now we're talking smaller chances. Ramping orders of unlikelihood."

Frick accepted another bucket of balls from one of the range kids. He spaced a dozen of these across the front lip of the Astro-turf tee-box and fished out his nine.

And in that book, Frick continued—"*Herzog*," I said—in that book there was another business card with another address, which led to some more graffiti.

"*People with no soul*," I said, nodding, taking another long pull of beer.

Which was the last line of another book Griegson owned, Frick said, bobbing in place, then lobbed a nine-iron out towards the nearest pin. It dropped onto the front edge of the green, then spun backwards down to the fringe.

"*Island of the Day Before*," I told him. "Umberto Eco."

"All right," Frick said. "All right. And in that book, we find yet another card."

"Structured magnitudes of impossibility. Forget the numbers," I told him. "There is no computation required. Three turns around this business and it just isn't nature."

"And we're not even through yet," Frick said.

Definitely not through, I told him. Another address, which led to more rooftop graffiti: *No symbols where none intended*, which is the last line from Beckett's book *Watt*. Which Griegson also owned, yes.

"Moving us into impossible land," I told him. "You follow me?"

Frick put his next shot a couple yards farther up the green, but pushed it right. The ball dropped and corkscrewed, then stuck on a bad part of the slope, twelve feet above the hole.

"Impossible land," Frick repeated. "And how many of these graffiti/book combinations did you and SaBe find?"

I told him the number. A big number. "Thirty-four and we had to stop. The two of us had to get some sleep."

Frick looked up at me sharply with these words, then forced his eyes back to the ball. Something he normally repressed was briefly released: an amped-up curiosity about SaBe's whereabouts at night, at bedtime. Guarded interests. Intrigue and leaderboards. How I hated this place, while saying nothing about it, just carrying on with the unlikely chain of books and business cards, graffiti and last lines. Looping in and out, from the Rough to the cabanas. Beckett to Flannery O'Connor to Martin Amis to Dostoyevsky to Janet Frame to a line on a hardware store out near the coastal highway and the rooftop banner that told us: *There's no need to say another word.*

Frick hit and watched the ball. I drifted back remembering SaBe crouched next to the shelf looking for this last one. Her eyes luminous, alive, curious, unresolved. She ran one finger down the books on the lowest shelf and breathed the words: *Big Sur.* Then we sat on the bed together and she read me Kerouac's words: *Something good will come out of all things yet—And it will be golden and eternal just like that. There's no need to say another word.*

Frick's ball settled to the left fringe. "Remarkable," he said, still listening but not watching as I fetched another beer and inserted a lime, as I sparked a reefer and sat puffing and sipping and continuing the tale: books to cards to roofs to quotes. A mad daisy chain. Onwards through Ellison and Nabokov, until SaBe and I had to quit. Until we had to sleep. Until we lost the will to figure it out. Until it was just a pattern that defied nature. All the while, both of us knowing where it had to end, spiralling through all of its turns until it reached the top drawer of Griegson's desk. The book he had been reading, or re-reading, at the very end. We might not have traced it that far. We might both have had to quit due to fatigue. But we knew that right there on the final pages of *Underworld* it ended with the single-word sentence: *Peace.*

Frick stroked a shot better than the others. I could see it the moment of contact, the soft sound of transference, all that club energy passed in a micrometre and a microsecond through the dimpled polyurethane surface and on into the ionomers and proprietary low-compression rubber composites of the ball's core, passing inwards and inwards as the ball soared, as it arced, as it scraped infinity.

Frick's ball landed three feet past the pin and bounced up, almost vertical in its hard backspin, seeming to quiver in place before falling, before hitting and rolling sharply back towards the flag, then dropping into the centre of the hole, the black heart of the game, the absolute zero of golf's obsession.

"Swe-eet," Frick said. Then he started laughing.

I grabbed a cart out front of the range and drove across Sunshine City to the security centre. Frick shouted after me when I left. But I just kept on stumping up the tier and was gone down into the lobby area before he could pack his clubs and follow. I heard him call out behind me: *Ah come on, Hoss, there's nothing in it. Patterns aren't meanings.*

Now I was swerving through traffic. Two-wheels into the planter getting around carts stopped for room service. Tearing up grass in front of the caddie shack.

I was thinking: so Frick's short game beat his approach play. So when he holed that final shot, after that entire story about Griegson's books had been played out, he turned to me and started laughing. That wasn't so unusual in itself: Frick finding humour in the moment. He had always been able to afford that luxury. What caught my attention this time was how sincere his amusement seemed to be.

He said: "Let me tell you something about Sunshine City."

I didn't want to hear. I was stoned again. I was bloated from two fast beers. I'd just decided that moment I was through with this place, really done and gone. I was leaving the same afternoon. Going to pack up my bag, my van, take some water, forget the money, just let me go. But here Frick was blustering on through some final detail. How they all liked to mess with each other. Head games were part of the leaderboard culture. A little gentle fucking with, Frick called it. So someone was messing with Griegson, undoubtedly. Everyone knew he liked to read. It was his weakness, this romantic business. Books. Frick rolled his eyes at me. So you hire some kid to paint signs on rooftops. Hack his mail-order account and get the cards inserted between strategic pages. It was a complicated trick, not impossible.

"But we don't *shoot* at each other, Hoss. Look around yourself for God's sake," Frick was leaned towards me now, breath smelling of toothpaste and breakfast cereal. Over his shoulder I could see flecks of pastel across the links green. The air tinkled with ice and idle conversation, cell phones twiddling and low whine of golf carts. "These people aren't *shooters*," Frick continued, voice low and urgent. "We don't think about taking lives. We don't think about life at all here, Hoss. That's one of the chief benefits of the place. We don't think life. We don't talk life. We just live it and talk about something else. Bad for stroke play, talking about life, Hoss. And don't feel sorry for the members either. They're not trapped here. They earned their way in. These people earned their right to be *golfers*."

I stormed off. I climbed down off the tier and into the lobby where there was a big picture of a new refreshments building planned for the end of the 9th hole on the second 18. The Griegson Turn it was going to be called, and by some fancy architect if my eye could be trusted, all sheets of glass and cantilevered timbers. There was a picture of the dead man up there in the corner of the poster. He was holding the trophy above his head, in his left hand. Huge-occasion smile stretched across his television features.

I stood staring at this for a long time, registering and not registering what was wrong. It was Griegson, no doubt, but with something skewed in the portrait. It took me a long time to get it. Then it came. They'd flipped the image. Griegson shot right, so he wore his glove on his left hand. I knew that intimately, having peeled the glove off his dead fingers to find the phone number that now, like everything else in the story, appeared to mean nothing. But here he was hoisting the trophy over his head in an ungloved left hand, or so it appeared. His gloved hand, which looked to be his right, hanging down by his belt.

"Sir?"

He was sixteen or seventeen years old. Range ball kid. He still had on the kneepads from the samurai suit.

"Yeah?" I slurred. Feeling the worst I could remember feeling in many years. Feeling the Rough in my skin, in my hair. Feeling the Rough in my internal tracks and approaches. In all my hidden traps and waterways. And realizing, just then, that the kid recognized it in me, being from the Rough himself.

"Just wondering if you're all right, sir," the kid whispered.

I stared at him. Red hair, scrawny. Underfed. A certain determination in the eyes. Angling and figuring. I said: "Where do you live out there?"

"Southeast," he said. "In the hills."

"You come in every day."

He nodded.

"You like it here."

He nodded again. There were people moving by, ignoring us. Members and caddies. Girls from the bar up top of the hill. I thought I could read a few things about my range kid here. He wanted to be one of them. He was probably in caddy training already. I wanted to tell him to flee, to get out before the place burns. Leave before the bullets start pouring in, or out, or both ways. It was surely coming and you look like a survivor, I wanted to tell him. You look like someone who won't desiccate and blow away in the heat of the outside air. Get outside. Stay outside. Leave the compound and don't come back.

But I didn't say any of that. I pointed at the picture instead, knowing well that I sounded blown. Hosed and ripped and bent. Fried. I said: "Just noticing the picture's backwards. This man shoots right, I happen to know it."

The kid grinned and nodded, inside on a detail I obviously didn't have. He said: "Well yeah. That's what makes Griegson so awesome. They guy shoots right, but he didn't always."

I heard myself say: sorry?

"Didn't always," the kid said, eyes bright with the wonder of it. "Griegson was a natural southpaw. Shot left all his entire life. Wrote left. Did everything left. Then sometime last year he got the yips and his score exploded. Griegson was scratch. Then suddenly he was shooting 72. Then 90, 92. It was bad. Some members take pills to break the yips. Some use meditation or therapy. Nobody has ever done what Griegson did. He switched over, bought new clubs. He started shooting right."

I was staring at the kid, struggling to process this information.

The kid just kept on nodding. "I know," he said. "It's unbelievable. Switched right and a year later he's number three on the leaderboard. Natural southpaw. The man is a god."

Behind him, I saw what he was talking about. The picture, the building named after him. That was the ascending deity of Griegson. But I didn't stand around to admire. I was out the door already.

Hoss careering across Sunshine City, lurching to a stop in front of the security centre, stumping inside. Where of course I had no clearance and would not be permitted to review anything. Unless I phoned Frick, that is. Who, to his credit, just told me to put him on speakerphone, then commanded the air in the way only he could. Frick communicating entitlement and authority for all the dudes from Therman Winkler and Huston

Armed Response. Frick's voice barked out of my phone: *Show this man anything he needs to look at. Do it now.*

I needed just two minutes of security camera footage. Yes, yes. I could have done this before. But it seemed too obvious. Now I clutched at the obvious. I needed the obvious. So: the 14th green, Thursday morning, before and after the power cycle. And here the images came, spooling up from some hidden vault below, images sharp but with an auto-archival quality, aged the moment they were recorded, belonging in the instant to deep memory, to times forgotten, or soon to be forgotten, to the part of us that fades and fades inexorably, heading for zero.

Griegson's long back and wide shoulders, bent to the task. He steps up to the ball. Then he steps away. He dangles the putter briefly in a plumb line. Then he looks off-green, almost directly towards the camera. Or over the camera and into the hills. And in the seconds before the screen goes blank, I see that his shoulders are heaving, that his face is crumpled, eyes shining with tears. He's holding a phone. He's dialling and listening without hope. Weeping. Now turning back to address the ball. *Dead already.*

The screen cut to black, a counter rolling, ticking off the five minutes of maintenance while I waited for the world to return as Griegson had left it. The world that might somehow reveal to me how a natural southpaw came to have a phone number written on his own left palm.

Sky still high and blue, ocean still flecked and agile in the distance. Dotted with sailboards from resorts farther down the coast that catered to that kind of thing. And here came my answer: Griegson in the trap, face-down in black sand. Wes at his side, feeling his pulse. Looking up past the camera into the hills. First anxious, then firming with resolve as he takes Griegson's left hand in his own, as he removes Griegson's glove. As the caddy takes a pen from his shirt pocket and begins to write on Griegson's hand. Wes committing some numeric detail from ink to skin, from skin to me. The one waiting in the future who will shake the dead man's hand and know the truth.

∞

I'd never wanted much. Even in the best of the good years. It was always about some comfort, a measure of friendship. I was unlucky in love, they said. One fortune teller. I swore I'd never go to another. One person announces a deficit of luck, which is something that doesn't exist in the first place, and people around me changed their tune. They said: you have bad luck in love. And hearing that, a person's life cramps around the notion, like a hand closed over a high voltage wire.

Of course there were always those moments of stepped-up yearning. Again, I'm just average on this score. Muddled in with the great mound of experience at the centre of the bell curve: I had my moments of wanting to punch out of the ordered life, the endless cause and effect of being an organism. I had my moments of wanting to see and touch something greater than the numbers that was yet possibly the source of all numbers too. Infinity, sure. The word. The idea. The elusive article of faith. And I knew only too well that admitting this kind of thing— scotched up at an office party, having a good time, a big case just complete—can lead to trouble, can get you on shit lists, can turn your career from a gentle draw to a parabolic hook, heading hard for the weeds. Saying something like: "But what about a number beyond the numbers, though. A moment of real understanding. Not the stats, right? Not the event probability or the compound risks. I'm taking about…a master key. An insight. I'm talking about a moment of seeing it all, the internal pattern. Infinity?"

I never said this: *Because aren't we all trying to bring that into exis-tence, somehow? Infinity. Longing for it, aching for it, crying for it in our private places?*

But everybody still stared back at me in the low light of a bar on the thirty-seventh floor of a hotel where the IAF jocks used to gather to drink, to be the quantum lords that we knew we were. As if my face had been transformed by that one drunken spree of words.

Their expression said it all. Hoss has the yips, the deadliest virus known.

∞

In Sunshine City, when it was all over, I sat in the van waiting for the red-and-white-striped steel poles at the main security gate to drop into their recesses in the roadway. I was facing east, into the rising sun. Frick nodded from the doorway of the guard hut. I gave him a half-smirk and waved my hands around, indicating the van. Two thumbs up. Nice ride. Brazilian made. Four-wheel drive. Huge front seats as if for the pilot of an inner-space shuttle. Dials and gauges all around. Club quality sound system. Plus these drink holders that would hold a two-litre cup of cola, just like back in the old days.

Frick hugged me hard in the garage after unveiling the thing. Cobalt grey, black leather. Water tanks in the back, full. Money in a slim executive briefcase on the passenger seat. Enough cash for me to drive wherever I wanted and to drift through as many days as I cared to imagine. Of course I tried to refuse it. And I was glad when Frick said *no way, not a chance, you take it.*

"I read your report," Frick said. "You ran the numbers. You rolled the reality bones, fair and square."

"Sorry about the sniper," I said. "A sniper would have been nice and clean."

"Well," Frick said, "You did say 92% probability the bullet came from Hill 231 where the casing was found."

Sure. But in the document this bullet was not sourced to a "sniper" but to an "accomplice." *78% likelihood 9 times out of 10 with an error margin of 4%: death is a category-4 suicide, under subsection 4.4 Assisted Suicides, under subsubsection 4.4.2 Assisted Suicide with Firearm, Projectile or Ballistic Device.*

I had to dial the number on Griegson's palm a final time to reach my conclusion that he had, in fact, killed himself. Sitting in the security centre, watching Wes write on Griegson's hand. Watching Wes's face, that stone-cold look. I realized he was writing in anger. Wes was blowing somebody's cover. He was pointing me in a particular direction, one where I might not have looked otherwise. I thought about that. My own blind spots, the places I might not look. I thought about the people Wes might hate and why. I thought about dialling the mystery number myself that one time. Familiar birdsong, that light breath. So close. So very close.

What did she remember, watching from the window? A puff of smoke. A lick of flame. A thump or a crack. And then, odd detail this one: a phone ringing. Somewhere, she said.

I dialled the number again. No answer. But this time I followed the forming hunch, the innumerate gut call. I climbed slowly to my one foot, put weight down on the peg, pivoted and blew past the hovering, suspicious guards and out to the cart. I drove to SaBe's cabana at a slow and deliberate pace. Parked out front and straightened my hopeless hair, wiped sweat out of my eyes. She was in the kitchen, watching a kettle boiling for tea. She didn't look up or frown when I walked in without knocking. She said hello without raising her head and I could see all that was secret about her to all of those members who hungered for her, hunted her in their minds, lined her up in their sights,

imagined her spatchcocked like a trophy skin carpet in front
of their fireplaces to lounge on, to stroke and soil. SaBe, who
must surely have considered options during the days since her
husband Scott was last around. In all these long days of her captivity. Perhaps even sampled here and there. But who ultimately
wouldn't have any of them. Not Frick. Not Griegson. Not if you
were number one on the leaderboard or number fifteen and
hard rising. Rigid with potential. She pulled back from them.
These people who lived life but chose to talk about other things.
And now I had the proof of it, and the reason too. The meaning.

The walls of SaBe's cabana were hung with photographs.
Framed and matted. The viewings of an achingly pure eye. The
long-absent Scott's work, almost surely. High skies and thin horizons. Desert landscapes and lonely highways. Outposts leaning
under tarps and sticks. Photographs of dusty children and hungry dogs. Random portraits, faces lined with bitter knowledge
and faint hope. A dead water pump. A fortune teller's caravan,
draped with corporate logos as was the style of the roving seer
in our era. And she had collected these, held them, wished to be
in them. Waiting for her chance, which did not come.

"You've looked better," SaBe said to me: "Would you like
some tea?"

"Did he phone you?" I asked her. "Griegson. Thursday morning, very early."

She lifted the tea bag from the pot. She said: "I don't like my
tea too strong. Do you mind if it's weak?"

"They all love you, don't they?"

She took honey from the cupboard, a silver spoon from a
drawer.

"The old guys. The middle-aged guys. The crook caddies and
security goons. Even the range kids in from their shacks in the
Rough. You give them all a whiff of something, don't you?"

She turned to the fridge for the glass bottle of milk and held it quivering over the cups. "Do you like milk?" she said. "I have cream too."

"And what a burden that is," I said. "To give people a whiff of the freedom you're too bored, too spoiled, too lazy to take for yourself."

She poured milk into both cups, her hand shaking.

"But Wes didn't love you," I continued. "Wes hated you hard for something you did."

Here came the tea, gurgling into the cups. Then a spoonful of honey, swirled into each.

"Did Frick put you up to it? Did he give you the order?" I said. "Did he say it was just in the spirit of the game? All part of lead-erboard culture in Sunshine City. Messing with a guy being part of the contest. *Just a little gentle fucking with.* Did you give Grieg-son a gentle fucking, SaBe? Once or twice. Maybe three times if you could stand it. Then listen to the phone ring and ring. Listen to Frick's stroke-play nemesis losing his mind."

She was stirring the honey while tears made their way down her cheeks to the corners of her wide mouth.

I took my phone out and dialled the number from Grieg-son's palm and watched it ring in her shirt pocket. The ringer was off. But just over SaBe's heart there was a flutter of irides-cent green. Killing envy. World-destroying desire. All of it right there. Vibrating with soft urgency in the valley between her breasts.

Impossible land.

I never told Frick all that I knew. My old college friend hugged me again in the garage. And again out at the guard hut. I couldn't say with any certainty that he'd arranged the book prank that gave Griegson the yips. I knew only that he probably had done so because he was very likely the only other person in camp with a bookshelf of his own, with a sense of what an unsettling dirge might be written using the final cadences from dozens of novels. Not a single word/ People with no soul/ No symbols where none intended...

What I knew with much greater certainty—call it 85%, good enough for me—was that when Griegson blew through the yips by switching left to right, he had Frick worried about local authority and leadership, faced with a guy who might pass him on the leaderboard twice, playing different ways. That sent Frick looking for new techniques. New black ops. New trickery and deceit.

As it was, unaware of all I knew, Frick was happy. Suicide it was. Suicide which was insurance-neutral and manageable from a morale perspective. Griegson drinking heavily. Griegson distressed. That story could play. So Griegson would rise to the pantheon and be praised, unite the community, calm the fears. And if Frick noticed me darting a glance backwards from time to time while I packed, he didn't show it. My own secret hope dwindling. My own yearned-for moment of blinding unlikeli-hood: SaBe running up the road with a suitcase. SaBe running for freedom, running to me out of the seams of infinity.

Thumbs up from Frick. The security guard popped his fist down onto the button and the steel bolts hissed home. The road was clear. I glanced once more in the rearview mirror and hit the gas. I disappeared into a cloud of dust the instant I left the perimeter. And then I was driving and blinking back tears, anguish, God knows what. I missed the true passage of at least three hours there, reaching for reefers and tossing them unlit out the window. Spoiled even for smoke. And then I was two hundred miles north and I'd eaten the sandwiches I'd picked up at the canteen, and I was parked at a crossroads with no partic-ular idea where I was. Mountains over there. Long expanses of burnt brown stretching west down towards the invisible sea. I was at a cinematic intersection. A road running precisely north-south under my wheels. Another crossing, stretching from the road rash of the western sky to the dark bruising of the east.

I got out. I paced. I made a tic-tac-toe grid with my shoe in the dust, right at the centre of the intersection. I stood in its various boxes, testing their feel. There was no real reason for doing this, that I could figure. But it allowed me time to vacate the present moment. So I found myself remembering SaBe instead, how tightly she had tried to hold me before I left, pinning my arms to my sides. Hoss idiotically resisting. I scuffed my shoes now in the silky dust and told myself that she would have dried her tears by now. Gone on to whatever Frick had in mind for her next. And perhaps that was Frick's bed, perhaps not. SaBe would return, in either case, to being what she had always been at Sunshine City: the heart of human misery, the reminder of transcendent possibilities forever withheld.

I thought of Griegson: face up into the hills, then turning to his routine putt. Crosshairs tickling the back of his neck. I thought of my last moments in his cabana, packing my clothes. Perhaps it had been Griegson himself who leaned in close, in those dwindling seconds, and whispered the idea. Something stopped me short in front of the computer, caused me to lean over suddenly and type SaBe's phone number into the password box on that file: *Tally of Scores*. And, with a harp-stroke of computer music, the file unfolded. It took a man of rare honour, I thought, to type his suicide note into the header of a spreadsheet showing detailed hole-by-hole scores over twenty-five years. I dropped into the chair in front of this data set, amazed. Winded by the size of my discovery. Griegson was no cheater. His handicap as a leftie had long been near zero, hovering as low as minus two for several recent years. Then it started to mysteriously rise. Plus 5, plus 15. When he switched and started shooting right (a particular column was annotated to this effect), his score shot even higher. Plus 20, plus 25. But then the tide had turned. Falling steadily, seeking zero. And getting there too. Bouncing along at the level it had been before.

Until Frick thought of SaBe and what she might do. And when SaBe got involved, then Griegson's score bounced again as if off a magic floor. Shooting 75, shooting 80.

Griegson was no wuss. I read those ranks of scores and formed a solid affection for the man. He'd licked the book prank, after all. That took guts. But when SaBe collided with his scores—either by arriving in his life, or by her leaving, it hardly mattered—Griegson saw he'd run out of radical solutions. You could only shoot left or right. There was no third option. It was of a different order, this prank. Love itself, whether he felt it for SaBe or merely saw in her what he'd lost those years before, that was of a different order. So the trick worked quite a bit better than Frick in his nastiest mood would have hoped or imagined. They didn't give the guy the yips. They gave him despair. And if, in choosing his way of surrendering to it, Griegson had tried to take the whole place down with him—tried to induce a crisis by which Frick and his little kingdom would collapse under the black hole weight of failed insurance policies—then it only proved to me that Griegson had a sense of humour too. Through the tears and exploded scores. Right to the end.

The suicide note itself was impressive. Griegson had been to school on last lines by this point, of course. But it was a good one even by the high literary standards of his library, I thought. Right there at the top of the spread, above the orderly columns of scores, six final words on the life from which he wanted freedom:

Last shot, a hole in One.

∞

The fortune teller's caravan arrived from the west. It had been coming for the past fifteen minutes, smudged out there long in advance of its arrival. I saw it. Then I heard it. Now it was here with its dangling and jangling crust of ancient, talismanic logos: hood ornaments and street signs, bottle caps and sports paraphernalia. Beer cans, tennis shoes, action figures. And pictures of once-known actors, athletes, singers, varnished to the fenders and the door panels. Icons of fame and obscurity.

He said: "Fortune?" Window down. Dirt-grey elbow sticking out through the beaded curtain he had hanging in the driver's side window. His face round and gaunt at once. A fat man starving down. Everybody off somewhere else in search of work, bread, water.

I told him no thanks. But he pressed. He said: "I'll give you a free read. You buy the fortune."

I laughed and turned away. My new van was there. Just a few paces off. I could be in it and driving away in less than a minute. I said: "What free read?"

"Free read on how you lost the leg."

I turned back to the man. What the hell. I nodded.

He said: "You were driving drunk."

"No," I said.

"Hey," the fortune teller said, "I'm not finished."

I rolled my eyes and waited.

"You were driving drunk in a car with a friend who was behind the wheel."

There was some way they did this, picked up clues from how you darted your eyes. I tried to keep my gaze steadily on him. But this was part of the trick too. You couldn't.

He sensed he was on to something. He scratched his chin, then said: "Buddy drove off a bridge."

"Wrong."

"Embankment," the guys said.

"Forget it, you're wrong."

"No wait," the guy said. "This is strange. I'm seeing something like a bridge, but it just goes part way, then stops."

"Look, you're the fortune teller. Can you see the past and future or not? No. No you can't. Everybody knows you can't. So why don't you just admit it? You're a fraud. You don't know anything. You make these statements like you're so sure of something but it's all just a crock. And you leave people thinking that you've told them something serious about themselves and it just screws people up. Unlucky at love. Bullshit. She liked me, all right? Only here I am driving around in the goddamn sticks in a van I'm all proud of and she's having a hot tub right now. Okay? Sipping champagne. So why don't you just leave people the hell alone? Why don't you get a real job? Because it wasn't a bridge, you moron. It was the off-ramp on the 580 in Berkeley that had the bridge decks removed for maintenance after the Castle Rock quake, a detail Frick's fucking onboard navigation system had not yet been updated to notice. You get me? So sure we were drinking, but the computer is supposed to tell you not to take that exit. That would be reasonable. If the world were reasonable. Which it isn't. So we drove off into the thin air. Is this all making sense to you? A car trying to fly but not having wings so we end up crashing in a gravel pit and Frick walking away. Me not walking away, for reasons you have obviously already noticed."

The sun was setting. I stood in the failing light, sweating with rage.

"Hey man, sorry about that," the fortune teller said.

"All right," I said. "So, as you can see, I'm not interested in hearing your thoughts on the future."

"Freebie," the guy said. "No hard feelings."

"Piss off," I said.

"It's short. It's really short. Not a prediction, so much, as a statement of relevant fact."

I looked at the guy through the beads. He had a not-unfriendly glint in his eye. He wasn't messing with me. He just thought I was funny. And at that moment, I had to admit I could see his point.

My shoulders rounded down. I exhaled. I went into my pocket and pulled out some bills, gave them to him. No, no. Take them. We all gotta eat. "Okay, give it to me," I said.

"You ready?"

"Don't start messing with me now."

"You're sure you're ready?"

"I'm in the van in ten seconds you don't start talking," I told him.

"All right," he said. "Here goes."

I heard a very faint rumble, very far behind me.

"Someone is following you," the man said.

Then he stuck a hand out the window, and I shook it. And he drove off slowly. The caravan shrinking down and dwindling and fading with the light, then disappearing from view.

I turned and looked south. Back down the road in the direction I had come. Back towards Sunshine City. Towards Frick. Towards the corpse Griegson left behind.

Towards SaBe.

Definitely somebody there. I had that certainty. Somebody approaching. On the horizon, right where the white sky fused in its furious heat to the cowering earth, right in that seam of infinity.

LOVERS

MARK ANTHONY JARMAN
THE DECEMBER ASTRONAUTS
(or Moon-base Horse Code)

> *The distance I felt came not from country or people;*
>   *it came from within me.*
> *I am as distant from myself as a hawk from the moon.*
> JAMES WELCH, *Winter in the Blood*

I WAS LOST in the stars, but not lost, my tiny craft one of many on a loop prescribed by others, two astronauts far out in a silk-road universe of burning gas and red streaks, and one of us dead.

Then the land comes up at us, the speed of the land rushing up like film and our Flight Centre men at serious blinking screens. Our valves open or don't open, the hull holds, the centre holds, little I can do. The dead man is not worried. I will not worry anymore, I renounce worry (yeah, that will last about three seconds). The angle of re-entry looks weird to my eye. I had to haul his corpse back inside for re-entry so he wouldn't burn up.

In the city below me traffic is backing up into the arterial avenues. They want to see us return, to fly down like a hawk with the talons out.

"Units require assistance. All units."

We are three orbits late because of the clouds and high wind. They want to be there if there is a memorable crash, our pretty shell splitting on the tarmac into several chemical flash fires engraved on their home movies.

We were so far up there above the moon's roads, my capsule's burnt skin held in rivers and jet streams that route our long-awaited re-entry. Up there we drive green channels riven in the clouds, ride stormscud and kerosene colours in the sky, then we ease our wavering selves down, down to this outer borough, down to rumpled family rooms and black yawning garages, down to the spanking new suburb unboxed in the onion fields.

I'm a traveller, an addict. I descend from the clouds to look for work, I was up there with the long-distance snowstorms. It's hard to believe I'm here again, hard to believe Ava became so uncaring while I was gone from the colony.

Ava's messages are still there. "This message will be deleted in two days." I press 9 to save it yet again. I save her messages every ten days, my private archives, my time capsule, a minute of her lovely voice.

"Loved your last transmission," Ava said in September. "It made me laugh! And I loved the pictures you sent! I can't wait to see you."

But then the change in October, the October revolution. We are changelings locked in a kingdom of aftershave ads and good shepherds, lambs and lions and the Longhorn Steakpit's idea of a salad bar.

Her messages were so very affectionate, and we'd lasted so long, so long, but in the end our messages were not enough. Our words were not enough. A week of silence and then a new message. I knew it.

"Some bad news," as Ava termed it. She'd met someone else, she'd had a lot to drink, one thing led to another. And I was so close. Only a few days more. But she couldn't wait for me. So long.

In the Coconut Grove bar in the afternoon I'm feeling all right. I'm good at clarity and appreciation, but I'm slightly out of time. Time slows and I lurk in it, I can alter it. Do you know that feeling? I drink and carefully move my head to study my world. Venetian blinds layering tiny tendrils of soft light on us, the purple tennis court on TV, an AC running low, the lack of real sky. It all seems okay, it all seems significant, it all seems deliberate and poised for some event. But only to me, only I know this mood, this valiant expectation, this expedition into the early realms of alcohol.

Perhaps I am not quite right, but I savour the strange interlude. I'm a lonely satellite in space, a craft drifting alone, drinking alone. In this room the music is fine, the hops have bite—the perfect bar moment.

Then the bartender cranks up the volume on Sports TV and snaps to his phone, "The girl who cut my hair butchered it. I didn't have the heart to tell her, *You suck.*"

And that's the end of my spell, the end of that little mission to Mars. And I was so enjoying it.

"Hey dog, you flew with that dead guy, didn't you? And then your girl dumped you. She's *hot.* Bummer, man." I wait until the bartender goes to the washroom to work on his hair and I exit without paying.

Maybe not the smartest idea, but I call Ava in Spain. She left me, but she's the only one who will know what I mean.

"What do you want from me? Why are you talking like this?" Her slight laugh.

Apparently I have some anger to work out.

Turquoise mountains at the end of the street remind me of Tucson or Utah. The mountains of the moon. I kill time walking. Funny to be on foot once more. The sun and earth—what are they to me? I still orbit Ava, but she's not there, no there there, so to what furious solar system do I now pledge my allegiance? I still orbit her blue-eyed summer-kitchen memories and the cordwood and pulpwood childhood in the north.

Need to change that orbit, need orbit decay.

In the building where she used to live they now deal ounces and eight-balls. I was gone, Ava's gone, the moon has changed.

Not sure I like the messages I'm picking up re the new frontier. No one foresaw this, crystal and crank smuggled into the colony, dealers and Albanian stick-up crews and crummy walk-ups, the adamantine miners working the face under Dwarf Fortress, all the single males earning big bucks in the catacombs and mineral mines, but with nowhere to go, the shortage of places to live, the exorbitant cost of milk, the new gang unit brought in, dead bodies on the corner with splayed hands and wrists smeared red with their own blood, and bouncers at the door working hard at that Russian look. With the economy in the toilet the Minister of Finance is studying the feasibility of holding Christmas four times a year instead of two.

At the reception for me and some other space cowboys the party crackers lie like ashes on my tongue. The fruit salad fallen from soldered tins; taste the fruits of duty. My long periods of radio silence and now the noise of crowds and halls of ice cubes.

My brother-in-law Horse the detective is at the reception with a woman he says has just moved to the moon from Babylon to escape the war. Delia looks nervous, as if still in a war zone. Her family made her leave her home, smuggled her over the border, they feared for her life if she stayed. Forget this place, they said of the only home she's known, it doesn't exist anymore.

"How do you like it here so far?"

Delia says, "People are very nice to me, but it's not what I thought." She shrugs. "All my life I wanted to see the moon, stared up at it. But I miss my home, my family, my car, my brothers, the path to the river."

"Can they visit?"

"No, it's impossible now." The family had money, but now it is all gone, they are bankrupted by the war, the stolen gold, the extortion, the journey to other lands. Her English is very good.

"How is the new job?"

"Horse can tell you better than I."

"Brutal," says Horse, "A ton of movement with the gangs, a lot of old grudges, eye for an eye. We just had a 27 before we came here."

"27?"

"It means he was already dead before we got there," Delia tells me. "Another young guy," she says. "They get younger and younger. Children."

Five phones ringing on the silent body, once so talkative, now so grave. How may I direct your call? How come it's so easy to become a body? He is past saving, his messages will be deleted in ten days unless someone who loves him presses save.

The woman from Babylon asks about my last trip in the light years, where I slept in far stars like fields sown with salt.

"Is it boring out there? Is it better than here?"

"It was wild, hard to describe, almost religious."

"What about when Curtis died?"

"I don't know, he was just dead."

Was it an accident or did he do it to himself? This question is not in the press. One time, after he was dead, I swore I heard a fly buzzing inside the windshield, that manic little taptaptap.

I turned my head slowly; there was no fly. I had wires to my skin, an extended excellent dream.

I hear Delia speaking Arabic on her phone. Her uncle is a consul in Vietnam with an Irish wife. We, all of us, have come so far from home.

No one else from the December class returned alive. There is a chance they are still out there, or else something is killing them, making them martyrs. Or perhaps some Decembrists stumbled onto a beautiful world, and chose to not steer back to this one. Why am I the only one who found a course home? And to what?

It's just survivor's guilt, the detectives insist. Take up golf. Some good 18-hole courses on the moon, especially the Sea of Mares, Sea of Tranquility, condos with fake pools stocked with trout fingerlings.

"You can rent an AK at the range," says Horse. "Or sled down Piston Alley."

Piston Alley is named for all the sled engines that have blown pistons on the long straight stretch. The engine runs the best ever just before the piston shoots out like a tiny rocket. I don't really want an AK-47.

In the NASA gymnasium the trainee astronauts play tag. Astronauts get lots of tang; that was the old joke. Poontang. When I was out there I craved smoked salmon and dark beer. The dead man went on for hours about steak and ice cream. I have a few too many bank loans. Curtis was outside when it happened, his air.

The woman from Babylon stares at me with her very dark eyes, says, "I wonder if perhaps you would help us in the interview room."

Did Horse put her up to this?

He says, "The Decembrists are famous with the school kids."

"But with these jokers you pick up?"

Horse says, "You've always been better than me at reading faces. You can let us know when it's a crock. We'll have signals."

Horse makes it seem like a job selling vacuum cleaners.

"Think about it. Something to do."

Something to do—he has a point. Maybe a distraction from Ava in my head. I have escaped gravity and achieved a kind of gravitas. Yet I feel like a broken shoe. I can't sleep (*night and day*), my mind locked on her with someone else (*day and night I think of you*), and the lymph nodes on each side of my groin are swollen tight as stones inside a cherry; no idea what that's about, what's next, what's approaching me.

They are plowing a new road by the graveyard, by the old settlers and the new settlers in the cemetery under Meth Mountain. The lumpy graves look to be making their slow way across the white moon's dusty field, the dead in their progress to us, their magnetic message under clay walls and organic reefs and the moon's Asiatic peaks just past the plywood windows of the closed mall.

Ava quit her job and got away, but when I filled out a Planet Change Request Form it was turned down by upstairs. I know it's not a planet, but that's the form they use. At the drive-thru window on Von Braun Boulevard I order a combo and a uniformed teen hands me a paper bag.

"Enjoy your meal."

I drive to the carved-up picnic tables by Lost Lake. Opening the bag, I find $6,000. They have handed me the day's receipts. Or gave something to the wrong car. Someone will be pissed off. And where are my fries? I'm not driving all the way back down the mountain.

Now, how to use $6,000? Pay down the loans or just buy a giant TV? I've always wanted a jukebox or to buy a bar in Nebraska. Maybe I will. I can learn things. Ava said, *Whosoever wants to be first must first be slave to all.* That night I sleep among the fences under stars where I rode so long. Perfect carpentry is a thing of amazing beauty.

Downtown I see Delia walking by the Oppenheimer Fountain. She seems shy. I feel her lovely eyes hide something, some secret limit inside her. Is she resigned to it? I like the idea of a secret, like her face.

"So I can just ride along in the car?"

"Hell yeah you can ride," says Horse. "That's it exactly. A goddamn team!"

I can ride, privy to the children selling ghost pills stepped on a few times, dividing the corners, eyes like radiogenic freeway lights. It's the Zombies versus the 68th Street runners, yellow flashes on a dark wall and the Indian Head Test Pattern, and from this world of instant grudges we pluck the sad-eyed murderers and take them into Interview Room #2, where we strive to arrive at some form of truth acceptable to most of us.

Everyone loves truth. Ava told me the truth, did she not? She loves me, she loves me not. It's a gamble, shooting dice while clouds boil around the sun, goading the dominos.

Who controls the corner, the zoo? We travel to the far corners of the universe, but we can't control the local corner, can't control the inside of our head.

In the interview rooms prisoners must be checked every fifteen minutes. Someone slumped there in a chair killed a son, a cousin, killed in the triple last time. Horse walks in with his coffee. It goes on, it goes on.

They seen you riding with Moonman and Mississippi and Ghost.

Seen *me*?

You been slinging dope?

I don't know no Mississippi.

Tight bags of meth hidden in the torn baby-seat.

Where were you rolling?

Nowhere. You know, just rolling nowhere.

By the fountain her gas mask matches her dress. Males never quite exist for me—only women. I don't carry a mask; the air inside is fine, but she is very cautious and keeps it with her briefcase. Five PM and the moon goes violet. Free Fanta for all teens at the moon-base chapel. She doesn't drink and I am a spastic snake.

At dinner she doesn't know she saves my life just by being there in front of me. I'd rather she not know my sad history, my recent heartbreak. It's so pleasant to meet someone so soon after Ava, but still, the joy is tempered a tad by the prospect of it happening again, of another quick crowbar to the head. But I resolve to be fun. After the attack on the Fortran Embassy I resolve to be more fun.

Delia says she swam a lot in Babylon before the war, and she has that swimmer's body, the wide shoulders. She says, "I am used to pools for women only, not mixed. I don't want to swim in the moon-base pool."

"Why not?"

"You'll laugh."

She doesn't want to swim with strange men, but also fears catching some disease.

"I was hesitant to tell you about the pool. I feared you'd laugh at me."

"No, I understand perfectly."

But now I want to see her in a pool, her wide shoulders parting the water, her in white foam, our white forms in manic buzzing bubbles, her shoulders and the curve of her back where I am allowed to massage her at night when her head aches.

Strange, Ava also had migraines, but I was rarely witness to them; she stayed alone with them in the whimpering dark and I would see her afterward. Beside me in her room, Delia makes a sound, almost vomits over the edge of her bed, almost vomits several times from the pain, her hand to her lips, her hands to her face.

Delia is very religious, very old-fashioned, jumps away in utter panic if I say one word that is vaguely sexual, yet she delights in fashion mags and revealing bras and cleavage in silk and she allows my hands to massage her everywhere when she aches, allows my hands to roam.

"How do you know where the pain is," she asks me, her face in pillows.

I don't know. I just know how to find pain.

At Delia's kitchen table we study maps in a huge atlas, Babylon, Mesopotamia, Assur, where she says her ancestors were royalty in a small northern kingdom. I love the small kingdom we create with each other in our intimate rooms or just walking, charged moments that feel so valuable, yet are impossible to explain to someone else. I saw her in the store, saw her several times in the middle aisles, knew I had to say something.

"I noticed you immediately, thought you were some dark beauty from Calcutta or Bhutan."

"You saw me several times? I didn't notice you."

"But you smiled at me each time."

"Everyone smiles at me," she says brightly. "And you whites all look the same," she adds, and I realize she is not joking.

Her white apartment looks the same as the other white apartments, windows set into one wall only, a door on another wall. I realize both women have apartments built halfway into the ground, a basement on a hill. Yet they are so different. Ava's slim Nordic face pale as a pearl and her eyes large and light, sad and hopeful—and Delia's dark flashing eyes and flying henna hair and pessimism and anger and haughtiness. Ava was taller than me, tall as a model. Delia is shorter; I find this comforting.

I close my eyes expecting to see Ava's white face, but instead I'm flying again, see the silver freighter's riveted wall, the first crash, then sideswiped by a Red Planet gypsy hack, a kind of seasickness as the Russian team ran out of racetrack, Russians still alive, but drifting far from the circular station lit up like a chandelier, their saucerful of secrets, drifting away from their cigarettes and bottles, from a woman's glowing face. So long! *Poka! Do svidaniia!*

The young woman in Interview Room #2 speaks flatly.
They killed my brother, they will kill me if they want.
We can help you.
She laughs at Horse. You can't help me.
Who to believe? I want to believe her. She got into a bad crowd, cooking with rubber gloves, the game. Our worries about cholesterol seem distant and quaint. She's not telling us everything, but we can't hold her.

"I've come into some money if you need a loan. It's not much."
Delia raises her dark eyebrows in the interview room, as if I am trying to buy her with my paper bag of cash. Maybe I am trying to buy her.
"And how am I supposed to pay you back? I have no prospects."

On her TV the handsome actor standing in for the President tells us we must increase the divorce rate to stimulate the economy. We need more households, more chickens in the pots. I am sorry, he says, I have only one wife to give for my country. We switch to watch *Lost in Space* re-runs.

At night I ask my newest woman, my proud Cleopatra, "Is there a finite amount of love in the universe? Or does it expand?"

"What?"

"Well, I didn't know you and no love existed, but now I love you, so there is that much more."

"Say that again," she asks, looking me in the eye.

I repeat my idea.

"I think you are crazy," she says. "Not *crazy* crazy, but crazy."

I am full of love, I think, an overflowing well. Perhaps I supply the universe with my well, perhaps I am important. Her full hips, the universe expanding, doomed and lovely, my mouth moving everywhere on her form. The bed is sky blue and wheat gold.

"How many hands do you have," she asks with a laugh in the morning, trying to escape the bed, escape my hands: "You're like a lion!"

She is trying to get up for work. My first time staying over. I am out of my head, kiss me darling in bed. Once more I can live for the moment. But that will change in a moment.

My ex on Earth watches our red moon sink past her city. The huge glass mall and my ex on an escalator crawl in silver teeth, at times the gears of the earth visible. We are all connected and yet are unaware. Does Ava ever think of me when she sees us set sail? We hang on the red moon, but Ava can't see us riding past.

"How many girlfriends do you have?" Delia asks, tickling me. "Many?"

"Just you. Only you."

"I don't believe you. I know you flyboys." She laughs a little at me.

"How about you?" I ask. A mistake.

She turns serious, conjures a ghost I can never hope to compete with. "My fiancé was killed," she says quietly. "He was kidnapped at a protest and they found him in the desert. His hands were tied with plastic. My fiancé was saving to buy me a house. My parents told him that I wished to go to school before we married and he didn't mind. My parents sold their property for the ransom, but the men killed him regardless."

I remember my parents' treed backyard; I tilted the sodden bags of autumn leaves on end and a dark rich tea came pouring out onto the brick patio. Do the dead watch us? There were bobcat tracks: it hid under the porch.

Horse says, You know why we're here?

I watch the boy's face; he is wondering how much to admit.

Got an idea, he says.

The rash of robberies and bodies dumped in craters and the conduit to the interview room and my irradiated bones that have flown through space and now confined in this tiny space.

You never sell rock?

Like I told you, never.

He's got a history.

Somebody's took the wallet before they killed him.

Holy God. Holy God. Dead?

The man is dead. We need the triggerman.

This the t'ing. I have no friends. I learned that.

The young man wants to pass on his impressive lesson to the interrogators, but he has misjudged, his tone is all wrong. He thinks he is good, world-weary, but he hasn't seen himself on camera, has no distance. The face and the mind, O the countless cells we represent and shed, the horseshit we try to sling.

Man, they had the guns! I was concerned with this dude shooting me in the backseat.

Down the road, what will haunt the victorious young tribes? They've heard of it all, but still, nothing prepares you.

"You have your ways," Delia says, "you can control me."

I wish. I can manipulate her, get some of her clothes off, but I need her more than she needs me.

She says, "I don't think I can control you." I can't tell if she thinks this is good or not. We spend time together, but I have trouble reading her, can't tell if she likes me.

Delia is not adjusting well to being here. She hates the lunar landscape, the pale dust and dark craters past the moon's strange-ended avenues. She is weary of the crime, the black sky.

"The weather," she says, "never a breeze, never normal, either one extreme or another. Killer heat, fourteen days! Boil to death! Or else so cold. Fourteen days, freeze to death! Cold then hot, hot then cold. And there are no seasons. At home summer is summer and winter is winter. Food here has no taste, has no smell. I hate everything and then I hate myself. All my life I wanted to meet the man in the moon and now I'm here."

"You met me."

"Yes, that's true."

I wish she spoke with a bit more enthusiasm on that topic.

She is losing weight since moving to the moon.

"This is not acceptable," she says to the waiter. "You would not serve me food like this on Earth."

But we're not on Earth. Forget Earth.

"I'll make you some of my own," she says to me later. Which she does, a creamy and delicious mélange at her tiny table in the apartment.

Sunday I bring my bag of illicit cash and we shop for fresh spices. We hold hands, touching and laughing in the store, fondling eggplants that gleam like dark ceramic lamps. We are the happy couple you hate, tethered to each other like astronauts. I am content in a store with her, this is all it takes, this is all we want now, red ruby grapefruit and her hard bricks of Arabic coffee wrapped in gold.

Romance and memories and heartbreak: One war blots out an earlier war, one woman blots out the previous woman's lost sad image, one hotel room destroys the other, one new ardent airport destroys the one where I used to fly to visit her. The only way I can get over her. We are prisoners, me, her, bound to each other like a city to a sea, like a kidnapper to a hostage.

Why did Ava leave me when we got along so well? It was so good. I think I lost something human in the blue glow of that last long flight. Will it keep happening to me? Now I am afraid. The Russians from Baikonur Cosmodrome never returned, the sky closed over them like a silver curtain, like the wall of a freighter.

They went away and I was inside my damaged capsule, inside my head too much, teeth grinding in ecstasy, quite mad. They had me on a loop, my destiny not up to me. We are abandoned and rescued, over and over. But who are our stewards?

We went backward to the stars. For months rumours have suggested NASA is near bankruptcy, bean counters are reorganizing; my pension is in doubt, as is the hardship pay I earned by being out there. Now we are back to this surface, back to the long runway and smell of burnt brake pads by the marshes and Bikini Atoll.

Me alone in the photograph, the other travellers erased. Or are they out there still, knowing not to come back? You can't go back to the farm once you've seen the bright lights, seen inside yourself.

One day I delete Ava's sad lovely messages. Why keep such mementoes? You burn this life like an oil lamp. You make new mementoes, wish they could compare.

I remember parking the car by the dam with Ava. The car was so small we had to keep the doors open as I lay on top of her, but the dome light had no switch. To keep us in darkness I tried to hold one finger on the button in the door and my other hand on Ava. That ridiculous night still makes me laugh, but I need to forget it all, to delete every message and moment.

"You are unlucky in love," Delia says. "The God is fair and distributes his gifts and clearly you have many talents, but not luck in love."

Is she right? I had thought the opposite, that I had inexplicably good luck that way, but now I wonder; she does seem to know me better than I do myself. I was lucky to know Ava, but now my thoughts are distilled: Ava was too tall, too pretty, too kind. What I thought was good fortune was bad fortune. Was I bad luck for the Russians? Did I kill Curtis? Strangely, I feel lucky to have met her, to have crossed paths in the long fluorescent aisles of the store. With my cash from the drive-thru I buy her shoes, an ornate belt, French dresses. She is very choosy, but I like to buy her things.

In her room when I squeeze her hard she calls me a lion. Says I will devour her. I want to devour her, her ample flesh. My tiger, I call her. My tiger from the Tigris will turn. Friday night and we don't talk, no plans do we make. I thought that was kind of mandatory. Are we a couple or not (*Is you is or is you ain't my baby*)? It is odd to not know.

Desire has caused me so much trouble in my life, but I miss it when it is not around. Living without desire—what is the point of life without desire?

Perhaps that is a question an addict would ask.

Perhaps I am not unlike that French youth—you must have read of his sad, sad plight—rejected by a circus girl with whom he was in love. A circus girl! I love it. The poor French youth committed suicide by locking himself in the lions' cage.

I was locked in a cage, tied in a chair, in a capsule's burning skin, hairline cracks like my mother's teacup. A rocket standing in a pink cloud and I am sent, her pink clitoris and I am sent, 3, 2, 1, we have ignition, my missions hastily assembled, mixed up, my mixed feelings as I move, my performance in the radiation and redshift. The officials and women are telling their truth about me. I was thrown like an axe through their stars. I was tied in a chair, a desert, waiting. When the engines power up—what a climb, what a feeling! And who is that third who hovers always beside you, someone near us? When I count there are only you and me together—but who is that on the other side? 1, 2, 3. 3, 2, 1.

Why can't Delia say something passionate to erase my nervousness? I *have* to live through someone else. Why can't I be aloof, not care? I used to be very good at not caring. But when Delia hates the moon I feel she hates me, when she says she has no money and that the moon is dirty! too hot! too cold!, then I feel I've failed her with my moon.

Why does she not say, Come to me my lion, my lost astronaut, I love you more than life itself, my love for you is vaster than the reaches of the infinitely expanding universe, oh I love you so much, so very much. But no one says this. Her expanding clitoris under my thumb. She is calm, she is not passionate. But she is there, I'm happy when she is near. After my trip I crave contact.

I am being straight with you, swear to God. I had a couple of ounces. He was on me—it was self-defence.

Did he have a weapon, Delia asks. How can it be self-defence if he didn't have a weapon?

Friends we question say the dead man was always joking, always had a smile.

We were sitting there, the kid says. The gun went off, the kid says, and he fell out.

It *went off.* Delia tells me they always word it in this passive way, as if no one is involved and, in a kind of magic, the gun acts on its own.

Government people contact Delia. Don't be afraid, the government people say to Delia, which makes her afraid. They visit her at her apartment, claim they are concerned that a faction in the war at home may try to harm her here.

Has anyone approached her?

No, she says. No one from home.

Has she heard from her uncle in Vietnam? they wonder. Is he coming here?

"They were very nice," she tells me, "they bought me lunch."

I look at the white business card they gave her; it has a phone number and nothing else. My hunch is that they are Intelligence rather than Immigration. She asks questions for a living and now she is questioned by people who ask questions for a living. Now I worry we are watched, wired, wonder if they hear me massage Delia's shoulders and her back and below her track pants and underwear, if they hear us joke of lions and tigers.

In the interview room: He owed me money so I hit him with a hammer. He was breathing like this, uh uh uh.

A day here is so long. At Ava's former apartment building I pick up my old teapot, books, and an end table from the landlord's storage room. The aged landlord's stalled fashions, his fused backbone.

"Young man, can you help me with the Christmas tree?"

Of course. I like to help. He was one of the first here.

"The moon used to be all right," he says. "Now it's all gone to hell."

He gives me a huge apple pie from the church bake sale. They attend church religiously, they'll be in the heavens soon.

And poor Mister Weenie the tenant evicted from his apartment down a red hall.

What was his life like, I wonder, with a name like Weenie?

Horse laughs when I tell them, but Delia doesn't get the humour.

Now it's on the books as The Crown versus Weenie. How he yelled in a red hall.

"I belong in there!" he hollered, pounding at the door closed to him. "I belong in there!"

Mister Weenie pounds at doors that once opened for him, and I wonder where we belong and who do we belong with. In times of great stress, says science, the right brain takes over like a god and the left brain sees a god, sees a helpful companion along for the ride, an extra in the party. Does Mister Weenie see a helpful companion?

My ex quit her job to move to Spain. Ava has always loved the sun, the heat in Spain, the food, the language, the light. On a weather map I see that Spain has a cold snap and I am happy, as I know Ava hates the cold. I want her to be cold and miserable without me. I am not proud of this part of me.

Delia reads from a childhood textbook that she found in Ava's belongings: "Our rocket explorers will be very glad to set their feet on Earth again where they don't boil in the day and freeze at night. Our explorers will say they found the sky inky black even in the daytime and they will tell us about the weird, oppressive stillness."

"It's not so bad," I say. "The stillness."

"It isn't at all beautiful like our Earth," she reads. "It is deadly dull, hardly anything happens on the moon, nothing changes, it is as dead as any world can be. The moon is burned out, done for."

Delia endured a dirty war so I admire her greatly. She gets depressed, refuses to leave her room. Where can she turn? Her Babylon is gone, the happy place of her childhood no longer exists, friends dead or in exile or bankrupt or insane.

My dark-eyed Babylonian love, my sometimes-passionate Persian—where will she move to when she leaves me?

Out the window are astral cars and shooting stars. Where do they race to? I know. I've been out there, nearer my god to thee, past the empty condo units, the Woodlands Nonprofit Centre for New Yearning, the Rotary Home for Blind Chicken-Licken Drivers (hey, good name for a band), the Rosenblum Retirement Home (Low Prices and Low Gravity for Your Aching Joints).

My happiest moments with my mouth just below her ample belly, I forget about outer space, her legs muffling my ears, a gourmand of her big thighs, her round hips, surrounded, grounded by her flesh; I have never liked flesh so much as with her. The world only her in those charged moments, my brain-stem and cortex and molecules' murky motives driven by her and into her. The devil owns me. No devil owns me.

The valves on my heart are wide open. I have no defences, sometimes I am overflowing with affection—and I have found this is a distinct disadvantage when dealing with others. I never want this to end; so what do you suppose will happen?

The crowd pays good money to file into the old NASA Redstone Arena, into the band's aural, post-industrial acres of feedback and reverb. The band used to be someone, now they play the outposts. We are happy to see them here.

The woman singer moans, *Don't you dog your woman*, spotlights pinwheeling in the guitarist's reflector sunglasses. She sings, *I pity the poor immigrant*.

We will remember, we will buy T-shirts, souvenirs, get drunk, hold hands on the moon. We will remember.

Later the ambulance enters the moon-base arena, amazed in pain and confusion.

The white ambulance takes away one body from us so that we can see and not see. Carbons linger like a love song for all the coroners in the universe. One casualty is not too bad. Usually there are more. An OD, too much of some new opiate, some cousin of morphine, too much of nothing. You pay your money and you take your chances.

Who calls us? The ambulance tolls for someone else. Who owns the night, owns the night music of quiet tape hiss and music of quiet riches and debts in messages and missives from the crooners and coroners and distant stars? I have learned in my travels that the circus girls own the night, and the Warriors and Ghosts and Scorpions run the corner. They have the right messages.

And come Monday or Tuesday the interview room still waits for us, will open again its black hole, its modest grouping of table and walls and the one door. But Delia books off work: the war, the government people, the questions.

Say that one more time?

Who do you think did this?

Dronyk.

Dronyk says you did it.

Who's bringing it in?

Who. That's a good one. Who isn't! Man, who's bringing it in. Can I have a smoke?

The room—it's like a spaceship for penitents; we climb in and explore a new universe, their universe. Fingers to keyboard: does he show up on the screen? A hit, a veritable hit, he's in the system, the solar system.

I don't want her to worry, but I want to know that she knows.

"Those government people asking you questions; they may not be who they say."

"I know that," she says. "I wonder if they are watching us now?"

We watch Delia's TV. In the upscale hotel room the actor states to the reporter, Friend, for this role I had to go to some very dark places. He was gone for a while, celluloid career gone south, the actor is hoping for an award for this project, a comeback in the movies.

Gone? I'll tell him about being gone. I went up past the elms and wires, past the air, past the planets. Where did he go? A piano bar, a shooting gallery in the Valley, a dive motel in the wilds of Hollywood? The actor went nowhere.

When you return to a place that is not your home, is it then your home? I insist she go out and then I fall into a fight on Buckbee Street in the fake Irish bar (yes, fake Irish pubs are everywhere).

"Hey, look who crashed the party. It's that rug-rider cunt who sent me to jail." The slurring voice in the corner, a young man from the interview room.

The brief noise of his nose as I hit him and he folds. Granted, it was a bit of sucker punch. Why oh why didn't I sprint out of the fake Irish pub at that point? I stuck around to find myself charged with assault. Aren't you allowed one complimentary punch at Happy Hour?

Now it's my turn to be asked the questions in Interview Room #2. I've been here before, know the drill, I know to stonewall, to lawyer up.

What the hell were you doing?

Wish I could help you, Horse. Really do. Beer later? Chops on the grill?

Mine may be the shortest interview on record.

Delia says to me, Stand against that wall. Face forward.

The camera flashes in my eyes.

Now please face that wall. The camera flashes.

After the fight in the fake Irish bar Delia gets depressed and doesn't want to see me for a week, lunar weeks, it drags on, which gets me depressed that she is depressed in her subterranean room and won't let me even try to cheer her up, have a laugh.

"No, I'm in a hopeless situation," she says on the phone. "I don't want a temporary solution."

"Everything is temporary."

"That is true," she admits. "Everything is temporary."

But, I wonder, what of Curtis? Gone, permanent. Ava? Gone. Is that permanent too? I feel myself falling from the heavens.

"Are you hungry? Let's go out," I beg.

"There's nowhere to go here. I've told you, I don't want temporary solutions."

"Can I come over?"

"I'm tired of questions. No more questions."

The other astronaut, Curtis—I wonder if I'll ever know for sure whether it was a malfunction or suicide. Curtis might have tinkered with his air and made it look like an accident, a design flaw, or his air went and it was horrible. I often wonder where I'd like to be buried; perhaps he wanted to die out there. Flight Centre instructed me to tether him outside to the solar array until just before we got back; didn't want him stuck out there burning up when we made our grand entrance. Maybe Curtis wanted to burn up, the first outer space cremation. It's almost poetic, but the Flight Centre would not see it as good PR.

You know who strangled the old man? You know who did it? A fuckin' stupid crackhead!

He is pointing at himself and in tears. It's Ava's landlord who is dead.

I fouled up good, says the aged addict. Using that stuff wore me slap out.

His aged face. He is sincere, his hard lesson. But he is somehow alive. His prints don't match his face, but I can read his mind. By the power invested in me. He is thinking like a cheerleader, he is thinking, I must look into the future.

Yes, I tell myself, I too must remember there is a larger world out there, a future. I too must think like a cheerleader.

"This has worked a few times," my lawyer says before we file into the courtroom. "You guys are the same build. Both of you put on these glasses and sit side by side."

The judge asks the victim, "Do you see him in the courtroom?"

"He bumped my table, he spilled my drink and then it all went dark. I had a bad cut over my eye. I couldn't see nothing. Dude was on top of me wailing all over me, and it went dark."

Wailing? I hit him once and he dropped.

"So you can't point out the assailant?"

"Hell if I know."

His girlfriend takes the stand, says, "It might be one of them over there. I thought he was going to kill him, beating him and beating him. I remember the third guy, that tall white-haired feller."

They cannot ID me. The judge throws out the case, my lawyer makes his money, the truth sets you free.

After my lawyer takes his cut I still have $3,000 of the $6,000 cash in the paper bag. She's so sad. Delia saved me, but can she save herself? Delia believes that her God takes care of her. I guess I don't need to buy a bar in Nebraska. With my cash I buy her a ticket back home to the Hanging Gardens, a visit, but I suspect she'll stay there or land a more lucrative job in Dubai and never return from the sky.

"You are nice," she says.

"Because I like you. I like you a lot."

"Thank you," she says. She never says, I like you. Just thank you.

The interview room is never lonely for long. *Who did it? Why?* Someone always wants to know. We come and go like meteors, Horse at his desk staring.

That's the one was running.

Did you see the shooter? Did you see?

I ran off, I didn't see anything.

No one sees anything.

Why did she leave when I was almost there? Who shot him? Who was the third guy? Don't know a name. I ran. Give me your money, I heard him say, then *Pop pop pop!* Man I was gone. No need for it to go that way. I don't want to do nothing with nothing like that. Maybe Eliot did it.

This is good, this is rich: a collection agency calls my voicemail using a blocked number. The young hireling tries to be intimidating. It may be the loan sharks or skip tracers or maybe the poor Burger King clerk at the drive-thru wants his paper bag back.

"Reply to this call is mandatory," the dork voice speaks gravely on my voicemail. "Govern yourself accordingly," he says, obviously proud of this final line.

Govern myself? I love that, I enjoy that line immensely, much the way the roused lions enjoyed the French youth's heartbreak as he walked in their cage, as he locked himself in their interview room. You sense someone else with you, you'll never walk alone, and the empty sky is never empty, it's full of teeth.

Maybe I'll re-up, sign on for another December flight, collect some more hazard pay, get away from everyone, from their white apartments and blue eyes and dark eyes. Be aloof, a change of scene; maybe that will alter my luck. I'll cruise the moons of Jupiter or Titan's lakes of methane, see if I can see what's killing the others. Once more I renounce worry! And once more that notion will last about three seconds.

One Sunday Delia phoned at midnight, barely able to speak.

What? I can't hear. Who is this?

A delay and then her accented Arabic whisper: I *have headache*.

I rushed over with medicine for her migraines and some groceries, sped past the walled plains and trashed plasma reactors in the Petavius crater. I was happy to rush to her at midnight, happy that she needed me to close the distance.

In her room I saw that she had taped black garbage bags to the windows to keep light from her eyes, her tortured head. I unpacked figs and bananas and spinach as she hurriedly cracked open painkillers.

"Thank you for this," Delia murmured quietly with her head down, eyes hidden from me. "I know I bother you, but this is hard pain. Every day I will pray for you. Every day I pray the God will give you the heaven."

JESSICA GRANT

LOVE IN THE
PNEUMATIC TUBE ERA

WE BAT OUR eyes more than everyone else. We are more batty. We love our parents more than they love us, and more than other people love their parents. We play piano. Well, one of us plays and one of us puts her hands on top of the other's while he plays, like a blind person. We say each other's names more than we need to. We are annoying. We are lovely. We cannot sleep in the same bed. Yes we can. We thought we couldn't but we can. We fall asleep and twitch in each other's arms. We dream of chess. We slide like bishops. We gallop like the letter L. We are not trying not to get pregnant. We are moving fast. We are catching each other's colds.

We can't figure out why everyone else is so calm. We try to explain how we *both* worked at Jiffy Lubes at opposite ends of the country, which is how we re-met, via Jiffy Lube, and this is where you are supposed to bat your eyes in amazement, people. No one bats an eye. Fine. We discover old scrolls that we wrote to each other in high school, back in the Early Pneumatic Tube Era. One of us was bossy in her scroll. One of us said, *I am disappointed you don't remember that I have a Math test fourth period and therefore cannot meet you in the cemetery to smoke a joint. Meet me after.* That was back when a PT message took five minutes to get across the city. We shake our heads. Now you can send a living butterfly to Dubai in ten seconds.

We did not lose our virginity to each other, but one of us lost our virginity in the other's house. One of us lost our virginity in a tent while the other roasted a marshmallow nearby. We mourn this. We remember getting high. We remember buying dope in a neighbourhood that was over our heads, danger-wise. We drove a white Jetta. Well, one of us did. The other rode side-saddle. *You are my knight on a white Jetta.* One of us preferred hash to pot. One of us did not prefer. One of us graduated to narcotics. One of us did not. One of us got a tattoo on the inside of her wrist that said: *It's cold in here.*

On the night of our prom, which we did not attend together, one of us played that song that the other was always requesting, the Kate Bush song from the movie *She's Having a Baby.* One of us played the grand piano while the other got all dreamy and draped herself across the top and tried to look what is called *fetching.* The one of us playing the Kate Bush song registered the one draped across the black surface but his eyes said, I'm concentrating on the chord progression. Right. And the other of us rolled over. Can't you see I'm in love with you.

Twenty years later one of us is having a baby and the other is the father.

This after a long and difficult attempt to get reunited in the Late Pneumatic Tube Era when cross-continental VacTrains cost a million bucks and there are no more white Jettas, only trucks operated by large men with difficult-to-get permits issued by Transport Canada. The Jiffy Lubes are few and far between. We, the Jiffy Lubers, wait in our respective holes in the ground for a truck to run us over. Oh for a truck to run us over! We arrange bottles of Pennzoil in pyramids. We wait. We are sentimental about the trucks when they do come. We are pale and deficient in vitamin D and full of longing when we watch them go.

How we finally get reunited is this: He sends a PT cylinder with an oil-smudged request for a special brand of filter that is really scarce these days and signs his name at the bottom. This request is unscrolled at a Jiffy Lube on the other side of the continent where she reads the signature with batty eyes. Could it be he. She has not seen him since they were eighteen and his parents moved west. She sends a scroll back that says only his name, plus a question mark. He replies, Yes, plus a question mark. It's me, she says, and signs her name. No question mark.

And they are off to the races. Exchanging scrolls like there is no tomorrow. Catching up. Finally, something to do in their underground holes! They find it unbelievable that they both work in holes. They find it unbelievable that they are both single. They play chess remotely. He teases her because she still doesn't understand how the knight moves. How the L can be sideways or upside down or mirror-imaged. *What the hell is your knight up to,* she yells in her scroll. She is still bossy in her scrolls.

He sends her a stick of gum, just like he used to, as a peace offering.

She sends him her underwear, just like she used to, but this time he does not reply, *Why are you sending me your underwear.*

He sends her a song he wrote, transcribed on staff paper. She tries to bang it out on the piano in her basement. She is unsuccessful. She cries alone in her basement because she thought she was happy, protecting her parents and changing oil, but what she is realizing is that she has been missing someone for years and that someone is him.

The next day he sends her a scroll that says: *If I could, I would play the Kate Bush song for you again, and this time I would not concen-*

trate on chord progression, but would break off mid-song to crawl atop the piano that you are so dreamily draped atop of, looking fetching. Your move.

She bats her eyes at this. Her move. Does he mean move your rook to h4, or does he mean move *yourself* across the board to *me*. Surely he means the latter. But how is a poor JL employee to move rook-wise across the country. VacTrains are out of the question, and she does not have a permit to travel above ground.

Well, you will recall that myth wherein Odysseus straps himself to the belly of a sheep in order to escape the cyclops he so conveniently blinded. Well, what is a truck travelling west if not a sheep. And what is Transport Canada if not a blind cyclops. And so the next time a truck drives over her head at the Jiffy Lube, she gets an apprentice luber, a kid named Cutler, to strap her onto the bottom of the truck. Are you sure this is legal, Cutler says.

Of course it isn't legal.

It is early December and cold. She is wearing her JL coveralls, her white cowboy boots, and a stocking cap. She assures Cutler that the large mud flaps with the picture of the girl looking fetching will protect her from the wind.

Cutler looks dubious.

Do I look fetching, she asks.

The truck pulls out. And she is riding its belly! Stones hit her back. She is not used to stones hitting her back. Faster and faster. She is not used to fast. Her eyes get watery. She is rushing away from her Jiffy Lube. She is rushing away from her parents. Her whole life she has been lifeguarding her parents who cannot swim and who live beside a pond that every year gets a little bit bigger. Do not think about that. Also, do not think about how Cutler has for many months coveted her job as Chief Luber. Do not think, do not think.

Hours pass. She has no water. Occasionally there is a puddle. Water is overrated. The straps dig into her ribs. Finally the truck stops and the trucker debarks to check his tires. Hey! He catches sight of a pompom dangling above the pavement. Hey! He bends down. Git. Git out from under there.

However she is strapped in so tight that she cannot extract herself and the trucker must cut her loose with an exacto knife. She hits the pavement. The trucker bats an eye. He cannot believe he picked up a stowaway in a stocking cap at the Jiffy Lube. What is the world coming to.

He buys her a coffee and donut and listens to her story of pianos and chess games and true love and uncrossable distances that might be crossed if, and only if, a kindly trucker will play a sheep and carry her west to her true love's Jiffy Lube.

He looks reluctant to play a sheep.

But she is black with soot and road dirt. She is bruised from stones and straps. She is thirsty and half-starved and, having already eaten her own maple dip, cannot take her eyes off his. The trucker, whose name is Ham, short for Hamish, buys her another coffee and donut and says, yes, fine, she can ride in the cab with him, in the back, which is like a little apartment, with a skylight and an ottoman. There is also a black curtain she can hide behind as they go through Transport Canada checkpoints.

And so it is that she is able to arrange herself like the Mud Flap Girl in the furnished back portion of Ham's cab, her feet up on the ottoman. The moon is bright as she scrolls and unscrolls her true love's scroll. She reads his message aloud, several times, until Ham says over his shoulder, okay, enough.

She asks if he remembers back in the Early Pneumatic Tube Era, how everything that came out of a PT gave you a shock. Remember that. And everyone who rode a VacTrain had staticky hair for days. And how staticky hair became cool. And everyone wanted staticky hair so it looked like they'd been in a VacTrain even if they couldn't afford one.

He says he remembers and what is her point.

Her point is that those shocks have not gone away in terms of the scrolls sent to her by her one true love. She is still all static-electric with excitement when she touches his scroll.

Ham says that is more than he needs to know. Then he asks why is she the one making the trip like Odysseus. Why isn't the piano player strapping himself to a sheep and coming to her.

Well, that is a good question, and one she can answer only by saying that she is black and her true love is white, and black always makes the first move.

Ham says, I think it's white that makes the first move.

She rescrolls the scroll. That's not how I learned it.

And she remembers how, way back in grade seven when he first taught her chess, she thought he was saying ponds, not pawns. Slow-moving bodies of water.

And he said the goal of chess, the whole point of chess is, are you listening, to protect your parents.

He meant the king and queen.

Right.

And one time she even caught him carrying his king and queen around in his back pocket.

Outside the truck, snow swirls. She starts to drift off. Ham is saying about an old TV show called *Fantasy Island*, how that was the start. The start of what, she mumbles. The start of the PT Era. Oh. The head guy, Mr. Roarke, the fantasy facilitator, he'd get a request via PT, and then the people who'd sent the request would follow up and go to the island. You had to actually go to the island to have your fantasies realized. In a plane. And a little guy named Tattoo would point and yell, The plane! The plane! And they would get a lay when they arrived.

Wow.

A lei. A flower necklace.

Oh.

And their dreams would come true. But you had to physically go. Is my point.

Thanks, Ham.

The truck pulls to a stop at a checkpoint and a slippery Transport Canada bishop approaches sideways out of the darkness. What is your business, she hears him say. But she is safe in her Mud Flap Girl posture, concealed behind the black curtain.

Ham pulls into her true love's Jiffy Lube. He, the true love, is underground, a bottle of Pennzoil Platinum at the ready. He notes the big trucker's boots retreating in the direction of the free coffee. He notes the weird straps attached to the anterior axle. And then, lo! Two white cowboy boots descend from the truck. A face bends down. That face is wearing a Santa Claus–type hat. The pompom is dirty. It is a familiar face. Now she—for it is a she—is sliding down into the underground hole the way someone in a warmer climate might slide into a pool. And in that instant, he knows her. She slides down into his underground arms. She wraps her legs around his waist and her arms around his neck. They are fused together in their identical JL uniforms. He backs up. He walks in a wobbly circle, carrying her.

And you know how this story ends because we already said at the beginning. Remember how you refused to bat your eyes. Our story is like a new kind of chess game wherein the pieces lurch towards each other in longing. Wherein there is no battle. Wherein there is kissing. Wherein the king and queen are left unguarded. Wherein the only bad guy is a Transport Canada official, and he is not so bad. Wherein Ham stands up for us at our wedding. Wherein one of us plays the song from She's Having a Baby and the other lies atop the piano, looking fetching, and, finally, being fetched.

ELYSE FRIEDMAN
I FOUND YOUR VOX

I FOUND IT in the park. The one behind the gas station. The one full of Filipino nannies. It was under the picnic table in the no man's land between dog people and kid people. The Filipino nannies walk dogs too. They fly halfway across the world to walk dogs. They stoop and they scoop. Golden retrievers. I found it under the oak.

I was excited when I saw it—a wink of pink. I thought: I'll just keep it in my pocket; I'll just get a case for it. I picked it up and pretended to look around for the owner. I stood and scanned the park with a concerned and inquiring expression on my face, but my plan all along was to palm it. And anyway it was just me and the nannies and the kids and the dogs. The kids have very faint Filipino accents. Have you noticed that? Probably not, since you've only been to this park once, I think. Just long enough to lose your VOX to me. Under a tree. The nannies wear hand-me-down T-shirts. On their chests it says Parasuco. It says Juicy Couture. Across their breasts it says ROOTS. I see them all the time. I eat my lunch under the oak. Turkey sub and a half-ration of Diet Coke-GT®. Sometimes I think about Mount Pinatubo. I think about ROOTS and eruptions and Juicy

Couture. Turkey is better for you than ham if you're worried about your weight. The nannies all have iPhones. And Custom Gloves.® Tight. You could pick up a dime in those things. I seem to be immune to listeriosis.

The plan for Pinky was to erase and replace, but on a whim I decided to check out what was there. I put it on Stray and listened for a bit. And you know what? I was pleasantly surprised. You have good taste in music, Louise S. Graham, 575 Gladstone Ave., Apt. 301, LSG@bestnet.canam. I am suitably impressed by your extensive and varied musical collection. In just under two weeks you have introduced me to a panoply of unique artists that I never would have discovered on my own, like that ear-tickling harp sprite, Blossom Topsy—so off-putting at first, but then so addictive. Or the ultra-raw Vic Chesnutt and his southern-fried cat-gut moan. I like the horns and howls of Neutral Milk Hotel. And the retro get-down-to-it-ness of The Hold Steady. Swarmbots Do Sally I had heard of, of course, but never really heard. And what of that "Walking The Cow" tune? Zowie, Louise.

People always talk about the importance of a good sense of humour. Women especially say that's the number one thing they look for in a man. This is not true, of course. I have a great sense of humour, Louise, but no chin, no gold card, and virtually no hair on the front half of my skull. A sense of humour is important though. Especially these days when planes keep falling out of the sky, and bacteria gobbles flesh and antibiotics with equal yum, and the colonized/cratered keep sneaking or suing their way out of quarantine, and a glass of water is just chlorinated piss. You have to laugh, right? If you work in a gas station you do. If you have a degree. If you're a polar bear, or were born with AIDS, or you live in Alberta and your name is Abdullah. If you spent all your money on what you believed to be a well-respected business college. Or neglected to stockpile the correct masks, anti-virals and inhalers last October. If your best friend was devoured by exotoxins, and six hundred of your six hundred and two cronies on NETworks are marketing avatars. Or the bed-bugs are still kicking after four professional sprayings, and the bumps under your left armpit might not be bites after all. That's why it was so great to find those Sarah Silverman skits under Vids, Louise. You have a good sense of humour, I can tell. No SNL. No *Funny Or Die*. No *PrankToob* shenanigans featuring someone's granny diving into an empty swimming pool, or some unsuspecting teen getting a surprise jizz shot in the face from a Kushner wannabe (I think it's sad that *Aaron Kushner's Celebrity Poppers* is the number-one show on VOX-TV). No, just a few of the better Silverman skits, which we both totally enjoyed and laughed at. It's amazing, isn't it, that she's still doing her thing, even in Stage-IV Isolation, even working the amputations into the act? Brave. And so cool, don't you think, that we have a similar sensibility when it comes to what's funny? By the way, Louise, I should probably mention that I was totally awed out by your incredible collection of 1970s soul. Al Wilson; Charles Wright & the Watts 103rd Street Rhythm Band; Marvelous Marv Johnson... I've never met anyone with so much soul.

Listen Lou, when I saw your podcast list, I knew you were something special. I admire the fact that you subscribe to *Bookworm* and *Ideas* and the LearnOutLoud Philosophy Series, and was pleased to discover that you have all 1,272 episodes of This Americanadian Life stashed away. Obviously, you're a brainy girl with a curious mind. I have to admit I was taken aback by the *What Not To Wear: Trends* podcast. But nobody's perfect, right? Flaws are what make people individual and charming.

God knows I have my share. Bites. Not bites. It's kind of cute that an intellectual such as yourself—a woman with great taste in music and a great sense of humour—would be interested in hemlines and frills and all that white after Labour Day stuff. I noticed that under Shopping, you have carts crammed with shoes and purses and tops and dresses (I like the baby-blue one, Louise), but no recent orders. I guess you just enjoy browsing. You are a female after all. And I don't want a clone of myself. I appreciate and celebrate our differences. I have a toenail fungus that causes the toenails on my left foot to repeatedly come away. That is one of my flaws. Also, I spend approximately two-thirds of my free hours gaming, which most people (erroneously) view as a waste of time. A quick perusal under your Extras headings shows that you played *Maze* only once, and that you never even bothered trying *Meltdown* or *Bacteria Blast*. That's okay. I'm not looking for a man with breasts and a vagina. *Bacteria Blast* blows anyway. And as for *Maze* and *Meltdown*, let's just say they're not exactly *Call To Arms: Iran* or *EverQuest Live*, both of which I'm sure you would appreciate once you gave them a try.

I'm working my way through your podcasts now. The words that filled your ears are the words that fill my ears. I take you to bed with me. The holes in my body absorb the same words as the holes in your body (except for the *What Not To Wear: Trends* words). I'm strictly a T-shirt and jeans man, Louise. I've actually managed to win quite a few T-shirts through competitive online gaming. A few years ago on Boxing Day I invested in a black leather Danier jacket, which I think is pretty respectable. I'm not averse to wearing a button-down shirt or a sports jacket, I just don't happen to own any. I have one suit. I bought it for my father's funeral. Itchy. Then I wore it to my mother's funeral. Hot. Then I wore it to a bunch of job interviews. Futile. Then I had it cleaned. It's somewhere in the back of the closet, wrapped in plastic. It's too small on me. The toenail fungus is not conta-gious. I hate that fucking suit. Pardon my French, Louise.

Speaking of words, a picture is worth a thousand, so they say. I counted precisely seventeen pictures of you under Photos. That's seventeen thousand words, and all of them WOW. You are beautiful, Louise. You have very bad skin, but other than that you look like a model. I'm so glad your skin is terrible (assum-ing it's acne and not VRSA). A girl that looks like you but with good skin could never be mine. Of the twenty-three pictures stored under Photos, three are of your cat (cute, but should you let him/her sit on your kitchen table with that F-94 Feline virus that's going around?), and three are of the Golden Nugget Hotel sign in Vegas. I see you had a good time there. I think it's cool that you stayed at the Golden Nugget instead of one of those tacky, modern monstrosities like *Las Vegas: Vienna* or that freaky *Guantánamo Bay Las Vegas*. Also happy (and relieved) to see that you went with a group of gal-pals, Louise. It took me a while to figure out which one was you. For some reason you turned your Tag app off, you naughty thing. Naughty gloves. Pick up a dime. A wink of pink. All of the Vegas people shots are group shots. You could have been any one of those laughing girls (except maybe the see-through-top blonde with the RealFeel boobs and the nipple-bling, who I'm sure is nice enough, I just don't believe she subscribes to the LearnOutLoud Philosophy Series).

Luckily, shot number seventeen is not a Vegas shot or a group shot. It's a cottage shot. It's you alone on a dock. That's how I knew you were you. You're alone on the dock and you're wearing a plaid shirt that looks very soft. Flannel. Not itchy. You're wearing shorts and canvas sneakers with no socks. Not hot. Your legs are bony and you have two bruises on your left shin. You look extremely satisfied. The lake is still and shiny and foam-free. You look entirely calm. The corner of the cottage is brown and rustic. The trees are pine and poplar. In the Vegas shots, you are laughing and laughing. Squinty eyes. Teeth. Adrenalin. In the cottage shot you are not smiling. Your mouth is a slit, open just a crack and you look completely happy and wonderfully fatigued. The toe fungus isn't contagious, Louise. The nannies all have iPhones. I am immune to listeriosis.

Last night we were in bed together. A brown out. A black room. Rain was pinging off the air-cleaning unit. I caressed you in bed. Pink. I touched you to my lips. I used my thumb to turn you on. Your mouth was a slit, open just a crack. Legs, bony. Flannel, soft. You looked extremely satisfied. I put myself against your mouth. You looked entirely calm. After, we listened to slow rain in a dark room. Droplets pinging off the air-cleaning unit. You looked completely happy and wonderfully fatigued. Across their breasts it says Juicy Couture. We stayed in bed for almost two hours until the power came on. I made turkey sandwiches with salt & vinegar chips on the side. Diet Coke-GT® has green-tea compounds that help burn calories. 575 Gladstone Ave., Apt. 301. It was a great night, Louise. My little pink, my sweet slender. I fell asleep without my pills.

ANNABEL LYON

REMOTE CONTROL

TRY THIS ON:

The year is 2013. You are an alien from outer space. You have an excellent spaceship with important flashing lights on the console and many tasty foreign foods for your snacking pleasure. You are passing planet Earth when you decide to do some impromptu research.

To a native, the couple you choose would not appear to be promising. You, however, have the advantage of being able to see slightly into the future, so you're able to pick them out before they've actually met and follow them through, knowing the outcome.

Your pet comes bounding into the room and jumps up onto your lap, where you stroke its silvery fur as you watch the wraparound video screens from your ergonomic swivel chair. It is not a dog and not a cat. It's a pet, okay?

The screens on the left side of the room show the man. The screens on the right show the woman. When they meet, it will happen right in front of you, as you sip your delicious alcohol-style beverage. You can have it this way because you're an alien.

Look at this man, now. See his head? Inside his head, chaos. Fucking *dank*, man. Words are swishing around in the oil in there, you're getting *boss*, you're getting *Tuesday deadline*, you're getting *injunction*, you're getting *drink, drink, drink*. You're getting *penury*. That's him in the elevator, rain in his shoes, breathing too hard. You get *dying, death, dead.*

Pet sighs like a person as you knuckle its spine.

Now the woman. Most of her thoughts surface as one word: *no*. She sits at a desk, paging through a file, making minimal, decisive marks with a sharp pencil. Before she leaves for the day, she will have bought two small companies, initiated three legal actions, bought her secretary a tasteful, expensive, congenial birthday present, run 10K on the company treadmill, and redesigned her firm's corporate logo and colours. Her clothes are silk. Her favourite colour is graphite. Her favourite word is *graphite*. Thoughts which do not come through as *no* come through as *graphite*. With these two words as her arsenal, she blows most problems to penny-candy shards.

She has a background in design and a foreground in law. She is the gun you always wanted.

The man in the elevator is now stuck in the elevator. The roil in his brain has thickened and darkened and reduced to a sauce below the level (marked by a line inside the brain-pan) of articulate speech. He is late, late, late. Still, his eye is drawn to the instep of the girl by the buttons, who has stepped right out of her pump to flex her toes. He wants to touch it, the ticklish pale curve. Lust brisk as pepper, succulent as salt. Surprising—this day of all days—as sun.

You, meanwhile, are trying to figure out if his elevator is in her building. Looking at the future is like looking at a night sky obscured by rags of cloud, black on star-spackled black, where the sweep is knowable but the details obscured. You decide not: his fake-walnut and Lysol to her exposed brick and hardwood. You hazard same city, though, from the blurred ashen view from her window and the rain on his clothes. With one curiously elongated finger you point to the screen and teach your pet: *rain*.

Pet yawns. Fast forward.

Rain makes Byzantine patterns on the woman's office window as she glances down, an hour later, and you had better believe that the difference between dribbling and Byzantine patterns is her exquisitely cool take on the world. She watches a man come out of the building across the street and hail a cab. When the birthday secretary offers her a coffee she turns, smiling automatically because she is a good boss, and when she looks back the man is gone.

In the cab, at the airport, he reaches into his coat to touch his heart.

"Fifteen fifty," the driver says.

His mouth tastes of salt. Is it possible, he wonders (an hour at his wife's—ex-wife's—lawyer's having restored language, just), that tears withheld long enough find other exits. Nose and mouth, like a head cold; a bittersweet crystalline residue on the skin.

"Take care of that," the driver says, giving him a Kleenex for his twenty.

Entering the terminal, he wonders if there really is such a thing, in law, as stalking your own wife. The judge obviously thought so.

"Going home," he tells the woman at the ticket counter. "No bags, no." Behind him, a dozen Japanese schoolgirls in knee socks and kilts and dark green blazers, the backs of their knees staring at him. He wants to kneel amongst them. *Home* is approximate. The woman behind the counter tells him his flight does not depart for another three hours.

"That's okay" he says, tears spilling over.

Pet's stomach growls in its sleep. This is so cute!

The man sits in the airport bar. The woman sits at her desk, working. You try to recall the picture you first had—a messy straddling—but as always the future fades as you involve yourself in the details of the present, and like a good moviegoer you surrender the image as both highly improbable and absolutely certain. All you have to do is wait.

Home, these days, is in the East. Home, for the man, is a white city, not this grey city where his wife—now ex-wife—has chosen to spill her sweet sticky days. He understands the ocean is beautiful to some people but he doesn't think he'll come here again. Also the injunction was fairly specific and he has a Tuesday deadline, at his job, at his home, if he cares to meet it. Plus his debts, his many little chickens, are over there. He is, at any rate, not really here: on his boss's war-map he is a pin in suburbia today, pitching to clients, not three thousand miles away getting waxed in this honey-coloured hole of an airport sports bar, click and slice of hockey on the overhead set. With luck he won't be missed.

He watches a Thai Air jet snug up to the corrugated tubing that will feed it passengers. He won't know how bad he is until he stands up. His fingers trace the facets of his chunky glass, glass so thick the hot little burnish of drink seems buried in it, until he realizes that, doing this, he has turned himself on. Furtively, he looks around at whatever might be watching—carpet, game, darkling day.

The woman, meanwhile, has accomplished more in one afternoon—well, you've already got the picture. Now, looking more closely, you begin to wonder if there isn't, indeed, something strange about her—the efficiency, the diligence, the *smoothness*, as though her maker touches her joints each morning with dots of lubricant and puts her back in the box each night. Odd, too, the way her mind runs so smoothly on its tracks, so straight and true. Even you, a higher being, are occasionally distractible. (Pet will attest.) But she, you get the feeling, walks through each day as through a minefield—head down, *forward, forward, forward.* You wonder if she is afraid; but, if so, she's squirrelled it so deep you can't feel it. If you were a poet you would say: her mind is a mansion of sealed rooms. You would say: only the halls are lit, and those on timers, to keep you moving. But what is in those rooms? Or, you might say: her mind is a library, where you request materials and they are brought to you, promptly and quietly, crisp and speckless; but you cannot get behind the desk and wander the stacks yourself. No leafing and fingering for you. What's the big secret?

"See you tomorrow?"

Startles you—the birthday secretary. You had been trying to guess between dead lover and dead baby from her shoes—black brogues. On the one hand, you think: the very shoes of the dead lover! She wears them still! On the other hand, you think: shoes of a woman befuddled past fashion by the tragedy of the death of her child. Or simply: expensive ironic designer articles that are sweet with that suit. But you've got the volume dialled up way too high from trying to hear the man over the airport hubbub, so that the secretary's voice comes at you from everywhere, like the voice of God. You quickly adjust, but too late: the silly woman has woken Pet. Pet arfs.

"Not until Wednesday," your woman is saying. Beneath the silky patience, a minute reassessment, like a chess piece placed one square to the left—*she's forgotten the conference.* The woman smiles as you realize that while she will continue to give her expensive presents, she will never trust details to this secretary again.

"All packed?" the secretary says. You don't dip into her mind, don't bother. It's written on the surface, the respect, the envy. "I love that *suit!*" the secretary frets, eyes darting. "You're really flying *tonight?* Am I losing my mind?"

Your woman gives her the rest of the day off.

And, yes, she's flying tonight, going to the airport straight from work, in fact. That briefcase behind the door is in fact a suitcase, laptop-slim, light as a cracker.

Four days in the tropics. She's wearing the suit. What else?

Where is everyone, that is what the man would like to know. Where are the other travellers? He is pacing the length of the terminal, angry, stuttering. Why are all these counters closed, that is what he would like to know. How is the economy ever going to pick up with all these counters closed? Where is consumer confidence, all of that? *What do they know that I don't? Why the hell am I always alone?*

"Fog," the taxi driver tells the woman, when she asks why it took him so long.

You quick-squiggle through the next bit, having some fun with the cars—zip! Zing! At the airport, keeping your thumb on the speed button, you watch the woman pop out of the taxi, give the door a comic slam, and toddle stiff-hipped to the glass doors which, rotating constantly, never come into focus. Inside the terminal, she does the business of picking up her ticket and checking in, darting and jerking like a spastic. You realize she has a mannerism: she reaches to push her hair away, fingertips tracing the curve behind the ear. She does this over and over. You didn't notice at the normal, slower speed.

Pet starts to vibrate and change colour. This makes you both a little anxious and a little wistful: Pet is no longer a young pet, you know it's normal at Pet's age, but still you remember Pet as a baby and it's the baby attributes you love—the warmth, the cuddliness, the little snuffling sound which means *cookie* or *stroke me*. You get preoccupied reassuring Pet (who comes out of these spells shocked and wheezing and desperately needing to *see* you) and let the big moment, the meeting, slip through on fast-forward. You glimpse the woman racing past the bolted ranks of plastic seats. In such a seat the man has come to roost. For a teasing moment—pure farce, this speed is actually good for it—their separate screens merge for the first time as she passes him on her way to the toilet. He doesn't look up. Hug Pet, kiss Pet, while the woman attends to herself in the cubicle and the man ponders his future. Their minds are harder to penetrate now: like the revolving doors, they blur at this speed. The woman is completely opaque, although the man's dark aura hovers like a cloud captured on time-lapse film, swelling and shrinking like a breathing thing, like poor Pet's own taxed little lungs. As the woman emerges from the toilet the man glances up. The next time you look they are speaking. If you were using the vocabulary of their Renaissance painting you would say the woman had taken the courtier's stance, the man's stance, erect but leaning slightly towards the seated lady (in this case, the man). You would call them *Swain and Maiden* or *Eros and Psyche*. After a blink the man, too, stands, and they toddle off together. The man's bad aura, you have time to notice, has deflated quick as a balloon, to a tiny, wrinkled black skin trailing off the back of his head—an apostrophe, a hopeful lick.

But a number of things are happening. First, you've lost sound: you turned off the chipmunk chitter of voices when you changed speeds, and now you can't get it back. Stupid machine! Second, you are losing your bead on the couple, or perhaps the fog is interfering with your reception; at any rate, they are getting smaller and smaller as they walk the length of the terminal.

If they turn a corner you will lose them. This isn't supposed to happen! Finally, most annoyingly, you can't rewind and replay. You can only go forward. The meeting, the first words, are lost forever.

Uttering sibilant alien oaths, you get the speed back to normal. You still can't hear them, but at least you've bought yourself some time. You manoeuvre your snazzy alien craft a little closer to the planet and right away their image snaps back onto centre screen. So it was a range problem. You curse yourself for not buying the upgrade when you had the opportunity because you were trying to economize. You tell yourself: next time, spend the money, cheapo! This is science!

They're back in the bar, and you find you can manage after all without sound. Their thoughts are clear as clear water, although their words, correspondingly, are distorted, like speech under water. You start to calm down. You'll manage.

Pet, recovered, tumbles from your lap and pads out of the video room.

There is, indeed, something primeval and aquatic about them now, about the way they listen to each other, feelers out, alert to every last delicate cell. You understand all flights have been delayed because of the fog and they are having a companionable drink, waiting it out. You understand it was she who approached him. Curious about a couple of things, you hit a sequence of buttons and wait. After a moment the screens go black except for your two subjects, lit now from within, like fish tanks in a pet shop at night. You see their skeletons and organs, the pulse of blood, the brain-coral, the shopping-bag lungs. His heart, you note, squeezes faster than hers—that was one of the things. When she reaches for her hair it is a glowing orange skeleton hand (you're using an orange filter) caressing the brain. The hair is invisible because hair—you know this—is dead. On this setting, all you see is what lives.

Changing filters, you observe brain activity. Hers is cool and constant, a few flares as she recrosses her legs or sips her drink, but mostly steady. His is a crackling web around a knot of blue light, locus and source of all his pain, lust, and hope, a light so small you could snuff it with a fingertip. His ex-wife is in there! His job! His desire to take this woman somewhere private, now, and bring her off! So very small!

This was another of the things.

The screen around them is not actually black, as you first thought, but dotted with specks of scribbling light so small you will think yourself dizzy before you realize they too represent life—billions of tiny one- and two-celled organisms, the kind that live on your eyeballs and in the interstices of your skin. You zoom in close, watch them billow in your lovers' breath, swim in and out of their ears, light up the surfaces of their invisible drinks and get themselves swallowed that way. Solar explosions of brain activity in both subjects interrupt your observation of the mites—you have to pull back to see that the man has reached out to smooth the woman's hair back for her. What you see, literally, is a skeleton shyly caressing another skeleton's skull.

Now words are coming through. But this is confusing. Are they both talking at once, saying the same thing? This is what it sounds like. Both heads are tipped back. Changing filters a third time, you watch the musculature of their faces, the meat. Both are frowning, face-meat like wood grain, like webbing; neither speaks. Quickly you turn their insides off and the lights back on, and, once tucked back into the cowlings of skin and clothes, you realize they're listening to a slurry overhead announcement, something about all flights. That's why the words in their heads are the same. You're getting *fog, cancelled, tomorrow morning.*

Their reactions are interesting. The woman is as delighted as a child. A problem to solve! For me! Already her mind is producing a checklist—*fax the office, call about reservation in St. Agnes, expenses will cover a hotel for tonight, will probably miss the first two lectures tomorrow, check programme for speakers and email request for speeches as a courtesy*, they'll notice her absence and she knows things wing back at you like boomerangs in this business if you're not courteous—

From the man you get, Fuck.

But these are just the top layers, the crust on the *crème*. Underneath, sweetness and tingling. Because it is all inevitable now, they can see it as clearly as you—this drink, the next, a lingering sobering considering supper in the marine-themed restaurant (so humorous for an airport!), the slow walk (as through a park at night, the wrought-iron gates, the scent of flowers, the turn in the path, the heavy moon, oh!) back down the length of the terminal, past the newspaper shops, book shops, smoked-salmon shops, T-shirt shops, coffee bars, maple-leaf-shaped-chocolate shops, foreign exchange, duty-free, Airport Improvement Tax consoles, to the glass doors of the Best Western which suckers right onto the airport like a leech. The dutiful enquiries—fog, you say? only one room available, you say?—the complicitous glance, the squaring of shoulders for the concierge's sake, as though to say: *As business associates, we'll grin and bear it.* The woman takes the key.

But you, you are unaccountably sad. You don't want what's coming next. Maybe it was Pet's spell (MORTALITY * * * MORTAL ITY * * * MORTALITY circling Pet's head like a halo, like a cinema marquee), or the sight of a skeleton making love to another skeleton, or the specks of living dust in their food and in their eyes. All around you! you want to tell them. Look all around you!

But, science. So you watch them fuck. It's an odd little show.

Your sadness becomes acute as you wonder if you should have paid more attention to other things, to details, to the glances and hesitations and tones of voice, the paving stones on this too-familiar road. You wonder if you've missed the story on these two (at each other like scavengers, now, the joy of glut) with your God's-eye views, your impatience, your probings and unpeelings, your fickle, flickering curiosities too easily satisfied. What have you really learned? You glance into the future, as far as you can, and see! the bright lines of their lives untwist and fray away from each other, phosphorescent worms tunnelling away into separate darknesses, soon now, oh, very soon. They have not manoeuvred themselves into a winning situation, these two. But you, could you not have spent more time with the man, explored the seeds of his rage and pain, his seedy lusts? Could you not have spent more time with the woman, found ways into those cool vaults, picked the slick locks?

You wish you could go down there, sit down with them and lay out the situation, say, *What the fuck, guys? What made the two of you want to get into a thing like this? Is it a pheromone situation? Do you know how unlikely this was? Do you?* This would really be breaking all the rules, but suddenly you think: what price rules? You imagine the dash to the driver's seat. (None of this "bridge" bullshit. You have a driver's seat. Leather! Yes!) You imagine the plunge through the atmosphere, feet-first and hair streaming stars, landing your smoking screaming craft alongside their jets—it is an airport, isn't it?—striding up to their room, all ten feet of you, gathering your robes around you as you sit yourself down on the end of their bed, gesturing elegantly with your very long fingers, and saying: *Look. Can I level with you? I know what's been going on here but I have these burning questions about your motivation. My species is a cool, rational, totally superior species, no shit, but unlike you we've kind of lost touch with our baser natures. You understand, I'm a scientist, it's for science. It's in the spirit of pure inquiry. What do you mean, how do I know? Six eyes, a spaceship, an exoskeleton, plus I just walked through your bedroom wall and Mr. Genius here wants credentials?*

He's gotten himself into her again. You watch his back, the regular surge and fall, surge and fall, as of breaking waves. You understand the ocean is beautiful to some people. But even if you could ask, they couldn't answer. They don't know themselves any better than you. All you can do is watch, admire the weird coupling compulsion until it bores you, and then change the channel. So you flip. (Pet is back on your lap; Pet has never really liked the nature shows anyway.) For a while, down in Bombay, you watch the world's leading mathematical physicist work on his unified field theory, and he's *this* close, man, cool as *kulfi.*

NOTES FROM THE WOMB

127.

I am inside my mother's womb. It's warm in here.

126.

My world is full of blood. I wonder what mother looks like from the outside.

125.

Mother talks to herself a lot. She wants to peel off the lines on her face one by one.

124.

I can leave anytime I want. All I have to do is stop breathing.

123.

Does mother think this sticky rope will prevent me from escaping?

122.

If I am a tiny, ignorant fetus, how come I know the square root of death?

121.

When I am eleven, I will jump off the roof of the Bombay
Stock Exchange. Hundreds of brokers will follow. We will all hit
the pavement together in a gorgeous smattering of skulls. But I
will be the only one that travels upwards again.

120.

Why do my words somersault into a parade of clouds?

119.

Look, I float. Perhaps I am a being of light and lightness.   ·

118.

My head is very soft. I can mould it into any shape I want. Just
before I am born, I will give it a good thump. My parents will
think I am deformed.

117.

At night I comfort God. He has nightmares about me. I promise
him I will not become a killer.

116.

Why is there is so much violence inside the womb?

115.

I will grow into a knife, an instrument of silence.

114.

Tiny micrograins of pills float towards me. Mother wants me
dead. I swallow them all.

113.

To her I am just a sound.

112.

I call mother's name in blue. She turns white when I do this.

III.
She wants a white piece of silk to cover me with in case
I am stillborn.

110.
Whenever she forgets to eat, I start munching on bits of
her tissue.

109.
Father smokes a lot. I inhale deeply and let the smoke freeze
my brain.

108.
Mother wants a girl. So I curl up and stay silent. Let her
think I'm dead.

107.
At times like these, I turn to the future for some cheering
up. Here's a tidbit that might be of international interest:
twenty years from now, Iran will be the only nuclear power
in the world.

106.
And Afghan women will play soccer with the heads of their
husbands.

105.
Mother threw up last night. She must have found out I'm a boy.

104.
I find it hard to wake up in the morning. There is not enough
light. I beg light to enter the womb but it is afraid.

103.
Nights are different. I dance in blood. Then lick my toes clean.

102.

My hands are curled into a fist. I start punching red water. It feels good. I hit myself and it feels even better.

101.

My tiny palms open. I want to grip something sharp and plunge, plunge, plunge. So this is how killers are born.

100.

I like numbers. They are always correct. Old God without emotion.

99.

Can I get you something, mother? Aspirin, tea, a soul? Tea, you say. Tea with a silver pistol to stir it?

98.

I lied to you before. I will not jump off the roof of any building. I will be pushed off by a girl named Lola. She is the same age as me. I can talk to her this very moment. She is in her mother's womb, too. She tells me she will be born blind.

97.

I tell Lola there's not much to see anyway. She calls me a liar. She says she can never trust me for as long as I live. We're off to a bad start.

96.

Lola, where are you right now? In Ibiza, she replies. In Rangoon. In Calcutta. In Tel Aviv. She says she can be in several places at once because her mother reads maps all day.

95.

Hold me. I'm scared. The truth foams at my mouth and calls itself Child Snow.

94.
When I am a year old, I will speak. The moment I utter my first word, I will no longer be a child. I will begin festering.

93.
When I am newborn, I will be small enough to fit in a ceramic pot. I am brown in colour. I will even look like baked clay.

92.
Mother, your hair winds around your neck in waves. Your hair, it smells of a long death.

91.
I can see myself in a reflection on the walls of mother's liver. I am a made-to-order cherub.

90.
I have enough fight in me to giggle in the face of bombs. If only mother could see me now: a silver grenade-pin between my soft, pink gums.

89.
I do not talk much, do I?

88.
But they will pull me out shouting and screaming.

87.
I wonder what father's womb would be like.

86.
Mother, your face is white. Like the hospital sheets you will soon cry on.

85.
I wish I could smile. I need balloons filled with love in all colours. Except red. Red balloons are filled with blood.

84.
I have heard father discuss cigarette brands with mother.
He only smokes Gold Flakes. She pretends to be interested.

83.
Lola tells me she was conceived by force. She wants to bring
peace to her mother, but Lola's mother keeps rubbing her own
belly, wishing it would get smaller and smaller.

82.
My own mother consumes gold shot after shot. She stares at
the walls and swallows gold. I get the feeling I'm not
wanted at all.

81.
She reads books too. Each time she discovers a new fact about
babies, she bursts into tears. The world is afraid of children.
Who wants to be born into such a horrible place?

80.
Lola just told me that there will come a day when cancer and
Alzheimer's will no longer exist. But hernias will be contagious.

79.
Wombs are tombs that so many of us have died in.

78.
When mother sleeps, I am wide awake. I try to soothe her sore
heart, but I am too little to reach it. It will continue to ache for
as long as I live.

77.
When mother cries, I rock back and forth like an old man in
an easy chair.

76.
Lola says that at her birthing, she will blind herself by closing her eyes extremely tight. I ask why. Lola says she never wants to see her father's face.

75.
Lola and I will become friends. We will cut our hands with blades, stare at the walls, and sing nursery rhymes.

74.
Mother wants me to know that if she gives me away, it is because she is not capable of loving me.

73.
I prefer lies.

72.
I now have a brother. Her words have cut me in two.

71.
Who am I? I am my mother's wound.

70.
What year is it? Perhaps I could strangle the centuries and force God to start all over again. His own children have forgotten him. They have sent him to an old-age home called heaven where he counts stars and thinks mountains are building blocks that tumble into the valleys.

69.
I feel for God. How would you feel if only the dead visited you?

68.
How would you feel if no one could bear to look at you because you are too bright?

67.

I'm a midget Nostradamus and this is what I have to say:
There will come a day when suicide bombs will be available in
supermarkets.

66.

I was a writer in a previous life. I wrote a story about a
clockmaker who grew an extra hand each time he repaired
someone's clock. The story never got published.

65.

Here's what some of the literary geniuses of the past are doing
right now: Chekhov is currently working as an anesthetist in a
plastic surgery clinic in Florida. He saw a play called *The Cherry
Orchard* and hated it. Bukowski is six years old in an orphanage
in Bombay. The nuns keep showing him *The Sound of Music*
and it's killing his soul. Luckily, Carver's with him, making
mundane observances like "the nun raises her hand and then
brings it down again."

64.

Someday, heaven will be full like jails. Only then can we rejoice.

63.

I just heard a shriek from Lola. Her mother punched her own
belly. Lola finds it hard to breathe. She asks me if she should
make the effort to live. I am about to answer, but it's too late.
Lola says she has made up her mind. She will live until she is
one hundred years old. Just to spite the world.

62.

I suddenly want to tell my parents I love them. Mother, if you
give me away I will find you. Father, if you cannot afford to
keep me, I understand.

61.

What colour am I? I know my skin is brown, but when I am held up against the light, will people be able to see through me?

60.

I wonder what my skeleton looks like. Will my bones shine as much as my skin does? If I had teeth, I would bite into my flesh and find out.

59.

Father tells mother that he could leave me at the doorstep of an orphanage. At least I will have lots of friends, he says. God will look after me because I am an orphan. Does father not know that God never visits orphanages? They make him sad.

58.

What if I were a little girl fetus? Would my thoughts be any different?

57.

Mother keeps staring at falling leaves. They are boats, she says to herself. Boats flying in the air. Rain will flatten the boats and turn them into leaves again. Dead wet leaves. Mother needs to cheer up. I feel like popping my head out right now and bursting into song.

56.

I long for trees. Long trees, dead on their backs. If I wanted them alive, I would have said tall. Trees have lost faith in us. Their roots are spreading underground deep and fast, and one day, on Thanksgiving, they will rip through the tiled floors of our homes and choke us.

55.

Lola smiles in her mother's womb. She thinks of how her hair
will move in the breeze as she pushes me off the Bombay Stock
Exchange, the way her skirt will fly and the soft hairs on her
legs will tingle. She will not feel a thing when I am gone. I think
I'm in love.

54.

When I am born, I will look at the faces that greet me with
warm eyes. "I am here," I will announce, "to warn you of my
charm." As they pick me up, I will steal their watches and
wallets.

53.

Beware. My ashes should not be mistaken for baby powder.

52.

A decade from now, people who commit suicide will be reborn
the next instant, automatically, with twice the number of problems and excessive body hair.

51.

When mother was chopping onions this morning, she
wondered what would happen if she just plunged the knife
into her stomach. Would I feel anything?

50.

I hold my umbilical cord in my hand. It is my first magic trick.
I will make it easier for them to pull me out. I shall send my
umbilical cord out first and ask them to tug hard.

49.

Help me, Lola. I can't sleep at night. Lola replies, I never sleep at
night. I will keep my eyes open for nine months because they
will be shut for life, she says. I want to be blind too, Lola.

48.
Dawn cracks. Cracks my skull. Fills it with mornings, with the warmth of trembling aspen.

47.
Father, when you drop me off at the orphanage, do not stare at me too long or whisper goodbye. Just pat my soft head a couple of times and trudge your way.

46.
When I grow up, I will buy an asylum. I will own all the mad people in it and set them free. They will wander the streets and talk to trees, sparrows, churches, and potholes. The world will finally be the way it should.

45.
How old am I? The months have passed and I have changed positions. I wish my parents did too. They still have a list of all the orphanages in the city.

44.
I will be a clown when I am five years old. I will work at night when the wind is howling. Little children will hold on to their pillows and I will peep through their windows and shine a flashlight on my bleeding gums. They will be too scared to brush their teeth in the morning.

43.
Don't blame me for being this way. I have nothing. I am a carnival of dancing knives.

42.
I know the words "I love you." They are sold in multiples of three and wear thin like famine each time they are uttered.

41.

At the age of seven, Lola and I will walk through a garden.
All the trees will have nightingales in them with their vocal
cords cut. I will start crying. But Lola will throw money at them
and ask them to sing nursery rhymes. Can you blame me for
being madly in love with Lola?

40.

If I had a twin, he would be nothing like me. That's how
generous I am.

39.

I am well acquainted with pain. It moves very slowly at first,
and convinces you it will make you stronger. Then it strikes a
blow so hard you find even snow heavy to lift.

38.

I have my own little moon in here, bouncing along these womb
walls, dipping itself in blood, and turning to a crescent when I
scream for knives.

37.

I hear voices all the time. Wardens telling me I will be locked
up as soon as I am birthed. I tell them I like isolation. Look at
me now. No chains and still I choose to stay.

36.

I want to smile like mother. Walk slowly like father. It shocks
me how human I am.

35.

Lola, will you marry me? Please stop, she replies. I've already
buried my wedding dress.

34.
Babies have very strange customs. They wiggle their toes and leapfrog to the moon. That's why so many go missing.

33.
I forced it out of mother today. I kicked so hard she lied and told me I brought her joy.

32.
I ask Lola if she thinks about me. I'm a like a plant, she says. I water you because you are there, but if you wither I do not hold myself responsible.

31.
If I wither, it is due to the soil I grow on. Look at mother. Each time she turns in her sleep, her eyes open a little and she curses me. Her dreams could curdle breast milk.

30.
My Lola dreams too. When she is asleep, an angel covers her eyes with duct tape to prepare her for the blind days to come.

29.
I could talk about Lola for as long as I live. She makes my heart bounce across walls that divide countries.

28.
Lola says that if I went to school nobody would be my friend. The teacher would take one look at me and hang me from a ceiling fan. Lola says she will be there to switch the fan on.

27.
But how will Lola and I find each other? Will we cry in the same frequency when we are born, will we not stop until we are inches from each other, and when our tiny little fingers touch, will we drown in our own sorrow?

26.

Listen, I hear Lola say. Let's play a game. You count to ten and die. She loves to joke around, my Lola.

25.

Lola and I just felt a surge of electricity. It's Einstein taking rebirth. He's split his soul into nine and entered several wombs at once. At least one of us will have straight hair, he says.

24.

Lola, when we meet I will give you a shoebox. I will put my eyes in it, my first gift to you. You fool, says Lola. Who wants to the see the world through your eyes?

23.

Do you even have a heart, Lola? Call Lola whenever there is a water shortage, she says. Lola's eyes will pump tears to the houses of the poor.

22.

How old am I, Lola? You are six months old and you have six wrinkles, she says. Lola has none at all. She is timeless. If Lola were to wear a watch, its hands would disappear. Speaking of hands, Mother Teresa wants to come back. But this time, with a hundred hands so she can simultaneously soothe the foreheads of a hundred children.

21.

I have a feeling I'm special. God was not paying attention when he created me. He was tending to his garden of angels. He was worried about them because they were growing from the soil with their heads bashed-in and holes in their bellies.

20.

I will form a gang of babies. We will smother mothers with diapers.

19.
Lola and I can still be saved. I want you to know that.

18.
How many trees can you climb, asks Lola. As many as you want,
I say. Good, says Lola, I like servants.

17.
I can't live without you, Lola. I take my mother's cord and wind
it around my neck. Lola yawns.

16.
To live, says Lola, you need to be in constant pain.

15.
I am a tiny animal begging for air.

14.
What colour are your eyes, Lola? They change colour, she says.
They are both black and blue from beating.

13.
And your nails? Oh, my nails are red, she says. I dig out my own
flesh from my thighs and face. I don't want to be beautiful. But
I will be born a healthy seven pounds. My body will weigh only
five. Two I will carry in my hand.

12.
Let's talk about something else, I say. What makes you happy?

11.
Birds, she says. Birds with big black beaks and tiny wings. So
that they go nose down into the earth and their beaks get stuck
in the mud and they get asphyxiated.

10.

She makes me laugh. When we are seven we will hold hands for twenty-four hours and laugh in the face of the orphanage nuns. Ha ha, we will say, we have no parents.

9.

Here's something else that will make you laugh, says Lola. I will travel to war zones and collect the sweat of soldiers in a glass bottle. Then I will create a perfume from it, born from nightmares and bomb explosions and severed limbs. I will call it the Scent of Fear, and feed it intravenously to all government officials.

8.

I love you, Lola. Your words are like snake spit.

7.

You are my only friend. I have no one else to call my own. Jump with me, Lola. Let's jump off that building together.

6.

No, she says. I will die at one hundred. I will sip my coffee, and swallow my last tooth with it. I will choke on it. Then my grand-children will slit my throat and fight for that last tooth. The winner will put it under her pillow.

5.

Lola, it's almost time now. In a few days we will exit the womb. I buy time like it is auctioned at half price, she says. Ticks, chimes, bells that make grown-ups fearful.

4.

I am now nine months old. I have no recollection of the months that have passed. I think I died but nobody noticed.

3.

I want to be young again. A small warm ball of misery.

2.

I love you, Lola.

1.

See you on the outside, she says.

OUTLIERS

WILLIAM GIBSON

DOUGAL DISCARNATE

I MET DOUGAL in Kits, in the early eighties, when I was first starting to try to write fiction. I was thirty-three. He was nineteen.

He's still nineteen. He's been nineteen since Halloween
night, 1972.

He went to a party that night in an attic apartment on Ste-
phens Street, and took acid. He'd done this plenty of times
before. In fact was a serious stoner, a 4th Avenue veteran. This
time, though, during a particularly intense rush brought on by
a guitar solo on a Quicksilver Messenger Service album, something happened. Actinic, the colour of mercury under a flashbulb.

He'd become discorporate. Discarnate. Had left his body.

He didn't know it, at first. He was seeing the room from
some very odd angles, but he took that to be the working of the
blue tab.

Then he noticed that the sad-looking guy across the room, in
jeans and a jean jacket and a lumpy red-and-blue plaid Chinese
lumberjack shirt, was him.

No doubts, no mere doppelgänger suspicions; it was him.
But it was him without himself, or rather he, Dougal, was without himself, or...

And then he started yelling. And that was when he realized that nobody there could hear him. Except maybe himself, across the room, his body and whatever was left in it, and that started to cry, long, wracking, shoulder-heaving, bereft sobs, face buried in its hands, seriously bumming the party out.

His body, Dougal told me, when I first got to know him, enrolled in Langara a week later and eventually became an accountant.

He spent the rest of Halloween night, and most of the next day, trying to get someone's attention, anyone's. He went back to the place where he'd been crashing, and tried to get his body's attention, but that proved too sad to bear. His body seemed near catatonic (a word he hadn't known at the time). Sunk in some unutterable depression.

The people at the house were getting worried that Dougal had messed up his head, and these were people it took a lot, in that particular way, to worry. They were wondering if they shouldn't take him to a hospital, or anyway the Free Clinic, but in the end they just left Dougal's body alone. It crawled onto the mattress on the floor and pulled his spare pair of jeans over its head and eventually fell asleep.

He went out walking, then, away from the sadness in that room, and he'd more or less been walking ever since, for about ten years, when I met him.

We went to a lot of movies together, once we got to know one another, and that meant the Hollywood, because he couldn't leave the neighbourhood. Couldn't leave Kitsilano at all.

I brought up psychogeography, when we were trying to figure out why he couldn't leave Kits, but to someone in his position it probably just seemed like some postmodern conceit (which it basically was). For his part, he had some fuzzy ideas about ley lines, from a book he'd read part of, in 1971, when he'd still been carnate. I told him I didn't think there were any. Maybe underground water, he suggested. The buried salmon streams, like the lost rivers of Kits. But I know where some of those are, and he crossed them without any problem. And anyway, he wasn't a ghost, just part of the reason why people have always believed in ghosts.

He didn't think people ordinarily discarnated when they died. If they did, he said, he'd have been able to see them, and you'd figure there'd be quite a few around, even if they were just all the people who'd ever died in Kits.

There were three other discarnates in Kits. A First Nations guy in a semi-rigid outfit woven out of cedar bark; a Japanese man with a derby, an old-fashioned black suit, and pointy little black dress-boots that laced to his ankles; and a mean crazy white girl named Mary. Dougal figured the First Nations guy was from a long time ago. He had a big polished plug of jade stuck through his lower lip, and two smaller ones through his earlobes. Dougal thought the Japanese man was from the 1920s, by his clothes, but I guessed ten years earlier, from the description. Mary just wore a white cotton slip. Hard to date. Long straight dark hair. She'd talk, sometimes, but not particularly to him, and she didn't make much sense.

He asked me why I thought discarnates had clothes at all, or, for that matter, bodies. I pointed out that naked ghosts aren't much a part of our folklore, but that in England, for instance, people see ghosts walking around in suits of armour and nobody thinks twice about it, at least as far as ghosts go. Nobody knows, I told him, and he shrugged, a skinny young man with centre-parted shoulder-length hair, with a jean jacket over his plaid shirt, the kind they used to call a rounder shirt. He'd never figured out how to take any of his discarnation outfit off, he told me. He'd been wearing it all that time. It just seemed like part of the deal.

Like the time-mirages.

I don't know why I couldn't see the First Nations guy, or the Japanese man, or Mary. I couldn't always see Dougal that well, either. Sometimes I thought I saw him best with a hangover; other times scarcely at all, just a Cheshire-cat grin, in the rain that didn't touch him.

But I really wanted to see those time-mirages.

Once, he said, he'd been down at Kits Beach at dawn, in a fog, and heard voices, a language that sounded like birds, and out of the fog had glided this war canoe, dark, almost black, with men bent down rowing, and two men up in the prow, standing, with spears, talking. They weren't First Nations, he said.

He thought they were Hawaiian. He said that there had been Hawaiian settlements over on the west coast of Vancouver Island, once, and I doubted him, but later I read somewhere that there are people who believe that. But this was a time-mirage, he said, not a war canoe full of discarnate people. Not just because they were out in the water, where he couldn't go, the same way he couldn't go much farther south than 16th, but just because it was different. Not like seeing other discarnates. There was a shiver to it, he said.

And on 16th once, standing in the middle of Arbutus with cars driving through him, he'd looked up into a Shaughnessy and a Kerrisdale that were nothing but the tallest evergreens he'd ever seen, little wisps of mist hanging, a couple of small waterfalls, and this elk, its antlers as tall as a bus, taller, and nearly as wide, looking back at him.

Another time, a sunny spring day at the top of 4th, the sunlight changed in a long smooth blink, and he saw deep snow, filthy with the soot of coal-burning furnaces and fireplaces. A mostly residential avenue, lawns where the stores are now, the white frame houses darkened with that same smoke, and an electric tram ascending the hill, like something out of some shabbier, more realistic version of Disneyland.

Then blink again, everything reversing.

You've seen Dougal, if you've ever spent much time in Kits.

If I could show you a photograph, you'd recognize him. There was a very bad Identi-Kit portrait of him up on some lampposts, once, though that isn't what I mean when I say you've seen him. The victim of an attempted rape had mistaken him for her assailant. Which really got him down, he said, seeing as how he'd been the one who'd saved her, back in that alley, getting repeatedly up in the rapist's face and screaming at him, in sheer disgust and frustrated disembodied fury. He'd been praying he'd give this asshole an embolism or something, whip some harsh discarnate voodoo on him, but it doesn't work that way. Though the guy had started batting at his own face as though there were insects there or something, then just stalked off, struggling with his fly.

Dougal figures the girl must have seen him then, and described him to the police. That was a good five years before I met him, but when he told me about it, I remembered the posters.

But if you spent any time in Kits, back then, you'd have seen him. He was always around. No choice in it.

He'd attended a lot of night classes, at Kits High, whatever they were offering, and had watched a lot of television, mostly in people's apartments. He could get in anywhere, but never really knew how. The world seemed solid enough; he could sit on a sofa, climb stairs, but if he wanted in, somewhere, he found himself in. He'd discovered a couple of places where people left the television on, when they went out, and if they left it tuned to something educational, they were on his list. He gave himself an education, that way. When the Discovery Channel started, he was an immediate fan. Books were harder. Impossible, really. He'd have had to read over someone's shoulder.

He went to bars fairly regularly, which was where I met him, and also to AA meetings. Said the new people in AA always saw him, figured he was there for the meeting, but the people who'd been going for a while usually couldn't see him. People would see him, nod, then not offer him their hand when they said the prayer at the end. Just the way some people in bars would talk to him at length, hit on him, even, then seem to forget him. Turn and walk away.

I don't know if he had any other friends, when we knew each other. If he did, he never mentioned them. He was always glad to see me, even if he was down, and he often was, though never much prone to self-pity.

His three fellow discarnates weren't much help, as far as company went. The First Nations guy was in his own space, totally, and the Japanese man seemed perpetually terrified of everything, including Dougal, and just ran away. Mary, the girl in the slip, he confessed to having had a thing for, initially, but she was just too crazy. Hung out in Tatlow Park around dawn, first light, scaring the shit out of the odd drunk who happened through there. He'd had to chase a profoundly inebriated UBC student out of the little creek there once, because the guy had seen Mary from the bridge and tumbled off, over the timber railing, landing on his face in cattails and frog-water. Which would've been, Dougal said, like drowning in a bowl of cold old spaghetti. Much harder to motivate this one than to freak that rapist, but somehow he managed it. But he'd seen a look in Mary's eyes, then, that he didn't like, not at all, and after that he wondered if anyone had ever drowned there before, in Tatlow Park, just around dawn.

We bonded, in large part, around cheesy science fiction movies. I explained my theory that the best cinematic SF is almost always to be found in very bad films, but only in tiny, brilliant, fractal bursts. We both loved *Blade Runner*, *Alien*, the first couple of *Terminators*. Hated *Star Trek*, hated *Star Wars*. Loved *Mad Max*. But really what we both wanted was Mick Jagger driving around some half-assed dystopian L.A. in a six-wheeled armoured car, painted red.

I worked out a deal, with a friend who lived on Cornwall, that allowed Dougal and me to more fully explore this genre. The friend would go out while Dougal and I watched videos I'd rent. That way we could talk without my having to worry anyone would think I was crazy. Except my friend, whatever he thought I was up to.

I rented Tarkovsky's *Stalker* and Dougal swore it had put both of us to sleep, but he was joking. He never slept. When he wasn't watching movies with me, and he wasn't that often, he watched everything else. Did the disembodied witness thing. He'd seen it all, he said. Said that if there was anything he'd ever heard of that he hadn't seen someone in Kits do at least once, he couldn't think of it.

The dystopian movie thing, I figured, for both of us, was actually about Kits.

A mirror. Inversion. Utopias are by definition unreal. Dystopias are merely relatively unpleasant. One person's raging dystopia is another's hot immigration opportunity. But there's something about living in such a thoroughly, however relatively, non-dystopian place. A place whose time-mirages, if you could see them, might mostly be quite pleasant. (Though if you were Dougal's First Nations discarnate, maybe not. More of that relativity.)

After I'd sold one or two stories, and not long after I'd met Dougal, I went to New York. Stayed in Alphabet City with someone I knew from Portland. New York before what my friend Jack calls "the regooding." If you were ready to put up with some relatively serious dystopia, you could live there, then. It wasn't about having enough money. It was about wanting something else badly enough, the secret semi-utopian flipside, the freedom of a splendidly broken metropolis. The sirens all night. Buildings torched for the insurance. A lawlessness, and the absolute need to abide by the real, the unwritten rules. Somehow I carried some of that home with me, as in a Dixie Cup. I'd never seen anything like it, and haven't since. And dipped into it as needed. In Kits. Building what I was always somewhat annoyed, later, to see described as dystopian fictions.

I saw Dougal last in 1998, across Arbutus from the Ridge Theatre, where the Vancouver Film Festival had just screened Abel Ferrara's adaptation of a story of mine, "New Rose Hotel." He'd liked it.

We'd gone across the street, afterward, so we could discuss it without people seeing me talking to myself, though I'm sure a few did. He was a huge Walken fan, Dougal. I am myself.

By that time, Dougal had started getting high. I had started not getting high, myself, some time before, and we seemed to be heading in opposite directions, that way.

I don't know how he discovered it, the thing with televisions. The old-fashioned kind, with the big glass picture tube. There's an electron gun at the base of that tube, and a powerful electromagnet. Sometimes I've wondered if he didn't see something about Michael Persinger's God Helmet, maybe on the Discovery Channel, and tried sitting with his discarnate head directly behind a television. Because that was how he was doing it. Getting high.

It made him less interesting company. Still likeable, but not as sharp. Less observant. Less funny. Muted. I don't remember what we talked about, that last time, other than Ferrara's movie, and Christopher Walken. I saw my wife wave to me, from in front of the Ridge. Said goodnight.

I lost track of him, after that, and didn't find him at the next Folk Festival, where I'd always seen him before. I kept expecting to run into him, after that, and didn't.

In his absence, which at first didn't seem like it would be permanent, I started seeing Kits differently. I'd remember something he'd told me he'd seen happen there, or notice something that had changed since I'd last seen him. I wondered about his body, the accountant who lived in Burnaby and was a tax consultant. (I'd helped him find that out. Yellow Pages.)

I sat in a Greek breakfast place on West Broadway one September afternoon and watched the towers of the World Trade Center collapse, over and over, on a flat-screen television he couldn't have gotten high with, and wondered what he would have made of whatever that was that I was watching.

I got an email from Dougal, on the eve of what we didn't yet know would be Obama's election. I was in Paris, with my daughter, about to return to Vancouver.

It was quite long, a single paragraph, all lower case, no commas. I read it, went out to dinner with friends, came back, read it again. Then, evidently, I managed to accidentally erase it from the Telus Webmail server. Election excitement took over, the flight back, then when I remembered it, looked for it, it was gone. The address forgotten. Some utterly unfamiliar domain abbreviation.

He said he was "down in Klong Toey" (he didn't use caps but I googled it) which he described as "this Bangkok superslum" and that he thought I "would really dig it" there. He said he and his "gf" were there "on business," but that they lived in Okinawa. Okinawans, he said (I'm not quoting, and this is all from memory), occupied something like the niche in Japanese culture that Cajuns occupy in American culture. Sexy, into magic, musical, foreign without actually being foreign.

He said that she was "typing for him," but didn't explain further.

He never mentioned his girlfriend's name. Described her as "a shaman." A female Okinawan shaman, twenty-seven years old, whom he'd met three years before, late one hot June afternoon at Kits Beach, under those big old trees where the beach curves off down toward the West End.

He'd been "doing way too much television" by then, he said, and was really feeling like shit, and to make himself feel worse had gone down to walk, disembodied, through sun-warmed flesh and the abundant evidence of the action of pheromones.

I imagine him, from what he wrote, walking toward Kits Pool, into the shade of those trees, and as he walks becoming aware of what he at first assumes is a time-mirage, that same shiver, and this around a small figure seated alone on a bench. Strange that anyone would have a whole bench to herself, that time of day, that kind of weather, and as he draws closer, he sees, without knowing it at first, that she sees him. Sees nothing else, in fact, this skinny, acne-scarred, cat-faced girl or woman, of deeply indeterminate age, in flip-flops, cut-off jeans and a black Hello Kitty tank top with white bra straps showing. She smiles, then, and something about her teeth terrifies him for an instant. But then she briskly removes her very large, very black sunglasses, and in her eyes he sees, simultaneously, the gathering darkness of thousands of miles of Pacific thunderheads and an utterly carnal desire.

Mine, she says, triumphantly, in no human language.

And he finds himself, shortly, in the back bedroom of a bed and breakfast in Kits Point, being introduced to the ins and outs of one particular kind of Okinawan shamanism, one centred around congress with discarnate entities.

Within days, they are on a flight to Narita. Many things being possible to the adept. Most particularly to one who has now, finally, at the end of a very long search, found her familiar.

He didn't do television any more, he said. Life was interesting. He liked Okinawa, but also they travelled. And what had I thought about *Johnny Mnemonic*, he asked? I hadn't been able to see it with him when it was released, and he'd missed it at the Hollywood. He'd recently seen it on DVD, he said, and thought it had its moments.

BUFFY CRAM

LARGE GARBAGE

THEY'LL COME AT night, the papers warned. They'll come haul-ing carts of empty wine bottles, all racket and ruckus, their skin the colour of city, the smog rubbed right in. They'll have no hygiene, no fixed addresses, no shoes or toothbrushes. Some will have no teeth. They'll come with their sores and their fleas and their nineteenth-century coughs, hacking and spitting, scratching and bleeding right into our gardens and backyard gazebos. Like disease they'll come, fast and unforgiving.

"A new breed of homeless. A sign of the new economic real-ity," the experts claimed, although it meant little to us at the time. We knew they were overeducated, unemployed, and migrating, east to west, across the country; we'd heard rumours of how they set up at the edges of wealthy neighbourhoods, living off the fat of the land, hosting late-night salons in other people's living rooms, but we all had our own economic reali-ties to contend with. Some of us had even been forced to lay off the help.

At some point we of Cherry Lane stopped reading the sto-ries. Sure, we fit the profile: a pocket of stately homes just at the edge of downtown, but our city was the westernmost in the country, set apart from the mainland by a two-hour stretch of ocean. We knew the last mainland city had been overrun, but we never believed they would find their way here, to our island, our city, our Cherry Lane. After all, we convinced ourselves, how would they afford the ferry fees?

My wife, my daughter, and I were seated in the formal dining room when they arrived. Ever since we'd let Lucinda go, my wife had been doing the cooking and she liked to separate our carbs from our proteins so that night it was all carbs: linguine with some sort of seed sprinkled on top and a side of delicate purple potatoes.

"Would this be a fingerling potato?" I asked mere seconds before they appeared outside our window.

At first there were only two. He wore a tattered tuxedo and pushed a cart filled, not with empty bottles, but with books. She was wearing mermaid-green taffeta, pearls and heels. The shoes were shaped like playground slides and not quite her size, so she weaved and wobbled like a child playing dress-up. There was a certain aura about them—not the mix of sex and decay I'd expected, but something almost noble, as if they'd been plucked from another time. They were both wearing pink sun-halos. Even the sunset had been recruited for this, their arrival scene.

My fingerling tumbled to my plate, scattering seeds everywhere. My wife nodded to my daughter, me, and we rose, moving to the window to watch the newcomers zigzag from the mouth of one driveway to the next, opening our recycling bins, the sturdy kind with wheels and lids. Creak-slap went those flip-top lids. Then the frenzied sifting—paper against paper against plastic.

"It's happening," my daughter said, the small envelope of her lips quivering, a certain mosquito pitch rising in her voice.

It was all too much for my wife—who swooned beauti-
fully, allowing me to steady her. Then I remembered the boxes
I'd stacked in front of our garage the day before, once I saw
the Gregorys had put theirs out, each one marked CHARITY in
Lucinda's thick black writing.

"What about the Large Garbage?" I asked my wife, tight-
lipped so she wouldn't see me tremble.

For some reason we, the residents of Cherry Lane, had taken
to calling the third week of September Large Garbage Week
when we could just as easily have called it the Annual Charity
Drive.

"I don't know why you insisted on putting that junk out so
early," my wife said.

"Because the Gregorys did," I replied. "And the Felixes."

"The Gregorys did because they left for Flor-i-da today," she
said. "And the Felixes did because *you* did." When she was smarter
than me in a particular matter she enunciated very clearly.

The three of us leaned towards the window then, holding
our breath, but it was too late. The strangers were tearing at
boxes, emptying them of clothing, holiday placemats and old
bed sheets. We looked at the tangle of high chairs, dismantled
bunk beds, retro skis and tennis rackets stacked up in front
of our neighbours' garages, all the things we unearthed from
basements and attics each September to prove our charity to
ourselves and to each other. *One man's treasure* and all that.

"Constantine," the woman called out from alongside our
house, voice like a pencil scribble. "This one's a veritable jackpot."

"Constantine?" my wife said.

"Veritable?" I said.

But by then Constantine had discovered Mrs. Felix's box
of books. "Proust!" he shouted, fanning the yellow pages. "Pinky,
come see!"

"Pinky?" my daughter laughed. "More like *Skanky*."

"Enough!" my wife commanded.

"What did we even put *out* there this year?" my daughter whined. "Anything of mine?" Her voice had risen to a whinny. "Mom, you can't just let them—"

"Why not?" I said. "Charity is charity."

"But I don't want to *see* it," Jennifer said.

My wife turned down the blind. I turned up the chandelier and we guided our Jennifer back to the table.

"Never you mind," I said, putting my hand atop my daughter's, a wink for my wife. "Now, what can you tell me about the tenth grade?"

"Eleventh," she corrected, and although my error made them both momentarily glum, they soon recovered themselves.

While my daughter talked about her newest elective, Money Management, and the horrors of a certain partner named Hez, we could hear them outside, hooting and clattering, hauling boxes down driveways.

"Your grandfather made his fortune in money management," my wife was telling Jennifer, "… foreclosures, refinancing, loss mitigation…" and Jennifer was practically gurgling with excitement.

I tried to follow their conversation, but I was elsewhere. I was stabbing and twisting up bite-sized nests of linguine, trying to recall my own Proust days. My Balzac and Sartre and Camus days in the Department of Comparative Literature, before Kathy and the School of Business. Before the MBA. I was arranging those pasta nests side by side on my plate because the appetite had gone right out of me, or rather, it had shifted farther down to become something that had very little to do with food. The truth is, I couldn't quite recall what was in those boxes. In my race to keep up with the Gregorys, I hadn't even opened them.

I sat back in my chair, one hand fogging up my glass of Merlot, gripping the edge of my mahogany table, trying to take comfort in the largest room of my—our—large, large home. Antique cabinets, upholstered chairs, cut crystal: everything so finely crafted. Everything so sturdy, and yet I couldn't help but see myself as the most tender inside part of that life: me as mincemeat, as mollusc, as morsel.

In the morning charity was strewn across our lawns. Clothing hung from gutters and tree branches. Old magazines and once-loved toys cluttered the sidewalks. I was standing underneath the "TWO HOURS MAX AT ALL TIMES" sign untucking parking tickets from my windshield wiper—one of the disadvantages of living so close to the city—and taking in the damage when I heard a chattering from under our hydrangea. I crept closer. It was tuxedo man, Constantine, reading—no, *reciting*—something to Pinky beneath a canopy of flowers. For a moment I envisioned them curled just so under a bridge in a large mainland city, inhaling exhaust fumes, scavenging for fish in diseased rivers, munching on gristly berries by the sides of highways. I felt a sudden kick of pride for having provided a downtrodden man with a flowering bush to sleep beneath—after all, it was *my* bush he'd chosen—and for a moment I longed for true charity, something beyond Large Garbage once a year. I imagined bringing this man into my home, giving him a shower and a shave, perhaps an old suit, perhaps a rudimentary lesson in entrepreneurship. Or if he wasn't interested in that, at least a proper fishing rod, some bait and tackle.

But this entire line of thought came to its snarled end when I noticed the woman was wearing something long, white and glittery, something familiar and poofy and then it hit me: this skank was wearing my wife's cotillion gown. I could see it then. How, in my zeal to best the Gregorys, I'd not only grabbed the boxes marked CHARITY, but also those marked KEEPSAKES.

"Hey," I shouted, coming across the flowerbed at them. And I kept on, "Hey-hey. Hey. *Hey*," until I was close enough to reach out and grab her. That's when I realized I didn't actually want to touch her.

The man stood and faced me. Now he was reading to me from the open book: "*Étonnants voyageurs. Quelles nobles histoires.*" French: I flinched. I could barely tell one word from another these days...

"*Nous lisons dans vos yeux profonds comme les mers,*" he continued. There I was, the enraged landowner, standing inside his orbit of stench and he could care less.

"*Montrez-nous les écrins de vos riches mémoires...*"

It was impossible not to hear it all as personal insult. I didn't want to recall my leisurely undergraduate days, reading Baudelaire beneath trees. Nor did I want to understand what this meant: that I had also mistaken my own box of keepsakes for Large Garbage.

Something was rustling in the man's pants just then and I looked down to find he was scratching and rearranging himself *down there*. He was bouncing his meat at me. My gaze jolted back up to his face. Then his hand, the same one he'd used to scratch himself, was coming towards me. I could see his crumbling yellow nails, the grime built up in the creases of his palms. For a moment it seemed he would make some apologetic gesture but then he opened his filthy crack of a mouth and said: "Would you happen to have any spare change?"

"No. No-no. No. No. No change. Sorry," I stuttered. I was a small angry man, a man of small anger. "This is our—*my* property and I command you to get *off*," I hollered. "Go-go. Please go."

He didn't run as I had hoped but turned to offer his hand to Pinky.

She looked at the stack of parking tickets pinched in my hand and said, "You shouldn't park in front of your house anymore."

She was right, but ever since Kathy had given Jennifer a BMW (and my spot in the garage) for her sixteenth birthday, I'd had no choice.

"What was it the Marquis de Sade said?" She was wiggling into her heels. "Social order at the expense of liberty is hardly a bargain." She stepped out from behind the hydrangea then, dainty as a debutante.

Constantine smiled. "Or, 'Miserable creatures, thrown for a moment on the surface of this little pile of mud,'" and then he looked at me just long enough to break the social contract. "You, sir, are you a miserable little creature?"

My mouth flapped: open, closed.

He threw his head back, laughing, and then they walked—no, sauntered—down my driveway. I didn't chase after them. I was stunned, speechless. And I was late. Again. As always.

I slammed into the car and headed for work, the previous night's parking tickets piled on top of all the others on the passenger seat beside me.

At the Department of Revenue I was hardly in the office door before man-faced Rhanda was on me.

"You're late," she said, and I couldn't help but notice in that particular light she really did have something like stubble. She was keeping pace with me down the hall, yapping and handing me memos. "The Schmidt case is being pushed ahead. Dan wants all the forms by noon. But he wants to talk to you first. ASAP. As soon as you're done with—" then she looked at her clipboard—"Hez? Yes, Hez. She's waiting for you."

"Hez?"

"Hez. Your daughter's friend?"

"Deal with this, would you?" I said, handing Rhanda my dirty travel mug.

It seemed Hez was there to talk to me about money management while my Jennifer was somewhere across town talking to Hez's father about the same thing. It seemed it was a competition of sorts. So I explained my position to her, then about taxation policy and departmental divisions and the various meetings I attended in any given week, but it wasn't good enough, somehow.

"Wait," she said. "So you don't manage any *actual* money?"

"I'm afraid it's not that simple," I said. "I'm more of an overseer really."

She waved her hand around. "So this is all just *files* and stuff? There's no actual *money* here? This office is more about paper pushing?"

"Well Hez, I suppose it is," I said and then I gave her the number of my brother-in-law, a banker, before showing her out.

I stopped by Dan's office.

He squashed his blunt finger up against the Schmidt file, a couple of eighty-year-old artists who had managed to evade property tax for more decades than I'd been alive. "Might I inquire when you were planning on dealing with them?" he did, indeed, inquire.

My tongue was fat and lazy in my mouth.

"Even the sweet and the old have to pay their taxes, Henry," he said, "but that's not what I really wanted to talk to you about." He pulled out another file, one I'd never seen before. "What I really wanted to talk to you about is this parking ticket situation."

"Are you aware," he asked, "that you received a summons to go to court several weeks ago?"

I was not aware.

"Are you aware of how bad this makes us look? Jesus, Henry, if you'd come to me at any point, any point before now, we could have dealt with this reasonably. Like adults."

And so, in the end, it wasn't the Schmidts. In the end it was the parking tickets. Dan insisted that within the office, my "termination" would strictly be referred to as a "leave of absence." He insisted I would receive a respectable severance package.

On the way out the door I saw Rhanda gossiping by the copy machine. Hiss-hiss-hiss, she was saying, while glancing over her shoulder at me, which is why I was inclined, against my own better judgment, to walk right up to her and rustle my own pants. One minute I was heading for the door and the next I was thrusting up while reaching down. I was scratching and rearranging and jiggling my bits at her. I was calling her a man-faced skank.

Cherry Lane was still, except for a small fleet of charity vans idling by the curbs. I hadn't been home at that time on a Monday for decades. The hybrids had gotten into the rest of the Large Garbage while everyone was at work. I stood on my doorstep watching the staff recover items from under bushes, off lawns and out of gutters. Where's the money management in this? I wondered. How exactly can these people afford to be volunteers in this day and age? I briefly considered helping but I was overdrawn, expired.

I called to my wife and daughter from the foyer but it was just me, *man alone*. I instinctively went to the den, kicked off my shoes, and clicked on the TV, but it was hours until prime time. I turned it off and that's when I caught a whiff coming from the couch pillows. It was gamey, oniony, slightly animal. A smell some part of me enjoyed, but a smell that had no place in my home. I lifted a pillow to my face and sniffed deeply. I must've drifted away for a time then, for I woke in the afternoon with that pillow sitting on my face, smelling more scalpy than ever.

I sat up with a start and noticed that all of the couch pillows were mussed, that the carpet was showing signs of heavy traffic—and yet, since Lucinda left, my Kathy had been so diligent, one might even say *obsessed*, with these kinds of things. She was always making sure the individual carpet bristles were set the same way.

I went from room to room then, sniffing, checking the window locks.

In the kitchen I found cheese and cracker crumbs. Cheese *and* crackers: carbs *and* protein. Upstairs, in the master bathroom, I found a bar of soap with deep, dark striations where dirt had settled in. There was a faint scum line around the perimeter of the tub, as though several dirty bodies had been washed there. Glued against the porcelain was a curly red hair. I was searching my wife's drawer for tweezers to collect the hair when I happened to glance out the window and see more hybrids, seven or eight of them, making their way slowly through the ravine at the back of our property. The men were wearing ratty suits and top hats, the women fur and silk.

Never mind tweezers. I was hauling down the stairs with that hair pinched between my fingers when my wife and daughter stepped into the foyer.

"Thank God you're home," I shouted and then my feet kicked out from under me and I slid down the last few stairs.

They were giggling in their matching yoga wear and the hair had escaped my pinch.

"They've been in here," I said. "Those homeless people. I just found a hair in the tub."

"Gross, Dad," Jennifer said.

"I think they've been taking baths."

They looked at me blankly then, all the giggle gone out of them.

"Well, maybe you should have considered this before you let Lucinda go," Kathy said.

"No, not *our* hair," I said. "One of theirs. A red one. Wait, I'll show you." I was patting the floor around me. I was pleading, "C'mon. Help me look."

"I've got homework," Jennifer said.

"I've got dinner," said Kathy, holding up a grocery bag and then they split off—north, south—and I headed for the computer.

That night it was all protein: breast of something covered in sauce with peculiar sausage as a side. The blinds were snapped tight but we could still hear them out there.

"People are calling them hybrids," I announced. Then in my best newscaster voice: "'The *New* Hybrid Class.'" I was the only one laughing. "They're really quite educated," I added.

Neither one of them had a response—just the sounds of chewing, scraping, swallowing.

My fork was poised somewhere between plate and mouth when I noticed the sauce was made from the finest paper-thin slices of mushroom. "What type of mushroom is this?" I asked.

"Chanterelle," Kathy answered.

"Such a lovely word," I said, to kill the silence. Meanwhile, I was wondering: How, exactly, was I different from this mushroom? I ate, I slept, I too grew larger, paler by the day.

Eyes on plates. Sipping, slicing, clinking of ice.

"Apparently they were once middle class," I said. "They were students, artists, professor-types, too-good-for-the-corporate-ladder types. And when they couldn't afford their passions anymore, they just…dropped out."

"Like your father!" Kathy said to her dinner plate.

"Passion," I said to mine. "Another lovely word!"

"Evidently they've been holding 'salons' in people's homes. Like if a family is away, they'll just go right in and read all their books and hold seminars. Apparently property values have really..."

But I was speaking to myself. They were involved in some sort of mother-daughter communication involving only the slightest eyebrow movements.

Kathy put her fork down, folded her arms across her chest and looked at me. My daughter, having missed her cue, joined in at the folding-of-the-arms part, fork still in hand.

I looked from my daughter to my wife: *my Jennifer, my Kathy*. It was what one might call an awkward silence.

A slice of chanterelle fainted from my fork, fell to my plate.

"What did you do to Hez?" Jennifer said finally.

"And how is it you can afford to be home from work so early?" Kathy asked.

I was still formulating a response when a bright, farm-smelling whiff passed my nose. "Do you smell that?" I asked, louder than I meant to, so loud Kathy startled. "That funny smell? Like a greasy scalp? I'm telling you, they've been in here!"

That night I told my wife about the tickets. She was on the bed rubbing lotion on her legs.

"How many?"

"Oh, I don't know," I said, "twenty, forty. It's nothing really."

"Forty!" she screeched. She rubbed more vigorously then, going over the same area again and again—now knees, now ankles, now knees-knees-knees.

"I'd planned to dispute them when I had a moment. I mean they can't give a man fifty tickets for parking in front of his own house! They can't just declare Cherry Lane a two-hour-max-any-time zone. 'Social order is hardly worth the price of liberty.' You know who said that?"

"Now it's fifty tickets?"

"What?"

"A minute ago it was forty tickets. Now it's fifty?"

I pulled back my side of the sheet and looked closely at the accumulation of bodily crumbs there. I couldn't, just then, be certain they were my own.

"I think the den needs vacuuming," I said.

"I think you're more and more like your father every day," she said.

"I think I'll be taking a flex day tomorrow," I said, and then I headed for the couch downstairs.

In the morning there was no sign of them, not behind the hydrangea and not in the ravine either. I headed for the basement and, as I'd feared, found two boxes marked CHARITY among those marked KEEPSAKES. Most of the keepsake boxes were Kathy's: the Montgomery linens tucked in with the Montgomery china and the Montgomery photo albums—boxes of dresses and shoes and ribbons and trophies for every occasion in a Southern girl's life. In among all that was a single box marked KEEPSAKES: BROWN. My family inheritance. I brought it out to the backyard.

I found six of my father's journals. The first one was from the France years, just after his PhD and just before my mother. It was written in scratchy black French. French: the language I could read and write but never quite speak, a taunting, cruel language, a language that had led me right up to the threshold of fluency and then shut the door on me in the end. I almost broke down. I did. My tears landed on the open page, drawing the ink up from the page, the page up from the book. I dabbed with my shirtsleeve but I was only smearing ink and history. I almost gave up and then the sentences I was reading began to loosen. Verbs and their conjugations, nouns and their complements, tense, vocabulary: it all started rushing back to me as if French, like a good woman, had been waiting for me all those years, as if no time had passed at all.

I read verse after verse about *la lune*, about grass blowing in the wind, women's hair blowing in the wind, hair luminous and flowing and silky and honey-coloured. Rivers of hair. Entire poems about a woman's eyes. Eyes like syrup, no, coffee, no, caramel, no, amber. The eyes of a seductress. Tantalizing, come-hither eyes. Page after page about a woman's curves, vast swells of flesh, heaving mountains, soft veldts, damp crevasses.

I closed the book. It was my mother of course.

My dear father. He had the heart of the poet but not the talent, which is why he devoted his life to the study of troubadours. One of only a handful of troubadour scholars at the time, he had gone to France to walk in their footsteps, to dig through archives and write a book about his findings. It was while researching a certain French family and their history of troubadour patronage that he met my grandfather and, eventually, my mother. My father was a scruffy American with a big nose and corduroy pants, but my grandfather was so impressed by the young man's interest in history he let his daughter marry him anyway. So began the Brown family tradition of "marrying up."

My father wrote the book, but not before one of his colleagues did, so he was always given second pick of the jobs and the conferences. He worked in a small, cluttered office at the local university until my mother left him—and who could blame her? He had begun to dress in head-to-toe brown as so many scholars do, but, given our name, it made him a target for ridicule. He would wear the same shirt-pant-cardigan combination until it was sour-smelling, at which point he would change the shirt or the pants, never both. He smoked and drank with his friends, scholars of equally obscure subjects: *Fifteenth-century Swords of the Middle East, Italian Rococo Hair Styles* and *The Ceilings of Rajasthan.* And he wrote terrible French poetry.

After hours of sitting in the grass reading my father's writing, I saw Constantine stroll into my yard.

"Hello," he said, not bothered in the least by our trespasser-landowner relationship.

"Hi." I couldn't seem to locate anger.

"What is the meaning of this?" He gestured to the clutter around me. I noticed he was covered in a noble grime.

"Reorganizing," I said, closing the box.

He gave an aristocratic shrug with his mouth—the first sign of approval I'd had from anyone in days.

"I'm going to have to ask your girlfriend for that dress back. The white one."

"That seems reasonable," he said.

I nodded towards the sandwich in his hand. "What's that?"

He cracked the bread open. "Pesto, brie, tapenade—"

"Is that grilled portabella?"

"It appears to be," he said, and ripped off a mouthful. Then he held the sandwich out to me, "Care for some?"

We shared the sandwich and a bit of conversation. Eventually he excused himself to look for my wife's dress and I carried my box inside. It was then, just after he had left, that I managed to locate my anger after all. Where exactly did a hobo like him get a sandwich like that? Just who did he think he was, breaking into the kitchens of the good people of Cherry Lane? I was just starting to think laying Lucinda off was one of the single greatest mistakes of my life—Lucinda, not just the maid, but the guardian of our home—when I noticed the stiff wind, the front door standing wide open, and more of that deep-skin smell. Only this time, it was everywhere.

I found body-shaped ruts down the centre of each bed, grease spots as dark as cheeseburger stains on the pillowcases. The bottom bookshelf, down where we kept our Joseph Campbell and Carl Jung, was in disarray. In the living room, the chess set had been hastily put back on the shelf. The TV was on Masterpiece Theatre.

After I told her about the mix-up with her KEEPSAKES, and the trouble at work; after she dragged my father into it and I dragged her mother into it, Kathy suggested I spend the night at a hotel. I chose to stay in the yard, though, where I could keep an eye on things.

I spent the early part of that evening reading my father's journals, falling deeper into French than I ever imagined I could, the language opening to me in new ways. At the bottom of the box, beneath the journals, I found my father's old scholarly uniform: brown pants, brown cardigan, brown shirt and tie, all my size. Putting those clothes on, I understood why my father wore them a week at a time; it's a quality you just don't find in clothes anymore.

The uniform must've filled me with strength and purpose, because I immediately got an idea. After writing out twelve versions of the same note, I walked up and down Cherry Lane tucking one into every mailbox. The notes were a call to action: *Tomorrow, 5 PM, my yard, be there*, or something to that effect. Then I got the idea to keep an eye on the Gregorys' house from inside the bushes.

It was nearly midnight when I heard them. I climbed out of the bushes in time to see a dim, shifty light, a candle or a Bic lighter, moving through the Gregorys' house. I crept across the yard on hands and knees and pulled myself up against the tall fence separating our yards. I could smell salmon grilling. I could hear the clink of wine glasses, the hot tub bubbling.

I didn't even walk around the fence; I jumped over and marched up the back steps to confront those hybrids for once and for all.

There were ten, fifteen, twenty of them. They were in the yard, on the porch, in the house. The ones in the patio hot tub were nude, debating intensely. Inside, the air was thick with cigar smoke. It was dark but for the moon and the odd candle. My clothes must've helped me blend in, because nobody noticed me at first. In the living room women and men were lounging about, sipping wine with their feet in each other's laps. They were passing a book—Rilke? Neruda?—taking turns reading verses aloud. The last woman to read finished the poem and asked, "What do you think it means?" closing the book gently. "Do you think he might really fail his lover or is he just afraid of his own mortality?" I was tempted to lie down with them, to speak about love and death while some young woman played with my hair, but I kept on.

Several of them were gathered around the dining room table attempting to interpret a tide chart. They had an almanac out, an atlas, a dictionary, a small flashlight. A petite redhead was at the kitchen counter dishing out food. "Niçoise?" she offered each passerby. It smelled delicious.

A man was drawing different constellations into the dust of the foyer mirror. Cassiopeia, Pegasus, and Chamaeleon: he described each one and then a huddle of women with tall hairstyles recreated the shapes by squeaking their fingers across the marble floor.

On the stairs, two men in coattails were debating the Bible from a purely literary standpoint. "From a purely literary standpoint, Genesis almost directly correlates to Aristotelian structure," one said as I passed.

In the upstairs hallway a couple was slow dancing to a song only they could hear. They were humming softly, voices in perfect harmony. Another couple was making love in the spare bedroom. I stopped before the open door. "You complete me!" the man yelled. "You complete me!" and then they collapsed in groans. A woman smelling of snuffed-out fires came up beside me then and passed me an orb filled with bright smoke. I inhaled once, twice, and began to feel impaled. Then, once I was a limbless black core, once I was only the body, only the parts of me that beat, she led me towards the master bedroom. Pinky was there, and Constantine. He was playing a delicate stringed instrument—a lyre?—and she was warbling operatically. They were accompanied by a woman with a wooden flute—a lute?

People were twirling and floating around the room in what can only be described as interpretive dance. The woman, my friend, led me forward and before I knew it my arms were swaying—now I was a tree, now a woman's hair, now grass in the wind. I was twisting carpet bristles up between my toes like meringue and reciting something, a French poem I had memorized years ago, a poem I forgot I knew.

I woke up late, alone on Bruce and Linda Gregory's bed, my mouth coated in red wine, Salade Niçoise ground into my hair. Except for a few minor details—couch pillows, crumbs, the odd carpet blemish—the house had been put back in order.

It was afternoon. Driveways stood empty and for a moment I thought my wife had accidentally locked me out until I found a stack of sandwiches and a glass of milk set outside the back door. There were three, peanut butter and jam, carbs and protein, hastily thrown together. I ate all three, one after another. Then I revised my notes in preparation for the meeting.

At five o'clock on the dot the neighbours filed into the backyard. They arranged themselves along familiar lines—the Andersons clustered next to the Smiths next to the Woodwards, families waving to families across polite distances.

I cleared my throat and mentioned that I'd been keeping an eye on the hybrids. "We all know they're sleeping beneath our shrubbery," I said, "but did you know they are also living inside our houses while we're at work?"

Alarmed murmurs.

"You may not detect the signs at first," I said, "but I suggest sniffing your pillows, checking the backs of bookshelves for volumes of poetry, philosophy, literary criticism. I suggest steaming up your mirrors and looking for messages written there."

They were whispering among themselves and I was beginning to sense skepticism.

"Now you might wonder how it is I know this," I said. "The truth is, I infiltrated one of their 'salons' last night, and what I found was rather fascinating. The funny thing is"—I tried to chuckle, but it worked itself into a frog, then a rattle, then a nineteenth-century cough.

"The funny thing is," I tried again, "I think these people may have something to offer. I think, when you find these clues I've mentioned, you might also encounter parts of yourself, long-forgotten parts: books you always meant to read, little notes you scribbled to yourself years ago. You might ask yourself, 'Who was I before all of this?' and 'When did *that* end and *this* begin?' You might reassess, I mean *really* reassess, and change your priorities. And you might start to wonder, 'Who's really free, us or them?'"

"Where's Kathy?" Mrs. Park asked.

"She'll be home any minute," I said.

"Why are you dressed like that?" one of the teenagers asked. Snicker, snicker went the rest.

"Well, I'm locked out and I haven't had a chance to—"

"You're locked out?" someone asked.

"Of your own house?" said someone else.

"What exactly is going on with you, Henry?"

"Hold on now. Hold on just a minute." I was that movie actor from It's a Wonderful Life, over-earnest, trying to control the angry mob. "I gathered you here to tell you about—"

"How long have you been living in the backyard, Henry?" someone interrupted.

"Wait,"—it was one of the teenagers—"didn't I see you sharing a sandwich with one of them yesterday?"

"You're getting this all wrong. This isn't about me. This is about our community and our way of life—"

Just then the back door opened. It was Kathy, home from work, and she was ushering the neighbours in the door. Like a funeral procession, each family stopped and whispered their apologies before entering my house. I brought up the back of the line. I whispered an apology too even though I wasn't sorry for anything, not really.

"You stay here," she said, her palm open on my chest. "I need some time." Her eyes travelled up and down my body, taking in my outfit. "Jesus, Henry," she said and then shut the door on me. I heard the twist of the lock.

An hour later the neighbours filed out—one bright goodbye after another. I could hear them out front, but I didn't go around. I waited by the back door until the sky grew dark from the east and the mosquitoes rose from the ravine. I waited for Kathy until the bedroom lights came on and moths clunked against the windows.

"Jennifer," I called up in a loud whisper, but she must've already been asleep.

I moved to the other window. "Kathy? Kathy?"

Finally a Kathy-shaped shadow came to the window, her triangle of hair, her small sad shoulders. *My wife.*

"Honey, I understand you're mad at me, but could you spare a little change? Just a little?"

But she just as quickly moved away.

The next morning there were only two sandwiches—no peanut butter, just marmalade—and water instead of milk. I tried to remember the previous day's joy but I was dirty and hungry and the tiny hairs of my beard were curling back on me.

I was working on a poem, something to move Kathy to forgiveness, when I heard the bright chirp of teenage-talk coming from the yard next door—not the Gregory side, but the other side.

I moved to the fence. I heard something about Jennifer first, some new boy she was dating. He was *way* better than her, they said; she was *totally* lucky. *That's my Jennifer*, I thought, *dating up!* Then their talk turned to me. Kathy was divorcing me, they said. I had lost my mind and my job and my wife all in one week.

I considered bribing them for entrance to their house. I could've finagled a shower and a shave, probably, maybe even one of their dad's suits. I could've headed downtown, talked to Dan, and apologized to Rhanda, begged for my job and fit right back into my old life, but I didn't. Instead I poked my head over the fence.

"Excuse me," I said. "When you say Jennifer's boyfriend is better, do you mean from a wealthier family or just more popular?"

They were frozen on the spot, baring their braces at me.

"Listen," I said, "I won't tell your parents you're skipping school if you give me some change. Just enough for a hamburger. And a coffee."

When Jennifer and Kathy got home later that evening, I was ready. I gave them a moment to get settled, to turn on some lights. Then I stood in the gazebo and yelled to the house. First, an invitation: "My daughter and my wife, my love and my life, please listen to what I have written. Please let me in my home. Please don't leave me out here alone." I saw their heads in the window and then I began to recite in my best approximation of French: "*La lune, la lune…*"

It rained that night, so I was forced to sleep in the shed between the lawnmower and the weed whacker. I could hear the hybrids in the distance. They were chanting something sounding like *heave-ho*, or *hobo*, or *let's go*. I read until I slept. I cried until my face was plastered to the pages of my father's diary.

I ate the last sandwich in the early morning, looking back at my house from the middle of the yard. This time it was only butter, stale bread, no drink. I knew what the next day would bring. I didn't want to be there to see it.

I looked at the building that had contained my life for so many years. Brick and mortar, wood and glass. I thought of my life inside those walls: a kind of mushroom sleep, happiness like a heavy lid. I tried to remember my wife as soft, the contours of her body, but all I could think about were bones, sinew, digestion, respiration—the materials and mechanisms that held her together. I noticed a place where the shingles had lifted off above the sunroom and it was as if I could see the future. There would be a leak in that spot soon. At night my wife and daughter would lay their cheeks in someone else's hair grease and dream of money and acquisition and accomplishment. Other people would read their books and sleep in their beds and Kathy and Jennifer would be forced to buy zit zappers and special creams to cure their mysteriously oily cheeks. They would buy air fresheners to cover the strange goat smells they sometimes found and they would straighten their bookshelves again and again, never knowing what went on while they were away because only a few ever do. Only a few are brave enough to admit that we're all living off each other, one way or another.

Meanwhile, I am moving south with Pinky and Constantine and the rest of the hybrids. We enter people's homes and, while the others deplete the food and drink the wine and lather on expensive shampoos, I find a patch of sunlight to curl up in with a good woman—Pinky, or the redhead, or the brunette—and she is wearing my father's sweater, and spooning me, wrapping me up in my father's brown sleeves, tugging me down, and my eyelids are filling with fire colours and I am drifting into dreams, dreams large enough to haunt the hollow rooms of another man's home, dreams of poetry and of history, of freedom and of motion. It is the future and I am right where I belong, dreaming troubadour dreams older than me.

PAUL CARLUCCI

THIS MORNING ALL NIGHT

THESE DAYS, OLD Jamie White takes his rum and rod to
Utmost Perch at four in the morning. He starts his day in the
kitchen, where he occupies a lone shaft of light, some dimming
beam offered by a stubborn star. He kisses Betty, his woken wife,
kettle steam wetting her cheeks as she pours tea into a Thermos
from which he seldom sips. He tips his hat to Jimmy, their son, a
bulb of boy planted on the couch, that rumbling snore soon to
furrow the pillows of Light Side College. Jamie likes the snoring
how he likes the tea, but these days he makes a show of appreci-
ating both. Things, he's learned, have a tendency to fade.

The constant night of Dark Corner is thickest in the morning, and that used to be all the advantage Jamie needed. There
are fewer stars in the early hours, and so the mammoth skyliners aren't yet netting, if indeed they're out at all. At least, that
was once the strategy. Things change.

Utmost Perch is a steep, rocky column about fifteen minutes from Jamie's front door. The Rambling Hills roll from the
house up to its base, and there the Perch climbs skyward, stands
tall like a monolithic utility pole from times prehistoric, those
forgotten days of myth and mayhem when giants used to

267

pluck the stars from the fabric of night with their hard, naked hands. They took only what they needed, Jamie's father used to yarn, and they were always sure to send a belch back into space, where heat and gas would provide anew.

There's something about poverty that encourages mythology. Jamie can appreciate that.

"Giants made the stars, m'son," the old man would slur, his breath thick with rum and smoke. "And giants want us to keep that sky well stocked."

Climbing the Hills to Utmost Perch, the tea Thermos forgotten on the front stoop and the snoring lost to the black of morning, Jamie quaffs his rum with one hand and twirls his nova rod with the other. He carries a rucksack full of bat jerky, gas-retarding gloves, and industrial, ultraviolet goggles. Also in the bag is his brand-new, cast-a-minute power reel.

The reel brings shame. His father would certainly sneer at it. But the old man is long gone, and, besides, he wouldn't understand what it means to cast off the Perch nowadays.

This particular star-stock used to be the most abundant of Dark Corner's once-bountiful sky. They used to call it The Broken Dozen, as if some astral housewife had overturned a batch of luminous eggs while baking bread. It lit up the whole valley back then. The Rambling Hills were like a disco dance floor, light glittering off the dew-drenched grass, and Jamie, unburdened by notions of age and oblivion, or the tyranny of depletion, would tumble across the undulating plain that unravelled from the edge of Spruce Grove. These days, he can't even see the forest, not even on the brightest of nights.

Back then, from way up the Perch, they could see Betty's home a mile or so into the grove. Jamie would spy as she washed clothes in a ten-gallon bucket while his father trawled the sky. Thoughts of the past always bring a tear to Betty's steam-soaked cheeks when she thinks of her quaint little home, the whole thing sucked up into that absolute night, nothing left of it but a well-lit memory.

The old days haunt Jamie, too. Catching stars was so easy back then. His dad would flick out a line, trawl around a few minutes, and in no time they'd be climbing down the Perch with a bag full of light.

These days, it takes hours for Jamie's line to even reach the star-bed. The darkness is heavy, defiant. Flashlights do nothing against it, and a creeping, dull roar, emanating from somewhere deep within, is the only sign of life or movement it allows. Jamie drinks between casts, his mind hobbled so as not to wonder towards the future. Giants may have made the stars, he sometimes thinks, eyes glued to an approaching skyliner, but it's giants, too, that steal them all away. And yet, knowing the score does nothing for his conscience: the rod still brings shame.

It's a sharp, cold morning, and Jamie is already drunk at the foot of the Perch. A fierce belt of rum, and he tallies this morning's offer. Skyliners are out in force, the moratorium of past months lifted because of fierce lobbying. They give off more glow than the stock itself, and Jamie has a hard time spotting his pool. He clips the nova rod to his rucksack and ascends the Perch, his calloused hands easily finding smooth, worn finger-holds.

Once ascended, Jamie finds the stump his father used to sit on. It was a throne back then; now it's just a haggard lump of wood. He digs mournfully in his rucksack, finds a piece of salty bat jerky, and, chewing on it, pulls out his goggles and gloves. He heaves a great sigh, one of those timeless, collective expulsions that travel around like electric current in search of some beleaguered conductor.

Time to provide, he thinks, his spirits quasi-optimistic from the excess of drink.

Noon, now, and old Jamie White has just one star in his rucksack. The skyliners head off into the black, fading from sight like phantoms after a kill. The rum is gone, and anxiety grows in its absence. He descends the Perch with knots in his guts. He traverses Rambling Hills with a tremor on his lips. One star in his bag, barely more in the sky.

He's been walking ten minutes, and, still, he can't see his house. The night grows hard around him, and he's standing on his stoop before he sees the front door. He grabbles clumsily for the tea Thermos, finds it and takes a swig in the hopes of masking his breath, then dumps the rest into the dark. He doesn't even hear it hit the ground.

He opens the door and holds out the bag, illuminating the kitchen table, where Betty sits drinking tea. He smiles, although she can't see; that morning's light beam is gone, its source likely netted by one of the skyliners, and the bag of light in Jamie's hand bleaches him out.

As for the source of the light beam, that faraway sun, it'll be served at one of Toronto's star bars. A waiter will hover over a table, the star in a fancy plate held up high, sand from far-flung beaches sprinkled around it. Wealthy young city folk, forward-thinking and upward-moving, will marvel over its beauty, will dine on its Platonian light, all the while trading statistics on rural abandonment in 2050.

Quickly—for this part, the employment of the payload, is always performed in haste—Jamie digs out his gloves and removes the star. The energy harness is mounted beside the coat rack, exactly where his father installed it decades ago. Jamie slides the star into the harness, and everything changes.

In the blink of an eye, the kitchen is awash in light. Jamie looks to Betty, sees the pupils dilate in her auburn eyes. A smile plays at her lips, coaxing the same from his. A film of promise settles over life in the beaten old house.

Jimmy, eyes bleary and salt-encrusted, strides into the kitchen with a stack of Light Side College program books tucked under his arm. Mother and father greet him warmly, pulling out a chair at the table, clearing space for the shaggy young man and his books.

"Good catch, Dad?" Jimmy asks, his thin lips twisted by a barely suppressed yawn.

"The best of the recent," Jamie lies.

Betty pours tea. Whether in times of worry or times of hope, times of family or times alone, tea, Betty feels, is an ever-necessary lubricant. "Pick all your courses, hon?" she asks.

"Yep. Just copying down the program codes now," he says. "I'll be sending them by post tomorrow, one week ahead of deadline."

Jamie reaches for one of the books and opens it randomly. This page is titled *Urban Design in Postmodern Societies*. Jimmy's quick, impatient hand marked the page with a check, and Jamie wonders why. Uncomfortable, he recalls the yawning gulf of darkness between the stump atop the Perch and the star-stock way out in the sky. Not all things are so completely out of his reach, he hopes. "What kind of designing will you do, son?"

"Urban design in postmodern societies, Dad," Jimmy says, his stubby fingers turning pages. "You'd like it, I bet."

Jamie is about to probe further, but the phone, restored to life by the star, begins to ring. Jamie shrinks from the sound. Never one for socializing via technology, he associates phones with bad news. It's Betty who moves for it, brushing a strand of shiny, blonde hair behind her ear as she lifts the receiver.

It's for Jimmy. He scrapes the legs of his chair off the warped, wooden floor, smiles briefly at his mother, and takes the phone from her. He faces the wall while he talks, grunting agreeably here and there. All smiles, he hangs up and wheels around.

"They've invited me down for next week," he gushes. "Orientation!"

Betty gets up from the table and envelops her son in an ambiguous hug. Jamie also gets up, slipping past the human entanglement of love and fear, and makes his way into the den. Standing next to a sagging bookshelf, he turns on the radio, causing the lights in the house to flicker.

He sighs, listens: "...appears to be only one star left. Despite pressure from lobbyists, who insist skywatchers are drastically underestimating what they, lobbyists, consider a self-replenishing stock, Minister Grady has reinstated the moratorium, saying it may be necessary to enforce it for decades."

Jamie turns the radio off and checks his pulse. He takes a number of deep breaths and heads to the kitchen after achieving a measure of calm. Inside, he finds mother and son still clinging to one another. Closer inspection shows only mother clinging, while son's eyes appear preoccupied, no doubt cataloguing a list of Light Side expectations.

Arms out and hands clasping, Jamie joins the desperation. His heart beats off Jimmy's broad shoulders. The boy's wild brown hair smells like pillowcases. Jamie suffers Betty's tiny hand pressed worriedly against the small of his back. Blinking back tears, he nudges her reassuringly with his elbow. Nobody says a word, and Jimmy gently struggles free of the embrace.

One star. One star, and the dark is casual tonight, not at all heavy, instead gathering at its core, stoking up to assume completely the land over which it's been yearning for years to consume.

One tiny star, and it twinkles unaffected by its solitude, ignorant of its colossal importance, innocent of its status, prized and pricey.

Outfitted with goggles and gloves, nova rod cast, Jamie slouches on the crest of Utmost Perch. Behind him, the stump is overturned, uprooted in a fit of drunken helplessness. He sees them, the skyliners. They are pirated, he knows, by outlaws on corporate payrolls. And they aren't far off. They push forward through the black, their sights set on Jamie's final catch.

His face grim and set, Jamie jerks his line, trying to force a snag. He clips the star once, sends it slowly travelling from its station. Cursing himself, he wheels in his line, now thankful for the cast-a-minute reel, and hurls it out again, begging the giants for an accurate cast.

The skyliners are alerted to his presence by the star's movement. A spotlight blasts him, and he knows these industrial rapists have a stockpile, knows they wastefully fuel their ships' instruments with stars caught during past excursions. Fearful of remaining in the light, he ducks behind the stump, careful not to loose his line.

And then he feels it. A current zaps down his line, travels through his rod and into his hands. Were it not for his gloves, he would surely be unconscious. Jolted instead by panic, he reels in the star, is mesmerized, as always, by the soft, white streak of its movement through space. But that beauty gives way instantly to terror: the star's wake is lit only by skyliners, and that light is piffling, bound to lose against the omnipotence of night.

The world, finally, is giving over to black.

And now the hurry. Jamie stuffs the star into his rucksack and staggers to the edge of Utmost Perch. He frantically searches for footholds, finds one, loses it, and falls to a plateau some ten feet below, twisting his ankle on impact. Ignoring the pain, thinking of the rusty all-terrain vehicle behind the house, he clambers the rest of the way down, cutting his palms to ribbons along the way.

An old man, he stumbles across the Hills. The skyliners rumble behind him, but he's too terrified to look over his shoulder and gauge the speed of their approach. He trips, falls, and rolls over, resigned to abduction by one of their tractor beams.

But they aren't behind him. The rumbling was simply the dark preparing to stake its victory.

He hurries home, using the glowing rucksack to light his way. Instead of charging indoors, he shuffles around the house, shaking the star free of the bag and slipping it into the engine of the ATV. The engine turns over, and Jamie shoves open the back entrance, yelling for Jimmy, telling the boy to hurry, for Christ's sake, there's no time to explain.

Jimmy, his soft features bent by fear, comes rushing to the back entrance. Jamie throws a coat at him and tells him to put his boots on. Betty comes out, her mouth gaping, trying for a question. Jamie pushes past her, running into the kitchen to collect Jimmy's books. He throws them at his son.

"Take them!" he screams. "Go!"

Jimmy stands there, uncertain.

"Go to your school now, son," Jamie says, his voice suddenly calm and commanding.

"Um, okay," Jimmy whispers, frightened and confused. "I'll see you all at Reading Week, then, right?"

"Yes, son," Jamie maintains. "Of course."

He ushers the boy over the threshold and slams the door in his face.

"Why did you do that?" Betty yelps.

Jamie sees her in the fading light of yesterday's catch. He takes her hand, still soft after all these years, and leads her to the kitchen table, sitting her down and preparing tea.

"Why did you do that, Jamie?"

The light flickers out before the tea is ready, and Jamie finds a seat next to his wife.

"If he hurries," Jamie says, collapsing into his chair, "they won't find him. Besides, breaking the seal hurts the value. They might not even be interested anymore."

They link hands in the totality of the roaring night. The pirates will never find them, Jamie assures her.

She squeezes his hand and strokes his thumb.

"No, Jamie," she says. "No one will."

SHEILA HETI

conceived with Margaux Williamson

THERE IS NO TIME IN WATERLOO

EVERYONE IN WATERLOO was an amateur physicist, and they
endlessly bugged the real physicists as the physicists sat in cafés
talking to each other. The amateurs would approach and put
questions to them; simple questions, obvious ones. Or else they
asked questions that even a physicist couldn't answer, or questions that weren't in the realm of physics at all, but had more
to do with biology or straight computation. People who know
almost nothing about what they're talking about are often more
enthusiastic than the ones who know a lot, so they do all the
talking, while the ones who know their shit stay silent and get
red in the face.

Whenever a real physicist would start to correct or explain a
point, the amateur would smile and nod, and would loudly pro-
claim that they'd read something about that in a magazine or
book recently. Then they would start explaining it and the physicist would listen, tight-lipped, or else abruptly put an end to the
conversation in frustration.

Then the physicist would return to the Perimeter Institute,
which was built on the top of a gently sloping hill, and sigh in
relief to be home again, standing at the chalkboard, working out
equations.

One afternoon in March, a rumour went around town that some boy's Mothers had predicted that a kid was going to blow up the mall on the left side of town, so all the teenagers got on their scooters and sped off towards the parking lot there.

As Sunni was leaving her apartment, her mother called out from her usual place on the couch and asked where she was going. Sunni returned and explained about the rumour, saying that she was really eager to see the mall be blown up; that she and her friends had so much pent-up energy—they were wild with energy and simply couldn't wait.

Sunni's mother felt a bit of regret that her daughter was going to watch the mall explode, but she didn't object. After all, if that was Sunni's destiny, who was she to interfere?

At the mall the teenagers spoke excitedly with each other, drawing together and apart, eager for the show to begin. They asked around to discover whose Mothers had predicted the explosion, but no one seemed to know. When after an hour the mall still remained standing, undisturbed, they each started checking their Mothers to see if they were the one destined to blow it up. It appeared that none of them was.

Now they began to grow tense and upset. It was not the first time something like this had happened. A week before, some boy's Mothers had predicted a fight, but no one had thrown the first punch. A month ago, there was supposed to have been an orgy in back of the other mall, the nice one, but after standing around awhile they had checked their Mothers and learned that the probability of their participating in an orgy was really low.

It started to rain, as a weatherman had predicted. Dispirited, the teenagers began to drift off. Only Sunni and a few of her friends remained, to finish the conversation they'd been having about film. They each had their own distinct opinions about art, but came together in agreement that surprise in drama was an inaccurate reflection of life; the best stories followed the path of greatest likelihood. Indeed, when you thought about the best stories down through time, their greatness and terror came from the fact that the most predictable and probable thing always occurred.

"Like in Oedipus," Sunni said, watching her friend Danny as he lit up his cigarette with an old-fashioned butane lighter whose flame danced high in the air. As the boy tried to snap it closed smoothly, a fumbling occurred, and it tumbled, aflame, onto Sunni's hand and her Mothers, igniting the casing in a sudden burst.

"Oh, *fuck!*" Sunni cried, batting her Mothers into the air; it arced, smoking, and dropped on the pavement, the lighter clattering beside it.

"Oh my God, Sunni—is your Mothers dead?" Danny gasped.

"Nope! Nope! Luckily no!" Sunni replied, picking it up. It was burning hot, and she tossed it from hand to hand. Looking down as it cooled, she saw that the screen had been melted into a squinty little eye. The keys were matted down to their wires, and the casing was tarry and charred.

"Still works!" Sunni announced. Then she got onto her scooter, feeling like she was about to faint, and rode to the parking lot around the other side of the mall, her Mothers propped behind the windshield. She kept glancing at it, but no glance transformed it from the twisted, charry mess it had been in the glance before.

In the back parking lot, she stopped her scooter and got off and doubled over, hyperventilating a bit, then ran a distance to throw up. This vomiting might have been because she was pregnant. Most of her friends were; they knew that there was a greater probability of having a successful career and a nice-looking body if they gave birth while still young, and their Mothers pushed them in this direction.

When Sunni returned at last to her Mothers and saw it there on the windshield, she was overtaken by a spell of vertigo. It wasn't clear yet whether its destruction was the worst, most tragic thing that had ever happened to her, or if this was the most exciting moment of her life. She only knew that she had never felt such dizziness before, and upon asking herself what to do now, then glancing down reflexively at her Mothers for the answer, she grew overwhelmed by vertigo once more.

Twenty years earlier, the citizens of Waterloo had grown enthralled by a book written by a physicist who had been invited to spend some time at Perimeter. The book was called *The End of Time*, and its author had argued in a persuasive and beautiful way that time did not exist; the universe was static. There were a slightly less than an infinite number of possible moments hanging about, like paintings in an attic, all real but out of reach, and each person's destiny was nothing more and nothing less than the most probable of these possible futures.

The people most taken with this idea led fervent discussions on how to best realize the theory in one's life. Like humans anywhere, they didn't want to waste their time. They hoped to reach their destinies as quickly and efficiently as possible—not their ultimate destinies, just their penultimate ones. And so it made sense to try and act as much in accordance with probability as they could.

The executives at the BlackBerry headquarters in Waterloo decided they would capitalize on this desire, and they began producing a machine they tagged *The Mother of All BlackBerrys*. It remained a phone you could email from, but it had an added, special feature: given ongoing inputs, it was calibrated to determine for each user what they were destined to do next.

"It will be a device that determines a person's most likely next action based on previous behaviours. If the input is one's life, then the outcome is one's life," an executive explained to the rest as they sat around a table.

"Brilliant!" said another executive, reaching for a Danish. And they all reached for Danishes, and toasted each other, smiling.

The Mothers—as people began calling them—were at once a huge success. They eclipsed everything in culture at that moment, like any great fad down through time. People in Waterloo consulted their Mothers at every turn, and it quickly became as impossible to live without a Mothers as it had once been to not check email. People wondered how they had managed their lives before the Mothers. They even bought Mothers for their babies.

If life became somewhat more predictable as a result, it was also more comforting, and soon the citizens of Waterloo didn't even notice that they were going in circles; that it was always the same thing over and over again.

The physicists, though nominally to blame for the proliferation of the Mothers, were largely skeptical and had a hundred doubts, so it was not unusual to be standing in a supermarket line-up and hear one of them testily provoke and challenge an amateur physicist who was checking his Mothers, if the physicist was having a particularly bad day. "So, do these Mothers calculate quantum or classical probabilities?" the physicist might ask; a question over which the amateur might stumble, only to regain his footing upon consulting his Mothers about whether continuing the conversation would be to his benefit, to which the Mothers would reply that the probability was low.

What will Sunni do without her Mothers? I sometimes ask myself a similar question. What would I do if I didn't know what was to come? If the inputs of my past were to disappear, I'd have no idea how I behaved in relationships past, and would

not know how to behave in them now. I would play it all differently, not knowing how I was likely to behave. I might forget
how much I once hated to be on a soccer pitch, but was forced
onto the field, and have avoided soccer ever since. I might, while
lounging in a park, say to the soccer players, while rising, *Do you
need an extra player?*

If you draw a line across a piece of paper, that is King Street.
Now draw a small, perpendicular line crossing King Street
near the centre. That is Princess Street. That is the part of town
where losers, misfits, and orphans hang out. It's where someone
crosses the street drunk, and someone else crosses the street
with ripped jeans and a lazy eye.

On either end of King Street, draw a square. These are the
two malls. The mall at the right end of town is in the richer
neighbourhood, near the Perimeter Institute, the University,
and the Institute for Quantum Computing—all those institutions representing the heights of Waterloo's excellence. The
other mall, the one the teenagers gathered at, is situated near
the Old Town Hospital, City Hall, and the more run-down
establishments that deal with humanities and the human body.

Now watch Sunni speed along the long line of King Street,
arriving within minutes at Princess.

Sunni was like all her friends and all her friends were like Sunni.
Their machines represented the part of the brain that sees
patterns and nothing but patterns. To that part of the brain,
everything fits. There is no randomness to life, no chance. If ever
their Mothers missed something, or something not predicted
occurred, it would correct for the future, learning from what
had happened and fitting this new thing into a better, more
complete image of the whole. In this way, if not everything was

already accounted for, Sunni and her friends had faith that in time it would be.

Sunni had always avoided Princess Street, since only losers hung out there. But since nearly every teenager whose Mothers broke wound up on Princess, it was where she decided to go now. She still had the instincts of someone with a Mothers, and wanted to waste no time before moving on to the likeliest next stage of her destiny. She parked her scooter and walked straight into one of the bars, pushing its red door open.

Two teenagers she had never seen before were sitting on tall stools, smoking and drinking, and upon entering Sunni could hear them whisper: *Doesn't she look like Shelly? No, but she reminds me a lot of my grade-four gym teacher. Actually, today in its entirety reminds me a lot of grade four.*

Sunni went to perch on the stool beside them and said hi, placing her hand below her slightly heavy belly. They regarded her blankly. Without waiting for a sign of their interest, she explained that she had lost her Mothers that day.

The boy nodded solemnly. Once your Mothers is dead, he knew, it's gone for good. The factory had shut down years before due to a lack of demand for the Mothers beyond Waterloo, and not a single repair shop in town knew how to fix the machines. The boy explained that the very same thing had happened to him four years ago, but told Sunni not to worry; life would not be as different as she feared. Having said this, he turned to face his friend, finishing up the anecdote he had been telling about his childhood, concluding, "And I still feel its reverberations today." Then the two of them put down their money and began packing their bags to leave.

"Wait! Wait! Where are you going?" Sunni cried anxiously, and the boy sighed deeply and said, "Relax. Personality is as static as time; it's a fixed law. People don't change. As long as you remember that, you'll be all right. Now we have to go and write in our diaries." And they left.

Sunni, still sitting there, glanced down at her Elders pin as it began to blink and beep. Then she jumped up from the stool and left.

Time is a measurement of change. The change in the position of quantum particles cannot always be known, because they don't seem to exist in any fixed spot. At the level of human bodies, we can see that time has passed because one moment I'm here at this bar, the next I'm at City Hall. But at the quantum level, everything is cloudy. This is the mechanism for the disappearance of time. The people of Waterloo liked the timeless theory because, deep down, they felt it. Their lives, in so many ways, reflected it. The science simply stamped their intuition with the air of authority and truth.

"No," said a physicist, standing in the park under the gazebo, to the twenty-odd citizens picnicking around her. "We *don't* all believe that time is static."

The picnickers smiled up at the physicist. They continued to eat their bread and sandwiches and throw their strawberries into the grass.

Though Sunni left for City Hall as soon as she received the call, she arrived a little later than everyone else. The other Elders were already there, waiting for the emergency meeting to begin.

The teenagers of Waterloo, whose Mothers had been receiving inputs since the day they were born, were believed by everyone to have a more accurate grasp of what the future would hold. Compared to their Mothers, their parents' Mothers were deeply lacking: twenty, thirty years unaccounted for. So a special place in Waterloo was reserved for the young. They were given much respect. They bore the official title Double Special Elders, since having a particular destiny is the essence of being Special. They were paraded about on ceremonial occasions and called in to advise the city on all the important matters.

Sunni crept quietly through the side door, up to her seat in the fourth row of the dais, which seated thirty across. Already Waterloo's 250 native-born teens were in their seats, and they glanced at Sunni and watched her take her place, though she had tried to make her entrance subtle. The mayor, standing at the podium before them, was in the midst of explaining the current crisis, but after two minutes, Sunni was still totally lost, so she whispered to the boy beside her, asking him what she had missed.

He replied quickly, "This morning Perimeter received word from Africa that all the problems in physics have been solved."

"*What?*" she whispered back. "Are you *sure?* The measurement problem and—"

"Yes, yes, *everything*," he insisted hotly. Then he rolled his eyes. "Don't ask me."

Sunni slumped back in her chair, stunned. The mayor was now on to the mundane, municipal details, explaining how much it cost the city to fund the institute, claiming that it would be humiliating for Waterloo to carry on the project of physics when the field was now kaput. He gestured at the two physicists who had come to explain the proof, should anyone want to hear it. He said that they represented the physicists who believed the institute should be kept alive—not because the African proof was wrong; it wasn't—but for reasons that he, the mayor, did not completely understand, though if one of the Elders wanted to hear their reasoning, the physicists could give it. As for the rest of the physicists, they were too preoccupied with going over the proof to attend the meeting that day.

"Would any of the Elders like to see the African proof?" the mayor asked.

Sunni looked around tentatively. No one else seemed to want to hear it, but she wanted to know, so she awkwardly raised her hand. The mayor nodded at the physicists, and the younger of them stood and went to the whiteboard and began drawing an equation and a little diagram. He turned to the Elders and began to speak. He was only a few sentences into his elucidation when the mayor interrupted him to exclaim:

"Aha—look! It's like an earthworm praying!"

At which point the young physicist violently threw his marker onto the ground and left the whiteboard and sat down beside his friend. He was too upset by the events of the day to push forward. It wasn't even so awful that a proof had been found; the pain in his heart was about how unsatisfying a proof it was. It just wasn't the beautiful, elegant thing that everyone had been hoping for.

Sunni wanted to ask the physicists what the African proof said about the unreality of time, but just as she was about to raise her hand again, the boy next to her leaned over and pointed at Sunni's Mothers, which she still reflexively clasped tightly in the palm of her hand.

"Is your Mothers *dead*?" he gasped.

Sunni, hiding it quickly beneath her sweater, replied with feigned ease, "Nah, it's just a new sleeve. My architect friend made it. He's cool."

"I wouldn't want a sleeve that looked like that."

"Never mind."

"You should take that sleeve off."

"One day I will."

Then the mayor turned to the teenagers and asked, "Should Perimeter be closed?" In this way voting began.

The first Elder spoke: "Yes."

The second Elder looked up from her Mothers, which knew that once you began talking about ending something, usually that thing ends. "Yes!"

The third Elder spoke. "Yes."

And on and on it went: yes yes yes yes yes yes yes.

Now it was Sunni's turn. She hesitated, glancing down at the blank screen of her Mothers, which she had pulled out again. It was still a twisted, black, charry mess. She took a deep breath, and said very quietly, though loud enough for everyone to hear: "I am no longer Special."

Then she stood up from her place on the dais and climbed carefully down the steps. It was a humiliating walk, one others had performed before her while she had watched in pity and fear. Behind her there rose a wall of whispering; it was the world Sunni had been part of, sealing itself off behind her.

She walked past the mayor and beyond the physicists, towards the doors at the end of the hall. Just before she slipped out, she heard the mayor announce the tally of the vote: it was unanimous. Perimeter was to be shut down within the hour.

"Fucking teenagers," the older physicist muttered.

Sunni stepped out into the breezy air of the afternoon, blinking in the brightness of the day. Her face felt oddly hot. She stood on the steps of City Hall, faintly bewildered. Her eyes rested on a tree that stood a short distance in the grass, and she watched it gently sway, moved by the breeze. What would move her, now that her Mothers was dead? With each day, she felt, her destiny would be less and less clear, and less and less would what was probable be the law that ran her life. She tried to imagine what other law might come to replace it, but no other laws came to mind.

Perhaps, she mused, she could learn about living from this tree—let the laws that moved it move her as well. At base, she knew, she was made up of the very same substance as the tree; she must be, in some sense, treelike. She stepped down onto the lawn.

At that moment, her attention was distracted by some vague sounds in the distance. She squinted. Soon she could discern a lethargic parade approaching from the far end of King Street. After watching a bit longer, she realized what it was: a small tide of physicists was flowing from the doors of Perimeter. They came closer, heaving down King Street with stooped postures, dazed, carrying boxes of computers, papers, and chalk, streaming towards their cars, which would take them back to the university towns from which they had come.

"How pathetic," came a small voice.

Sunni turned around and noticed that sitting cross-legged beneath the tree was a scrawny boy around her own age. From the first glance she could tell that he was a loser, but such a loser he wasn't even a Princess Street loser.

"They don't have to leave," he said.

"But it's their destiny." Sunni replied, moving closer. "I was in the meeting. I saw it happen."

The boy looked up at her skeptically, pushing his bangs away. "Destiny? What a word! These physicists don't believe in the future. Most of them don't, anyway. I know it. I'm good friends with some of them."

"But—" Sunni shook her head. "If there's no destiny, how can you know what's going to happen next?"

The boy, whose name was Raffi, frowned. He paused a moment, then went on to quietly explain, barely raising his voice above a whisper, so that Sunni had to move closer to hear.

He told her that last year's Bora Bora proof, which contributed to the African proof, revealed that not everything that comes to pass can be known in advance; rather everything is in a continuous state of co-creation and co-evolution with everything else. The future is utterly non-computable and non-predictable—possibly not mathematical, in essence, at all. No future can exist until it exists, since we are all creating reality together in a radically flexible present. "Like, things can happen all sorts of different ways," he said.

Sunni sat back hard against the tree. She was flustered by all that this boy was saying. But the Bora Bora proof was impossible! Absurd! She turned her head as the Double Special Elders began emerging from the tall doors of City Hall and spreading across the lawn, heads bent low over their Mothers as they decided where to go next. She was about to say something when, in the distance, a blue spiral burst into the world, lighting up the sky. Sunni felt like she was going to vomit, felt like her insides had been scooped out with a spoon.

"It's the action," Raffi said quietly. "It's coming closer, I see."

"What action?" Sunni asked.

Raffi said slowly, looking at her again, "You're a Double Special Elder through and through. You didn't even know."

Now another explosion burst blue in the distance, near the mall on the left side of town. A high-pitched radial whistle was emanating from the spiral, and Raffi got up like a smooth animal. He bent over and started rummaging in the large duffle bag that had been lying beside him in the grass.

Sunni pushed herself closer to the tree, scared. In the distance, a physicist in a red overcoat turned around and began walking towards them. Raffi looked up to answer the question on Sunni's face and said, "It's a Spiral. We might know how to handle this." The physicist came near and Raffi walked off with her, in the direction of Perimeter and through its front doors.

Now Sunni was alone. She found herself, for the time, watching the Elders, many of whom were gazing into the distance where the spiral still hung. Sunni observed them glance down at their Mothers to make sense of it; to know how to respond. But their Mothers had no valuable insight; could not fit the spiral into the pattern; had never known such a thing before.

Get on your scooter and go home, was the instruction that appeared on their screens; an instruction applicable to many situations, and the most common one.

The teenagers made their way to their scooters, seemingly sure in their movements, for somewhere inside they felt a reassurance: it was not that their Mothers lacked insight about this new thing, but that the question they had posed to their Mothers about the explosion was not a pertinent one. What happened in the distance had nothing to do with the patterns in their lives. It had nothing to do with all the ways they were Special.

They got on their wheels and, like the physicists, sped off from the heart of town.

Sunni looked up as an acorn fell from the tree and landed on her head. She thought about what she knew.

With special thanks to physicists Sean Gryb, Aaron Berndsen, Lee Smolin and Julian Barbour

HEATHER O'NEILL

THE DREAMLIFE OF TOASTERS

IN THE SUMMER of 2075 a female android named 4F6 stopped on her way home from the pharmaceutical factory and stood looking at the stars. As she gazed up, visions flashed above her.

Androids were designed, half a century ago, with superior eyesight to humans' so that they could work on the tiniest computer parts. A side effect of this provision was that when they looked up into the sky at night, they were able to perceive thousands more stars, thousands more configurations and astral phenomena than the average human eye could ever discern. When they walked at night, they could not help but look up into the sky and marvel. In fact, this was the easiest way to tell an android from a human. Androids were the ones on the street with their briefcases dangling at their sides, staring at the stars in wonder. For this reason, androids were no longer given driving licences—it led to too many accidents, this ability to be struck by perfect things.

4F6 imagined the stars were a group of ancient coal miners with lamps on their helmets being lowered by elevator into a deep dark hole. Imagining in this way was not typical of robots; but 4F6 had known she was different from other androids for a long time. Once, during rush hour four years ago, she had been shoved onto the subway tracks and, as she hit the rail, an electric current had surged through her. Since that time, her electrical currencies had been too high.

She had already experienced some peculiar side effects from her accident. She was able to turn on lights just by looking at them. And unlike other androids, she was able to tell when something was funny. She was forever explaining jokes she had overheard from humans to the other androids she worked with. They couldn't understand them at all. To them jokes were merely equations with slightly incorrect answers. That was one of the reasons humans avoided befriending androids—they found them cold.

As 4F6 was standing there, peacefully looking up at the stars, she realized that another android in a tweed suit was standing right beside her also staring up at the night sky.

Naturally, they introduced themselves. Androids were always very cordial as this greatly increased workplace efficiency. 4F6 liked BX19 immediately. She liked his brown eyes and his pale skin. He told her that he worked transcribing trials at the courthouse. He began to repeat verbatim one of the cases he had sat in on that day. A man was on trial for murdering his ex-wife's new boyfriend. He had strangled her boyfriend with his bare hands and now showed no remorse. Then he told her the story of a man who had held up an atom bar and only got away with fifteen proton tablets and had subsequently been sentenced to fifteen years in prison.

4F6 was moved by these stories. She had never had anyone say such things to her. The only kind of talk she ever heard was from the other androids at the pharmaceutical factory who spoke solely of formulae and the periodic table of elements. All this talk of murder and love, to her, was like poetry.

Somewhere within 4F6's circuitry there stirred a desire to reach out and touch BX19. Androids often mimicked human behaviour out of curiosity. They had, of course, tried kissing and lovemaking, and certain androids claimed they had felt something, but it was the general consensus that they were unable to feel anything at all while engaging in such activities. 4F6 herself had never been kissed before.

"Please kiss me," she said.

BX19 leaned over and did as he was told. He was just being polite, but when his lips touched her lips, 4F6's heart felt like it had dunked into her stomach. When that happens with humans, it is just a sensation, but with an android, every emotion has a mechanical reaction. Miniature wires and bolts fell from inside her chest into her stomach. 4F6 felt the metal parts moving around in her belly, as if they were the insides of one of those alarm clocks she'd seen in a museum. But later that night, lying in bed, the discomfort she was feeling in her stomach was the furthest thing from her mind. She replayed the kiss over and over, until her short-term memory projector snapped off as she drifted into sleep.

The next morning, as 4F6 was gaining consciousness, as she lay in bed staring at the ceiling, she felt something fall from between her legs. She pulled off her blankets and rummaged through the sheets, searching for the errant part. Her hand touched something cold and metallic. She pushed away the thermal duvet and there, wrapped in her bedding, was a tiny stick-like figure.

Its skeleton was made of wires and tiny screws and bolts. It had a small spring for a spine and frayed, spliced wire grew out of its head like hair. It had tightly wound wire for a neck, and where a heart would go, there was a tiny valve that looked as if it could be cranked. The little thing started to move its arms in the air over itself. It was obviously some sort of robot, but it didn't look human the way androids did.

The little thing looked at 4F6 through the holes in the minuscule spark plugs he had for eyes. There was an awful darkness and limitlessness to those eyes.

Could this be a baby, her baby, conceived from her first kiss? The gestation period for the tiny robot had only been a day. 4F6 had never heard of robots making robots—perhaps on a factory assembly line, but never without being told to and never in a bed, and *never* as the result of a spontaneous kiss. She knew that something horribly wrong had happened.

Although androids didn't really know what it meant beyond the softer skin and crooked teeth, they wished to be human. They considered themselves inferior and got tongue-tied around people. Whenever they saw a human, they couldn't help but think: he invented me. Humans did not know what their origins had been. Some of them believed in God and searched for the meaning of life in the Bible. Androids, on the other hand, had no Bible, no Koran, no Talmud. The closest thing they had to a creation myth was the original grant application that the Department of Artificial Intelligence had requested for the funding of robotics research in 2015. Every android had a copy of this proposal. It was a bestseller among androids. It said that the applicants of that grant wanted to create a robot capable of operating all of human kind's other inventions, thus significantly reducing the workday. There was never any debate about the origins of existence or the meaning of life among androids.

But now this baby robot had been created by some unknown force, independent of man. 4F6 knew that this would not be taken lightly.

She worried that if the scientists found out about the baby there would be a mass android recall. The scientists would tamper with their insides, making sure that no other android would be capable of experiencing love as 4F6 had, because it was love that had created the little spring man, she was sure. They would take away the androids' ability to be amazed by stars, too, for good measure. Without these abilities 4F6 would only be an appliance—a machine.

She wrapped the tiny robot in a sock and put him in her briefcase. She called in to work to say that she would be a little late that day because she was going to stop at the Android Servicing Unit to be recharged. Instead, she took the bus all the way to the edge of town.

When the bus reached the end of the line, she walked down an empty street, and as she walked she convinced herself that what she was about to do was necessary for the safety of androids everywhere. It was not an easy task, this convincing. 4F6 was programmed to know when to yell and when to whisper, when to fuel up and when to rest; but in this matter, she was not certain what she knew at all. Had anyone been watching her, they would have seen a woman walking along haltingly, as though looking for a street address she wasn't sure existed.

4F6 had been to the dump many times before. It was a hobby of hers. She enjoyed estimating how many pieces of debris were contained within each pile, but she was not interested in that today. She had no desire for calculating. She took the baby robot out of her briefcase and threw it over the fence onto a heap of garbage. That's where it belongs, she thought: it was junk—a broken, incomplete thing.

She repeated this to herself over and over as she waited for the bus, boarded it, and returned to work. Several years earlier she had had her temperature regulator exchanged. In the moments while she lay on the metal gurney, her chest-plate opened, the old part removed and the new part not yet inserted, she had really felt fine and complete. The little wire thing that had fallen from her was not even half the size of the temperature regulator, yet back at the factory assembly line, as she stood making calculations on her clipboard, she had the sensation of being empty. As much as she considered the matter, it did not make any sense to her. Yet there it was.

At the dump, there were seagulls circling above, crying out as though in pain. The tiny robot, lying on his back, wished that one of the birds would swoop down and pick him up in its claws because he wanted so badly to be held; but the seagulls, yanking apart plastic bags and perching on top of old refrigerators, seemed interested in everything at the dump except him.

As it started to get dark, the little robot began to feel more and more alone. He stood up on his feet, which looked like tiny salad forks, and stumbled over the garbage. He passed a coat rack that looked like a thin man looking out to sea. He passed an old shoe, piles of books and tin cans, green metal chairs, and couches with cushions covered in coffee stains. Then, amidst all of it, he saw something that comforted him: a toaster. The robot hurried over and wrapped his arms around it, circling its electrical cord around his body. He lay there, entwined with the toaster, and in this way, he tried to assure himself that, somehow, he was loved.

When the stars came out, so numerous and fantastic, the little robot was so struck by the utter mystery of the universe that he forgot, at least for those moments, that he was alone in the world.

As he gazed up at the stars, he was moved by quizzical thoughts, thoughts that, could he articulate them, might take the form of such words as *Why am I here? How big is the universe? Why am I me and not someone else?*

Although androids all over the world had been coming up with infinitely complex answers for over fifty years, the little robot was the first to ask a question.

OLIVER KELLHAMMER
CRUSH

"H-E-E-EY, WILLEE BOY!"

I was back in that dream again; the one where I'm standing on deck, watching my disembodied stomach get tossed like a vomit-filled handbag over an endless expanse of waves.

"Will-*ee!*"

My inflamed eyelids cracked open to an assault of fluorescent light. "*Cool-White.*" Whoever invented that colour? It makes everything look so dingy and sick. But then again I *was* so dingy and sick. Perpetually nauseated, sick of the world and sick of myself. The ghost of that barf purse still hung on my retinas like a bad hologram. The thrum of the ship's engines seemed louder than ever; boring through my pillow, jiggling into my brain. The bedclothes reeked of diesel and intestinal fermentation. A wretched night at its wretched end. I reared up onto my elbows. Through the salt-splattered Plexi of the porthole, a sallow dawn making its way across a graphite horizon. Another tedious day yawning out in front of me.

"Will-*ee!* Way-kee, way-kee."

That little Filipino birdman fuck. I hated being called Willy, especially by the crew. The name's Williamson. Stefan Williamson. But I let it go. Besides, Rodger was a sweet old creature; a kind of mechanical intuitive who basically kept the *Tethys* going when the remote diagnostics didn't—which was most of the time. He did so entirely by ear, sensing the nuances the computers had missed, always tweaking potentiometers with his tiny screwdrivers. It was amazing he was still on the payroll. Head office had no idea he'd gone blind.

In the interstices between crashing waves, I heard him down the corridor, clattering the breakfast dishes in the galley. Maybe the weather had calmed down a bit. That was about all I could have hoped for. The warm, armpit smell of his coffee soon suffused the cabin's chill, then the heaviness of pyrolizing animal fats. I forced the bile down my throat and pressed my feet to the humming steel floor. It was time to get up.

We'd left the Strait of Juan de Fuca almost eight days before. The pummelling had begun as soon as we'd entered the open ocean, a conveyor belt of gargantuan waves that had been building unimpeded across the width of the Pacific. Nausea and delirium had once again confined me to my cabin. I felt worse every time I signed on for one of these fish-stick trips and now it was getting so I could hardly stand it any more. Pretty embarrassing for a marine biologist. But I wasn't here to do any actual science. Drone trawlers didn't need *captains*, let alone biologists. Maybe that was what was twisting my gut. I was on board so C-Corp could call what they were doing "research." To the rest of the crew, I was just a dickhead.

I wobbled down the shifting corridor, steadying myself against the bulkheads like some glue-sniffer coming down off a toot.

"Will-*ee*, You're *up*!"

"Yes, I am," I sighed bitterly. I could barely see Rodger through the aerosolized grease that hung over him like a cloud of blue ectoplasm. He was scraping something viscera-like off a skillet. The fluorescents were really buzzing now, drilling into my temples. My stomach started to tremble again and I thought I'd better try to tame it before it did the full-on loop-de-loop. I grabbed my chipped blue mug and poured myself a coffee from the battered aluminum urn. I had an odd nostalgia for that thing, its worn Bakelite spigot—old and comforting, a traveller through time from the dawn of plastic.

"So we're almost there, hey Will-*ee* Boy?"

"Maybe so, Rodge." I was hedging, noncommittal. I didn't have a clue if what he was saying was true. But I should have known. It was annoying how the crew always knew stuff way before I did. Even old Rodge. He was blind for fuck sake. Our destination was supposed to be secret. Nobody but me was supposed to know where we were headed. That way the competition wasn't going to get tipped off. Those were the C-Corp rules. "Total Quality Assurance," they called it. I hadn't been given any activation updates. Not that I'd paid much attention.

The coffee was oily, scalding, with a hint of reheated decay, and immediately it triggered a spasm just below my sternum. Maybe I was taking things a little too quick. Clunking the mug down on the wood-grain Formica table, I gazed bleary-eyed across the ladder that lead up to the bridge's port side. It was like I'd never seen it before. It's true, I'd hardly been up there lately, though technically I should have been, as the guy who was somewhat in charge. But I wasn't inclined to play pretend-captain. The *Tethys* was tethered completely through her satellite link to the C-Corp headquarters over in Taipei; her navigation systems, engine revolutions, trawl deployment, and haul processing systems were all remotely controlled. The crew was just there to clean up the messes. And there were always messes.

C-Corp's headquarters glowered at us from every e-pad and computer display that we had on board. A giant, oven-mitt-like tower, clad in a titanium skin that reflected the viridian, subtropical hills around it like a funhouse mirror or a surrealist terrarium. I had no idea if the building, or even C-Corp, actually existed. For all I knew, we could have been being controlled by some buzzed-out geek-for-hire pubescent squeezing us in between rounds of *Pony Play Porn* and *Slime Mould Apocalypse*. I wouldn't have known the difference—nor did I care, as long as my pay credits kept on rolling in.

I don't know what it was that came over me, but I found myself heading over to the ladder and hauling myself up, gripping hard on the handrails to compensate for the ship's lurching and the maddening morning weakness of my legs. It was only eight rungs up, but by the time I reached the top, I badly needed to sit down. Pushing through the bridge door, I was hit by a curtain of stale smoke, like from a recently extinguished garbage fire but with notes of old sweat and melted styrene. A swarm of Cheeze Kurls lay strewn over the instrument panel and onto the floor. I brushed off the Naugahyde captain's chair and fell into it, my life force spent as if sucked by invisible vampires.

The debris of many nights' partying crammed every available surface with bottles, cans and plastic cups, cigarette butts leaching their amber exudate into the drinks' dregs, scrunched-up packages of Mild 7s, a riot of gutted chip bags—it all made a perversely cheery contrast to the panorama of monochrome ocean that heaved ceaselessly beyond the expanse of rain-spattered windows. Looking down, I noticed a crack pipe, its scorched glass tube with the little wad of Chore Boy still jammed into the end of it, lying forlornly on the console in front of me. I slipped it like a bad little friend into my shirt pocket.

Maybe it would come in handy again, I reasoned; it could help with my nausea, maybe even cheer me up. I'd missed out on the nightly revelries so far, locking myself in my sour-smelling cabin, watching the walls spin from my dishevelled bunk. Drinking and bumping with the crew might have helped me pass the time. Not that long ago, that would have been a lot of fun. But lately I'd been trying to prove something, only I'd forgotten exactly what.

Besides, I'd got the feeling the others didn't much like having me around anymore. Maybe I was tainted by the hopelessness all over my face. I'd stopped trying to hide it, stopped trying to pretend that everything was okay. Who'd want to be around that all the time?

I tilted up the grease-smeared screen of the GPS:

latitude 50 degrees 21 minutes north

longitude 130 degrees 44 minutes west

Still off the northwest coast of Vancouver Island. Somewhere beyond yesterday, obviously, but outside the window it looked exactly the same as everywhere else we'd been on this godforsaken stretch of North Pacific—the roiling waves, the leaden sky, an occasional seabird skimming its way across the spray. A restless, endless surface of churning possibilities. No place and everyplace all wrapped up in one. Yet a little red blip was throbbing in the middle of the screen; a new blip, the blip we'd been waiting for since the beginning of the trip. C-Corp had made its move. It was time to get ready. It now seemed so sudden and yet it hadn't come soon enough. The momentum that had somehow propelled me up that ladder had vanished into a sucking tiredness. All I wanted now was to get back to my bunk. I felt my chest tighten, the panic enzymes rising into it like poison sap. Clicking closed the bridge door, I started back down. There wouldn't be much for me to do. My job was just to stand out there on deck, supervising the rape of the ocean. A mere formality. I'd click a few boxes on my e-pad and call it done. Nothing more was required. I used to be a *biologist*, a guardian of marine biodiversity, a keeper of this goddamned blue planet. Now I was just a stooge.

Rodger had been waiting for me down in the galley. He'd laid out a plate of breakfast—a glistening, greasy expanse of violated animal rights, the acid-green reflections of the Cool-Whites dancing crazily in the pale yolks. I pushed the plate away.

"I'm sorry, Rodge. I'm gonna have to take my time."

Rodge was really making an effort. It wasn't his fault I'd been acting like a dead man, not talking to anyone for days. Poor old Rodge. He sighed and went back to his Braille edition of *Playboy*, its grimy manila cover flaunting nothing but a black bunny logo in a sea of raised nubs—well worn, I noticed. A few moments passed and he started to snuffle, his milky, rheumy eyes twitching beneath their drooping lids, his fingers caressing the pages—left to right, left to right—as if he were stroking a kitten. For a second there, I thought he was crying. Maybe he was, but he remained engrossed. The great thing about Rodge was that, though he'd be sitting right there in front of me, he never made me feel scrutinized or compelled to make conversation. Each of us could drift privately through our own thoughts, yet still keep each other company. Something had changed with him, though, in the past little while. Something in the tone of his sighs. He seemed a little irritated. Maybe it was me.

I scooped a little milk simulacrum into the lukewarm coffee, absent-mindedly tracking the von Kármán trails of white powder as they spiralled off the back of my spoon, first clumping then disintegrating into the sludgy brown continuum. What the hell was I doing? Once upon a time, I had wanted so badly to make a difference. I wanted to save the whales. But whales were long gone. Now I was here. Monitoring a fish-stick expedition.

Fish sticks. The world was just jonesing for them. And every marine biologist I knew, at least the ones still working, the ones who hadn't yet given up in disgust, were being hired to find more fish to make them with. Trouble was, the world's supplies had already been pretty much wiped out. Along with a lot of other things. Sea turtles, of course, which had vanished ages ago. Corals, more recently. But the sea was vast and the sea was deep and here and there, hidden in the blackness of the abyssal trenches, were pockets of sea life, as yet unexterminated. Protein was protein and pretty much anything could be ground up and pressed into the golden breaded goodness of a fish stick. So standards got dropped as well as the nets. But lately, as the trawls got ever deeper, some strange, hideous, and unbidden things had been brought up in the hauls. Head office was concerned. Lawsuits had to be avoided. *Quality is number one*, they kept telling us. After profits, anyway. So I'd been detailed to keep an eye out on deck to make sure nothing too libellous got sucked into the hoppers. Even fish sticks had their limits.

Zee, the main deckhand, stuck her head around the corner. Well, not "her," exactly. Zee was only a few paycheques away from completing her transition. These days, Zee had kind of an Eldridge Cleaver, *Soul on Ice* thing going on, the fuzzy little beard, the Ray-Bans, a short, tight 'fro.

"I've told the guys to get ready," Zee said, to no one in particular. She looked way over my head, avoiding my gaze, then quickly ducked away. Zee'd been kind of distant with me lately. We'd never had a *thing* or anything, but on past trips we'd hung out together in my cabin, reading our favourite passages from Samuel Delany to each other, or maybe listening to a little Schnauss and laughing over the clips of Japanese model-railroad porn I'd been archiving on the company server. And yeah, we smoked a bit of crack. But we did it ironically.

Now Zee was all, "When I became a man, I did away with childish things," in her stuck-up, Jamaican lilt, like she barely remembered who I was. I missed her though, just the same.

Rodger sniffed again, then snapped closed his *Playboy*, pushing himself back from the table, the black leatherette seat-cushion hissing a bit as his bony little bird-man frame rose up out of it.

"Well, Will*ee* Boy... eet's time to go to work."

A statement, not an invocation. With that he shuffled down the corridor, patting the wall from time to time, reassuring himself of his well-worn route back to the engine room. His head bobbed like a little grey mushroom on a jerking blue armature of coveralls, the *Playboy* rolled up tight in his saggy back pocket. He seemed to have become much more stooped since I'd last paid any attention to him.

Back in the dead of the previous night, some intern over at C-Corp or whoever the fuck they had running the *Tethys* at that point (or maybe even an algorithm designed to replace any last vestige of human intelligence) had uploaded an encrypted message to the pinprick of light that was locked in synchronous orbit high above the ship. The satellite dutifully responded by booting up our multi-beam finding module, which in turn lowered its transducers from a bulge in the hull. From then on, every topological nuance, every stone, every crenellation, every mound of benthic mud beneath us was being scanned, geo-tagged, and streamed back to the C-Corp headquarters, without, I might add, the slightest need for my scientific ministrations. Software had replaced me—in tiny, bite-sized pieces. But I was okay with that. I wasn't exactly on top of my game and I really needed this job. My credentials were all that mattered now. With a biologist on every C-Corp drone, they could beat the restrictions. They could call what they were carrying out a "research fishery." This was the great old scam going back to the days of "scientific" Japanese whaling. And look how that ended up. Fish sticks were an unavoidable by-product of marine research.

In the lightless infinity, a mile below our thrumming hull, we'd passed over the lip of a deep and sinuous canyon. It plunged like an enormous ass crack into the dimpled expanse of continental sediment. At the very bottom of it, where the pressure was so intense it would crush a human being into a mass of primate jerky, the sonar had already registered the presence of fish flesh as yet unexploited. But C-Corp was on it. Here is where we would lower the trawls.

I knew this was probably going to be another freak show. It'd been that way most other times we'd fished that deep. The benthic zone, they called it. What lived down there wasn't good looking. These creatures were extremophiles that thrived in perpetual darkness, on a diet of, well, each other. They weren't exactly the kind of thing most people had in mind when they thought of how a fish should look, especially one they were eating. That's where the fish stick came in. The great equalizer. It could make even "ugly" taste pretty good.

Mostly we hauled up bristlemouths—slimy, jet-black things with demonic, pin-prick eyes and mouths that gaped like wind socks, full of black, bristly teeth. Their scaleless, jellyish flesh and soft, cartilaginous bones made them the perfect fish-stick feed stock. Still swarming in the deepest ocean trenches, the bristlemouths formed the mainstay of the business. Unprocessed, nobody could stand to look at them. Yet mashed up and deep fried into golden breaded fingers, they got schnarfled up like there was no tomorrow. Kids in particular liked their sweet, amorphous taste. C-Corp fish sticks had become the pride of public school lunch programs right across North America. Prison management corporations, too, bought all they could get their hands on. Supermarkets were rebranding them into three different price points: *Value Meal, Weight-Minders,* and *Grand Gourmet.* Same stuff, different packages. It was a miracle, really. Our industry could hardly keep up with the demand.

Though we were after the bristlemouths, C-Corp hadn't been too choosy about what got minced up and extruded. The machinery would take care of it, make it all look the same. But lately there'd been some "incidents." Employees having psychotic episodes because of stuff they'd come across. Being out there on deck during a benthic haul could feel like wading around in the hell section of a Hieronymus Bosch painting— a mucousy, black conglomeration of umbrage, writhing and snapping and lashing all over the place, while the deckhands scrambled in their rubber overalls, gaffing the big stuff and zapping anything else that looked too ornery with their electric stunners. Some of the creatures would be locked in death grips, trying to swallow each other, even as they were getting pulled from the ocean.

Creatures. Well, yes. They were creatures, all right. Along with the bristlemouths there'd be the viper fishes, gnashing their needly fangs, the gulper eels, which were basically all mouth, the vampire squids, the bulbous dreamers, and lots of other species I couldn't even begin to identify, some of them most likely new to science. Not that science mattered. I just stood there giving my blessing, watching it all get dragged, flopping and bleeding, into the processor's churning maw.

Worst of all were the twisting balls of hagfish. Eyeless, finless, the colour of faeces, they didn't even have *mouths.* What they did have was something much more primitive, designed for simultaneous boring and devouring. They'd eat anything, dead or alive, swarming over their prey like leeches then drilling into it through the eyes and anus, ripping through the insides, the skin jerking and twitching as they went on with their repulsive business. Sometimes they'd come bursting out through the side of a fish already on the conveyor belt. Then we'd *really* have to get busy with the stunners.

But even the rape of the sea could have its beautiful moments. During the night hauls, I would stand out there, gazing at the myriad seething creatures, gasping and dying all over the deck, many of them flashing bioluminescent pores as the life force seeped out of them, bathing everything in a cold goblin glow like the Cherenkov radiation emitted by nuclear fuel rods. Maybe I'd be listening to a little Schnauss on my headset and thinking about how strange life was, how ephemeral.

That's how it was all supposed to go. That's what I anticipated, sitting in that galley at that grubby little Formica table, its edges chipped like a poor kid's fever-scarred teeth—staring, just staring into the murk of my coffee, searching for something, some sign, that might help me imagine myself as anyone but a puppet scientist stuck on a clockwork ship, a man who'd sold his soul for fish sticks. I wouldn't be needed for a while. The crew knew exactly what to do. They always knew: Rodger, Zee, and the Vietnamese deckhands who'd turn away whenever I came by. I'd just wait. Wait like I always waited and wonder how I'd got so cold inside.

The whine of hydraulics from out on the deck, the *woomph* of the trawl's steel doors shifting, then the clattering of bobbins and floats against the mantra drone of the great spools winding out their kilometres of cable—the machine-music prelude to the slaughter I'd heard so many times before. Until one day soon, when it would all be over. There'd be nothing left to catch in this heaving, ancestral ocean.

There were a couple of hours to kill before the haul came in. The air of my cabin hung sour with last night's sick, the sheets on my bunk all sweat-sodden and twisted. A half-empty Schweppes bottle sloshed like ancient urine amid the torn-open blister packs on the bedside table. On the floor lay my Wilby's (1961) edition of *Fishes of the Pacific Coast of Canada*. I'd found it when I was a small boy back in Victoria, out behind a Goodwill store in a box of broken hairdryers. With its gold embossing and olive linen cover, it had seemed impossibly old to me even then. By the time I'd first opened it, the species it described were already mostly extinct. Climate change and rogue drift nets had pretty much taken care of that. I used to like stroking the frontispiece, a glossy, full-colour plate of a breeding male coho; an amazing, vermilion thing, turgid with testosterone, all hooked jaws and flared fins. It might as well have been a triceratops. Gone forever, before I was even born. Now, I couldn't stand to look at it. I nudged the book under my bunk with my foot.

I settled into the orange fibreglass chair at my bureau, my thighs already aching from keeping me upright for more than a few minutes. Firing up my tablet, the C-Corp building throbbing menacingly on the log-in screen, I entered my password and dropped into the command line, down, down, descending through the file system, opening directories like so many nested Russian dolls until I was deep inside the server core. And there, hidden in a heavily encrypted backwater, was my little jewel: 3369devotchka.tar. The only thing left that could still make me smile. I unzipped it into my home directory and a row of little vidcons tiled themselves neatly across the screen.

I slid on my headset and clicked on the first one; my favourite vid of all: *Yamanote Crush*.

A gawky, antelope-like woman, wearing nothing but a pair of vintage Manolo Blahniks and a Japan Rail conductor's cap stands in the middle of a vast model railway landscape that replicates in obsessive miniature the vicinity of Shibuya Station. Her bony legs tower over a dense skyline of Lilliputian buildings, painstakingly outfitted with even minuscule transceiver masts and microwave repeating arrays, all modelled exactly to scale. The trains, streets, traffic signals and swarms of tiny pedestrians have all been perfectly and laboriously crafted. She bends over a section of the train track and picks up a green-and-silver E231-series engine from the Yamanote Line, gently, as if it were a cute little animal. Cuddling and kissing it, she begins playfully to lick the fuselage with her pointed, liver-coloured tongue, then rubs it across her tiny breasts and mouse-like pubic mound, glancing up at the camera occasionally as if receiving direction. She carefully places the engine back on its rail then rears up and crushes it beneath her stilettoed heel, slowly and precisely, an odd, sad look of affection on her face, her soft cooing punctuated by sounds of fracturing styrene and the skittering of tiny metal wheels.

She picks up another piece of rolling stock, this time a 205-series six-door passenger car, which she proceeds to fellate in an exaggerated manner before similarly treading it into toy-train oblivion. After a few more train cars, she turns to the buildings, demolishing them in an apoplectic frenzy, shrieking and stabbing at the shoebox-sized department stores and office blocks, her lustrous scimitar heels stomping the ruins into puffs of electric-blue smoke and plastic smithereens that fly in all directions. Sated, she strides across the flattened vista; she licks her lips, cheeks flushed, a sheen of fresh sweat on her pale Asian skin. From off-camera, we hear hoots of male encouragement followed by polite applause from an unseen studio audience. She bows modestly and exits the right side of the screen.

I had watched *Yamanote Crush* so many times that I knew every second of it by heart. And so did Zee. "Comfort television," we used to call it. Everyone clings to some sort of ritual, I guess, and *Yamanote Crush* was part of ours. Back when we were together. Well, not *really* together. But now the shrieking and the crushing and the shattering didn't seem so funny anymore. Not without Zee. I saw a deadness in the eyes of the model I hadn't noticed before. I took off the headset and let the vid restart its infinite loop, letting my heavy eyes wander down to the bureau drawer beneath me. Sliding it open, I took out a few of the sample vials I had stored in there, each bundle tied neatly with red elastic bands. I barely recognized the wax-pencilled depth readings and accession numbers, so carefully marked on the white plastic lids. It was as if they had been written by a different person. Orderly. Precise. A self I no longer recognized. Each one held a precious sample of Foraminiferous ooze; the microscopic exoskeletons of dead plankton that had been raining down to the bottom of the ocean since the beginning of time. This used to be my research, my passion. Back when it was still possible to have passions. The ooze told the story. It told what happened; how everything in the sea had changed over so few years. One of the vials wasn't labelled. I pulled it from its bundle and held it up against the tablet screen, still pullulating through the last few moments of *Yamanote Crush*.

It wasn't ooze in there, but a tiny, white lump.

Old friend.

I slipped the crack pipe from my shirt pocket and packed it with the contents of the vial. My fingers scrabbled through the drawer for a lighter among the pens and sticky notes and then, tilting my head back, a flick of flame, the first taste of numbing smoke:

Oh, yes.

Bzzz-Bzzz-Bzzz-Bzzz. Better. Sharper. Everything gleaming, metallic, electrical, hissing, a warm, blue glow soaking into every cell of my being. My neural nets entwined in the great mitochondrial mother, humming in the sea of her energy, her vistas of eternal pleasure—unicorns, thousands of them, copulating on waves of purple grass; the arteries in my head rushing; shining alpine streams of synaptic lubrication; ozone-electric fire burning away despair like autumn leaves. But then. Too soon. Fading. Vanishing. Into the rearview mirror of my mind. My mirror ball of pleasure. My mind's eye. The third eye. Closing.

"Wil-l-e-e!"

"Willee Boy!"

The blind, the bird, the blind man, the bird-man. Rodger. What the fuck? Dull pain billowing in from all directions, gravity snapping at my limbs. A word coagulating in my throat, bitter syrup; choking me, gasping, back into the world of streaming tears and the little bird-man standing at the door, wanting something, waiting, wanting and waiting for me just to say:

"What?"

"They need you, Willee Boy, They need you out on deck."

They needed me? Nobody needed me. Not ever. What was this? Old Rodge. Suspended there in the doorway, the fever aura of Cool-Whites flickering nastily above his bobbing, bird-man head. Standing right there in the cold, hard inevitability of now. Everything played out, wound out, bagged, tagged, and slagged. Back into the tar pit, I am the tin man. Oil me. I am the slug man. Boil me.

"Willee. Come on now. Now!! They need you!"

Urgency. I was needed. How nice. But maybe he had something else in store? A plank perhaps, for me to walk? No. Not old Rodge. He wouldn't be party to something like that. Or would he? But getting out of the chair wasn't possible. Not close to possible. Not just now. The world was still too viscous, too strewn with impediments, unstoppable forces over which I had no control. I closed my eyes and let myself sink back inside, drifting back into that warm, internal ocean of smooth, dark oil. Infinite, infinite warmth.

Then Rodger at the back of my chair, shaking it. Shaking me. Shaking my shoulders. Oh, for God's sake, why? Why now? Me, a different person, watching my non-self get handed its yellow rubber overalls by a wizened little bird-man; a blind man who could see everything. Next, he was helping me into my faded red float-coat. I myself looking out from inside someone else's eyes, a former shell of me, following the bird-man hovering down the corridor, feeling his way past the steel bulkheads and their drippy palimpsests of paint. *Schumpf*—the door opened onto the cargo deck.

Rodger's hand on my back, pushing me out. "Go!" he said, standing in the threshold, shivering in his greasy blue coveralls. They were blue like something long extinct. An indigo bunting, perhaps. Poor little bird-man. Wind-spattered veils of rain, heaving sea. Writhing mounds of silver and black, dying all over the deck. Little crimson freeways of blood braiding across the rusted expanses of diamond-patterned steel. The Viet deckhands gaffing and stunning and shovelling squirming *product* onto the conveyor belts of the processing chutes. Winches squealing, hydraulics moaning. The universe of killing unfolding as it should.

Toward the starboard bow, I could see Zee, now in her orange immersion suit and visored black-knit cap, standing over something, looking down. I made my way over, halting and starting, the rain lashing across the shifting deck in sepulchral blasts, my legs buckling and dragging like half-empty sacs of iron filings. At least I was getting more in my own head, my thoughts congealing as the hyper-chilled rain slapped against my temples. As I got closer I could see Zee was crying, tilting up her Ray-Bans and wiping her eyes with the back of her hand, the wind blowing her tears and the rain across the mahogany moons of her cheeks.

"Jesus Fuck Willy, what da hell we DO wi dem?"

Behind her, the Viets had stopped what they were doing and seemed to be waiting for me to say something, do something. Zee broke into a deep guttural sob, collapsing into my arms. I'd never seen her like this. I hugged her, stiffly, ambivalently, my hand patting her substantial shoulder with the mechanical efficiency of a sewing machine.

There were three of them lying out there on the deck; the first rigid on his back, the dark blood seeping like old wine from the gaff-puncture in his neck. The other two, clearly female, were convulsing—maybe from decompression sickness—I don't know—wheezing grotesquely, grasping at their throats with tiny, delicate hands. They were the size of babies, really, perfect little people, not of this Earth. Not the one I knew, anyway. I pulled off the first one's helmet. Such a wise little face; his skin grey, his mouth a frozen funnel of pain. We waited a while, Zee and I, neither of us saying anything, both alone with our thoughts, looking out across the vast dullness of the empty Pacific. In the end, when we were sure that they were dead, we threw them back into the sea. One by one. It seemed the kindest thing to do. The simplest too. Maybe they had relatives down there, someone who could grieve for them. We tried to put it out of our minds. And never spoke of it again.

WARRIORS

LAURA TRUNKEY

FIRE FROM HEAVEN

A Dystopian Suite

IN 1939, RUSSIAN electronic technician Semyon Kirlian witnessed flashes of light between electrodes and the skin of a
patient receiving electrotherapy. Determined to capture the
interaction, Kirlian re-enacted the procedure, but this time
placed a photographic plate on the electrode and rested his
hand on the film while he administered a shock. This was the
beginning of Kirlian photography—a process Semyon and his
wife, Valentina, claimed was able to record the energy force
emanating from animate and inanimate objects, including
coins, leaves, and the pads of fingertips.

In 1944, the C-squadron of the South Alberta Regiment made
a reconnaissance into Bergen-op-Zoom. German forces had
recently abandoned the town and the Canadians were wel-
comed as liberators. During celebrations in the *Grote Markt*—the
Main Square—a young boy crawled across the hood of a Sher-
man tank, jarring the Browning bow-gun. The gun fired into
the crowd, killing two teenage girls. Gunner Gerald Morris ran
towards the girls and bent to lift them from the ground; as he
did he felt a burning sensation in his right foot that soon spread

to his calf. His leg would be amputated less than a week later. He was twenty-five years old.

In 1970, Gerald's wife, Sally Morris, gave birth to a daughter, Daphne, in Saint Michael's Hospital in Lethbridge, Alberta. During her labour, Gerald felt severe cramping in his right calf. He sat in the waiting room with his prosthetic in his lap, massaging his empty pant leg. There were only twelve minutes between his daughter's arrival and his young wife's death.

In 1997, Daphne Morris's novel, *The Galaxy of Harvey Monk*, was published. The book followed an elderly space traveller on his mission to find the shadow-self he had lost on a distant planet during his youth. It was dedicated to her father, who had died from lymphoma the previous year.

In 2015, in Bam, Iran, four important men stood among ruins that had been a mud fortress, an earthquake zone, a modern city, and—most recently—a battlefield, and raised their pens to ratify a ceasefire that none of them expected would hold. As they signed, blue flame overtook their bodies, emanating first from their backs and then from their legs, and within minutes (though water was thrown and efforts were made to beat back the flames) they had been consumed entirely, but for a wrist and hand of one, feet from two others, and a head—shrunken—of the fourth.

Because Gerald Morris, inspired by the Kirlians' phantom-leaf photographs, had duplicated their machine in an attempt to document the energy double of his right leg; and because his theories on phantom selves became the stuff of Daphne's bedtime stories and stayed with her after her father's death; and because as an elegy to her father she had made Harvey Monk's shadow-self—once located—malfunction, enveloping him in flames; and because Daphne's book—published in a limited run of five hundred copies by a small speculative fiction press, now defunct—was carried in the butt pocket of one Marcus Spark all through his awkward teens, the pages tattered and smudged; and because Marcus Spark in his adult years (book now toted in various briefcases) served as a member of the entourage of an important man from a powerful country who had become a pile of ashes (and one foot); and because as the event played out before his eyes he did not think to run for bottled water or an extinguisher, did not think to roll, or drop, but only stopped and recalled Harvey Monk, who had been enveloped in much the same way, and turned into much the same thing: because of all this, at six that morning, the telephone rang in Victoria, Canada, in the home of Daphne Morris and her daughter, Helen.

From the Kirlians to Gerald Morris, from him to Daphne and Harvey Monk, and then to Marcus Spark, who was so impressed by how *right* D.F. Morris had gotten the whole event—from the colours of the flames, to the smoke (thick and yellow, almost liquid), to the greasy ashes and extremities left behind—that he became convinced that The Galaxy of Harvey Monk was not fiction, but a depiction: an accurate account of something D.F. Morris had witnessed, or, at the very least, had heard of second-hand and thereafter researched thoroughly. And so, while the other members of the various entourages of the four departed-yet-still-important men were contacting scientists and physicians and swarms of the typically significant, Marcus Spark tracked down the phone number of a one-time sci-fi writer and present-time mother of one, Daphne Fern Morris.

HELEN—SEPTEMBER 2014
It's just a blur at the edge of things: blades of grass, the wings of seagulls swooping the garbage bins, Mom's head turned

towards the remaining treetops of Beacon Hill Park. Like whoever's in charge up there was doing some kind of kindergarten
art project and outlined the world with scraps of blue wool. But
I just see it with my bad eye, and even then only when I focus
hard, which I try to avoid doing when Mom's around because
the second she sees me staring it's either a) the end of the world
because the surgery didn't work, or b) the end of the world
because now I've got glaucoma. "One in four cataract patients."
She's been reduced to one of those motion-sensor alarm systems and all I have to do is walk near her to set her off.

"Helen, should I make an appointment with Dr. Frey?" she's
asking now. And this time I've brought it on myself because I
have my hand in front of my face and I'm waving like a retard.
But there are sparks leaping between my fingertips—light blue,
cobweb-thin, and tingly as static.

At least with her eyes on me they're off the crew stringing
cable from the Douglas firs, building scrap-metal watchtowers
among the top branches. Or, more precisely, off their ringleader:
the bare-chested man with the scar on his neck. Mr. Clarke from
across the hall says the tree platforms only protect the fir ter-
mites, allow them to multiply, mutate, and decimate the rest of
the island's trees. That the real problem is these bleeding-heart
sympathizers. But Mom claims he's wrong, that the Herons are
the only ones doing good for the parks. It's obvious by the way
she stares at them, though, that it's not the trees she's mooning
over, but the biceps of the Heron honcho. Even now her gaze is
shifting slowly towards the group.

"The doctor? I'd rather vomit." Dr. Frey has these thick lips
that collect spit when he talks, so that by the time he's finished
one of his spiels it's all beaded up and ready to drip on you. And
besides that, minus the blue, my eye is fine. And if it weren't for
the pirate patch over my good eye and the fact that my mother

is escorting me to the first day of seventh grade I might even resemble a normal human being.

"I'd just like to meet your new teacher." The supposed reason she's with me, but it's a lie. Mom knows Mr. Perry well enough to chase him from the Safeway meat section to the bakery just so she can press her hand on his arm and spew off about windstorms and water levels and the price of produce as he gazes at her all wide-eyed amazed. But she's not coming in to flirt either, which might even be preferable. She's coming to deliver the one-in-four-glaucoma-risk lecture and to impress upon him the importance of me looking like a pirate until the doctor gives me some reprieve (presumably after I have suffered irreparable damage to my social life).

"Daphne," Mr Perry says, somewhat breathlessly. He combs his fingers through his hair and dumps the stack of math books off the chair beside his desk. "And Helen." An afterthought.

I stand at the aquarium and try to tune it out: "Of every four…" When I do look I see this thick blue around Mom, like the edge of her is puffed up and leaning into Mr. Perry and sort of licking at him—which is pretty disgusting if you stop and think about it. And so I watch the fish instead—the tetras Mr. Perry claims he bought when it was legal to import wildlife from overseas. Their fins glimmer, and I'm still standing there watching them when Morgan and Emily arrive, dressed head to toe in red, including so-long-it-must-have-taken-all-summer-to-grow-them crimson fingernails that they flutter at Mom when Mr. Perry finally walks her to the door. I keep my eyes on the tank, even as Mom blows kisses at my head and sweeps a blue sparking wave towards me.

"Hey," I say, when Morgan and Emily wander over. Like I don't give a shit that our trio is now a pair and neither of them has returned a phone call since the middle of July. Like I haven't noticed that they're dressed like mini versions of the Beacon's spaced-out followers. Emily smiles, but Morgan just smirks.

"What the fuck, Helen." She yanks off the eye patch and slingshots it at the aquarium, but Mr. Perry is erasing pencilled pornography from math-book margins and doesn't look up. I grab the thing and shove it in my pocket, but all of a sudden Mr. Perry is attentive.

"Helen," he says, pointing at his right eye. "Remember."

At recess Morgan and Emily are out the door before I've even made it to the cloakroom for the pride-and-joy bruised apple Mom bought as a first-day treat. They're on the side steps, but when I sit down Morgan says, "We're trying to have a private conversation here." Which is what she used to say last year—to the other girls. The Freak Squad and the Ordinary Nobodies.

"Fine." I stand up and walk past the portables to the chain-link fence at the edge of the field. Grass-green and aquamarine, and puffs of turquoise through the petals of the daisies. The arrow on the terrorist alert sign at the edge of the field is half-way between amber and red, and someone has spray-painted *Burn in Hell Raghead* on the boarded window of the house that belonged to Mr. Abdul, last year's pock-faced custodian. Then Morgan and Emily are by the goalpost and Morgan is whispering something in Emily's ear, and rolling her eyes, and laughing, and looking away. Emily's blue is so faint it's like there was no wool left and all she got were some strands of thread, and Morgan's is puffed up like Mom's except that near her head there's this streak of spitting orange.

"Morgan, your head is on fire!" Which I honestly believe it is before my brain catches up with my stupid big mouth. I flip up the patch for an instant and see just her thick black curls.

Half the kids on the field are turned towards me, the pirate loner. Morgan turns too, whipping her head from side to side, a shower of sparks, red whirls licking at her ears and down her neck.

"Fuck, Helen," she says. And louder, to make certain I can hear her. "Freak."

DAPHNE—MARCH 2015

The doorstep of "The Emily Carr," Daphne and Helen's apartment building at the corner of Simcoe and Douglas, looks onto the cluster of lodgepole pines that fringe the Beacon Hill soccer pitch and the rusted football tackling-sled tipped sideways behind the bleachers. Beyond this, to the south, a pale strip of horizon divides sea and sky at Dallas Road, and the Olympic mountain range rises in a wash of greys. These are the things that have always been.

But other things have changed. The Herons, a rotating roster of men and women from the Elk Lake commune, now live on platforms among the branches of the park's last standing Douglas firs. In the north of the province, entire forests have been destroyed because of fir-termite infestations. Daphne sides with the Herons. She has little sympathy for the city's cover-of-darkness tree-felling campaign—especially now, with reports that the demand for silver-streaked termite wood has skyrocketed in the Asian market. She has memories of those trees; when Helen was a toddler they used to collect eggshells from beneath them, dropped from the nests of the real herons. The park road is lined by rows of stumps, and though it is said that the chopped trees were burned, she has seen new fir desks and coffee tables in the offices at the legislature. In fact, she once sat in a silvery fir armchair while waiting to deliver a stack of proofed correspondence to the Minister of Forests—temperate responses to outraged environmental advocacy groups about the city park clear-cuts across the province. Her co-workers and neighbours would be appalled if they knew, but sometimes she bakes batches of shortbread cookies with jam-filled thumb-prints—birds' nests—and at night ties bags of them to the lower branches of the firs for the Herons' breakfasts.

Beneath the closest of these tree platforms is the strip of cement that was a water park before the restrictions, and before seventeen Canadian geese fell from the sky (paralyzed, but still in V-formation) during a lightning storm that saw the city lose its power for eleven days. The birds did not recover, and Daphne was hardly surprised when Helen came home from school a week later with theories about the Muslim community add-ing poisoned breadcrumbs to the piles of offerings left for the birds, targeting them because of their patriotic name. Though Daphne tried to talk some sense into her daughter, Helen said she refused to be part of a conversation in which her mother sided with terrorists.

Children these days seem to Daphne to be more impres-sionable than before. And this is what worries her. Helen and her classmates turn their televisions on each morning to see whether the terror alert is amber or crimson, hide beneath their school desks once weekly during simulated terrorist attacks, and have gas masks stuffed inside their lockers. It's not surpris-ing that the Beacon, with his alarmist preaching, has found an army of supporters. She wishes he had set up camp elsewhere, but his green-plastic pre-fab garden shed is less than three blocks from their home, beside the bronze Terry Fox monu-ment at Mile Zero. Although she isn't certain if it will make a difference, she has forbidden Helen to go near the man. She is worried about her daughter joining the Beacon's throng of crimson-clad teenage followers who pace the strip beside the cliffs like zombies, droning about the apocalypse to all who will listen. In fact she is worried about Helen going near Dallas Road at all. The tides are rising and the cliffs have been paved along the top with cement, but she knows that when storms come the ramparts will crumble and those nearby will be swept out to sea.

As Daphne waits on the doorstep of her apartment building listening to Helen's frothing about being dragged to a *fucking war zone* to be killed by *fucking terrorists* she thinks of these new things: the Herons, the Beacon, the lightning storms, the rising tides. These are what make her believe that anything is possible. That a man named Marcus Spark is coming to fly her and Helen to Iran. That Daphne is being sought for her expertise regarding classified matters. That she, a woman who has spent the last two decades typing letters in defence of programs and policies she doesn't believe in, is finally being asked her opinion.

POVED—OCTOBER 1944

Today the Moscow doctor and my husband discussed my treatments. Beside them I sat in my blue dress—a fox, a wolf, and me a sheep already slaughtered. On the desk: thick volumes, water glass half-empty, yellow handkerchief, and at the edge a photograph—an imprint of a hand, thick smudge of prints with gauzy luminescence spreading outwards. I touched the fingers with my own before the doctor moved it from my view.

"What is that?" My husband took the paper into his hands; this the doctor allowed.

"From Semyon, the electronic technician. Just a photograph he exposed with an electrode. His hand." The doctor traced the shape in the air.

"The Blue." I had my husband's wrist, pulling it towards me, asking him to share. But he did not.

"Poved and her colours." He patted my thigh, his fingers bristling. "Everything a colour." But he is wrong. Nothing is coloured now.

DAPHNE—FEBRUARY 1995

The elderly woman in 11-D offered Daphne a stick of Juicy Fruit before takeoff. She unwrapped it first, her fingernails pressing moon-shaped grooves in the centre. Then, before the plane had even levelled, the woman fell asleep with her head tipped back and jolting towards Daphne's shoulder, her smell a mix of disinfectant and bad perm. It was a reprieve—no one talking at her. Even the stewardesses scuttled quickly past, eyes averted from the tears.

Across the aisle was a kid who reminded Daphne of Ben Adelman from third grade (the boy who had instigated a fist-fight when he declared *Your dad's so old he'll be dead before you finish high school.* Daphne had given him a jab to the stomach for the cruelty of the statement, a broken nose for making her realize it could be true—Gerald already just months from sixty then, with more hair showing through the neckline of his undershirts than on his head). This Adelman doppelgänger was equally chinless and beady-eyed—Game Boy clutched in fat fists, a smirk as his feet stabbed into the back of his father's seat. Daphne wanted to lean over and smack his face: *Appreciate what you have, you little punk. Because someday you'll be alone on an airplane wanting to buy back seconds from a God you don't believe in.*

She should have gone home when Gerald first told her: "Harvey Monk is on his way out. Dying of cancer." "Are you still telling those Harvey Monk stories?" she'd asked, but in the beat of silence that followed she'd realized what he meant. "What did the doctor say?" Her roommate's mother had breast cancer, and Daphne knew about things. She knew about chemo and radiation. She knew about juice diets. She knew about visualization and meditation and the power of crystals. But there had been no doctor. Gerald had diagnosed himself.

Daphne had called Mrs. Neang, who she hoped still spied on Gerald over the fence. And Mrs. Neang had assured her that each morning Gerald filled the birdfeeders and just the day before he had delivered grocery bags of tomatoes to the neighbours. She claimed he still unhooked his leg from time to time to the delight of her grandchildren. *Don't worry, Daff-a-nee.* And she had stopped worrying. Besides, the next time she called, "cancer" seemed to have been abandoned.

There had been nothing malignant until Christmas, when Daphne arrived for a visit to find the house furnished with little else than stacks of labelled boxes. Gerald had even dismantled his machine and filed away the photographs that had always papered the basement walls. And there he was, sitting in his gutted study, watching the Discovery Channel and eating dry-roasted peanuts from the Melmac camping bowl because the Corningware was ready for Daphne to take with her when she left. And he hadn't looked sick at all.

"Cancer of what?" she had demanded.

And she had written down his answer and slipped it in her wallet so as to read it to the doctor, to illustrate the extent of her dad's instability. "Bones, blood, marrow. I don't know where it started, but it's everywhere by now."

Somewhere in the back of the plane a baby was crying, and the Adelman double twisted towards the noise, his eyes daggers and his fingers in his ears. Her dad had always said: *before you board, count the babies.* Like he could cure her fear of flying through his faith in the kind of God who spared infants from tragedy, a God who was rational. He'd eye the strollers in the security line, pointing them out as he clutched his empty pant leg and hopped through the metal detector.

Only a month earlier, they'd waited together in the snow for Daphne's cab to the airport. He had grabbed her shivering arm and insisted she count the babies. Standing there on the doorstep in front of the Neang kids' snow angels, there was so much Daphne could have said. But a week with Gerald was draining and she had just wanted to press fast-forward. She had been thinking past the flight home. She had been thinking about what she'd tell the doctor when she called his office, begged him to drag her father in for some tests, to prove him wrong.

Two weeks later, after an exam on medieval devotional prose, she had come home to a message from Gerald on the answering machine: his diagnosis. And she had tried to be calm and efficient. She phoned her landlord and her professors. She culled her possessions into a single suitcase. It was when she realized she had no clean socks that she lost it. Lost it in a way that made her throat ache, made the man downstairs throw shoes at his ceiling. But Gerald had said: you're not going anywhere, young lady. He'd said: we'll see each other soon enough. And he'd sounded so good she let herself believe him.

On the plane she realized she couldn't remember her father the way she wanted to. All she saw was a shrunken moon-coloured person on a hospital bed bleeding from his ears. Her dad in his final moments. Her dad as the matter-of-fact nurse at the Regional described him.

And then the plane hit turbulence and Daphne did the thing she always did: her legs hugged to her chest, knees pressed into her eye sockets, humming. *Any particular tune you're after?* Gerald had asked, but still his hand would be there on her arm. As she was thinking about that hand, its absence, she felt a weight below her elbow. And when she opened her eyes, there he was, floating past the airplane window. No moon-person and no old man either, but Harvey Monk himself, ready to fight the forces of evil on distant planets. He had a fishbowl over his head and a jumpsuit like a bag of Jiffy Pop—puffed up and silver. His hand was raised and he might have been waving or he might have been doing the countdown to liftoff.

The only goodbye she ever got.

MARCUS—MARCH 2015

"Harvey Monk felt a searing pain below his knee, like the sting of a nest of hornets, and looked down to see a flame—thin and blue, the width of a wisp of candle smoke—shooting from his leg. And yet his pants were not on fire."

Marcus read this passage from The Galaxy of Harvey Monk repeatedly on the plane to Victoria, and reads it again when Daphne and Helen are in the car—a 2012 Chevrolet Levatio, the only biodiesel vehicle manufactured in Canada before GM closed the Oshawa Car Assembly for good. Marcus keeps his voice low so that the men in the front seat can't hear. He glances at Helen.

"What do you think of that?"

Still turned sideways glaring at her mother, she shrugs her shoulders.

Daphne, her body a fruit basket of all things swollen and ripe, is so unlike the D.F. Morris Marcus imagined that he feels awkward around her. He is directing most of his attention towards her sullen and mostly mute kid who he has sat between them as a barrier.

Outside the car window, past the conference centre, the Empress Hotel slumps sideways—propped against a row of metal girders. The place is deserted now, the view nothing more than the wall that holds the ocean at bay, and besides, who comes to this city anymore? Only the transients escaping Prairie drought and Eastern ice storms, their tarps and shoes spilling from the once boarded, broken windows of the Crystal Gardens. Even with the car windows rolled up, Blanshard Street smells of human shit. Further on, members of restless flocks stand waiting their turn in the line-ups outside St. Andrew's Cathedral and the Temple Emanuel.

Marcus remembers taking the Port Angeles ferry to Victoria on a high school band trip. He had marched down Douglas with his clarinet in the Victoria Day parade, and afterwards he and his friends had followed a group of local girls along the Inner Harbour, talking loudly about the quality of their asses. They meant to snare the girls with these compliments, but the redhead called them Yankee pricks and wanted to know why all Americans wore tube socks pulled halfway up their calves. Before his group left the next morning he bought a six-inch wooden totem pole in a gift shop, and didn't notice the *Made in China* label until his mother thanked him for the gift and peeled it not-so-discreetly off.

He wants to ask Daphne about Harvey Monk's spontaneous combustion. But he'll wait until the jet, when he can send the aides to the back, out of earshot. There are two of them, the skinny one driving, the other seated in the passenger seat—trying to look busy with stacks of paper but holding on to every word. And what if she did invent the entire thing? What good would his expert be among the scientists then?

"Science fiction writer?" they repeated when he pulled the book from the side pocket of his suitcase.

"A witness," he clarified.

They drive past the soggy garbage dump that was once Swan Lake and continue up the highway to Elk Lake, which the younger aide informed him has been taken over by a group of back-to-the-wild environmentalists. A tarp city with communal meals of steamed skunk cabbage and twig tea. Clothing is optional, by most accounts, and instead of attending school the kids learn from their elders how to construct water-filtration systems and start fires with sticks. Marcus has read about similar groups across this country and his own, and tries not to speculate on what they are preparing for.

"So what was this classified thing that happened?" Daphne asks.

But instead of answering, Marcus flips to another section of Galaxy.

"'Everybody has a self made of matter, and a self made of energy.' Did you research this? Was this something you determined on your own?"

"It's fiction," he hears Helen muttering. "Like as in, not true."

"My father discovered it through the use of Kirlian photography." But she says it with a little smile playing at the corners of her mouth. Why? Because it's something that's obvious? Or is Helen right, did she really make all this up?

Marcus skims the paragraphs as field after defended field flips by through the windows, a row of soldiers standing at the edge of the highway guarding carrots and sheep.

GERALD—AUGUST 1994

In London, before they shipped me home, I woke one night with a cramp in my leg so goddamned unbearable that I grabbed the closest thing to the bed—a crutch—and pounded at the mattress until the Scotsman wrestled the thing away. The nurse with the mole above her lip got the job of changing the bandages but the stump wasn't the problem and I told her so in no uncertain terms.

In bed last night it was worse. The dreams in their usual sequence: using up all my rounds putting Kraut horses out of their misery, mangled heaps of them littering the roads. Mason and I coming to on the side of some ditch in Holland, flowers covering us like we were a couple of corpses. Liberation of Bergen-op-Zoom, the Browning triggering in the town square and two pretty girls dead on the ground. In my dream I'm leaning over the bodies and it happens just the same as it did then—some kind of raging inferno inside my boot so that I'm stamping it on the ground and shrieking like a lunatic. I woke feeling like someone was pounding my calf with a meat tenderizer.

Even still, it took less than thirty seconds before my mind was in focus, the covers were off, and I was hopping down the stairs to the basement. Because for the past three months there's been nothing more than an itch. I had the machine out, the lights off, was feeling around in the dark for the film, but by the time my stump was propped up on the damn machine the pain was just a throb, fading even as I flipped the switch. Three images of the stump, and then one of my arm thrown across the film when I slipped as I pressed the charge.

I sat in the La-Z-Boy and watched infomercials, hoping for another cramp. Every time I closed my eyes I saw Mason dragging me by my armpits into the goddamn tank, and ripping off the boot. It sure as hell wasn't trench foot or some kind of diabetic infection; it was burned right up.

I finally decided not to bother waiting and processed the film. And it was clear just as soon as the negs were on the light table. Three stumps, a shadowy blur of luminescence—nothing like the phantom leaf and nothing new either. But here's the thing: in the image of my arm were these wild flares, sparking and tangled. A giant asteroid of a fuck-you barrelling towards an old and crippled man.

HELEN—MARCH 2015

There's nothing to do on the jet but stare out the window and there's nothing out the window but dust. Like Iran is one giant sandbox. Like I should be bouncing in my seat, barely able to contain my excitement.

Mom said to lose the attitude, and then she abandoned me for Mr. Spark and his classified whatever. She's spent most of the trip up front, whispering with her biggest fan. And when she's not whispering? She has her legs gripped to her chest and her head shoved into her knees, humming. Which would be embarrassing if there was anyone around who remotely mattered.

During one of these musical interludes Mr. Spark comes up the aisle to inform me that though we will be landing on a U.S. base, we won't be staying there. Meaning, of course, we will see Muslims. And not just first-world Muslims like the ones in internment camps in the Interior—who aren't exactly real Muslims anyway, waving maple leaves and writing love poems about Canada that are constantly in the paper, the women not even in hijabs. These will be Muslims with explosives strapped to their chests, ready to detonate themselves and fuck virgins in heaven—maybe virgin sisters of the women they threw rocks and acid at in life, the women they lit on fire.

Is it unreasonable to expect someone else to be alarmed by this? Someone like *my mother*, whose responsibility in life is to protect me? Or Mr. Spark, who must be somewhat important if he can get a private jet to the Middle East when practically no one can even afford a plane ticket across the country? Important, but definitely not intelligent. For proof: Mr. Spark claims that there is "absolutely no reason to be agitated." That the Muslims he has in store for us are learned men and women, and pacifists every single one. Muslim pacifists? Excuse me, I want to scream, but Canada has been on red-alert for a year straight and all *our* Muslims are under armed guard. What kind of person willingly travels to a country composed entirely of terrorists? But I only stare at him and shake my head slow, like I'm not naïve and just because he has a monogrammed briefcase doesn't mean I'll buy his bullshit. And then I notice the flares that spit and crackle around his head. The blue is dim in places, faded to nearly nothing at his shoulders. It almost looks as though there's a wisp of smoke hovering near his collarbone, but before I can tell for certain he wanders off.

Three times I use the bathroom in the cubicle up front, and twice I walk there quietly enough to overhear the Top-Secret conversation. Once Mr. Spark is asking Mom about cases she has come across in *her research*. And does it always occur in the same way, with a greasy pile of ash? At which point she puts her hand on his arm, shakes her head, then turns to me and says, *Yes honey?* with her face arranged in this aren't-we-all-having-a-great-time kind of smile that I swear makes me puke a little inside my mouth. And the second time Mom is talking about Granddad, and how he only had one leg. Which has to do with exactly nothing. Mom an expert? News to me. And a science fiction writer? Hard to imagine anything more embarrassing.

As the plane starts its descent, the fence that surrounds the army base comes into view, and then so do specks of vehicles and people on the cement. I can see it now: my mother sitting with a group of Muslim sci-fi fans, all shedding their veils and cheerfully sipping tea. Which would be something no one at school would believe for an instant. A picture of Mom in a chador on the front of the newspaper. Science fiction ending the Jihad.

POVED—OCTOBER 1944

The soldiers came at night to kill our neighbour, Sanya. The shadows had matted into heavy dark; there was no moon. I heard boots on the stairs—the cries of Sanya's daughters. Pressed against the window I watched the men: swarmed by a whirled and clouded Red. Sanya thrown to the ground—dear

Sanya—the Blue sparking as it struck. The shots: a pair of crimson ribbons blazed a path through the night. The blast of sound and then the Blue of Sanya a river running past, over stones, along Gertsena Road and spreading until there was Sanya in the trees and Sanya with the pigeons, Sanya with his wife on the stoop. And still the sky blazed arcs of fire.

In the morning the fire raged still, so that I had to walk the children across the street and to the corner before I let them race to the schoolyard. My husband—hands to my hips he pulled me to him, reminded me he had said that trouble would find Sanya, but that the children and I would be safe. Safe from the soldiers, he meant, but of soldiers I was not afraid. I had watched from the doorway as Sanya's daughter stood at the edge of the steps, the sky-fire scalding her. I asked him please not to pass Sanya's house. I was afraid for my own.

But I watched my husband's path along the street; the arcs sparked towards him and still he did not slow. And that evening I saw the Blue of him had been singed. He was impatient with the children, his tongue grown sharp.

Was it not right to warn the others?

MARCH 2015

The armoured jeep driven by Marcus Spark stops in front of the ruins of the Arg-e Bam, where a tarp city of government men and women, of scientists and physicians, stands over four mounds of ash and extremities. Marcus Spark holds the passenger door open for Daphne Morris and her daughter Helen, but Helen's face is pressed against the tinted window and she makes no move to leave her seat.

Helen's eyes throb with a vision that slowly takes shape— an orange maze that blazes in the sky, arc after arc of fire that spits and bristles. And because she cannot see a path to the large white tarp that is clear, she clutches for her mother's hand, yanks her hard towards her.

A second vehicle pulls to a stop beside the ruins and an important man—a man seen often on television and in newspapers, a man who was second-in-command to a heap of ashes—exits. With the slam of his door Helen turns, sees his sharp, thin frame, and something else: a thin blue that changes to red at his shoulders, a mass of writhing scarlet. The shape of him is charged, rearing up.

She closes her eyes, as if not seeing will make a difference.

POVED—OCTOBER 1944

One must not confess to colours. For the doctor will strap you by your legs and arms. He will carve your sight away with wires, until the world is grey and flat and you are as blind as he is.

And now our sons march across Europe—our continent a constellation of flames—the world seared of Blue. It cannot be long before our children are burned. Until they ignite. And who will see it coming? Who will see?

DAVID WHITTON

TWILIGHT OF THE GODS™

I WAS IN my happy spot, near the Level 5 washrooms, staring out the porthole at the rebel fighters, who, through stupidity or desperation or something else entirely, were taking a stand against our gunners—but I didn't feel happy. I used to love these trademarking sorties: the non-stop action, the adrenaline high, the constant threat of obliteration. Used to love hovering over the peninsulas, our engines blowing across the lagoons so that the water rippled and swelled and the locals scurried for their lives into the forests and bunkers and crumbling strip plazas. On a really dark night you could see flares from the methane farms, little fairy lights that made you feel like your chest would burst from the joy and beauty of it. But something had changed. For the past few months, I'd gone to my happy spot, or I'd go down to the processing floor and scrape algae from the hopper, or whatever—I'd do all the things that used to rock me out—and feel nothing. Not happy. Not sad. Just nothing.

"You think it's true?" Sigrid said. Her eyes were glued to the porthole, where snipers, standing behind trees or crouching along the dark-green shoreline, took potshots at us. "What the leaflets said? You think these assholes eat kittens?"

"I guess they might," I said. "If they're hungry enough. I guess they might do anything."

Sigrid gave me a withering look. "As a *delicacy*. Do you not read the leaflets? As their *preferred* fucking meal." She grimaced and spat and scratched at the top of her head. "I swear to Betla, if I ever caught one of them doing that, I'd eat every single one of their asshole children, bylaw or no bylaw."

"Yes," I said. "Well, that's completely reasonable. I mean, if you can believe the leaflets."

Sigrid picked a clump of algae from her hair and dropped it onto the floor. She had no patience for my moping, no patience for any kind of human frailty. "You know," she said, "it's no wonder you're having problems with women. All this angst and introspection is distasteful. We don't want to have to wine and dine you. We like easy wood."

Through the porthole a boy, maybe ten years old, messy brown hair, baggy T-shirt and shorts, ran out from the underbrush waving a rifle over his head. He shouted something at our barge, then took aim and fired. A sad, futile gesture. A suicidal gesture. The *Skanderbörg*'s gunner was forced to reciprocate, and the boy slumped to the ground in a puff of pink mist.

Sigrid snorted. "Last time I saw such a crap army was in the old Falkland empire. They should just give up, enjoy the benefits of being conquered."

"Mmm," I said. "I don't know."

"What don't you know?"

"I feel kind of bad. For the people here."

"Hans. Babydoll. You're just looking for reasons to be unhappy, aren't you? They're separatists. They made their decision."

"I know, I know, I know." And I did know, too. They'd made a conscious decision to oppose the Enforcement barges. They understood the risks. It was their own fault. And yet—and here's where it got complicated for me—they still did it. It seemed perverse, and then suddenly it made sense, and then it went right back to perverse.

"You know Lodewijk, in HR? He was telling me, the other day. This girl he knew growing up? She fell into a fjord, nine years old, and drowned. Sad, sad, et cetera. But here's the thing. Her parents, the kid's parents, were so fucked up and distraught by the whole deal that, instead of giving her a proper pyre like any normal family, they saved up and shipped her body over here, to some sort of shit separatist clinic that performs back-alley rebirths."

"Oh, yuck."

"Yuck is right. But it gets worse. Apparently the surgeons, or whoever did the procedure? They botched it, and the kid came back all wrong."

"Wrong like how?"

"Wrong like she just sort of sat there all day, flopping around, and wouldn't say anything to anyone, and occasionally shrieked for no reason, and then, six months later, after all that worry and expense and hardship, shot her face off with her father's old Forsøgsrekylgevær."

I felt myself let out a little involuntary shudder. It was stomach-turning, this rebirth stuff. "Mortals playing Odin," I said, shaking my head. "It was bound to end badly."

"Yes, sure, yes, but anyway, the point is, that's what these people are like. They prey on vulnerable Danes. Which is why," she said, poking a forefinger into my belly, "it's our duty and our privilege to pound them into smut."

It was day two of the sortie and, knock on wood, things were running smoother than normal. Usually by this point in the mission we were balls-deep in chaos. Thanks to constant rightsizing and budget cuts, the barge—actually, the entire fleet—was falling apart around us. You'd fix a rotor and a pump would fry. You'd fix the pump, you'd overheat a generator. But today? Not so bad. There had been a few equipment fires here and there, and a couple of non-mission-critical systems had seized for an hour when Windows Cerebellum had had a panic attack, hid billions of data files, then nodded off in a self-administered narcotic stupor, but nothing we couldn't manage.

By noon, in fact, everything that needed doing, chore-wise, had been done, and we were at loose ends. With some free time on my hands, I thought I'd see if my latest sort-of girlfriend, Piroska, wanted to play hooky, maybe sneak off to a nice, cozy missile crib and plunder each other's persons.

I found her alone in Waste Recovery—a putrid little room near the men's fo'c'sle. She stood by a panel marked "Urethra," out of which a translucent rubber shunt, dripping with condensation, carried the computer's urine into a porcelain tub. Inside the tub, the piss would be analysed and scrubbed, then cycled back into the walls to keep Cerebellum's brain squishy, but P's sole job requirement, as far as I could tell, was simply to hang out. So strange to see a foxy woman in a shithole like this—before Piroska the unit had been run by prisoners and thralls—but she didn't seem to mind it. I stopped for a second and watched her. She wore a white lab coat and enormous mirrored goggles that gave her the look of a housefly; her hair was tied back in a face-stretching bun. She stood there, placidly smoking, a cig plugged into the side of her mouth, a pile of spent Kvalitet Milds at her feet.

I rapped on the doorframe.

Her face went sunny when she saw it was me. "Hey there, mister!" she said, in a sing-song voice. "What's up?"

"Thought I'd see what you're up to."

She shrugged and cocked her head at the piss pipe. "The rookie gets the good jobs," she said.

Piroska was new to the barge, recently transferred from a Venezuelan zinc scow. And that was all I really knew about her, other than that she possessed pretty green eyes and long, black hair and smelled—faintly but stirringly—of Glade PlugIns. The moment she'd come aboard, all the men had gone stupid, washing their armpits, combing their beards, doing all manner of ridiculous shit, but she'd floated above it all, oblivious.

I slid up to where she was standing, wrapped an arm around her waist, and gave her a surreptitious workplace smooch. She snuggled in, pushing her pelvis against my leg, letting me feel her crotch heat.

"So, listen," I said. "I was wondering, do you have a break coming up?"

Piroska's shoulders stiffened; an awkward silence fell over us. She took a drag from her cigarette, dropped it on the floor, mashed it with her heel. Her eyes shifted back and forth: thinking, thinking.

"Umm," she said. "I mean, maybe today's not the greatest."

"Why not?"

"I mean, I don't think. I don't think we. I think we're."

"I'm sorry?"

"I think that maybe we."

I waited for her to go on, but she just stood there—a bubble of anxiety. I wish I could say I was surprised about that. It was, however, a pretty typical conclusion to one of my advances. In the few weeks we'd been together, and especially on the rare occasions we'd been alone, I'd felt this intense heat from her, this need and hunger. Just last Wednesday, she'd hauled me into a closet and fucked me like a mongrel dog. But when it was over, she'd pulled away, breathless, confused, tucking her top back in and patting down her hair, and the next time I saw her, in the Level 4 mess decks, she acted like she barely even knew me. It was as though two different people occupied her body—a lunatic and a librarian. She was oversexed one minute, antisocial the next; sensitive then heartless in the bat of an eyelash. She couldn't make up her mind about anything. She laughed at all my jokes, but she laughed too quickly and way too loudly, like she didn't really get them. Small wonder I was smitten.

"What's going on with you?" I said. "You're on and off like a light switch."

Piroska broke from my arms and ducked under the shunt to put it between us. When she spoke, her voice was cold, toneless. "I'm not going to talk about this at work," she said. "It's not appropriate."

She turned her back to me, then stepped over to the tub, pulled a tongue depressor from the pocket of her lab coat, and swished it around in the computer's urine. Examining it up close for a moment, she frowned, dabbed the piss on the end of her tongue, then went over to a wall-mounted data station and pushed some numbers on a keypad.

"All right. So. Fine," I said. "I guess that's it." But she just kept punching buttons, pretending not to hear.

I tried not to brood about it. I tried not to let Piroska's flakiness consume every waking minute of my day, but it was hard because, by day three of the sortie, there was still nothing to fix or tweak or clean in our little corner of the *Skanderbörg*. All we could really do was sit around the coffee room wondering how to occupy ourselves. Sigrid spent the morning dusting her collection of Swarovski unicorns and meticulously rearranging them into tableaux that would maximize their cuteness—unicorns rubbing noses; a mother unicorn and her babies. She laundered her bras, styled her hair, phoned her mom in Detronto. Me, I made a peanut-butter sandwich and watched a bootlegged holodisc of *Gerd Nygaard's Man vs. Elk*, and then— a measure of my boredom—watched a bit of the separatist slaughter on our closed-circuit TV.

These separatists. They had, at one time, been part of a fearsome and powerful corporation-state, the scourge of the southern hemisphere, but now, because they couldn't bother to cough up a few kroner to unlock the chemical-rights management that the Denmark Corporation had lawfully, peacefully, and reasonably imposed on their water, they were reduced to agrarian hopelessness, cut-rate electronics sales, and an untalented dictatorship. So sad. And so unnerving, too. Life can turn on an øre if you're not careful.

"Hey, Sigrid," I said.

Sigrid was studying her face in a hand mirror. She pulled at the skin beneath her eyes, sighed, tucked a pink plastic dahlia behind her ear to see if it made a difference. "In my heart I'm a princess," she said.

"Hey, Sigrid, I was just thinking. Have you ever felt like you could've done better?"

"Better than what?"

"I don't know." I glanced around at the sweaty little room, at the drab industrial furniture, at the assortment of souvenir coffee mugs from different parts of the world. "Better," I said.

"Yeah, well, we could've done a lot worse too."

"Mmm," I said. "I suppose."

"You suppose. Come on now. We've got good pay here, decent benefits, reasonable vacation. Lots of folks would give their left æggestok for a job like yours."

And that was true enough, as far as it went. Sigrid was sometimes partially right about a certain number of things, and this could've been one of them. These jobs weren't bad compared to most. We could have worked on a Venezuelan zinc scow, after all. But it wasn't all blue skies and puppy dogs, was it? There was also a lot of unproductive stress aboard the *Skanderbörg*—a lot of job dissatisfaction. The crew was overworked in unchallenging ways. They felt unappreciated, expendable. Just last week, Gerrit in Livestock had his forearm chewed off by a breeding pig. Do you think he got a personal day? His team leader sent him down to Pharmacy, and he was back at work the next morning. A month before that, Karel in Weapons died in a freak Krag-Jørgensen blowback event. Rather than sending him off in a funeral raft, however, the bean counters at head office decided they'd dump his body in trademarking fluid and squirt the slop over some separatist chinchilla ranches in the eastern territories. Put that kind of stress and dissatisfaction in a small, poorly ventilated area like the *Skanderbörg*, toss in some recreational drugs and a constant fear of job loss and death, and what did you get? A volatile situation.

"All that peripheral stuff," I said. "The holiday bonus. The dental. It can be a bit of a trap, can't it? It lulls you into a false sense of security, keeps you from doing the things you really want to do."

"And what is it, pray tell, that you want to do?"

"I don't know. Something meaningful. Get out a bit, see the world."

"Oh, come off it. What's there to see that you can't watch on holo?"

It didn't take much thought. "The sex caves of Chernobyl. The ruins of the L'Oréal Pleasurelands. The Great Wall of Price-WaterhouseChina. Shall I go on?"

Sigrid barked out a joyless laugh. "Your problem is you have no problem. It's a luxury of the underemployed. But comes a day when—" She stopped, bracing herself against the arm of her chair. "What was that?"

A series of loud, chiming reports, like firecrackers maybe, or bursting metallic popcorn kernels, was issuing from the stern of the barge, and the blue hull breach warning light by the fridge began to strobe.

"Fucking hell," she said. "That can't be good."

A moment later the loudspeaker crackled, and an amplified throat cleared itself. It was Clausen, our skipper.

"Umm, hello?" he said. "Sigrid? Hans? You there?"

I glanced over at Sigrid, who just rolled her eyes and shook her head. She couldn't stand Clausen. No one could stand Clausen. He was vain and stupid and indecisive, like all commanders. "Yep," I said. "We're here."

"What, uh, what's going on down there?"

"Big bang, strobey light."

"Umm, okay, would you mind checking it out? Something's, I think, fucked up somewhere."

"All right," I said, trying to shut down the conversation. "Sure. Fine. Whatever."

Sigrid moaned and mashed the heel of her palm into her forehead. Her face turned blue, then pale, then blue, then pale, in the warning light. I'd screwed up—I knew it as soon as I'd given in to Clausen. I should have lied, told him we were in the middle of some other, more pressing disaster.

I shrugged out an apology, set down my coffee, and stood up. And Sigrid? She plucked a long, blonde hair off her knee, examined her cuticles, then dug some grunge out of the corner of her eye, but finally she stood up too. Then, slowly as possible, we went out to the processing floor to take a look.

Maybe I'd just been in the job too long, you know? Maybe I'd grown old and lazy and witless, no longer tuned in to the things that needed my attention. But, after several long seconds of half-assed examination, it was clear, to me at least, that nothing was wrong in our section of the *Skanderbörg*. The processing floor was just as we left it—a disgrace. Wrenches and screwdrivers scattered everywhere, buckets of stagnant seawater, plates of mossy, partially eaten sandwiches. A broken ping-pong table stood in one corner, piled high now with wrappers and pistachio shells and unemptied ashtrays. Not up to Enforcement standards, but definitely normal.

Sigrid, though, had other opinions. Picking her way through the debris, she'd stop, shake her head, and say things like, "This is it. Time's up. Time to pay the bill." She'd sniff at the air and say, "Something's gone sour." At one point, she grabbed her head and screamed. All of which wasn't as disturbing as you'd think. A few years back, Sigrid had contracted Mongolian Gonorrhoea on shore leave, and, since then, once or twice a week, she'd have auras, vomiting, seizures, and psychotic/spiritual episodes. I assumed this was what was going on now.

She inhaled deeply, pointing toward the stern. "It's coming from the hopper."

"Okay." I couldn't smell a thing, but decided to take her word for it. "My proposal, then, is that we get as far away from the hopper as we can."

"Come on, you pussy. It's time to face our destiny."

"What destiny?" I said.

She shot me a sour, disgusted look. "What are you, a soldier or a little girl?"

"Hold on, I know the answer to this one. Little girl?"

She jabbed me in the gut, then pushed me toward a knee-high vent that opened into a wall of pipes. This was the entrance to the hopper room. One at a time, we ducked down and shuffled our way through a warren of grease-caked machinery until, half a minute later, we reached the hopper. And I'm not afraid to admit it: I was worried. I mean, usually I loved this room, even if it did smell of fish heads and whatnot. But today? My heart was pounding, my armpits soaking. Every nerve ending was keyed into the possibility of my ruination.

I stepped into the room, looked around cautiously. Just as before, nothing seemed particularly out of place or strange in here. Like always, a loud, continuous burbling filled the joint. And the hopper—which was basically just a churning green pond sunk into the middle of the floor—looked fine too. Dim overhead lights bounced off the water and flickered on the pockmarked walls. It was a veritable spa.

Sigrid, of course, being Sigrid, didn't worry about safety precautions. She charged right into the room, randomly flipping wall switches, pushing buttons to see what would happen. Only as a last resort, after nothing happened, did she turn her attention to the hopper.

She circled it slowly, thoughtfully, sucking in its aroma.

"There's something down there," she said.

"Something like what?"

She got down on all fours and squinted deep into the amoebic murk. "I don't know," she said. "Like a turtle or something. But it's not moving."

"A turtle? It must've chewed through the filters."

"Whatever it did, it really wanted to get in here."

I peered into the water and moaned. There was something down there all right. A black, turtle-shaped something, undulating in the gloom. "Little turtle, do you have any idea how much work you've caused us?"

Sigrid went over to the drainage valve and wrenched it to the open position. There was a muffled clunking sound deep inside the hopper, and the water flickered, but that was it—the level didn't drop.

"We'll have to drain it manually," she said.

"Of course," I said. "Why should anything ever be easy?"

She horked up a phlegm ball and spat it into the water. "Fuck, man, get some perspective. It's just an itty-bitty turtle. What if it were, I don't know, a cuttlefish? What would we do then?"

"Yeah, yeah, yeah. Big scary cuttlefish. Whatever."

I'd heard this talk a thousand times before. Sigrid loved animals, land and sea, with a murderous passion. Cats, turtles, wolves, elephants . . . she'd save any one of them before lifting a pinkie to help a human. Any one of them, that is, except a cuttlefish, a creature for which, for reasons she would never explain, she nurtured an almost psychopathic hatred.

"Well?" Sigrid said, glaring down at her watch and then up at me.

"Well what?"

"Are you going to get some pumps, you lazy yob?"

All that anxiety over a turtle. Sweet fucking Odin. It was so typical of the kind of distorted thinking patterns I fell into. I tried to predict the future, I discounted positive outcomes, and I catastrophized minor events. The old Hans would've had none of that. He would've embraced his annihilation. But the new Hans? He was weak, just like Sigrid had said. He was limp-dicked and useless. The new Hans had fallen in love with breathing.

When I got back to the processing floor, I went straight over to the ping-pong table, then spent miserable minutes rummaging around underneath. Last time I'd checked, the manual pumps had been stashed there, but typically, so typically, they'd gone missing. Misplaced maybe; stolen probably, by some amphetamine-addled seaman who'd traded them for dope at our last port of call. I just sat there for a moment, staring mindlessly, furiously, at the floor until I heard someone knocking softly on the doorframe.

"Hans?"

I peered out from under the table to see Piroska standing in the doorway.

"P!" I said. "What are you doing here?"

She shrugged and smiled, riffling a hand through the back of her hair self-consciously. "Einar gave me a couple hours of liberty, if you can believe it, so I thought I'd drop by."

I pulled myself off of the floor to get a better look at her—because Piroska didn't look like Piroska anymore. Her hair was up in elaborate, old-fashioned loops on the top of her head. Her lips and cheeks and eyelids were smeared with artless blobs of makeup, garish reds and blues, like a child's idea of a pretty lady. And her dress! It was an emerald-green number with puffy sleeves, tightly fitted waist, and cleavage-squeezing bodice. I might have thought she was joking if her expression didn't seem so sincere.

"You look aggravated," she said. "Is this a bad time?"

I thought about Sigrid, toiling away in the heat and stink of the hopper room. She'd be wondering what the hell was taking me so long. Emergency protocol demanded that I get back there right away, with or without the pumps, but because I was a people pleaser and because I couldn't stop looking at Piroska's breasts, I said, "No, not at all. This is a beautiful time."

She strolled into the room, craning her neck to peek around corners and just generally check out the state of things.

"No Sigrid?" she said.

"Hopper."

Piroska stood in front of me and pressed a hand against my sternum. She glanced up shyly, as though gathering courage, then quickly looked away.

"Umm," she said.

"Yes?"

She reached out an index finger and began to draw little infinity symbols on my chest. "I know," she said, slowly, choosing her words carefully, "I've been giving you mixed signals lately, and there's, well, there's sort of been a reason for it."

"And what might that be?"

She sighed. She looked down at her feet, then up at my face, then down at her feet, then up at my face. Her chin quivered, as though she were about to burst into tears. After a minute or two, she shifted from one foot to the other, coughed twice to buy herself some time, then said, "I'm, uh... I've been umm..." She shut her eyes and forced out the words. "Technically?" she said. "I'm, uh, technically I'm, uh...dead."

Her body tensed up: bracing itself for my reaction.

It took a second for the information to sink in. I didn't quite hear it, I didn't quite hear it—and then I heard it. And my first instinct was to step back, to put some space between me and the dead thing.

"Okay," I said. "Okay, okay, okay, okay, okay."

There was a long pause, neither of us knowing what to look at or how to behave. My body still wanted her, I could feel it, but my mind? My mind said no way. From the time I was a kid, I'd been told to stay away from rebirthed girls. They'd seen things no human should see. They stunk of formaldehyde. They were walking cadavers, incapable of love or joy, sadness or sympathy. They were thieves and liars and con artists, all of them.

She lifted a hand to my chest. "Say something," she said.

But I had nothing to say. My head was full of noise. For one thing, I was distracted by the hand, still pressed against my sternum. Did I like it there? Was I grossed out? I couldn't tell.

"How," I said, "How did you. How did you come to be—"

"Marauders."

I lost my balance for a second. I thought I'd misheard. "You mean, *Hungarian* Marauders?" I laughed—a socially inappropriate thing to do. But it was just that I didn't quite believe her.

She nodded.

"So does that mean you're…?"

"A hundred and seventy years old," she said.

"Fuck me." Then, catching myself: "Sorry."

"It's okay. It's an understandable reaction."

The Hungarian Marauders had been a notoriously vicious and well-organized band of thugs, CEOs, and drug dealers that, until about a hundred years ago, had sacked and rebranded the better part of the Central Eurasian Republic. I'd learned about them during "Conquered Nations Week" on the V!K!NG! Network. Their brutal business practices had taken on an almost mythical status over the years, and it was well understood that if it hadn't been for the benevolent intervention of our armies, they would have overrun the world like so many plague-ridden rats. Piroska had been part of all of that. I had to admit it: beneath my disgust, I was a bit awestruck.

"So, I mean, why did they…?"

She shrugged. "My mom was the CEO of a rival multinational. Typical encroachment issues—she was trying to muscle in on Marauder territory. I was a warning." She pulled her hand off my chest and showed me her wrist. "See?" A faint, serrated scar cut across the base of her palm, separating the pale skin of her hand from the even paler skin of her forearm.

"What am I looking at?"

"They cut off my hands and feet," she said, "and left me in the road to bleed out."

So many things were beginning to make sense. The troubles we'd been having, Piroska's hesitation and mixed signals—it was all clicking into place. She was afraid, quite rightly, of my revulsion.

I scanned the room, hoping for something concrete and mundane and familiar to latch on to. The first thing that did it was my coffee mug. It was sitting on a clipboard, which was sitting on a toolbox, which was sitting on a battered metal side table. The mug was burgundy, gleaming in the fluorescence. On it, an illustration of palm trees and nineteenth dynasty Viking sodhut dwellings with the words, "Get Away From The Everyday—Try the New York Archipelago."

Dead girls have too much baggage, I thought. They have issues. They bring these into the relationship with them. Never go out with a dead girl.

"What are you thinking?" she said.

I was about to say something then. Something important. Something heartbreaking and perceptive and devastating—but I couldn't quite find the words. And then it was too late because, one split-second later, everything in the room—Sigrid's stuffed animals, toolboxes, chairs—lifted into the air and flew around like frightened birds. Ratchets and hammers and wrenches narrowly missed my head as they whipped past. Piroska too—she tumbled by and glued herself to the wall, which had magically turned into the floor. My own feet floated off of the linoleum. I spun around and around, helplessly, until I smashed against the wall beside her.

The room went black.

And the walls began to weep.

How long had I been sleeping? An hour? An afternoon? I had no way of knowing. But my sleep had been full of dreams. I'd been lying on a roadside, floating in a pool of gently lapping blood. My hands and feet had been severed from my body and placed on top of my chest. Up above—a warm, blue sky, a circle of lazy trees. A tiny kestrel flew by, once, twice, then lit down on my face and tap-tap-tapped on my forehead.

My eyes flickered open.

Up above, I saw a ceiling, but not the one I remembered. This new ceiling was plastered with unicorn calendars and dotted with electrical outlets, from which ceramic lamps, still dimly glowing, dangled by their cords. The holoframes up there had broken loose and were projecting at random spots across the room: Miss Copenhagen posing in her swimsuit on top of a table saw; three puppies in a bucket suspended midair. Directly above my head, a fire extinguisher swayed dangerously by one thin strap, foam leaking from its hose and dripping onto a spot between my eyebrows.

I didn't want to move. If I moved, even a finger, I might find out what parts of me had been broken or punctured or hacked off, and I didn't want to do that because right now I was feeling okay, if a tad confused. I scrambled to place myself. I was lying, it seemed, in a pool of cool, gently lapping water, covered in wreckage. A caged blue emergency light flashed on, flashed off. Out of the corner of my eye I could see, not an inch from my head, a generator that had at one time been stored under the ping-pong table. From somewhere nearby came the sound of drizzling water—a sprinkler maybe, or a crack in the hull.

"Hans?"

This was Piroska's voice—tinny and distant. I'd forgotten all about her. I'd forgotten about everyone. For however long, it had been just me, my mind, floating in the shell of my body. Now there was someone else to worry about.

"Hans? Are you okay?"

I pulled myself out of that swaddling bath and raised myself onto my elbows. And now I saw the room. It looked like it had been thrown into a blender: everything battered and scattered and fucked. Straight ahead, P was in the exact posture I was in—raised up on her elbows—staring back at me with a look of horror on her face. Her green dress was soaked through with blood and sprinkler water, and a screwdriver had skewered her shoulder.

"What happened?" she said.

It took me a while to formulate a reply—up to now I'd been all sensation, no thought. "I think. I think we've. I think we've capsized."

"No," she said, "what happened to *you?*"

Slowly, she lifted a hand to her ear, indicating for me to do the same. But when I did, all I felt was nubs of jagged cartilage and a warm, tacky liquid. Not at all what I was expecting to feel.

"Oh, crap," I said. "Not again."

I groped around in the water beside me for something that might resemble my ear, but it was too dark in there and there was too much chaos.

"What do I do?" Piroska said weakly. "How do I help you?"

"Don't worry about it," I said. "It's no big deal. They'll just grow me a new one in Pharmacy." Being brave, being nonchalant, because clearly Piroska was falling to bits. And who could blame her? She had issues with severed body parts. Behind my brave face, though, I was just as freaked out as she was; in all my years of trademarking, I'd never capsized before.

A warning klaxon—signalling desperation, signalling last resort—screamed through the barge so loudly it made my teeth clatter. Then, through staticky speakers, Clausen's voice.

"Oka yev erybo dy, theb arge h asbeen hit. Ma keyo urway to theemer gen cy e xits inan ord er lyfa shion. Ab and onsh ip. Rep eat. Ab and onsh ip. Th ere's b een so mesort of exp lo sion."

"What did he say?" Piroska asked, still oblivious to the screwdriver jutting from her clavicle.

"Not sure. Something about an explosion. I think he said to abandon ship."

This last bit lit a whole series of fuses in my brain. *Explosion* triggered *bomb*. *Bomb*, of course, triggered *shell*. This in turn set. off *turtle*, which set off *hopper*.

Sigrid.

"Oh, shit," I said.

Piroska immediately sensed what I was thinking; probably she'd been thinking the same thing. She looked at me, eyes searching, mouth agape. "She's trapped," she said.

I hauled myself off of the floor and slowly—from the spasm that shot through my leg, it looked like my right knee had blown, too—hobbled through the sodden trash. Piroska was right behind me. Together we picked our way past overturned generators and piles of battered equipment until we hit the wall of pipes. Capsized as we were, the vent that led to the hopper was now up near the ceiling. We used the pipes as a ladder, climbing, slipping, climbing again, until we reached the vent. Inside the tunnel, we crawled under ruptured pipes, dodged geysers of trademarked water, slipping and falling and gashing our arms and legs. Behind me, I could hear Piroska groaning from the effort. And I was groaning too—from the pain, from the fear, from the certainty that all certainty had been flushed from my life.

The hopper room was dark when we got there—dark and quiet and smelling, weirdly, of barbecued steak. The contents of the hopper had spilled out so that the room was filled with waist-deep water. One blue emergency light, submerged in the water, strobed weakly, pointlessly.

"That smell," Piroska said. She coughed, then gagged, then turned away, and in a moment I heard her vomit splatter across the tunnel floor.

Crazy with panic, I pulled a miniature Maglite from the pocket of my coveralls and trained it on the surface of the water.

At first I saw nothing. Just the gentle bevelled pool, rocking back and forth with the movements of the barge. Then an object of some sort. A chunk of metal, maybe—or, no. A chunk of shell. A charred remnant of turtle shell. And then another. And then another. And then—

"Oh, fuck, fuck, fuck," I said.

A waterlogged boot. I moved the Mag-beam to the right. The boot was attached to a leg. Which was attached to a torso. Two legs, a torso, and—yes—two arms. Everything intact, everything looking good. I shifted the Mag-beam further to the right.

"Sigrid?" I said. "Sigrid?"

Now here was a strange thing. I couldn't find her head. No matter how hard I strained my eyes, I just couldn't see a head. There was a neck, sort of, but beyond that? Nothing but water, with a pink plastic dahlia floating on top.

"Sigrid," I heard myself say, "come here." I reached out an arm to pull her in. "You better get out of there."

No reaction from Sigrid, but I heard Piroska moan.

"The fuck is wrong with you?" I heard myself say. "The barge is sinking. We have to get out of here."

Still no response from Sigrid. Not a twitch.

I banged on the wall. I was getting pissed off. "Come on, you lazy bitch."

"Oh, Hans," Piroska said.

"What's wrong with you? You pansy. You wuss."

"Oh, Hans."

"Get over here right now. You fuck. You shit."

Piroska was tugging on my elbows, on my shoulders. She wrapped her arms around my waist and pulled as hard as she could, but I just kept shouting insults at Sigrid. My throat was hot and raw; my eyes were filming over. Every cell in my body was burning. It felt for all the world like Sigrid had been ripped straight out of my flesh, so that all that remained was a huge screaming wound. I was loss—every bit of me was loss. My organs, my brain. My soul was loss. My rank, Løjtnant, my serial number. My name too—Hans Rasmussen. My name was loss.

I *should've been there.* That's what I kept thinking, over and over, until it wasn't even thinking anymore, but just meaningless sounds. I *should've been there. I should've been there.* Because if I'd been there, maybe I could've done something that would have kept Sigrid's head from being blown off. Or, failing that, I could've arranged it so that my own head would be gone now too, and not the thing that it was: a vat full of guilt and self-hatred. But I hadn't been there. No. I'd been distracted by a pair of Glade-scented breasts. Breasts—to make matters worse—that belonged to a rebirth.

Piroska and I were back among the wreckage of the processing floor. It had been five minutes, maybe, since we'd discovered Sigrid's body, but already the water had risen to waist height; sitting on top of a filing cabinet, it knocked against the soles of my boots. All I could do was stare—stare at the green steel walls, which, now that the ventilation system had cut out, were slick with lung exhaust; stare at the peanut-butter sandwich that had flown through the air and glued itself to the ceiling.

"Hans, we have to get out of here. We have to hurry."

All around me I could feel Sigrid's soul as it flitted through the room, preparing for the long flight to Valhalla. It reminded me that her body, or what was left of it, was floating all by itself in the dark water. It felt criminal somehow to leave it there, all alone. Surely we should just stay here with her, let the lagoon rise around our necks and leak in through our nostrils until all of our sorrows had ended.

"What's the point?" I said finally.

"What do you mean, 'What's the point'? To live."

"For what? There's nothing out there."

I pictured my happy spot, the Level 5 porthole. Its view at this moment would not be the peninsula, not glorious displays of Viking military power, but seaweed and mud and whatever else was at the bottom of this crappy lagoon. Separatist refrigerators. Old TVs. The husks of their weaponized Segways. It was beyond all understanding. When a separatist's turtle bomb could take down an Enforcement barge, you knew: anything could happen in this world.

"What are you talking about?" Piroska said. "What are you talking about? Do you think Sigrid would want to hear this? Do you think she'd just give up? Do you think she'd just lie there like a little bitch?"

Trying to manipulate me. Trying to get me all worked up, plying me with insults, reverse psychology and jabs at my manhood so that I'd have to stand up and prove her wrong. But I was beyond all that. I was suicidal and serene.

"Your pep talk," I told her, "won't work with me."

She let out a panicked, involuntary throat noise and grabbed at my knee, trying to pull me off the cabinet. "Please," she said, "Please. You don't know what it's like."

Her knees gave way and she dropped into the water.

"You're all alone, and it's grey and foggy and cold, and you can't lie down, and the eagles, the eagles are always circling, waiting for you to fall," she said.

She sobbed and moaned and clutched at her chest as though she couldn't get enough air. Snot dripped from her nose and off her chin and onto her soaking wet dress. Her makeup had splattered across her face like she'd been shot with paintballs. But what could I do? It was either what I wanted or what she wanted—and selflessness was stupid in a situation like this.

Compassion was stupid. I hung my head and rubbed my temples, hoping the barge would just blow up and I'd be spared the decision.

"Please!" she said.

"Not again!" she said.

"*Please!*" she said.

"*I'm talking to you!*"

"Soldier!" she said. "Snap out of it!"

This last got my attention: it didn't sound right. I looked up.

Hovering in front of me, in the spot where P stood, but an inch to the right and slightly out of phase, like a palimpsest, was Sigrid and her scowling face. Yes, yes, it was her. Same ruddy cheeks, same broken nose. She stared at me in a kind of sarcastic appraisal. I sobbed with relief. She was still with me, at least for a little while.

"What the fuck?" she said. "Crybaby. What's with the tears?"

"Hello to you too."

"Yes, yes, hello, salutations, whatever. So tell me, what's the deal? You're just going to give up like some pussy-whipped little gearbox?"

"Hey," I said, perking up considerably, "at least I'm alive. Unlike some of us."

Sigrid suppressed a smile. "Yeah, well, we can compare dick sizes all day, but all that's going to get us is drowned. The point is, and the reason I've come to see you, you've got an opportunity here, an opportunity that some of us don't have anymore, which is to continue to exist in this so-called mortal realm, and all the possibility that that entails, and you'd be a complete røvhul not to take advantage. But just keep an open mind, okay? There's shit coming your way you can't possibly prepare for."

"But how? I mean, how can I go on? How can I just leave you?"

"Oh, for the love of Mímir! I'm just meat now, babydoll. You'll get over it. So up off your ass and grab a sidearm and a fucking snorkel or something. Do you hear me, soldier? It's going to get wet, that I guarantee."

I wanted to grab her, to lay hands on her one last time, to prove I wasn't dreaming. To say a proper goodbye to my brave and noble friend. But when I reached out to touch her face, it was Piroska's cheek I was cupping.

"Okay," I said. "Okay. What the fuck."

I jumped down, ploughed through the water and debris until I found our emergency lockbox, then flipped it open and pulled out two double-action combat revolvers and several rounds of ammunition. Then I waded over to a sideboard and grabbed two knapsacks. I handed Sigrid's knapsack to Piroska, and gave her Sigrid's gun.

"We have enough food for two weeks," I said, "and enough bullets to kill about three hundred people. We each have a portable filter for trademarked water, an insulated blanket, a sewing kit, and a bunch of other stuff that I can't remember. Provided we don't get shot, and maybe even if we do, we'll be alive for the next two weeks. Beyond that, well..."

"Two weeks sounds good," Piroska said. "That's two weeks without the eagles."

I scanned the room, looking for the door that led out onto the corridor. It was more than halfway up the wall, impossible to get at without some sort of ladder.

"Filing cabinet," Piroska said, reading my mind.

We went back to the filing cabinet and, throwing our shoulders into it, managed, after considerable thrashing, to prop it against the wall. Next to it, we jammed a metal folding chair, and, on top of that, a plastic mead cooler. Hoisting our gear, we climbed the makeshift staircase and peered out the doorway at what lay beyond.

The corridor was now more of a well-shaft than a walkway, throbbing with blue light and echoing with the voices and frantic footsteps of crew members and thralls in other parts of the barge. Five metres below us: a pool of murky brine, the bodies of four seamen floating in it. Up above: an almost sheer face, with no obvious footholds and no chance of respite. We'd have to claw our way along the slip-free grating that covered the corridor's floor until we got to the farthest passage, twenty metres straight up.

"Okay, I said. "Okay. Fuck. Okay." I turned to Piroska. "Are you feeling lucky?"

But Piroska's mind was somewhere else. She opened her mouth as though about to say something, then sighed and bit her bottom lip.

"What's going on?" I said.

She stared intently at a spot somewhere around my Adam's apple. "I need to ask you something, and don't take this the wrong way, but I'm pretty instinctive sometimes about people and I feel like the question needs to be put out there."

"What?" I said. "What?"

"When we've landed. On the peninsula. When we've landed on the peninsula. Umm, which side will we be on?"

Out in the corridor I could hear the other crew members, my brothers and sisters, wailing and shouting and just generally losing their rag. Insults. Outrage. Outright panic. A family still, but a family gone cannibal.

"Wow," I said. "What a question."

She grew bolder: "Because I know we could never really talk about this before, for obvious reasons, and I realize we haven't known each other that long, but I sense an ambivalence, I guess, in you. It took me a while to put my finger on it, but yeah: a lack of commitment, I guess, to the mission here." She paused meaningfully. "Or maybe I'm projecting."

The separatists, those hayseeds with their homemade guns and half-assed goat farms, had murdered my best friend and robbed me of my home. Their idealism and independence and blah, blah, blah had destroyed everything I'd known and cared about—had, in the space of a few seconds, wiped away the last twelve years of my life. Not, actually, that I blamed them for that. How could I? We'd trademarked their water and slaughtered their child armies and fucked up their farms—and they'd done what any other right-thinking people would have done: they'd responded in kind. Maybe, well, maybe their actions weren't as perverse as I'd thought.

"Okay," I said. "Okay." My mind was humming—it was the first time in months or years that I hadn't been on autopilot. I grabbed Piroska by the shoulders and looked deep into her eyes. "The separatists. They'll need some sort of statement, some sort of indication that we're, you know, cool. So when we get out there, shoot as many of our own officers as you can. Try to find Clausen; we kill him, we're rock stars. Just don't stop shooting, all right? And forget about the lifeboats; when the ammo runs out, we swim. It's a risk, but what the hell, huh?"

Her eyes were glistening. "What the hell."

I kissed her for luck, shouldered my knapsack, and, together, we headed for the exit. We'd only just taken our very first steps, though, when the *Skanderbörg* let out a sickening wail, and we stopped dead.

"What was that?" Piroska said, gripping my arm.

It was an animal sound, of pain, of desolation. "I don't know," I said. "I'm sure it's fine."

The truth was, I did know, but there was no way I was going to lay that on Piroska. It was a bad thing to hear, man, very bad—a full-on hull breach. A "Cascading Skrog Failure," they called it in Nav school. We had thirty seconds, maybe less, before a high-velocity wave train overwhelmed the processing floor; when that happened, we'd be doomed. We'd be lost to the lagoon.

I turned to poor P, smiled in what I hoped was a cheery, untroubled way, and stared into her pretty green eyes. "I love you," I said, as earnestly as I could. "I realize it's kind of a weird time to say something like that, but I thought you should know." I didn't mean it. I didn't love her; not yet anyway. I just thought it would be a nice last thing to hear.

"Well, wow," she said. "I—"

The *Skanderbörg* lurched. Piroska dropped to the floor and slid away. Then it lurched again, harder, and I dropped—the room's chattel shifting with me, and on me, and raining down around me. And then, before I could regain my footing, or locate P and lock hands, a surge of freezing seawater enveloped me and I was floating, floating, pushed along by tides too strong to resist. I rose and rushed forward; I fell and raced back. The seawater, swarming with life, choked with motes, pulsed blue, then black, then blue, then black. When it was blue I could see things: a glob of gulfweed swimming by, a crystal unicorn cartwheeling gently through the gloom. When it was black I just dreamed, and wondered, and waited for death. All the stuff in here, all the bullshit stuff of everyday life—the clamps and squeeze tubes, the sidearms and pleasure sprays and cans of Lille Söd Sild—was transformed. The very air! The air had turned into water, and, suspended inside it, these once-familiar objects, now made mysterious, bobbed and drifted and spun.

I saw Fenrir, the wolf, thrashing his way through the brine. Such a terrifying sight. As huge as the stories had said, and as vicious and drooling and fierce. He turned, gave me a disconcerting once-over, then continued on his way. If I followed, he seemed to be saying, he'd lead me to Ragnarök, the end of the world, where, as the prophecies had told us, he'd wrangle with Odin, kill him dead, and eat him whole. All was not lost! If I followed the wolf, he'd lead me to shore. But whose side would I fight on when I got there? Who'd even have a turncoat like me? I supposed I'd figure that out. Because everything had changed, the world was starting anew, and it wasn't about alliances anymore, it wasn't about vision statements or corporate synergies or brand protection—not for me, anyway. It was about standing up, blood-caked and broken, and stumbling into battle.

PASHA MALLA
1999

When I woke up this mornin'
Coulda sworn it was judgment day

"I WOULDN'T FUCK ♀ if he was the last man on Earth," Sonya told her friends, drunk and searing with challenge, that New Year's Eve before the end.

This was just before midnight, seconds before the world and all that was in it went spinning into the new millennium. Out came the tequila. Then it was "Ten! Nine! Eight!" and at "Happy New Year!" Sonya downed her shot spluttering and snorting, the booze scorching her nostrils, and almost instantly the whole night—the whole century, it seemed—swelled up from somewhere and everything went careening into a great vertiginous swirl of noise and light, and the next thing Sonya knew she was waking alone to the year 2000 and a head full of thunder. And everyone was gone. And the city was empty. And it was the end.

It was just Sonya. There was no one else left.

But, wait. That was not entirely true.

On the radio, on every station, inescapable on either AM or FM, was the artist formerly known as Prince, now known as ♀,

365

beckoning all female survivors to join him at Paisley Park. "Cum 2 me," he swooned. "All u ladies, cum, let's start a new human race." And then he'd play one of his own songs.

Jesus. What if ♀ *was* the last man on Earth? What a nightmare. And if there were other women out there, scattered around the continent and perhaps even the world, hearing in this message some sort of salvation—well, they had to be stopped. And so Sonya was driving her leased Accord over the border to Minneapolis to intercept these women, to talk some sense into them before they stumbled, naked and duped, into ♀'s candlelit boudoir—a place Sonya imagined as all chiffon and gossamer and satin, and a heart-shaped bed with that weird bluesy nymph sprawled upon it with a rise in his silk pyjamas and a rose in his—*Christ*—teeth.

Holy, Debbie could not wait for ♀ to make sweet love to her and to implant in her womb his seed. *Oh my god oh my god oh my god*, she thought, speeding up through the great icy swath of North Dakota, fists pounding the steering wheel, each inch-long fingernail painted "Devil's Kiss Red" to match the rouge on her cheeks and the fire in her loins (and, sure, heart). Her bangs were a perfect crusty arc, "Erotic City" wailed from the stolen Corvette's plastic speakers, and in her lap, like an incubating egg, nestled the grenade. OH. MY. GOD.

Zipping westward on the her snowmobile, bundled tight head to toe, ♀'s voice ringing through the headphones in her helmet, Mrs. Mendelbaum tried to imagine who he might be. His voice was somehow…humid. Sultry and dripping. The music slinked and humped and awakened in Mrs. Mendelbaum a peculiar tingle she hadn't felt for decades. But this was no occasion for tingles! In times like these it was important to think rationally.

People needed to come together. If people did not believe in God at least they believed in other people. And while Mrs. Mendelbaum had no uterus, she did have a lot of love to give. She would not be much for repopulating the earth but she was a damn fine listener and a purveyor of really great hugs, things she knew mattered as much as the ability to procreate, if not more. For what sort of world was it to bring a child into without love? And Mrs. Mendelbaum tended a great simmering volcano of the stuff in her chest, ready to spew caring and compassion in pure, sizzling geysers of molten hope.

Over bridges and through empty states Esme drove her mother's Audi, the thermometer dropping as she made her way east. She knew what the guy on the radio wanted. And now, why not? It wasn't that Carlo hadn't been The One, with his frantic grappling and the salami smell of his neck. Or that since the first occasion she'd allowed it back in October, at every opportunity he thudded his crotch into hers for forty seconds—and then he retreated gasping, like a waiter whisking away a bowl of soup before Esme had even had a taste. Not to mention that maybe three weeks prior there'd been this: "Shit, I think the condom broke"—that same waiter splashing soup into her lap. No, none of that mattered. There was no more Carlo. There was no more anyone. There was nothing left; nothing mattered at all. It was only Esme and the fat grey ribbon of highway, desolate save the few abandoned shells of tractor-trailers at rest stops every few counties—oh, and the voice on the radio, providing directions. Here was a toll, unmanned, and Esme blasted through, the barricade splintering over the hood of the Audi. She cheered and veered across the highway and back. The world was hers: seventeen years old and free. She honked the horn. She cranked the stereo. She stomped on the gas. "Fuck everything!" she screamed, as loud as she could, speedometer fluttering between 80 and 90. But maybe now with snow and ice on the road she should ease up, so Esme did and breathed, and then hesitantly checked the rearview, half in fear and half in hope of seeing another car reflected there, closer than it might appear, following behind.

"I just wanna let all ᴜ women know, each and every special one of ᴜ, first off right now that I know how lonely ᴜ ʀ feelin'. But ʙ 4 you start to feel like no one's left, know I can feel ᴜ out there. And I know ᴜ can feel me 2. And that's why I'm telling ᴜ all right now, all ᴜ women left on Planet Earth, that we're gonna make somethin' special 2gether again. I want each of ᴜ 2 look out at the stars 2nite and know that we're all lookin' at the same sky, and I want ᴜ 2 pick just one star and imagine that I'm lookin' at it 2. And wherever ᴜ ʀ I want that 2 ʙ ᴜ ʀ guidin' star. I want it 2 ʙ the star that brings us 2gether, that brings ᴜ 2 me. And I want ᴜ 2 follow that star as long as it takes ᴜ, all the way 2 me, cuz I'm waitin'. I'm waitin' here 4 ᴜ, women of Planet Earth. We gotta cum 2gether. Because it's not over. We're not thru. Cum 2 me. We can make it. If ᴜ believe in me, 2gether we can believe in love, and I believe in ᴜ."

⚥? What was ⚥ supposed to even *be*, wondered Sonya. She pulled up her jeans and stepped around the puddle of ale-coloured pee she'd left in the middle of the highway, shivering in the icy air. ⚥, ugh.

Back in the car, hangover settling into a dull throb at her temples and a mossy paste in her mouth, Sonya pictured him shimmying about in doilies and fabric cropped from his grandma's plush sofa. "The Artist Formerly Known as Who the Hell Cares," Sonya had called him the night before. "It's not just that his music sucks," she'd ranted, "or that he's totally ridiculous.

It's more the hypocrisy that gets me. He's a raging misogynist, *and* a homophobe, yet he'll throw on garters and high heels and prance around like a drag queen. He doesn't love women, he's just confused. And '*Pussy Control*'? Come on, that's just offensive."

Now *this*—this Armageddon, or whatever—and here she was sliding behind back into the driver's seat of the Accord and continuing south into the United States. The winter was everywhere: thirty-below and the trees lining the highway garlanded with snow, and instead of sky there was a sort of absence above, grey and hanging there, emptily.

Sonya had always said the thing she craved more than anything was to be alone, mercifully alone, making art in some cabin secreted away in a deep dark wood. She would live on berries and delicious forest creatures roasted on spits; there would be much chopping of wood and a surfeit of profound existential thoughts sublimated into oil paintings and sculptures. And now here was that chance, offering itself up like a free, post-apocalyptic lunch.

But she couldn't exist out there in peace while the planet was being reinhabited by a race of velveteen maniacs with symbols for names, all those toddlers wailing away on sparkling toy guitars, performing cunnilingus in the air, pooping into sequined diapers. And so Sonya would stop it—and only then, knowing she had done right by the world, could she retreat to a life of hermetic bliss, away from everyone and everything, and live out her days in perfect, silent, uninterrupted solitude.

Oh, here was a "funky" song, thought Mrs. Mendelbaum in her snowsuit. She'd even heard it before, maybe, and turned the volume up just a touch—riding on the highway now, the snowmobile sliding along, ever mindful of black ice. What were they saying, though? Something about the future. "Something

something the future will в..." Will be *what*? Was there a future? Wishing someone would tell her, Mrs. Mendelbaum shivered and looked out through her visor at the world. She was *so close* to Minneapolis—close to everyone, close to the future! But looking up the sky did not look like the sky of the future. It struck her instead as still and lifeless, a great pale corpse slumped over the world. How depressing; it was enough to make her want to take a break. Also she had to pee.

Esme passed a Taco Bell, Carlo's favourite restaurant. Carlo, lurching Carlo: all chicken soft tacos and pico de gallo and that clumsy slug of a tongue. But, aw, so sweet—he'd made a piñata for her, after all, for her birthday (though he'd filled it with condoms, and when they'd tumbled forth she could have sheared him for wool, his grin was so sheepish). Was it only last night that he'd worked at her button-fly—for, what, *ever*?—before Esme, like a prisoner unlocking her own cell for a cute but hapless warden, snapped it open: here you go!

She'd wanted so badly for it to be good with Carlo, and when it wasn't she could only trust it would get better, later. She could wait; she loved him. But here was later, Esme thought, gazing through the windshield. Later was nothing at all.

♀ was singing again: "Until the end of time, I'll be there 4 u." She vaguely remembered what the guy looked like from the jacket of an LP that might have belonged to one of her mom's boyfriends—Tom or Roger or Luis-Enrique, Esme wasn't sure. And despite what appearances might suggest, apparently ♀ wasn't gay. Just sort of elfin and a little *purpler* than Esme was used to (Carlo wore mainly camouflage and black denim).

Maybe a guy like ♀ would be good—tender, experienced. She'd lose herself to it and him and afterward he'd hold her whispering, stroking, whispering. And if they had a kid, what would it look like? She tried picturing it, but all that came to mind was a little Carlo nestled in her arms, swaddled and cooing, gazing up at her with wide, astonished eyes.

Esme slid her foot off the accelerator, pulled her hands from the steering wheel, and closed her eyes. Slowly the car decelerated and began to list to the right, toward the shoulder, and blind to the world Esme thought about how she was old enough to do almost everything adults do: she could drive and almost even vote, though now—typical!—there was no one to vote for. There was only ♀. And not even *him*, just a voice and a promise.

At the crunch of gravel and ice Esme's eyes snapped open and her hands grabbed the wheel. She jerked the car back onto the road, sweat squelching in her palms. Breathing, now, breathing, with the car locked tightly into the lane and her foot steadying the gas. In the rearview, a little black blip emerged from the point where the grey of the road vanished into the endless snow—not a car, something smaller. A motorcycle, maybe.

Esme stared, unsure whether to speed up or brake. She was reminded of when she was eight years old during Christmas shopping season and her mom had disappeared at Sears. In that split-second of abandonment the world had expanded, reeling outward from her, infinite and unknown. Here was that again, but now, also, not just the threat of space, but a stranger in that space, and her alone, defenceless.

Seeing a service station ahead, Esme pulled in. She shut the engine off and the radio died with it, silencing ♀ mid-line: "Until the end of time, until the end of—" Immediately the cold began to creep into the car. Esme shivered, wrapping her arms around her shoulders, wishing she'd worn more than a sweatshirt.

The only sound came from the road: whoever was out there was buzzing closer. It became a drone that lulled Esme's thoughts back to herself, and there she found the pulse of a different kind of imminence—something within her, awakening, changing: the end of one thing and the terrifying, glorious beginning of something else. And then, flinging the door open, she leaned out of the car and barfed into the snow.

How many times had she dreamed of it, Debbie wondered, reapplying mascara in the rearview, steadying the wheel with her knees. Would they kiss and kiss? Would ♀ take her face in his hands and hold her like that just stare into her eyes—would he sing? But they had all the time in the world, didn't they? There would be time for everything... Debbie started to scream at this, at the endless boundless future; from deep in her guts roared great primal yowlings of happiness and potential and everything, everything, her face tingling through the mask of foundation and mascara and lipstick and eyeliner and blush. Dreams really did come true and no one could tell her to shut up or try to stop her, she thought, patting the grenade in her lap—but hold the phone, a sign from the radio! Debbie cranked it, wailing along as the sky deepened into night: "None of them got what it takes / 2 B a future baby mama."

"Ladies, ladies. Each one of U—keep keepin' on. I'm here. I'm waitin'. Each one of U is special. This is the future. We're the future. All of us, 2gether. We're gonna B 2gether. If U R hearin' these words it means it's meant 2 B. I want all U women, every one of U, 2 know each of U is special. I want U 2 think of me and us 2gether and how it's gonna B: champagne and candlelight. I'm runnin' a bubble bath. If I were in your arms 2nite—"

Sonya clicked the radio off. The planet didn't need this lacy goofball's sperm!

Soon enough it would be over, she told herself. No one would show up to ♀'s lair and the world, such as it was, would go on without him. Alone in her cabin in the woods Sonya could exist and paint, undisturbed and happy. But as she imagined this life, saw herself puttering through the trees, she began to wonder. Would it be worthwhile if there was no one to see her doing it, or to even tell? What would she paint in such a place? Owls? Who would even know and how would anything matter to her, alone, in some loggy cabin?

Head pulsing, Sonya found herself lulled by the steady growl of the Accord's cruise control, the sweep of the road under the car. But slowly this became something more sinister. With her foot off the gas it didn't feel as though she were driving at all; the highway seemed more like a conveyor belt, hauling her through an abandoned world of ice—toward Minneapolis, toward Paisley Park, reined in by ♀.

Wow, thought Mrs. Mendelbaum, finally, a service station—just in time! But, wait: was that a person sitting there in the parking lot, behind the wheel of a silver coupe?

"Imagine U could rid the Earth," Debbie sang along to the radio, easing her thumb in and out of the metal loop of the grenade's detonator, "of anyone U choose. Which ones would U need the most? And which ones would U lose?"

People. Two women. Just outside Minneapolis, leaning on the hood of a silver Audi in the parking lot of an ESSO, there they were: one big and one small. At first Sonya barely thought anything of it. But then her brain caught up: *People!*

The Accord hit a patch of black ice, fishtailing as Sonya cranked the wheel this way and that, now spinning across the highway, now turned all the way around and facing north, toward Canada, now Mexico, now the Pacific Ocean, now the Atlantic—and finally, slowing, the car slid back across the highway and bumped up against a snowbank, and rested there, and was still. After a quick check—she was fine—leaving the engine idling and the car half in the ditch, Sonya plunged into the world and staggered toward the women.

They turned toward her, faces open. "My," said the older, fat one, her look of worry mirrored on the face of the other one, a teenager in a hooded sweatshirt. They were eating Snickers bars and drinking Gatorade. Where should Sonya start? With her standard anti-? rant?

But it would have to wait: the matriarch was coming at her, arms out, hauling Sonya into her great duvet of a body. It actually felt sort of good there against and between and within her breasts; nothing said, nothing to say. And then she was released.

"I'm so happy you're okay. That looked very dangerous." The big woman stroked Sonya's arm. "My name is Mrs. Mendelbaum. This is Esme. We've just met."

The girl held up a Snickers and said, "Snickers?"

Had anything ever tasted so sweet and fake and good? And here was a Gatorade, that phosphorescent potion of synthetic magic. Sonya gulped down half the bottle. Who were these people? Hangover angels? She raised her eyebrows at Esme, who was clutching a little cardboard packet she'd clearly pilfered along with the candy bars—Tylenol, maybe, or something stronger.

The store in the service station appeared to have been looted, the door splintered as though body-slammed until it gave. Beside the pumps rested a snowmobile with the bumper sticker Live to Sled, Sled to Live.

"That was my ride," said Mrs. Mendelbaum. "We'll carpool."

"So it's only us left?"

"Not sure, my dear. I expect anyone else is on their way to meet the gentleman on the radio. Won't it be wonderful, all those people?"

"Yeah," began Sonya, finishing off the Gatorade, "about that."

"Yes, love?"

Sonya looked into the woman's eyes, wide with hope; beside her Esme traced a semi-circle in the dirt, back and forth, with her toe, sneaking glances at Sonya and then at the ground, clutching the stolen meds in her hands as though they were the antidote to whatever had happened to the world.

"It's just—"

Sonya stopped. With a roar a cherry-red sports car came barrelling down the highway, speeding past in a great plume of exhaust. It screeched to a halt about fifty yards along, then came whining back in high-speed reverse. While Sonya and Mrs. Mendelbaum and Esme stood gaping, their breath forming clouds in the frosty air, the driver eyed them through the open window.

"More friends!" shrieked Mrs. Mendelbaum. "Hello! Snickers!"

A figure in a cream-coloured cocktail dress stepped out of the car—very tall, very elegant—wrapped herself with a fur stole pulled from the back seat, and carefully tottered toward them in high heels. But before the ceremonial Snickers could be shared, the newcomer, billowing syrupy gusts of perfume, produced a deodorant-sized metal canister and menaced it at them, eyes narrowed behind lashes tarred with mascara.

"Is that," began Mrs. Mendelbaum.

"A grenade yes and I'll fucking use it asshole," screamed the woman, shaking the cylinder at them. "You think you're on your way to see him?"

"Ew," sneered Sonya—but here was Esme, clutching her arm with one hand, stashing the little packet in the front pocket of her sweatshirt with the other.

"On your knees bitches! Hands on your heads!"

Mrs. Mendelbaum wavered. "Will you blow us up?"

"Shut up. Debbie's in charge now. Got that? *Debbie*. On your knees!"

"Sure thing, Debbie," Sonya said as she knelt, squeezing Esme's shoulder before she laced her fingers together over her scalp. As the snow stung through her jeans she realized that her headache was completely gone.

With the three women genuflecting before her, Debbie seemed unsure what came next. And before she could figure it out, a gravelly, dyspeptic rumbling interrupted from above— not thunder; this was longer, more sustained. Everyone looked up. The sky had gone a deeper grey as night descended, and from the cloud cover nosed a 767 or some such thing, maybe a mile away and a few hundred feet above the snowy farms and fields, wingtips blinking.

Mrs. Mendelbaum jumped to her feet. "We must be near the airport!" When she wasn't blown up—Debbie was staring slack-jawed at the plane—Esme and Sonya rose as well.

"Let's go," said Debbie, making for the Corvette—and then paused: it was a two-seater. With a sigh, she gestured at the Audi, then Sonya. "We'll take that thing, I guess. You drive."

With Mrs. Mendelbaum riding shotgun and Esme cowering in the back seat, Sonya followed Debbie's orders: "Left! Right! Straight! Now turn here!" And by the time the Audi peeled onto an off-ramp that ran parallel to the end of the runway, only a few dozen feet above them the plane—roaring, landing gear lowered—was angling at the earth.

"Stop here, everyone out," said Debbie, so everyone filed across the highway where they stood in a line at the fence separating the road from the airport.

The plane's front wheels nuzzled the tarmac, bounced slightly, then nestled again and began to roll. Brakes screeching, the 767 tumbled down the runway toward the terminal, slowed gradually, then stopped.

"Excellent landing," noted Mrs. Mendelbaum.

As the engines died down, the doors swung open and out flopped inflatable slides. One after the other, women appeared—one in a burka, another in a sari, and two slender figures in shimmering salwar kameez; here were the pastels of business casual, the great canvas frock of Bavarian peasant stock, a head-wrap and dashiki, a young girl in a parka, a pasty, mincing lady in a Union Jack tracksuit—they all slid one by one to the tarmac until two dozen women clustered shivering together on the runway.

"People," said Sonya.

"People," agreed Mrs. Mendelbaum.

"Would you all please just *shut up*," hissed Debbie.

Then at the open hatch of the plane appeared a final woman, waving, in an official-looking uniform and matching hat. She bowed. The crowd applauded.

"The pilot," whispered Mrs. Mendelbaum to no one in particular.

This woman swan-dived down the slide and did a tricky flip to land on her feet, much to the delight of the other passengers. Debbie shook her head; beneath the stole her cocktail dress clung like a wet Kleenex to her body. She threaded her fingers, nail polish flaking, through the links in the fence; the other dangled at her side holding the grenade. Meanwhile, the pilot had stepped forward to address the group.

"Okay," said Debbie, "we're going in."

"I beg your pardon?" said Mrs. Mendelbaum.

"Climb the fence, Grandma."

And so they did: Esme dropped easily to the other side, and then Mrs. Mendelbaum, snowpants and all, was hoisted up and over, tumbling into Esme's arms; next was Sonya, and lastly Debbie, who threw her stilettos to Mrs. Mendelbaum, tucked the grenade into her brassiere and climbed, barefoot and muttering—and then snagged her pantyhose at the top of the fence. The passengers noticed Debbie, like some stranded Yeti up there in her furs, and began waving and cheering encouragement.

Dropping to the airport side, Debbie collected her shoes and announced, "Okay, you're my hostages. Don't do anything stupid."

"Stupid how?" asked Sonya.

"Just stupid. You run, everyone dies."

"Gotcha."

"Women of the world, I'm sittin' here still waitin' 4 U 2 cum. I just wanna—ladies, I can't wait 2 B with U. But the bubble bath is goin' cold and I'm wonderin' where U R. If we R gonna make a life 2gether we gotta start it soon. It all depends on us. It's time. Cum 2 me. Please. I'm just feelin' so alone."

"My name is Debbie. I've been an Artist-Formerly-Known-as-Prince fan since I was twelve years old. I've watched *Purple Rain* over a hundred times. I own every album on vinyl *and* CD and I have concert videos none of you have probably even heard of. So if there's anyone here who thinks they're a better person than me to go to Paisley Park then you better stand up and say something now."

No one moved; the grenade complicated things. All the women sat unspeaking in the orange vinyl chairs of the airport lounge. Debbie stood wide-legged by the Help Desk, the run in her stocking a thin pink fissure from ankle to inner thigh. At her feet, on their knees once again, were Esme, Sonya, and Mrs. Mendelbaum.

"Yeah, I didn't think so. So what's going to happen is that I'm going to take these three with me. And if I get a whiff that any of you are trying to follow us I will blow everyone up." She juggled the grenade from one hand to the other. "The old lady first."

Mrs. Mendelbaum's eyes widened. Sonya patted her arm. "You got that?"

After a few whispered translations, nods rippled around the room.

"Good then. Glad we're understood. Let's go, ladies."

But as Debbie was kicking her hostages to their feet, a voice called out: "Wait."

Debbie whipped around. "Who said that?"

The pilot stepped forward, wings on her lapel tilted at a haphazard angle—the plane crash-landing. In her eyes was worry; in her accent, Germany. "There are others. Guardians of the city."

"Who?"

"They are known as Diamond and Pearl."

"His old dancers?"

The pilot shrugged. "They are blocking Paisley Park. They do not believe in his mission. Did you not receive their facsimile communication?"

"They're sending *faxes*?" said Sonya.

Debbie glared at her.

The pilot reached into her carry-on luggage, a blue leather satchel bearing an airline's insignia, and produced a folded piece of paper.

Debbie took it and read, tapping the grenade against her leg. Sonya watched uneasily, afraid one vigorous strike might set the thing off. At last, Debbie lowered the page and licked her lips. "Well, we'll see about this," she snarled. And then, turning to Sonya, Mrs. Mendelbaum, and Esme: "Let's ride, ladies."

Minneapolis was burning in the starless, moonless night. The streetlights stood dead and unlit, office towers and homes sat in blackness, smoke billowed from buildings, and gunfire rattled in the snowy streets. "Drive!" screamed Debbie. "Drive!"

And so Sonya tore through the outlying suburbs, Mrs. Mendelbaum huddled with her head between her knees moaning, "No, no, no," and Esme stared straight ahead, her face a starched sheet of terror, arms elbow-deep in the pocket of her sweatshirt.

"It's D&P!" screamed Debbie. "Those whores trying to stop us getting to him!"

As they advanced toward downtown, a vicious pop sounded by the gas tank. "We've been hit," wailed Mrs. Mendelbaum.

"Nope," said Sonya, slowing the car down, "just blew a tire."

"What are you doing?" screamed Debbie, mascara streaking her face like war paint. "Are you crazy? Don't stop!"

But there was no choice. Sonya got out of the car. The back left wheel was already withering into a black rubbery goop. In the distance something like a bomb went off and a flash of light doused the neighbourhood; a few shots followed, then silence. Sonya's breath puffed from her face in clouds; she shivered and clutched her elbows.

Debbie came and stood beside Sonya, eyeing the flat. Mrs. Mendelbaum rolled down her window and stuck her head out to evaluate the damage. "Tire's flat," she said, nodding sagely.

Esme hadn't moved since they'd entered Minneapolis, and still sat petrified in the back seat, eyes tracking at once over everything and nothing, hands still hidden inside the pocket of her hoodie.

"If you want to keep going," Sonya told Debbie, "we'll have to walk."

Debbie's mouth opened, but no sound came out—her jaw just hung there slackly, her expression that of a stunned child watching a prized balloon lift into the heavens. The night was silent for a moment; everyone waited. Slowly into Debbie's eyes seeped that old look, a hungry, focused sort of lunacy, and her mouth snapped closed with a clack of teeth. She looked from Sonya, to Mrs. Mendelbaum, to Esme—but they were passing glances, because now she was off, shrieking, the grenade raised over her head, high heels ticking on the asphalt as she vanished into the night.

"Goodbye, Debbie," called Mrs. Mendelbaum from the back seat.

Sonya got back into the car and sat there, staring out the windshield: the darkness was broken by sporadic pockets of light from the flames of burning buildings. Things felt still again for a moment—but once again that was short-lived, as a fireball, like an orange fist thrust righteously into the sky, rose up from the Home Depot at the end of the block. The air was thick with smoke and ash, and debris rained down and went scuttling along the street.

Coughing, Sonya pulled her shirt over her face. "Anyone have any ideas?"

Esme leaned into the front seat and turned on the radio.

"People," came ♀'s voice, meek and exhausted, "u have gotta listen 2 me. This ain't no time 4 hate. I'm—I'm here. I'm waitin'. I don't wanna die 2nite." There was a pause, then, and Sonya was sure she heard a sniffle—was he *crying*? "This is a song I wrote," he finally spoke, "and it's called 'Just as Long as We're 2gether.' I hope u listen to it and I hope it means somethin' 2 u."

The music began and everything slowed down. Outside things seemed to settle; the flames leaping from the Home Depot dwindled. The only sound was ♀'s voice over the shudder of instruments, the patter of drums. It was a sweet song. Everyone listened.

By the chorus all three of them had joined in: "Just as long as we're 2gether / Everything's alright (everything's alright) /

Everything's alright (everything's alright)." While Mrs. Mendelbaum provided subtle harmonies, it was Esme's voice that moved Sonya the most: beautiful but fragile, at once knowing and innocent.

Then the song was over. They waited for ♀ to speak, but only a light hiss of static played from the radio. Everyone in the car waited for another blast from outside, or rekindled gun battles, but none came. And there was something about this silence that didn't feel like an interlude—whatever battle had been raging seemed to be over.

Esme touched Sonya on the arm. She was pointing out the window at an alleyway off the main street. "Can you—"

"Do you have to pee, dear?" asked Mrs. Mendelbaum, with a look of empathy that spoke of her own ongoing urinary dramas. From within her snowsuit she produced a squashed roll of toilet paper, and with it a similarly flattened pack of Dentyne. "Gum?"

Once everyone was chewing she told Sonya, "Pop the trunk, I'll change the flat."

Out on the street, the three women stood together and scanned the shadows for threats—holding their breath, listening. Nothing: no explosions or gunfire or sounds of any kind. The city was still and cold. "Go pee," whispered Mrs. Mendelbaum, blowing into her hands. While she dug out the jack and spare and got down to business, Sonya and Esme walked arm in arm into the shadows, huddling together for heat.

Before she squatted, Esme reached into her sweatshirt pocket and pulled out the cardboard box she'd stolen from the rest stop. Sonya's guts did a little tumble at the sight of it.

Esme's voice trembled out of the shadows: "Do you know how these things work?"

Daylight was just breaking as the Audi crossed over the Canadian border, spare tire struggling alongside the three chrome-capped wheels. On both sides of the highway were great walls of trees, pine and birch, larch and poplars and cedar, everything heavy with snow. Esme had fallen asleep, draped across the back seat. Ms. Jorgenssen (she'd reverted, in a blaze of self-satisfaction, to her maiden name) was a jumble of half-removed snowsuit, head lolling against the window, drooling steadily. The radio was off. The only sound was the gentle purr of the engine, and the forest was pierced here and there with spears of light from the rising sun.

Where were they going? What were they looking for? Sonya wasn't sure. She was just happy to be driving, out in the world, alive. There was no one else on the highway. She was confident they wouldn't see anyone. It was just the three of them. And maybe that was enough.

Looking once again at the blue dot on the testing stick that Esme had stuck to the dashboard with gum, Sonya recalled, how, only hours ago, her heart had fluttered at the sight of it. There had been something so proud and brave and terrified about the way Esme had fixed it there, and afterward Mrs. Mendelbaum had hauled them both into her arms for a mildly suffocating group hug—and then, releasing them, been reborn as Jorgenssen.

In the rearview mirror Sonya could see Esme sleeping in the back seat. The girl lay there, curled up, with the hood of her sweatshirt pulled over her head. From it a wisp of hair had tumbled out along her nose, hanging by her mouth, and this wavered as she breathed: with each inhalation it clung to her face, was released as she exhaled, trembled for a moment, and then was sucked back in.

The car moved steadily over the road, through the forest, the snow glittering in the rising sun. And here on the dash was hope—that little blue dot. Sonya thought again of the log cabin she'd long dreamt about. It could be tucked away anywhere along here, behind and among the trees, out of sight and secret. It would be a quiet, simple little shack, and warm once they got a good fire going that lit the room golden, smoke curling up from the chimney.

They'd find a supermarket or convenience store along the way and load up on groceries. Later that day when they reached this place, down some dirt track to a clearing in the trees, inside the three of them would cuddle under woolly blankets while their dinner heated on the fire. They'd spoon steaming Chef Boyardee Ravioli and Chunky Soup straight from the can, pass everything around so everyone got a taste. The food would be good and real in the way that bad and fake things are often so good and so real, in the way that when people come together sometimes that sort of thing is just what you need.

NEIL SMITH

ATHEISTS WERE ALMOST
RIGHT ABOUT EVERYTHING

THE OTHER DAY, Bobby Henzel and Nanami Kazikuyo drew
up a list of things that Heaven doesn't have. Lung cancer, dollar bills, hair dye, winter parkas, compact discs, marijuana, pork
chops, contact lenses, condoms, tooth decay, email, governors,
houseflies, cow's milk, photocopiers, handguns—all these dis-
parate things and many more found their way onto their list.
The last item the two teenagers added to this inventory was god.

Heaven has no god.

But one thing the great beyond still has is anger. As a result,
an anger management class is held weekly in Heaven at the
Ben Franklin Center for Continuing Education. The Ben Franklin looks creepily like the high school outside Chicago where
Bobby got gunned down last month by a skinny blond kid he'd
never seen before in his life. That school was also long and squat
with three stories, a flat roof, a mix of red and yellow bricks, and
a mural on one wall.

The mural here at the Ben Franklin is an expressionist explosion. Paint splatters, splashes, drippings. The artist had a hissy fit
and flung paint at the wall. That's what Nanami says as she eyes
the mural early on a Monday morning. A sure sign of anger. "And

why an anger management class?" she wants to know. "Why not an anger flinging class?"

Bobby and Nanami climb the stone steps of the Ben Franklin, enter the building, and wander down its hallways. The halls are empty save for a few stragglers because it's already 9:20 and the workshops started at nine o'clock. Soon Bobby is sweating. His armpits are growing dank because he has a queasy déjà vu feeling. Any second he might turn a corner and bump into a blond stranger brandishing a pistol.

Nanami slaps closed any lockers left open as she walks past. Bobby concentrates on the slates hung on the wall outside each classroom. Written in coloured chalk on each slate is the title of the group session held inside. The slate he's just passed reads: "Why We Can't Milk Goats: Theories on Sterilization in the Afterlife." He's looking for "Coping with Anger: Untwisting Your Knickers." The anger management group had better be in a classroom nearby. He doesn't think he can walk down another hallway. Already this one seems to be contracting and expanding. One second it looks as narrow as a bowling alley; the next it balloons to the size of a basketball court. Somebody hand him a paper bag because he might start hyperventilating.

Nanami is chattering about the only discussion group she's attended so far in Heaven: "Not All Deaths Are Natural." It was held at 22 Wormwood Road where she and Bobby share a room in a high-rise residence reserved for the murdered.

"People just bragged about how they died," Nanami claims. One-upmanship. Whose death was the most gruesome. Who suffered the most. "Mrs. Lebowitz was the worst. Okay, so her husband buried her alive in a steamer trunk in her backyard. But she was practically in raptures describing how she'd broken off her fingernails picking the lock from the inside. I lied that my killer had put me through a wood chipper semi-conscious, and that shut her up."

Bobby turns to Nanami. She has a half-smile on her face. She's made up that story about Mrs. Lebowitz, the old lady who lives next door to them in the murder tower. His roommate is testing his credulity again. (The other day, she claimed that a neighbouring building was reserved for people killed in embarrassing freak accidents. Rubbed out by a runaway grocery cart. Drowned in a bowl of party punch. A brain aneurysm caused by a cotton swab inserted too deeply into an ear canal. "Really?" he exclaimed. "Cotton swabs can kill?")

But now in the hallway, that half-smile of hers quickly fades. Nanami sees Bobby's sweaty forehead. His sudden pastiness. "What's wrong?"

Bobby turns away, embarrassed by his frailty. He steadies himself against the wall, one hand resting against a slate that reads: "AWARE: Atheists Were Almost Right about Everything." His legs go wobbly. The hallway tilts. He drops the canvas bag carrying his sketch pad, and his pencils scatter across the floorboards like a game of pick-up sticks.

Down on his knees he goes. Nanami crouches beside him. "Put your head down, Henzel." She pushes his head to his knees. "It's a dizzy spell. It'll pass. I got them too when I first came to Heaven."

He stares at the cracks between the floorboards. "I'm sorry."

"Don't be. This is a perfect excuse for missing that anger session. They're probably group-hugging as we speak." She pats the back of his head. A little too hard, though. Her clunky plastic ring denting his skull.

"The group leader's probably telling everybody, 'Quash that anger! Just be nice!' But niceness is overrated," Nanami says as she crawls across the floor gathering Bobby's pencils. Being nice, in fact. "Take you, for instance, Henzel. When you lived on Earth, you were probably Mr. Young America. Didn't talk back to teachers. Didn't spit in public. Girls in your classes must have had secret crushes on you, written your initials in the margins of their math books. Blogged about you." Here her voice goes high and lilting: "'Bobby smiled at me in the cafeteria lineup today.' But where did all that niceness get you?"

Bobby lifts a clammy face toward this girl. Mr. Young America? Smiles in the cafeteria? What's she talking about?

"It got you here," Nanami says. "The same place as me, and I was obnoxious to everybody."

They hear shoes squeaking in the hallway. Bobby's head jerks sideways. His heart thumps. He half expects to see his skinny blond murderer. But no, it's an Asian man with a ponytail. When the man turns the corner, Bobby mutters, "I think I saw my killer, Nanami." He puts his head back down, mumbles to his knees. "I think I saw him on the 727 that brought me to Heaven."

"What?!" Nanami cries. "Why didn't you tell me before?"

"I only caught a glimpse of the guy on the plane. I can't swear it was him. Maybe my eyes were playing tricks." Bobby sits up. "Maybe I'm losing my friggin' mind."

"You're not losing your mind, Henzel," Nanami insists. "If anybody around here is going mad, it's definitely not you."

Behind them the door to a classroom swings open. A head pops out. Closely cropped curly hair. A black man with skin light enough to reveal a smattering of dark freckles across his nose and cheeks. "What do we have here?" he says in mock surprise. "Two young people ready to regale us with stories of a godless yet fruitful life!"

Bobby has elected himself secretary of the meeting. But instead of taking the minutes, he draws caricatures of the members of AWARE, whom Zachary, the group leader, jokingly calls "barbaric heathens." Zachary looks like a superhero with his broad shoulders and a tight red tracksuit that shows off his muscles. Bobby is sketching him, no easy task given how hyperactive

Zachary is. As he talks, he waves his arms and bounces around the classroom, his sneakers squealing. Zachary is complaining about medication in Heaven. "The only drugs available here are homeopathic. Sugar pills. People pop them for warts, insomnia, jock itch, hay fever. And, depressingly enough, they work. All very homeo*pathetic* if you ask me."

Twenty or so people are sitting around the classroom in moulded chair-desk combos. The man next to Nanami, a hefty guy who seems to be wearing his desk like a corset, nods vigorously. Behind Bobby sits a young woman knitting, her needles click-clacking. Taped to the walls of the room are caricatures of American presidents. Theodore Roosevelt hugs a mangy teddy bear. Lincoln's top hat sports a bullet hole. Washington swings an axe at a cherry tree.

"So Heaven isn't a place of scientific rigour, I grant you that," says Zachary. "But nor is Heaven home to the supernatural. Nor is Heaven home to the Christian god! What did Thomas Jefferson, my favourite Atheist president, say about the Christian god?" Zachary glances at Jefferson's caricature: the third president of America is tearing the Bible in two the way a strongman will rip apart a phonebook. "My man Tom said that god was a being of terrific character: cruel, vindictive, capricious, unjust. Is the It cruel, vindictive, capricious, and unjust? No, the It is simply blasé. The It gives us a home and food, and the It lets us be."

"Who's It?" Nanami asks.

"You don't have the floor yet, young lady," Zachary replies, a bit petulantly. "I have the goat, so I have the floor." From the teacher's desk, Zachary picks up a foot-long crucifix with a blue toy goat nailed to the cross. He brandishes the goat crucifix like a magic wand. "But because you're new here, I'll answer your question. The It is simply this place."

Bobby crosshatches shadows onto his drawing as Zachary likens Heaven to a mammoth underground fungus whose

spores inch up through the soil to spawn the apartment towers, the subway, the thrift stores, the schools, and all the rest. "I
believe the It to be an organism," Zachary says. "When a crack
in a sidewalk slowly fills itself in, the It is mending itself. Just as
a scab on your knee heals itself."

He points the goat toward Nanami's knee, which is covered
with a bandage. She scraped her knee on the weekend when she
fell while jogging along a forest trail.

"But is the It some omniscient, omnipotent god?" Zachary
continues. "Is the It magic? I think not. Not any more than your
healing scab is magic."

"Are we part of the It?" Nanami asks.

"Did I say I was ready to take questions yet?" Zachary ad-
monishes.

Nanami looks at Bobby. Rolls her eyes.

"Okay, then, yes, I shall answer. Are we part of the organism?
A kind of living cell? I think so. This is not magic, mind you. This
is nature. The nature of the It. The nature of Heaven."

Bobby has sketched a big toadstool beneath Zachary's feet
and is now drawing a cross-eyed goat peeking over the man's
shoulder.

"The It isn't like that megalomaniac god in the Bible. That
cruel, vindictive, capricious, unjust god never existed, thank
god. That's why we Atheists were almost right." Zachary's
voice grows louder, more irate. "Unlike the Christian god, the It
doesn't give a hoot whether we believe in the It. The It doesn't
care if we pray to the It. The It doesn't want to hear our tedious
confessions. The It doesn't read our dreary thoughts. The It
doesn't care if we covet our neighbour's ass. The It doesn't
mind if man lies with woman, man, or even goat. And the It"—
here Zachary pauses, a smile frozen on his face—"doesn't give a
flying crap if we take Its goddamn name in vain."

A few chuckles from the participants.

"What about murder?" Nanami asks. "Does the It care if we kill?"

Zachary walks toward Nanami. With his face twisted into an exaggerated scowl, he raises the goat crucifix above his head as if to bludgeon her with the thing.

She cringes and slides down in her seat.

"Hey!" Bobby yells. "Hey!"

But Zachary just smiles sweetly and hands the crucifix to Nanami. "Please enlighten us, young lady," he says, "with your own beliefs."

What does Nanami believe in? Getting even. At least that's what her story seems to be about. Getting even with those damn Mormons back in Utah. Standing at the front of the classroom, she seems less bold, less poised than when she's alone with Bobby. She speaks softly, pauses often. She slouches. She glances out the window. She keeps fiddling with the goat crucifix and finally lays it down on the teacher's desk.

When she first moved to Salt Lake City in grade four, Nanami tells the members of AWARE, she thought the Mormons were called Ladder Day Saints. She pictured them, on the day of their death, climbing giant, wobbly ladders to Heaven. These Mormons believed in an afterlife, something her parents dismissed as rubbish. She wanted to believe too. An afterlife! So storybook magical! But she learned no rung of that giant ladder had space for a Japanese girl.

"For these saints," she says, "if you weren't white, you were of another species. They looked at you and saw a panda bear or a water buffalo." Within a couple of years, she no longer wanted a spot on their ladder.

She glances at Bobby, who smiles at her so she'll keep talking. He's drawing her skinny legs, her knobby knee with its droopy bandage. (The other day he drew a close-up of her scraped knee, the skin torn and pimpled with scabs. That drawing is the only sketch of her she's let him tape to the wall of their room. "My bloody knee feels more like me than my face does," she said.)

At the front of the classroom, Nanami is badmouthing the Mormons. You had to be a gullible chump, she insists, to believe that the church's founder, a con man named Joseph Smith, dug up golden tablets in his backyard that were scrawled with a message from god. Tablets nobody but Mr. Smith could see. "And the man was visited by an angel named Moroni," she says. "Moroni the Moron Angel."

Nanami picks up a piece of chalk and prints these slogans on the blackboard:

Jesus Is Lard.

Praying Is Begging.

Apes Evolved from Mormons.

She wipes her chalky palms together over a garbage pail. Tells the group she used to print these same sentences in indelible ink on bathroom walls across Salt Lake City. "My angry phase," she says, throwing Bobby a wry half-smile.

"But the Mormons got their revenge," she adds.

About five months back, a Latter-day crackpot by the name of Cage Young climbed onto the roof of her school for some target practice. Nanami looks away from the class, out the window, and slowly utters: "You shall not drink coffee or tea, Mr. Mormon, but you shall shoot a girl in the head."

A sharp intake of breath from the knitter behind Bobby. Zachary, seated three rows away, claps his hands once. Holds those two hands together in front of his mouth. You'd swear this Atheist was praying.

"Why did Cage Young do it?" Nanami asks wistfully. "Did a voice tell him to? The voice of god, maybe?"

The murdered girl looks at the floor. Then back up at Bobby. Her eyes blink. Then she grabs the goat crucifix. Raises it above her head like George Washington's axe. Whacks the thing against the teacher's desk.

The blue goat pops off, does a triple axel, lands across the room in the garbage pail.

For a few seconds, there's silence. Everyone stares at the garbage pail. Even Nanami looks amazed.

"A miracle!" Zachary finally cries. "We were wrong after all, people. There is a god!"

That night in the murder tower, Nanami wakes screaming from a nightmare about the sniper. In fact, her screaming triggers Bobby's screaming. So they both awake yelling their heads off and thrashing with their covers. Their hearts thumping. Their hands clammy. Their eyes wide in the dark.

Mrs. Lebowitz, the old lady in the next room, comes rapping on their door. Her voice tremulous, she calls out, "You two all right in there?" They're killing each other, she must think. They're ripping each other's throats out.

For an hour afterward, Bobby and Nanami sit on Nanami's bed with their desk lamps on. Their throats are raw from screaming. In the voice of a two-pack-a-day smoker, Nanami talks about hating Cage Young. He's a eunuch of a man, she says. He has no balls. He has bullets where his testicles should be. How unfair, she says, that she knows so little about a ball-less man who played such a pivotal role in her life. "All I know about him is his rage," she says. "When that bullet entered me, so did his rage."

She goes on to say she loathes Heaven. The place reminds her of the community her grandparents retired to in Florida. Every day is like Sunday. Mind-numbingly mellow. She gets weepy and starts dabbing her eyes with the corner of her pillowcase, and Bobby doesn't know what to say. When his depressed mother used to get sad and teary-eyed, he wouldn't say much either. He isn't a talker. He's at best a mumbler. But he used to sketch his mother when she was in these moods, and that's what he does with Nanami tonight. His sketch emphasizes the wire-hanger skinniness of his roommate's collarbones and the choppiness of her hair. He draws a smoky cloud over her head, smudging the graphite with his fingertips. When Nanami asks what that cloud is, he says, "Sorrow." Then, with his pink eraser, he rubs out the cloud and tells her she can sleep now. "Sorrow's gone," he mumbles.

She looks at him, that slack-jawed deadpan of hers, and says, "That's the stupidest thing I've ever heard." But she does slip back under the covers. She does fall back to sleep.

Bobby, however, does not. He lies on his bed in the dark and stares at the full moon smiling at him through the window of their room. Heaven may not have gods or guns or magic, but Bobby likes to believe in these things. Tonight he imagines the doily moon as his god. The moon is his It. The It is magical. The It transports him back to a high school outside Chicago. The It arms him with a pistol. The It whispers in his ear, eggs him on— "Thatta boy!"—as Mr. Young America stalks the hallways for a stranger to kill.

JAY BROWN

GLADIATOR

NIGHTS ARE THE worst part at AtGen. RTI5N is narcolaxic, meaning sleepiness makes you feel like you need to pee, and so every forty-five minutes or so I find myself in my gown hovering overtop of the urinal in the Gastro Ward lavatory trying to squeeze out a few drops. That's when I'll bump into Polly, who's on YL96B, which they're calling final phase. The peeing thing on YL96 is physiological—standard diuretic and not so severe. It's sticker-grade warning at best. It's always good to see Polly and to get the low-down on the YL trial. He's stuck it out from YL8 and onwards, from back when the juice caused dermal complications in people with more than one-fiftieth Polynesian gen. stock. They've shaved all of the growths off his face and arms, though you can see where they used to be: scars like oval liver spots above his lips and on the backs of his hands. He's such a goer he even had them leave one on, like a badge. It's a wobbly knot of flesh connected by the slenderest bit of tissue to the joint of his right thumb.

"Clifferton," he says and nods at me.

"Polly-boy."

We go about our business.

Just above each urinal's motion detector is the AtGen fountain of life symbol, the three wavy lines falling onto the raised
cup of a tulip. It's backlit by a throbbing blue LED. You get the
story behind that at the Participant Inductee Hall where they
screen you before admission. There's a row of quiet little rooms
with a single leather sofa and a pitcher of Herbavit Water inside
each of them. You get to go into one and have it all to yourself
for fifteen minutes while they play the welcome vid. It shows
how the AtGen militico-pharma model goes all the way back
to Napoleon. How, once you sign the appropriate paperwork,
you'll be a part of the AtGen family, and how at AtGen we all
work not just for ourselves but also for a better, richer, safer, lon-
ger-lasting world.

Why? Because the world was once a beautiful place, says this
tired, grandfatherly voice, and still is but it's been buried under
horrible things. It's like going to the dump and finding your
high school sweetheart's sweater, which smelled like her fresh
skin that time when you held her under this tree they show in
a now dark and lonely field. Her sweater's all balled up and covered in rotting food and tilting at the lip of the incinerator. Hold
up, operator! Meanwhile, such images of suffering and wast-
ing: emaciated and naked bodies heaped in frozen piles, enemy
combatants stringing up the still-smouldering corpses of dead
soldiers from a rusty iron bridge, children—little children—in
some kind of sandy tent and like zombies with flies on their
mouths. Thunder, darkness, then a sunrise and a giant cheer, a
close-up of a handshake behind a podium, a husband and wife
opening the door on their new home and their little boy dancing for joy in the kitchen, a field of purple canola flowers and
a cow munching by a fence, a man and a woman (wearing a
familiar, and now laundered, sweater) walking slowly, romanti-
cally, away from the camera, towards the cow which continues

to gently graze and gives no sign at all that it could charge and trample them—which is a thing, don't ask me why, I sometimes worry about when I imagine standing in a field next to one. At the very end it shows a simulation of the AtGen headquarters in Laval rising from the ground like how a flower grows and unfurls its leaves and petals. The soft blue rain comes down through the sunshine. A hum you barely knew was there rises in volume until your glass of Herbavit is dancing on top of one of the subwoofer armrests and you can really feel the force of all the possible beauty there is in this world.

You come out of that room crying, I swear to God. Saying: I want that. Want the field and the woman, the safe, loving cow and rain and not to sleep anymore on the floor of my mother's tiny habitable with ears chafed raw because of the earplugs, because of her snoring. Thinking how I've been so alone and all confused and no amount of long walks back and forth to the noodle shop on the far side of the Barlow Bridge seems to make me feel any better. I want to help. I'll do what it takes.

Beside me, Polly grunts and a short, powerful blast hits the porcelain back of the urinal and a fine warm mist settles on my right leg below the gown.

"It's late?" he says. "Or it's early?"

"I don't know."

Johnny, the night monitor, and a special kind of asshole, is standing there behind us in regulation gloves with plastic over-slips and a counter-contagion mask, waiting to take notes in case one of us faints or passes blood. He coughs but doesn't say anything. Doesn't flip to the clock page on his auto-jot and say 1:09 or whatever with that flat, tired voice of his. It's like he's watching soup and not two Participants whose blood samples and night sweats pay his wage. If someone like Johnny has an opportunity to tell us the time then he should be *happy* about it.

It's been ten weeks now since all of the hoopla at the beginning and I admit that there are times when it's easy to get a little bit blue, to feel a bit disconnected from everything and taken for granted. It becomes easy to forget—while lying in my cot for an hour, say, waiting for a MedAssist bot to de-intubate the clot-thinning thingamajiggy from my neck, or when Dr. Ryan vetoes the anti-nausea meds because of the chance their chemical signature might throw off some particular reading or another—that we're all part of something bigger here. Front-liners in the war on human suffering. And we've all been assigned our particular battles. And just because we spend most days lying by ourselves in a dim room, waiting, it doesn't mean we're actually alone. Maybe in body, but not in spirit.

That's why it's good that I ran into Polly. Just the sight of him brings it all back to me—the purpose and the meaning of what we're up to. It's real warriors like him that help me see it plain. That and the cut-outs on my ward-bedroom wall with all the faces of those kids diagnosed with Post-infantile Explosive Diverticular Cirrhosis—PIED.C—especially the one of the little girl with the big brown eyes and the messy bed-head who (I like to think) looks like me, looks like the sort of kid I'd worry about after I dropped her off at school, even though I saw her walk past the hall monitor at the door and I knew that she was the teacher's favourite and had lots of great friends. There's so much that can go wrong anyway. I'd carry her down the stairs until she was six or seven because I'd be too scared of her falling and cracking her fragile little head on all of those millions of sharp corners. If I had a kid I'd care about her so much, too much. A smotherer, that's what I'd be. She'd always be screaming at me to leave her alone, already, she's *fine*.

AtGen Pharma has a lot of contracts for the infant and juvenile stuff since that's the biggest guaranteed market—that's where the love is. So it's them we're saving, Participants like me and Polly, lab-cruisers like Kelly the vat-queen over in Neuro, Alphonse who runs the oscillator in the blood lab, the guys in Marketing who transit through the facilities every now and then with a flash-cam, all the way up to headquarters where Kasper Silex himself sits on his deserved leather chair looking out the window onto his good work. We're here for all the mothers and fathers and brothers and sisters and grandmothers and so on, gathered around the kitchen table while their little girl— herself innocent of this diagnosis they've all just heard from the doctor—sleeps away upstairs. Thinking, how will we tell her? She's too little to shoulder all of this weight. Who should have to live through that? Who will help her? Who will help *us*?

"…help us?" I murmur, worked up by the image of that poor family.

Polly cocks a spidery eyebrow but lets it go.

How I imagine myself sometimes is on the shore of the inner harbour in front of the sleeping city—it's me and Polly and the rest of us vs. these giant things stepping out of the water, lurching, dripping. Lymphoma and Ward's Syndrome and PIED.C: we've got the guns but they keep coming. They're coming for all the children in their cubic habitables in Grovener's Grove and Sweetgrass City and the Sour Bun Villages and we have to stop them. Throw a little RTI2 in the bazooka, Corporal Cliff, Dr. Ryan tells me, see if that slows them down. No? How about this, then? Or this? I don't think I can make it, Sarge—I can't feel my hands. I'm itching under my skin. There's too much blood accumulating in my vitreous…Will you shut up and look at 'em, Cliff! You effing did it. I look and sure enough the hulking corpse of PIED.C is collapsing down into the harbour muck like a deflating blimp.

He's a fine old codger, that Polly. Tells me he'd probably be getting up to go to the can a couple of times a night even without the YL. Prostate like a buffalo. I laugh back and both of us just stay standing there one hand up against the tiles for five minutes, waiting to see how much we're really going to get. When I was lying in my cot it felt like I had a grape coming down the pipe but now there's just an ache in my gut.

"If either of you is feeling dizzy you need to report it," Johnny says.

As if we were children, and not well past the need for that in either of our trials anyway. 96B is basically market, for God's sake. I'd like to remind Johnny just who's front-line indispensable on this experiment and just who's not. Any jackass can pen-tab his notes into an auto-jot. But who has what it takes to stand between the rising monsters and the sleeping city?

"You hear the latest on the monocytic leukemia thing?" says Polly, ignoring Johnny.

"Which one?"

"M5."

"Oh man, that's Jessalyn, right? Who'd she attack this time?" Jessalyn, the longest-standing trial Participant, has seen so many androgen bumps she's got whiskers growing out of her ears and a libido like a bonobo ape.

Polly lowers his voice for effect. "It's Andre, the new kid. He doesn't seem to mind."

Even though it's kind of funny, thinking of poor Jessalyn grinding against Andre in an idle blood lab makes me sad. It's not pretty, but you have to find love where you can.

Polly takes note of my mood. "Seen Violet around?" he says. He's got a way of cutting through the B.S. and putting his stubby finger right on the heart of things.

"Oh, you know. Not lately."

"You know what I mean."

Polly's voice has that fatherly tone and both of my eyelids twitch involuntarily. They sting. I'm supposed to report quick, unexpected emotions to Johnny but to hell with it. "I don't know…I'm waiting and all…"

"She's coming. Hold on, Cliff." He turns and looks me hard in the eyes. "Stay the course, Clifferino."

"You know I will."

"It can't be more than days now until they put you on the next one…the '16, right?"

"Just days, yeah. Gotta be."

At the sani-station Polly does a sly little finger moustache with chest-chop to me in the mirror, which is the Nazi sign— meaning Johnny. His extra thumb bobbles against the back of his hand. Then he shuffles on out.

RTI5N being the night formula they switch me to RTI5M after seven AM, which has a bit of a kick to it because of the Dextromethorphan and the Thoramone. It makes my skin flush and elevates my pulse but when it feels like I have to whiz buckets I really whiz buckets. I catch a few sweaty zzzz's in the rec room, which is floor-to-ceiling vid-papered. If I've got it to myself I always punch in the enviro-code for "Space." I lean back in the recliner with a pack of Frambroise Punch held over my burning face and the room arcs slowly across the methane lakes on Io.

Noon, Dr. Ryan comes in to take a vial and check my stats with a vital-bot.

"Do you know who I am?" he says. Back on RT06 I had morning dementia and tried to throttle him with a twist of my IV tube. He overcame me easily—inability to grip being another early side effect (thus the Thoramone)—and we joke about it now, but he's never stopped asking that before stepping out fully from behind the bot.

"How are you feeling?" He's got Johnny's notes on his auto-jot—zapping through them with one hand, taking my pulse with another. A real pro.

I think real hard if there's anything I need to share. "Itchy, I was itchy last night on my ankles."

He mutters some doctor-speak into a mini mic stuck into his collar like a gleaming Tic Tac. "Mmm-hm. And...?"

"Maybe a bit downbeat."

Murmur murmur. "And?"

"That's it. I guess. I'm pretty sure that's all."

Dr. Ryan punches some code into the extended arm of the MedAssist bot which spits out a line of paper that he'll stick to the board outside my curtain when he goes.

"What are we looking at here, Doc?" I say. Basically meaning: how much longer until we're on to RT16? I don't think I'll last much longer.

"Everything's fine, Cliff. You just keep doing your job. You're doing great."

He slides the auto-jot into a pouch on the front of his jacket and sets the bot to dolly up its wheels. He pats me on the thigh. It's always over so quickly.

"Doc?" I say, "do you think we're getting close?" I wish that I had more to offer than itchiness, like pronounced and worrisome lymphedema or even just some shortness of breath. "Do you think I'm the right one? You know, did you get the right Participant?"

He's ready to go but he sits back down on the edge of my cot, which creaks with added weight. He looks me right in the eye. "Cliff, you're exactly what we need. You test like a dream. From a trials perspective let's just say you've been blessed with the

Cadillac of lymph systems. And we're getting close. I'll send you the paperwork sometime this afternoon. We're gonna see big results on this next one. You should be proud."

He says a few things after that but I can't remember what. A new permutation for the RT means a new contract. A new contract means Violet.

As part of the purity code we're not allowed any cosmetics, but a little bit of sugar and water keeps the wave in my hair down nicely. I check the floor for any tissue wads, make up my cot and then sit on it, waiting. I've got an assortment of gowns in my locker and I've saved the purple one for her because it's the one I was wearing the first time we met when she said I looked noble, like a gladiator, or an actor in a movie about gladiators and she's this groupie come into his trailer for an autograph. "Gladdy," she says, when she's feeling playful, "my brave Gladdy." Or: "You know how cute your teeth look when you're mumbling in your sleep, Gladdy?"—the time I fainted when she came in because I sat up too quickly. Or, just before putting my name to the contract: "What a large pen you have, Mr. Gladdy."

To tell you the truth, that little girl with the messy hair—it's mine and Violet's kid, is how I think of her. Ours from the time after I've done my bit here, when RT goes market and we can roll everything I've saved into a deposit for a nice little habitable over in Sour Bun Village IV. Let's say I'm here another twenty weeks or so—it'll be enough. I'll come home from the office of my new job and Violet will be asleep on the couch with a baby on top of her—a baby who's safe forever from PIED.C because of her old man. I'll make dinner, something steamy and healthy. There'll be a balcony—doesn't have to be a big one—and while whatever's cooking is cooking I'll step outside to feel the updraft curl off of the cooling concrete and watch the

sun sink down on the Pacific. Things will have worked out for
me. When, from the vantage point of the fifteenth floor, I see
some loser on the Barlow Bridge heading for the noodle shop
I'll feel lucky.

"Ring ring," comes her sweet voice from outside my curtain
around three o'clock. "Anybody home?"

"Why nurse," I reply, "you seem to have caught me at a moment of indispose."

She peeks through the slit, her hair is in two loose pigtails
held together with bee-shaped clips. In one hand she's got the
contract, in the other she's got a plate of little pink sugar cookies.
"Trust me. I've seen it all before."

Then she comes over to me and kisses me on both eyes, my
nose and cheeks and lips. After two weeks of nothing but Dr.
Ryan and the bots touching me let me tell you...We have to be
gentle, since I've got a heparin lock plugged into the veins on
my left wrist, its IV plug-in held back with an elastic.

"I miss you so much when you're not around," I say. "Like, I
imagine you and me on this cot floating through space forever."

"I miss you too, Cliff."

"Sometimes I wish we could. Just float off into space like
that. Just the two of us and our own concerns and that's that.
Together, you know? And not just like this. All Violet, all the
time. I'd even take a bit more Violet, a bit more of the time."

Her face does this hardening where her soft lips get sucked
inside and she breathes big breaths through her nose, not looking at me. Sometimes I say the wrong thing and it hurts her and
she closes down and what starts as something nice is ruined by
my own stupid neediness.

"Me too, Cliff. Absolutely. It's not easy for me either. But how
would you like it if I sneaked off from my job to see you here,
and while I was seeing you Dr. Ryan popped by for a baseline
med adjustment?"

I know what she means: How would I like it for her to be fired and for Johnny to be the one who presents me every twelve days or so with a contract like this one. Would it be the same to put my fingers under the elastic hem of *his* nylon slacks? Would I like *him* to be the one who caresses my tender parts for half an hour while Violet highlights job ads at Tim Hortons?

"No," I say, chagrined at the image of my beautiful girl being sized up by pimply counter-boys holding giant nougat and almond crullers.

"Then why talk about the impossible? Just," she breaks off a piece of cookie against the plate with her long blue nails, warm to me again, and raises it to my lips, "enjoy the moment."

And it's good. There's a skin of smooth icing on top of the biscuit. The whole thing crunches honestly in my mouth. Another thing to remember for always. Inside I'm living for the day when I'll wait out in reception for her to finish her shift, me dressed up in my tan cords and a blazer. When I'll take her to dinner and I'll have the waiter bring out a plate of these very cookies with a ring hidden under the mound. The way her eyes will look when it's me popping the sweet into her mouth.

"Oh! You've got crumb on your lip, Mr. Sincere. You really are the messiest little Gladdy I know!" She paws it away.

"But do you understand? Do you understand what I'm trying to say?"

She sighs, and sets the contract, its paper and pen, down onto my lap. She taps the dotted line and I scrawl my big loopy "C.G." When it's done she takes it from me and pushes it away from both of us on the table. She pulls my head towards her and presses it into her stomach and I can't see her face but I can hear her sad voice where it travels through her body, "I think I do understand, Cliff. At least I want to." Then she steps back and unclips her phone from her earlobe, swings her ID badge around the back of her shirt and begins to undo her blouse.

I know I'm not going to get further than a hand on one of her naked breasts, a feel, maybe, of the hole where a bellybutton piercing used to be, before my blood pressure rises above 135 and the monitor starts dinging and Violet shuts us down for another two weeks until RT17. Maybe even three. It's torture. It's all torture, but it's my private battle. It belongs to me.

Come Tuesday morning Dr. Ryan and a phlebotomist administer the first dose of the RT16 right away into my neck. "Take these too." There's a small mound of grey and yellow capsules in two different clear-plastic Baggies. "One of the yellow after the shot and two each of the grey whenever your hands get shaky, if they get shaky. You," Dr. Ryan says to Johnny, who's standing by the doorway trying to look important, "help him watch his hands." He winks big at me and taps the grey-capsule Baggie. "There's a lot riding on this, believe me. We've got high expectations."

All morning Johnny watches me like a hawk, but the '16 goes down smooth. Nothing burns. In fact, it's like I've got a line of menthol running under my skin. I shrug my shoulders. Everything is monitored with special attention the first day. I breathe into a plastic pipe mid-afternoon and a bot examines the saturation of the drugs in my lung tissue. My meals are more like tests. I have to wait a full minute after each bite of cornmeal mush and hamburger and let Dr. Ryan listen to my stomach through a stethoscope.

Wednesday I'm back in the rec room flipping through a pile of old *Pyrogrrl* comics. Over by the games tables there's a small group of testers who've flung the vinyl cover off the foosball table and Nathan and Aretha, both late-stage kidney trial Participants, are twisting weakly at the long rubber handles from their wheelchairs. Andre, the new kid, has both hands gripped around the table's rubber bumpers, while Jessalyn runs her nails through his hair with long forceful sweeps of both paws. His eyes are closed. When he opens them he's got a look on his face that's difficult to read, like he's afraid Jessalyn will tear out his hair if he moves. Or maybe he's just flushing from the U450 mini-bump they've got leaking into his feed tube. Either way, he looks over at me in my chair at the same time I raise my head from my comic. I think of how much I appreciated Polly the other night as I give Andre the thumbs up. We all need someone to look to for encouragement and support. It's going to be okay, Andre-ski. Stay true.

That's when Johnny clears his throat and says, "Grey pill." Sure enough, my hand has a bit of a shake to it. When I stop flipping the pages the comic trembles in my grasp. Johnny fills a plastic cup with water and hands it to me and I pop two grey pills. Down they go. I'm a pro so it's no big deal. I even clown it up a bit for Andre who's still looking. I give Johnny my patented over-the-glasses eyebrow raise like, "That okay with you now, chief?" and with a big exaggerated yawn go back to Pyrogrrl dousing the Finnish parliament buildings with nitro.

In about a minute the shaking stops, which, I have to say, is a really impressive reaction for a consumable. I'm holding up my hands to Johnny to show him the result when it suddenly becomes difficult to breathe. Like I've got a chunk of something in my throat that the air is whistling around. I cough but it's still there. The next thing I know I'm retching on the floor. My heparin lock snags and rips out of my arm, but that's the least of my worries. My vision tunnels with little white lights dancing all around the edges. I hear feet on plastic flooring, the chang-chang of the alarm, and then it's like my life is on a vid display, I'm watching it all from across the room for a few seconds until something switches off the program that was me.

The next thing I know I'm on a gurney in a hallway I don't recognize, Dr. Ryan hanging over me. I'm being pushed along. "Whew, Cliff," he says, when he sees my eyes are open. "Whew. Boy oh boy, you really did us there. You really... you put a scare into me." His ears are all red and there's a vein standing out on his neck.

There's some kind of ventilation bag over my face and I can see an old-fashioned direct-to-vein IV in my arm. The kind they hang the drip from on a metal cart on wheels. Dr. Ryan looks from one eye to the next. "You can hear me, right?"

I nod and the ventilation bag crinkles.

"Fine... See this?" He waves his fingers in front of me. "How many?"

"Five," I croak.

"Fine. Look, Cliff, this is a serious setback. I'll have to leave you in a minute. You wouldn't believe the forms. My week, I'm sorry, my week is basically fucked."

The gurney taxis towards a set of doors with light streaming through them and Dr. Ryan takes a quick look at my drip and then turns back to me. "All right, Cliff. Take care, right?" He gives a reassuring tug to my gown and then starts talking to someone else on his ear-set.

In the next room, Mr. Jeffries, who admitted me almost three months earlier, raises an auto-jot to my ventilation bag. It's got all my stats on the screen. He flashes through a few pages until we get to "known medical concerns," which I tabbed in myself when they were checking for suitability at the initial assessment.

"Vanillin," he says. "You're allergic to vanillin. How anybody be allergic to vanillin?" He taps the word forcefully into the keypad and it appears beside my allergy stats: VANILLIN. His thin face overtop of me is full of blood. "Or, more to the point, how can anybody not know they're allergic to vanillin? Not much on the sweets, Cliff?"

It dawns on me then that they've brought me past the inner perimeter, where, as a test patient, you can't go without a full counter-contagion body bag. That it's all over, then. That I'm out.

Violet. Andre. Little girl with the messy brown hair. Polly. I'm sorry.

Mr. Jeffries begins arranging with someone on his ear-set for a wheelchair to be delivered to his office ASAP. I can hear that other voice—you know the way you can—like a little bee trapped under a glass. There's a garbage bag on his desk with a paper form stapled to it. It's got my own handwriting on it from when I filled it out months ago on the other end of things. I remember taking the time to really make sure it was all legible, to impress upon these people with my carefully printed r's and q's just what sort of man I was. It looks ridiculous now. I've always had the worst handwriting. Mr. Jeffries looks up at me while he's talking. From the gurney his head is sideways. The whole room is leaning. Vanillin. Who knew?

The upshot is that three weeks later I'm able to walk around again just fine. Upstairs, downstairs. I'm back sleeping on the air mattress in my mother's living room. As for Violet, she hasn't once returned any of the texts I drop her from my pearl. The sweetheart symbol that lights up when I select her from my contact list has gone out, meaning she's clicked it off. What did I do? How am I supposed to know? Daytime, I walk the path along the inner harbour that winds through the park towards the downtown bridges. It's not a special life. I have money left over from the trial still but I can't think of where to put it. I fritter it away on mocha-whips at the Caffeine-arena in Sweetgrass City and mope along the pebble trails.

One Thursday afternoon I'm in the park close by my home. Draped overtop of the wooden fence that surrounds the play area is some kid's single woollen mitten waiting there to be reclaimed. It makes me feel so sad I almost pick the squishy little thing up and bury it in the sandbox so I don't have to look at it ever again. Someone has a family. Someone else's little girl is curled up on his lap while he toasts her delicate hand between his own two rough paws.

As I'm standing there thinking this I hear someone calling me. "Clifferino, hey hey."

It's Polly. His hair has grown back and he's walking normally, but it's still him. He's got these two Alsatian pups yoked together on a single leash. They're straining forwards on their giant paws, sniffing the rotten leaves like maniacs.

"Polly. The colour's really come back into your cheeks."

"It's just a trick of the light," he says. One of the Alsatians lifts a leg and urinates on the other Alsatian who doesn't seem to mind. Polly shakes his head and pulls a rumpled T-shirt from out of his backpack to wipe the one dog down. "Christ, what I don't do for these guys."

"I saw YL97 went market. Congratulations."

"Yeah, SylvaBen. That pretty much wins the war on impetigo." He puts the T-shirt into an empty grocery bag. "What about you? Catching any rays in your free time?"

"Ah."

"Hmm." He kicks a little bit at the stones on the path. "You know we all really were shocked, just shocked, Cliffy... Guy that came after you was complete trash. He didn't last two days. Between you and me and these pups here, they're not gonna see quality like what you brought into the bargain anytime soon."

What he's saying, Polly, he's saying to make me feel better. I can see him thinking it through before he says it—poor Cliff, what do I say? Polly's jacket is a new Dupont clear-film jobbie and he's fidgeting with the metal flap at the elbow where it caps the plug, snapping it open and closed.

"What about Violet, Polly? Did she say anything?"

"Ah, kid, forget her. Look at us out here. We got the sunshine and later on I'm gonna walk these guys all the along the shore, right under both bridges and back. Remember that old macaroni kind of smell in the vid room? Taking a dump and having to call Johnny in for a look before you flushed? That stuff's in there. We're on the outside now."

Polly knows he didn't answer my question and we can both feel it hanging there. He looks down and so do I. "Would you look at that? Some little tyke lost his mitt."

Reception at AtGen has no idea who I am at first. I wait in line like everybody else, enjoying the free donuts and Herbavit. But as soon as I press my thumb to the ID patch my stats scroll across the woman's screen.

"We've processed your payment, Mr. Gordini. You should have received it weeks ago."

"No. Um. I mean, yes. I have the creds. I'm good. But Violet Mitchell. She was working with me in the gastro ward."

"I'm sure you understand that we can't release information on any of our staff. You'll have to…"

"I have her chat code keyed into my pearl."

"…leave a message in the general system."

The guy behind me, a hulking heavy-breather who must know he's about fifty pounds past the cut-off point for any trial, starts pressing into my back. The receptionist looks up at me, then at him, and warns him back behind the yellow line. "All I can tell you is that she's over in Military this month. That'll have to do, okay?"

She didn't have to tell me that. We both know it. She's got a kind face, this receptionist. All of these people, day after day, wanting. If I'd only lasted to market, she would've said, "Cliff!" when I walked through the sliding doors, motioned me forwards with the wave of a comrade. It's good to see you. How've you been? I'm great, Shirley, I would have said. I can't tell you how good.

There are no beds in Military, which is divvied up mainly into chemical and physical divisions, most of that buried underground and stretching for miles—they say—right out under the Georgia Strait. And no lineups around admitting, either. No screening or welcome video, just desperates who wander in from God knows where and come out seven hours later with 500 creds in their pearlchip and piece of plastic permanently grafted onto their calf. Or blind for a month in one eye. Or don't, once in a while, come back out at all. It's a very deep waiver you sign. They don't call you a Participant here. They call you a Body.

They put me in a Supersuit. Seamless NanoFab that sucks tight over my body like a wet T-shirt. Boots and a helmet. It's the helmet they're checking, I think, or maybe it's the gas. They don't tell the Bodies anything.

Even though it's made of glass and you can see out of it just fine, the test chamber is claustrophobic. I mean, I'm not particularly sensitive, but it's really not much more than a tube just big enough to fit one person standing up. If I fell down in here the walls would catch me before I hit the floor. The glass is maybe half a foot thick and when they close the door behind me after I step in I can hear bolts slide into place with a whir. Then it's very quiet, just the sound of my own breath, in and out. It always screws with my mind to listen to my own breath like that. What happens if I forget to breathe, and then begin to suffocate?

And what makes it work, anyway, when I'm not paying attention?

It's me in the room in my tube, shielded from these three people whose names I don't even know, who themselves— just in case, I guess—are wearing little plastic masks over their mouths and noses. They look up at me and then down at a screen glowing in front of them. Then up, then down. Before I know it, there's a fog between us and I can only see them like shadows. The tube is full of gas.

The question is: what angel comes to tend to you when it's over? When the gas leaks up under your chin and, before they can flush the chamber, curdles the skin around your nose and eyes? Who wipes your forehead with a cool cloth and says it's okay? That you did good and the world's going to be a better place and we know that you helped? Everybody knows.

"Please raise your hands over your head and then lower them repeatedly," says a voice inside my helmet, so I do.

"Please simulate walking."

I walk the way a soldier might. For five foggy minutes I imagine I'm on this giant battlefield, stepping over bodies. The guns have stopped and it's just me now with a head full of the terrible stories of the things I've seen and the things I've had to do. And my family when I come walking through the door, when I come bleeding and bruised. How they thought I was dead, how my little girl upstairs dreaming in her pyjamas will look when I peek in at her through the bedroom door, the light in the hallway spilling in just enough to see her. And my love, her hands on my face and her own full of tears and kissing me and the cold tip of her nose against my cheek. And bringing me home. Thinking that I'm a part of something. I'm a part of something and it's bigger than myself. And it's worth fighting for.

MATTHEW J. TRAFFORD

THE DIVINITY GENE

I.

JESI

From Poplopedia, the original free encyclopedia

The term **Jesi** refers to any of the viable human offspring created from the DNA formula released by **Dr. Maciej Wawrzyniec**
on October 17, 2006, at 9:57 PM (GMT), believed to be the accurate genetic code of **Jesus of Nazareth** (see also **Jesus Christ**).
The term can include the miraculous or biological descendants
of Jesi, although the latter are also referred to as **demi-Jesi/
semi-Jesi, quadrajeez, octajeez,** etc.

ORIGINS OF THE JESI

Dr. Maciej Wawrzyniec, a **Polish geneticist** who attended
the **International Academy for the Advancement of Science**
between 1962 and 1968, posted a 144-page document to no less
than 18 known Internet forums at 9:57 PM on October 17 of
2006. Referred to as **The Post**, this document had been downloaded over 80,000 times by 6:00 AM on October 18. The first
section of the document expanded upon his research into the
standard cloning procedures of the early millennium (see

somatic cell nuclear transfer), and outlined his instructions for how to choose the suitable woman to carry the **Second Coming of Christ**. The second section of the document, in 98 pages, gave the full genetic sequence for the DNA of Jesus Christ.

The cloning method proposed by Dr. Wawrzyniec and later practised by several private companies, national governments, and educational organizations, now known as the **Dr. W. Method**, requires an **egg donor surrogate mother**. One per cent of the offspring's DNA, the **mitochondrial DNA**, therefore belongs to the mother. Dr. Wawrzyniec's document outlined criteria for selecting the **New Mary** (see also **Semper Virgin, Mulier Amicta Sole**), including genetic history, IQ, religious affiliation, age, sexual history, and "moral orthodoxy." His wishes were ignored.

By November 23, 2006, the **Newcastle Centre for Life** (**United Kingdom**), the **Microsoft Corporation**, Professor **Hwang Woo-suk** (**South Korea**), and the national government of **Russia** had each announced their intentions to generate one clone of Christ. The women chosen to carry these four original clones were kept under 24-hour surveillance and medical care, and the video feed of each woman during the duration of her pregnancy was broadcast over the Internet (for archives of the videos, see **www.watchthejesi.org/archives**). Under the aegis of the **United Nations**, many world leaders made statements against the cloning of Christ, the most vocal of whom was **President Bush** of the **United States of America** (click here for a copy of his **speech**). After the events of the **Munich Miracle** (see below), this outcry against the cloning stopped. Dr. Wawrzyniec had become the most recognizable name on the planet (although, as the North American Consolidated Press quipped that December, still the hardest to pronounce). He had, however, disappeared from the public arena by then and become a recluse. He had no further known involvement in the development of the Jesi.

The source DNA for the Jesi remains a subject of some controversy, and as Dr. Wawrzyniec never revealed how he procured his base genetic sample, nothing definitive can be said. There is consensus, however, in scientific, religious, and academic circles, that the DNA used was indeed that of the historical Christ.

BIRTH, EARLY LIFE, AND PROPAGATION OF THE JESI

The first Jesus was born in July of 2007, to the South Korean mother (for the birth dates of the other Jesi, click **here**). According to the doctors present, the mother did experience the normal pain of childbirth, but the baby did not cry. Ethnically, the baby appeared **Middle Eastern**. Three days after the South Korean Jesus was born an assassin successfully shot the mother, although the shooter missed the child. A witness held the silent child to his mother's side, and the baby suckled at her breast. Reportedly, the woman's wounds were healed and she returned to life. Many dismissed this as global myth; however, later events imply it may well be true. The assassin remains at large, and no group or individual has ever claimed responsibility.

The four original Jesi grew and learned at an accelerated speed, which was unexpected. According to the **four Biblical Gospels**, the original Christ had grown as a normal child. The Jesi appeared adolescent after only one year. This may have been due to an imperfection in the cloning process (see **Dolly the sheep**, **premature aging**, and **telomeres**). When questioned about it, the Jesi simply responded: "Things have been changed." Other than the incident in South Korea, no miraculous behaviour was noted during the first two years of life. After several articles about the **Divinity Gene** and coverage of the drastic increase in pressure from anti-reproductive technology activists to prevent future instances of human cloning, the media buzz died down somewhat. Public interest in the Jesi resumed in May of 2009, when the **British Jesus** showed his capacity for granting **miracles**.

At a photo op with **Prince Harry**, the British Jesus (named **Hugh** at the request of his surrogate mother, a fan of British actor **Hugh Grant**) was approached by a tearful woman of **Argentinean** descent, pleading that she was a "pure vessel" meant to carry a Christ-child. The Jesus touched her and said, "**It is done.**" She reportedly took three pregnancy tests that afternoon, all of which came back positive. On February 14, 2010, **Valeria Paz** gave birth to the first **Miraculous Jesus**. (Gestational time of Jesi embryos is not accelerated, for unknown reasons.)

Following the successful fertilization of Valeria Paz, many women the world over sought to be impregnated in a miraculous manner by the various Jesi. For approximately the first year it was the standard for the "**Pilgrim Wombs**"—women who sought to carry a Jesus clone—to be virgins, due to the Catholic doctrine that holds that the mother of Jesus Christ conceived without having sexual intercourse (see **Virginal Conception**). When it became clear, however, that the Jesi would grant pregnancy to anyone who asked for it, women of any sexual history or creed became mothers of Jesi using the miraculous method.

By June 2013, it was estimated that there were at least 700 existent Jesi, and the numbers have grown exponentially from that point forward. All of the known Jesi are male. Jesi conceived miraculously show the same advanced rate of aging as the cloned Jesi, for unknown reasons. The Jesi, before the age of 12 (the equivalent of the mid-thirties in a normal human male), are often sexually active, and many have reproduced biologically. These unions have thus created **hybrid Jesus-human**

children, and have effectively mixed the **Jesus DNA** into that of the human species. Given the miraculous capabilities of the Jesi (discussed below), many prominent members of the scientific community have come to accept the theory of **Intelligent Design** in some form, and to regard the addition of the Jesus DNA as the most significant advance in human **evolution** since **homo erectus** became **bipedal**.

MIRACULOUS CAPABILITIES OF THE JESI

The first known miracle enacted by a Jesi, with the possible exception of the resurrection of the South Korean **birth mother** (see above), is the impregnation of Valeria Paz (see **propagation of the Jesi**, above). After this event, the four Jesi became celebrity figures in their own countries and worldwide, performing miracles in public.

The first instance of healing the sick (the Munich Miracle) occurred at a long-term care facility in **Munich**, **Germany**. No media representatives were present at the event, but later accounts from witnesses confirm that on June 3 of 2009, no less than seven Jesi converged at the facility at 3:00 AM, arriving on foot (it was later speculated that the Jesi **teleported** to Germany, a power they have since demonstrated on countless occasions).

The Jesi restored mobility, speech, and muscle mass to three men: **Hermann Gottleib**, **Paolo Abbaggio**, and **Henri Dauphin**. All three men were quadriplegics with reduced brain function, the result of having ingested an unidentified toxin in 1964 while students at the International Academy for the Advancement of Science. The fact that the three injured men had attended the Academy concurrently with Dr. Wawrzyniec did not go unnoticed. Internet discussion boards were filled with speculation: about the role of the Academy in the invention of the cloning process and the procurement of the base genetic sample; about whether or not Dr. Wawrzyniec may have been exposed to the toxin but been genetically immune (see: **survivor's guilt**), as well as whether he may have created the toxin, or whether he had any extraordinary knowledge of the toxin at all; and about the three men themselves, their personal histories, nationalities, and fields of research before paralysis.

The possible reasons for the miracle were not explored in depth outside of the blogosphere, however, as most mainstream media chose to focus on the fact that seven Jesi had been sighted in Munich, when only four were known to have been created. Privately funded investigations and media pressure for the responsible parties to come forward, as well as questioning of the Jesi themselves, led to the admission that Jesi had been created clandestinely by the **Coca-Cola company** in **Fort Oglethorpe, Georgia**, and, with the assistance of unsanctioned government funds, at the **Harvard University Stem Cell Institute** in the United States and the **Tehran University of Medical Sciences** in **Iran**.

In 2010, the seven Jesi walked across the Strait of Georgia in British Columbia, Canada, carrying torches and inaugurating the 21st Olympic Winter Games in Vancouver.

The first case of Jesi **resurrection** occurred in 2011, after a suicide bomber detonated explosives strapped to her chest while hugging the **Microsoft Jesus** in **Israel**. His final words were "**And so it is done.**" The world went into mourning.

The other Jesi refused to make any comment on the death of their brother. Three days later, the Microsoft Jesus showed up for his scheduled function at a hospital in Palestine. When questioned he simply said, with one of the few genuine looks of surprise ever recorded on a Jesus, "**And on the third day, I rise again.**" Faith in the Jesi increased, including a dramatic rise in the number of ordained religious, and the total number of Jesi-bearing pregnancies (both miraculous and biological) more than doubled.

LETHARGY OF THE JESI

An unexpected phenomenon associated with the Jesi is the utter lethargy and unresponsiveness that sets in approximately 10–12 years after birth. The term "**zombie-god**" has been used by more than one commentator, though "**lethargized Jesi**" is now considered the proper designation. The lethargized Jesi follow simple instructions if asked, but they do not speak, eat, or drink; nor do they respond to requests for miracles.

The lethargy of the Jesi is what led to their eventual enslavement. The first widespread use of the Jesi was in minefields. After the assassination attempt in Israel (and several others that followed) it became clear that the Jesi could not be killed. A full-blooded Jesus in the state of lethargy will respond only to simple commands (a half-blood or demi-Jesus tends to experience severe depression in later life, which can be treated with **conventional anti-depressants**). When asked to walk through a known minefield, a lethargic Jesus will comply. When the landmines detonate, the Jesi are generally destroyed, but will return to the field three days later.

Once the Jesi began their **de-mining** work in **Afghanistan**, **Eritrea**, **Ethiopia**, **Serbia**, and along the **Thai-Burmese border**, the **civil rights controversy** concerning the humanity of the lethargic Jesi became a high-profile international issue. The debate is ongoing: **the UN legal unit** works tirelessly in the defence of the lethargized Jesi, but because of the sheer number of them there is little that can be done. The lethargic Jesi are most often used for dangerous work such as de-mining, demolition, and working on offshore oil rigs. In the early phases of lethargy, the Jesi are often used in hospital emergency rooms to heal fatal traumas. Other contested commercial uses for lethargized Jesi include medical testing, pharmaceutical research, and military development. It is also believed that organized crime rings have abducted lethargized Jesi, and sold them into prostitution, used them to create counterfeit currency, and forced them to perpetrate torture and commit murder.

GOD-CONSCIOUSNESS AND RELIGIOSITY OF THE JESI

A long-standing theological question in various **Christian** sects has been the original Christ's possession of **God-consciousness**, the total and complete knowledge of his **divine personality**. The Jesi have never commented on this issue or any other aspect of religious doctrine, despite requests from literally every leader of a **world religion**. To date they have refused to engage in any kind of formal religious teaching at all, including the telling of **parables**, for which the original Christ is renowned. They will not make any absolute statements about faith or the specifics of the **afterlife**. When questioned, they tend to simply say, "**All that has been said before.**" Their patience is indefatigable and they are never caught in any kind of rhetorical trick. Another characteristic possibly related to God-consciousness is that all the Jesi have been (and continue to be) perfectly multilingual in every known language living or dead, including sign languages, pidgins, creoles, and regional dialects, regardless of lack of exposure in their early childhoods.

At various points in the past twenty-three years, religious groups have responded to the Jesi with denial, outrage, acceptance, paranoia, obsession, and devotion. The sheer range of reactions exceeds the parameters of this article, from proclaiming certain Jesi as godheads to denouncing all Jesi as idols (see **the Papacy, Protestant Christian reactions, Judaic reactions, Islamic reactions, Hindu reactions, other religious influences of the Jesi**, etc.).

IMPLICATIONS AND AFTER-EFFECTS OF THE JESI

The implications of the Jesi in terms of sustainable human population growth and gender equality in the species are largely unknown. However, given the seemingly limitless power the Jesi have in early life, there seems to be a consensus that no single problem will prove insurmountable.

In May 2020, in **Poland**, the remains of Dr. Maciej Wawrzyniec were discovered by a tourist who had become lost during an "extreme hiking" tour in the mountains. Autopsy confirmed that he died of exposure to the cold. On his person was a handwritten note dated December 2009, part of which read, "You have desecrated the one true thing that ever existed, and made my life's work profane." The death was ruled a suicide, as the note went on to give instructions for the disposal of his body should it ever be found. In accordance with his wishes, he has not been resurrected.

[*last updated June* 18, 2029]

2.

Last year was a good year for me—I made it into *People*'s 100 Sexiest Men Alive for the third time, became the world's seventeenth-youngest billionaire, and was interviewed by Barbara Walters as one of 2006's most fascinating people. You might have seen the interview: Barbara said, "Convince me that you awe not as despicable as evwyone thinks," and I said, "Barbara, I'm much more despicable than most people can even imagine, and that doesn't bother me at all." That line got quoted a lot. And then of course there was my profile in *The New Yorker*: "Jordan Shaw and his Cabinet of Human Atrocities."

This year, things are taking a drastic turn for the worse. It's the dreams I've been having. Real horrifying shit. Angels on meat hooks getting their guts torn out and ground up into sausages. Packs of black dogs ripping old people apart in the hospital while the nurses watch and laugh. I wake up with my heart pounding like I've just done an eight-ball of coke, and if there's one thing I'm still scared of in this world it's dying alone in my bed.

It's destroying my life. I can't hold erections, I can't keep down any solid food, let alone the rich stuff I normally eat, and I haven't taken a photograph in months. It's guilt, plain and simple. And that's the fucking kicker. I'm as Catholic as the day I was confirmed. No matter how much blow I snort, no matter how many Sundays I sit home with my thumb up my ass, no matter how many dumb-ass blondes I stick my dick into, I'm still an altar boy at heart.

And dumb as a box of hair. Shit.

I don't believe in god. I *don't*. My mother started me off Catholic, kneeling all the time, worrying rosary beads like rubbing them would make her life any better than it was, constantly muttering prayers to her magic man in the sky. She kept a strict home, so we weren't supposed to even *think* about touching meat on Fridays. Not even fish—she didn't want to take chances. Every Friday we had mashed potatoes, boiled turnips, and baked beets. You can imagine what a treat that was for a kid.

So one Friday when I was nine years old, I took all the quarters I'd been saving for a couple of months, and after dinner I pretended I was going to a friend's place and headed straight to Burger King. I bought the most gorgeous, juicy Whopper you've ever seen and bit into all that beef, clear grease and ketchup all over my face. On the way home I had to pass by Our Lady of Perpetual Help. I was scared shitless, thinking god was going to strike me down for transgressing his laws and walking right past his doorstep. And nothing happened. I licked my lips and I knew then that my mother was an idiot and that god didn't exist. I don't remember anything else that went through my head, but I got my first hard-on, a real stiffy in my jeans. Just the little-kid kind, but it was my own little miracle.

Barbara Walters asked me when I first became fascinated with human evil. Was it when I worked developing crime scene photos for the NYPD? When I started taking my own photos in less-developed countries? I fed her some bull about studying the Holocaust in high school, and having a friend who'd been the victim of abuse from a stepfather.

And when, she wanted to know, did I decide that physical pleasure was a worthwhile pursuit in and of itself? When I made my first million at the age of twenty-six? When my stocks in anti-depressant medications tripled? I told her my body is the only thing I know for sure is real, the only thing I trust, and physical pleasure is the only happiness I really understand. Did I identify as a hedonist? Not exactly. Just someone who likes to have monthly caviar hot tub parties, spleen massages, orgies. Don't I need some kind of higher gratification, for my mind or, dare she say it, soul? I don't believe in the soul, nothing eternal about me. And for my mind, I have my photography. Although I see it as a kind of visual pleasure, not so distinct from my purely physical delights. Isn't it contradictory, then, that I'm most well known for photographing holy religious relics? No, Barbara, not at all. They're very beautiful, and in some ways are exactly the same as the things I collect myself. "Ah," said Barbara, off camera, "I promised my producers not to mention your abominable collection."

The New Yorker guy didn't even pretend to like me. I could see the look of disgust on his face the whole time, and I kind of got off on it. When he went to shake my hand at the end of the interview, which we had in my apartment so he could see all my pieces, I shot my hand forward and grabbed his wrist, hard. His eyes widened a bit and he looked scared, and I leaned forward and kissed him. I could tell he was a fag. I told him if he gave me fifty bucks he could blow me. He said no, acted offended, but I could tell he was thinking about it. That's the shit I love. That's humanity. I don't really like sex with guys, but I don't mind it, either. The closest I've ever come to transcendence is when I'm blowing my load, preferably in someone's face. And if that someone is a preppy-looking Ivy League journalist fag who hates himself for paying to blow someone he finds morally repulsive but physically attractive—well that's just pure gold. I wish I had a picture of him licking my spunk off his lips.

He didn't mention it in the article, of course. He omitted a lot of things. "The Cabinet of Human Atrocities"—that was his name for my collection, but he left most of the good things out. Things he mentioned: the elephant footstool with the zebra-skin seat cover; all the ivory; the gorilla-hand ashtray; two of the illegal meals I've eaten and photographed (manatee steak and panda veal); some of the serial-killer stuff I've collected; the Aztec human sacrifice artifacts; and, surprisingly, the blanched skull of a Tutsi man, which I smuggled out of Rwanda in '94. Things he didn't mention in the article: all the Nazi memorabilia (that surprised me); my copies of the Bernardo tapes; the pickled body parts from Ground Zero and my piece of shrapnel from the second plane; and my prize possession—the one from Poland. He didn't ask me any of the questions I usually get when people see that: how does it work, what happens if I unplug it, am I ever going to try to wake the kid up. This guy didn't even ask me how I got it, and given what I've learned since, I wouldn't have told him.

My photographs of holy relics are just the public face of what I do. I photograph lots of things: concentration camps (my favourite is a piece of graffiti in Kaunas Fort IX reading *If God exists, he's going to have to beg ME for forgiveness*), that theatre in Russia where the government gassed the entire audience just to take out the Chechen terrorists inside, mass graves, all that kind of stuff. And porn you need to see to believe. And lots of people know about what I do, the kind of things I like to collect. I'm not a good candidate for religious photography.

But back in 1991 I was travelling around South America, chewing coca leaves, looking for torture devices on the black market, trying to bang as much Latin pussy as I could. In Chile I ate a traditional indigenous dish similar to *cabrito guisado*: they slit the throat of a live goat and let the blood pour into a pan loaded with garlic and herbs. When the blood congeals, it's sliced and served, like Jell-O. It had been technically illegal since the eighties, thanks to a law the city-bred animal-rights activists pushed through, but in the mountains no one cares. When I got to Venezuela I wound up in a little town called Betania, in the arms of a television journalist named Sonia Mañana, with long straight hair and perky tits. I wanted to spend the Christmas holidays in bed with her, so on December 8 I let her drag me to church for some feast day. I wouldn't have gone for anyone else in the world, but she had the best ass I've ever had the pleasure to be inside. I was only twenty-three years old, and couldn't help myself.

The cathedral was Gothic and stunning as shit, and I spent my hour walking around at the back, tuning out what was going on up front, studying the architecture and the stained glass, taking pictures. It had been a long time since I'd been inside a church, and I realized I'd been missing out on some very pleasing, gory, artwork. In one of the side altars, they had a bloodied piece of gauze that supposedly came from the side of Archbishop Romero when he was assassinated in El Salvádor in 1980. How it ended up in Venezuela I'm not sure, but I was fascinated by it because it looked exactly like something I had in my collection at home: a T-shirt sprayed with blood that I'd bought off a kid who'd been beaten up at school by his brother and his friends. Next thing I knew, there was a scream from behind me, and I turned to see a nun yelling that the host was bleeding.

I snapped a photo. If you were to look at this picture now, you would see a rosy glow like aurora borealis all around the host. Sure, it's weird, but it's not a miracle. I can show you any number of pictures I've taken in my kitchen or my backyard with similar wonky lighting effects. It could have been bad film. It could have been a reflection. It could have been anything.

The priest quieted everyone down and went back to mass, but when he finished no one would leave. They all just sat there, praying. I saw Sonia give me the look of death, so I just kept lurking on the sidelines waiting for something to happen. A few hours later the priest brought out the host, and I had my Nikon 570 at the ready. This part is true: that host dripped blood into the chalice like the priest was squeezing an orange. And I got it all on Kodak 35-millimetre ISO 800 film.

Since then, people keep asking me: Jordan, you saw the miracle, how can you not believe? It's such a profoundly stupid question. I don't know what happened in that church, but I don't think it was divine. I've seen monks in Asia do weirder things than make bread bleed. And I haven't joined any of their honky-tonk religions.

This is what happens next: Sonia never touches me again—she becomes this totally hardcore devoted Catholic. The priest takes the host to Bishop Pio Bello Ricardo of Los Teques. The Bishop sends it to "experts" at the Medical Institute at Caracas for analysis. The experts come back with the following information: the red substance on the host is blood of human origin, containing red and white corpuscles, and doesn't match the blood of the priest. The blood stays fluid for three days, then begins to dry up, leaving a small red spot at the centre of the host. The host stays totally dry on one side—the blood doesn't go through it. I sell my photos to *Time* for $75,000, which makes my name as a photographer of relics and miraculous phenomena. This leads, eventually, to Petr Grabowicz.

In 1995 I was in Italy. I was there for my own reasons—Nero, gladiatorial relics, Pompeii—but also photographing the supposed Eucharistic miracle at Lanciano. Catholics believe that during the mass the bread and wine change, not in form but in "essence," into the body and blood of Christ, and that when they eat and drink of these they receive the whole Christ—body, blood, soul, and divinity. "Miracles" like the one I saw in Betania and the one in Lanciano prove and reaffirm this doctrine for them. And pictures of it sell like smut.

I had had some trouble after Venezuela—the Church got wind of who I was and didn't want me poking around all their sacred bits of flesh and snapping photos. What saved me was a bishop in Mexico permitting me to photograph some relics there six months later. The reason he allowed me to was because I happened to know he was screwing two sisters and supporting his children by each of them, which I discovered by fucking Lucia while he was with Mercedes. He issued a pastoral letter about me, saying: "God has been revealing Himself and his Truth to mankind through flawed instruments since Creation, and the Church has always held these messages to be True and superior to the flaws and human failings of those who bear them. The Mystery and the Power of any Holy Relic cannot be tarnished by being photographed or recorded by any man-made technology, and the morality of the photographer is certainly irrelevant. Such pictures can only serve to further evangelize and spread the Word of Christ." After that, no bishop ever denied me access to anything.

The relics at Lanciano are the granddaddy of Eucharistic miracles. They supposedly date back to 700 AD, when a monk named St. Legontian doubted the presence of Christ in the Eucharist. One morning, at consecration, he was shocked to discover the host change into flesh, and the wine change into blood. The relics were placed into an ivory tabernacle and guarded by the monks. They hardened but they never decayed.

In the seventies, a priest decided to have them tested by science. Dr. Odoardo Linoli, a university professor-at-large and head physician of the United Hospitals at Arezzo did a series of tests, and verified everything with Dr. Ruggero Bertelli from the University of Sienna. They found: the relics are real flesh and blood of human origin; the flesh consists of the muscular tissue of the heart; the blood from both samples is AB positive. They did not find any evidence of preservatives or mummification techniques.

So in 1995 some priest wanted to write a book about the whole thing in English, and hired me to take the pictures. End of story.

Except: my second night there I was in the hotel bar, drinking scotch that was older than I was, when a man in his late forties with flyaway hair approached me. Sometimes I get recognized; there's a small circle of people around the world who collect the same kind of macabre things I'm into, or sometimes it's a human rights activist who thinks I'm deplorable, or sometimes it's someone who thinks they have something I want. I'm always a little bit wary, but this guy was different. There was an air about him—not quite menacing, but it certainly didn't put me at ease.

I asked him what he wanted, and he said, just like it was nothing, "I want to steal part of the relics of Lanciano."

I was surprised, to say the least. I'm not known for crime. I've broken laws, sure, in terms of smuggling or hunting endangered species, but I've never outright stolen anything—I've never had to. But it made sense to me immediately—I would have access to the relics in order to photograph them, and anyone who wanted to find out could have known that. I sat back and let him talk.

"I'm not going to tell you my name, nor what I want with the relics." He had a heavy Eastern European accent I couldn't place, though I thought it might be Czech. "I don't need very much of them, so little in fact that no one will ever know." He took a clear plastic dish like an earplug container out of his pocket, and a metal instrument that looked like it belonged to a dentist. "You will find a way to remove the glass surrounding the relics, and you will scrape the flesh and the blood into this dish. Scrape very lightly—I only need a little of the material—but make sure it is visible to your eye. Don't gouge the relics—I want you to treat them very reverently, no matter what you believe. Bring me the dish, and your work will be done."

"Why should I?"

His eyes narrowed and hardened a little. "I know who you are, Mr. Shaw, and I know what kind of thing it is that interests you. You have more money than I could ever hope to provide you with. But I have something to offer you which I do not think you will able to refuse."

"What's that?"

"First, a plant of my own creation. I am a geneticist. I have created a plant that is a hybrid of tobacco, marijuana, and coca plants. I believe you will find the effects when ingested most unique and most pleasurable."

"That sounds great, but you know it's not nearly enough. Second?"

"Have you heard about the Petr Grabowicz case?"

I was surprised for the second time. Of course I knew what he was referring to. Anyone who collects the kinds of things I do pays close attention to the international news. Just a few weeks before arriving in Italy I'd been fishing around near Kassel, Germany, where a man had advertised that he wanted to eat someone, and received a response from another man looking to be eaten. The two met, had sex, then together cooked and ate the one man's penis—all the while videotaping the spectacle. Then the castrated man was killed—according to his wishes—and his new friend continued to dine on him. The best part was that the cops had a hard time pressing charges at first because the whole thing was consensual, with signatures to prove it. I was trying to buy the dishes and cutlery they'd used, but someone else snatched those up before I could talk to the right people. All I ended up with was a static-ridden copy of the videotape.

But Petr Grabowicz, he was a six-year-old kid who had died three months earlier in Poland. In a little town near the German border called Swinoujscie, a homeless person dressed up as a fairy and walked out onto a pond where the local children were skating. He told them he was the pond fairy, and if they didn't give him money he would cause the ice to melt so they would fall in. When the kids didn't buy it, he cut a hole in the ice, grabbed one of the boys from the pond, and drowned him.

"What about it?" I asked the self-proclaimed geneticist. He leaned into me and whispered into my ear. By the time he finished my heart was pounding. I looked at him, and he stared right back at me, expressionless. I finally asked, "So why do you want these relics so badly?"

"I've told you not to ask. I don't approve of your collection, but I think I understand the principle behind it. There was a time in my life when I wanted to use the wonders of the natural world to reveal God to the world. You are using the horrors of humanity to reveal the evil of the world. I'm a man of faith and science—and you are not. I'm doing this only because I believe it's for the greater good, and that if I am successful even you will come to see the light of true knowledge and redemption."

The whole heist appealed to my utter love of corruption. I arranged to photograph the relics one-on-one with the head priest of the parish, who balked when I asked him to remove the glass. When I told him I'd arrange for a sizable donation to be given to his parish every year in perpetuity, provided he give me ten minutes alone with the relics, he lifted the case off and left. He came back ten minutes later, to the second. I'm not sure when he figured out I was lying about the money, but I never heard from him again.

The thing is, I didn't know the guy was going to do this fucked up shit with it. Cloning Christ. Apparently they've got four different women pregnant with freaky Christ babies. I knew he was crazy when he mentioned Grabowicz and Cryogenic Stasis Units in the same sentence. But I thought he was just a religious nut who wanted to steal the holy relics so he could eat them or sell them on eBay. Harmless. But when that Internet post went up last October, and everyone was all abuzz, I knew it was him. I knew what I'd done. And I knew everything was going to hell.

I haven't felt guilty for anything since I was nine years old. And now these dreams. Last night I was being eaten alive by locusts. Night before that I was in Africa, slicing open the distended bellies of starving kids, pulling out smooth gold stones and eating them. What's so frustrating about it is that I'm totally doing it to myself. I must be. I've been to every shrink in New York and some in Europe, but not one of them can make these dreams go away.

So God's finally won. I believe in you now, you prick. You've made my life a living hell and you've sent the dreams to drive me crazy. You want me to kneel down and pray? Fine, I can do that. But don't think for a second I buy your bullshit about forgiveness and eternal love—there's no repenting everything I've done. You're just a nasty son of a bitch who's holding all the cards and wants to see me squirm. But I'm still right about life. I'm still right about all of it.

3.

Magda Wawrzyniec, struggling with the weight of her swollen stomach onto bent knees, her skirt bunching slightly so that varicose veins show in her calves, the blue histories of the strain of her seven pregnancies, now eight, kneels at the prie-dieu before the monstrance and lights a candle for the soul encased inside her. She is praying Hail Marys, thinking of the Virgin and the greatness of what can fill a womb, praying that her own child—a son, she hopes, God's will be done—will do great things for the Glory of God. She is thankful that she has lived to see 1946, that so many she loves have survived the terrible war, that her husband is alive.

When her prayers finish (she imagines them as flying up to Heaven tied to the feet of doves, like the carrier pigeons her grandfather used to raise), she gets once again to her feet with the help of the railing, and begins her walk home. Just as she opens the church door and feels the cold night search and embrace her, she lurches and her shoes are suddenly wet. Her first thought, upon releasing her font onto the threshold of

God's house, is that this might be a sin, and her second thought is *Dear God no please no not now it's much too soon.*

Consciousness ebbs away from her as her feet slide out from under, as the young priest with the mole on his cheek comes rushing out to answer what she realizes now are her screams. When she wakes up in the hospital they tell her it has been three days (impossible), that the baby is small and weak but expected, miraculously, to live, that she cannot have any more children. Her eyes flutter and she whimpers and they reassure her again that the baby is going to be fine (thank God), was born in the church, baptized Maciej Magnus, and given last rites.

She lets herself go under again, praising God, sending up a prayer of thanksgiving carried by six of the most beautiful doves, hallelujah, hallelujah.

Maciej's father is considerably older than his wife. He was born in 1882 and apprenticed as a baker at fourteen, waking well before the sun and rolling dough to the rhythms of the rosary, saying the prayers in Latin for twelve hours each day. He has married twice and fathered fourteen children. His first family, his child bride and their six beautiful children, were knocked out by a bout of scarlet fever that he himself barely survived. Magda had saved him from his misery, and now, walking to bring her and the babe home from the hospital at last, he marvels at what a man can experience in sixty-odd years. Glory be to God.

His face is deeply creased, and his eyes widen with wonder as he reaches out for this son, who he knows will be his last and who almost did not exist at all. His forearms are marked with burn scars from years with the oven, and holding the sleeping Maciej, he marvels at how pale and soft his son seems, as though he could knead him into a pretzel or a bagel or a hot cross bun, as though there were no bones or blood inside him, just soft, doughy flesh. His eyes are just two tiny raisins and yet Tomas sees something of himself there, like looking at a memory of a reflection in a dusty mirror.

Magda looks pale and tired and frail, and for a moment so much like his first wife Agnes that he cannot speak. When the moment passes he says "Magda, thank you for our son. Thank you for Maciej." Magda smiles at him, and when their eyes meet he knows she will come through.

When Magda dies seven years later Tomas puts his fist through the drywall of their small two-bedroom apartment. This breaks his hand and he is unable to work at the bakery for a month. Sitting at his mother's funeral, Maciej thinks about his father's swollen hand and his mother's hands, how she used to run them through his hair when she put him to bed at night, and how now she cannot move them at all. He believes his mother still exists, in every way, but he does not understand why her spirit can no longer work to move her body. His father cannot move his right hand and his mother cannot move her right hand— the symptoms are the same but the causes are totally different. He makes a note to ask Father Krzysztof about this. He thinks about Christ and the Glory of the Resurrection. He will receive Confirmation this month.

Maciej is not sitting with the rest of his family at this solemn occasion. He has been an altar boy for a year now. This is something Magda was very proud of, beaming when she told the other mothers in their building and telling him that he was a good son when they were talking softly alone together. The family, and Father Krzysztof, thought it would honour Magda for Maciej to serve this role at her funeral mass. His robe is scarlet, with a white cassock over top, but he is careful to use the black sleeve of the shirt he is wearing underneath when he wipes away his tears.

Tomas's hand does not heal well, and as the month wears on things are getting tighter around the house: tone of voice, eyes, belts. Maciej's closest sibling is eight years older, and they are the only two children still living at home. Tomas is old and his hand does not heal and money is scarce, and so after two months Tomas goes to live with his eldest son and his wife, and the sister goes to live with her older sister and her husband, married three months before Magda died, but no one can take in a child of Maciej's age and appetite, and so he is sent to live with Father Krzysztof and the priests in the church where he was born. When he leaves, Tomas lets tears stand in his eyes because he is sad to be separated from his son, but there is pride on his face because Maciej will honour God and this will honour their family.

Maciej is thirteen years old and kneeling in the church in handed-down pants that are shiny and thin at the knees, and he is contemplating the Crucified Christ. He has sinned. He has, once, cheated on the German homework that Father Krzysztof insists he do. He has tried a cigarette he found while sweeping the church, smoked it in the lot behind the rectory. And twice in the past week he has given in to the flurry in his chest and the sweat in his palms and abused himself. These acts weigh upon him gravely, and he knows he must confess them. He gazes at Christ on the cross, the Face twisted with suffering, the Wounds bleeding, the Agony. How Christ suffered and died for the sins of Man, so that all might be redeemed. He thinks: *How much of that suffering am I personally responsible for?* And the answer comes to him as though his guardian angel whispered it in his ear: *all of it*. Maciej gasps as he realizes the fundamental truth of this: even had Maciej been the only human being to ever live, Christ in His love would still have come down and suffered and died, for Maciej alone. Because it could have happened that way, it is as though it did happen that way. Maciej begins to weep.

Father Krzysztof smiles and places his hand on Maciej's shoulder. "I'm not sending you *away*, my little Francis, I am sending you *to* somewhere, *to* education, *to* a greater understanding of Creation." My little Francis, after St. Francis of Assisi, is what Father Krzysztof has taken to calling Maciej, whose interest in the natural world, in how birds fly and animals run and how plants grow, whose interest in science has always been as unwavering as his faith. Maciej who always beamed when he learned of natural phenomena mirroring Revelation—the sand dollar, pale fragile discs with five holes to represent the five wounds of Christ; the Easter Lily; the Passion Orchid, again with five bleeding, wounded tips; the Crucifix catfish, *Arius proops*, in whose skulls men saw depictions of the crucified Christ, whose very bone structure contained a thorn from Christ's crown and the shape of a Roman soldier's shield, whose otoliths, small skull bones used for balance and discerning gravity, rattled in the dried skull to represent the dice used to gamble for Christ's clothes.

Maciej does not want to leave the church, his home, does not want to leave Poland. But he is obedient. "Will I become a priest or a scientist?" he asks Father Krzysztof, whom he wants to make proud. "How will I choose?"

The Academy looms up from the German countryside like a blister, all glass and steel and chrome among rolling hills of tall grasses and wildflowers Maciej recognizes and knows well, both by their Latin names and for their symbolic relation to the Virgin Mary: eglantine and honeysuckle, aphananthe and gromwell, peonies and Job's tears. It is 1962 and the tenth anniversary of the International Academy for the Advancement of Science. Only fifteen boys are selected each year, and Maciej is the only student from Poland, and the only Catholic. He stands at the gate with his single battered suitcase, a gift from Father Krzysztof, containing his few clothes, a wooden crucifix that had belonged to his mother, and his hardcover copy of the *Lives of the Saints*. He presses the suitcase to his nose and tries to smell the church vestibule, the dust of the rectory, the liquid wax of the devotional candles, the thick incense of ritual. He smells only leather.

In his first year he takes the school-wide prize in genetics, for cross-pollinating a lady's slipper orchid and a weeping birch. He names his creation *Cypripedium betula*, and is it regarded as a small miracle, since no one, anywhere, has ever successfully bred a flower and a tree before. It should not strictly have been possible, but his proofs are incontestable and the resulting plant so beautiful that when it germinates, they plant seedlings all around the campus, and Maciej notices a new measure of respect in the eyes of his teachers. A third-year student, Hermann, goes out of his way to break ranks and congratulate Maciej on his achievement. His hand is warm and large as he pumps Maciej's arm and tells him, "At this rate, you will be famous before you even graduate."

"That isn't what I want," Maciej tells Hermann. "All is naught but for the Glory of God."

By his second year, Maciej is bored with most of his fellow students. They sit around the laboratories, dissecting cabbits and squittens that seem overly simplistic to Maciej. *Why would anyone try to genetically merge a cat and a rabbit*, he writes to Father Krzysztof, *let alone a squirrel? I fear many of my colleagues merely wish* to create abominations: *they foresee a world of square trees and seedless watermelons, acid-free tomatoes and strawberries reddened with genes from shrimp. The study of genetics could be so much more, could bring us closer to what we were in Eden. I feel so alone here.*

He keeps the letters Father Krzysztof sends him tucked inside his *Lives of the Saints*, in the front cover of which he has pasted a periodic table of elements. He rereads these letters at night under the soft light of a sixty-watt bulb before he prays and consigns himself to sleep. *Loneliness is placed in the human heart by God, little Francis. St. Augustine said, "My soul will not rest, O Lord, until it rests in thee." Loneliness is what forces us to introduce ourselves to strangers, drives us outside of ourselves. It can lead to us to find love with our fellow human beings, a pale reflection of the love we have for God. Do not despise your loneliness, little Francis. It is a gift. And do not commit the sin of pride, thinking you are better than your colleagues. Make friends there. This Hermann you have mentioned seems to respect you and your work—seek out the good in him and turn a blind eye to the bad.*

From this point on, Maciej makes a point of taking meals with Hermann, talking to him in the afternoons and occasionally playing chess in the evenings. Hermann is the residence don on Maciej's floor, and it is considered an honour for a second-year to be invited to play chess in his don's room.

One night in spring, when the chess game is over and the lights from the courtyard shine fluorescent into Hermann's room, the older boy breaks the silence of some minutes and asks Maciej what he is thinking.

"Of how to make a cow yield human milk," Maciej answers, "and how this could benefit mankind."

"Always with such heavy thoughts," Hermann says, reaching over to tousle his thin, mousy hair. "You should learn to lighten up."

"And I'm trying to isolate the gene for human kindness. Although I think that it must be a sequence rather than a single gene. But just think, Hermann! If I could increase people's genetic capacity for sympathy, empathy, kindness itself! Think of the increase in Christian Charity I could bring into the world."

"If there is a gene for kindness, my friend, you definitely have it." With this he takes Maciej's hand and brings it to his rigid crotch. Maciej draws it back so fast a rush of air blows past his ears.

"Maciej, relax," Hermann whispers, laughing. "If you don't want to touch it, that's alright. But take yours out and let's have a pull together. I have some magazines hidden inside an old chemistry textbook." He grins.

"You should be ashamed," Maciej hisses. "Self-abuse is a terrible sin."

Maciej comes home from class the next day, opens the door to his room and places his books on his desk. He feels unsettled, his skin has goose bumps and he can taste bile. He looks around his bare room, trying to figure out what might make him feel so anxious. Finally he sees it; his mind catches on to what his physical senses had already noticed: his mother's crucifix, in its place above his bed, is hanging upside down. This takes his breath away. His left knee is shaking uncontrollably, his face grows cold and pale and prickles with sweat, until the spell breaks and he lunges up onto the bed and takes it off the wall. He slows his breathing, thinks of his mother and Father Krzysztof, and says the Prayer Before a Crucifix in Polish and Latin. He puts the icon back in its place, right way up, and moves towards his textbooks with purpose.

Maciej's revenge is preemptive and swift. He thinks a week of stomach pain will make Hermann repent for his actions, suffer appropriately for his desecration. He extracts the venom of a dugite snake, *Pseudonaja affinis*, the most poisonous snake in the laboratory, and he mixes it with the toxins of three different plants. His work is methodical, measured, toiling under a single light until the rising sun illuminates his elixir with the soft golds and reds of dawn.

It is not difficult for him to mix his concoction with gravy, or pour it over food, not unusual for him to bring Hermann his lunch, all smiles as though nothing has happened. He says nothing when Hermann loses his appetite half way through the meal, or when two other boys finish what Hermann has left.

Maciej is not, strictly speaking, a biologist. He has miscalculated, misjudged. By dusk the three boys are struck with a mysterious illness, not expected to live through the night. He does not come forward with any information about what he has done. He does not sleep, but prays for the three boys, and for forgiveness, all through the night, imagining his prayers carried on the feet of birds, large black ravens, circling higher and higher to Heaven. The three boys do not die that night, but the doctors say none of them will ever move a muscle again. They are taken away the next morning.

Three weeks later Maciej receives a letter from Father Benedykt telling him that Father Krzysztof has died. There is no money to bring Maciej back for the funeral. He is very sorry.

Maciej vomits after he reads the letter. He had sent no word since the night he spent making the poison. He was hoping to make a full confession the next time Father Krzysztof could visit, or he could get home. He turns on the cold-water faucet and lets the water pool in his hand, cups it to his mouth and rinses what he can't spit out. Everyone he has ever loved has left him. Why does God take all those who love him? Who will be proud of him now? What is he working for?

He rereads his letters from Father Krzysztof obsessively, ne-
glecting his studies. He reads the priest's concerns about the
foreign policies of Britain and America, the comparisons with
Rome. He remembers the parish baptismal font, the adults con-
verting at Midnight Mass at Easter, the way the Joy of Christ's
Light can brighten a face. He wishes he had seen a miracle. He
wishes he could show miracles to others: the way a tree draws
water from the ground, fifty feet into the air; the way a kidney
purifies the blood. The perfect symmetry of a double helix.

He thinks about how he has been using science to try to help
people, to help relieve the temporal suffering during this life, to
help reveal the glory of God through the physical wonders of
the world. But how much greater would it be to use science to
reveal God directly, not through the medium of creation at all?
Show people not merely the miracles that surround them in
nature, but literal miracles like those in the pages of the Bible,
enacted in their own lifetime? Show not merely the reflection
of God, but His actual face made flesh?

What then?

"How fleeting are the wishes and effects of man! how short his time! and consequently how poor will be his results, compared with those accumulated by Nature during whole geological periods!"

CHARLES DARWIN, from *On the Origin of Species*

JAY BROWN's fiction and non-fiction have appeared in many publications across Canada, including *Vancouver Review*, *This Magazine*, the *Globe and Mail*, and *Grain*, among others. He lives in Victoria.

PAUL CARLUCCI came from an infinitely dense dot. "This Morning All Night" received the Honourable Mention in *Vancouver Review*'s inaugural fiction contest in 2009.

DOUGLAS COUPLAND was born on a NATO base in Germany in 1961. He is the author of twelve novels and a variety of non-fiction books including a recent biography of Marshall McLuhan. He also maintains a practice as a visual artist and as a designer. He lives and works in Vancouver. Website: www.coupland.com

Like most of her characters, BUFFY CRAM is a hobo who can't decide where she lives. Her fiction has appeared in *Prairie Fire* and *The Bellevue Review*. In 2009 her short fiction was a finalist for a Western Magazine Award and *Cutbank*'s Montana Prize in Fiction. Her non-fiction has earned a National Magazine Award. She believes very intelligent homeless people will soon take over the world.

ELYSE FRIEDMAN is the author most recently of *Long Story Short, a Novella & Stories* (Anansi). She has published two novels, *Then Again* (Random House Canada) and *Waking Beauty* (Crown U.S.), and the poetry collection *Know Your Monkey* (ECW). She resents any future that doesn't include her, and predicts it will be just as sad, funny, beautiful and monstrous as the past. Website: www.elysefriedman.com

WILLIAM GIBSON no longer lives in Kitsilano but is a Kitsilano loyalist. His next novel is called *Zero History*.

JESSICA GRANT is the author of the novel *Come, Thou Tortoise*, published by Knopf in 2009. Her first collection of stories, *Making Light of Tragedy*, includes a story that won both the Western Magazine Award for Fiction and the Journey Prize. She lives in St. John's, Newfoundland.

LEE HENDERSON is the author of the award-winning short story collection *The Broken Record Technique* and the novel *The Man Game*, winner of the Ethel Wilson Fiction Prize. He is a contributing editor to the art magazines *Border Crossings* and *Contemporary* and has published fiction and art criticism in numerous periodicals. His fiction has twice been featured in *Journey Prize: Stories*. He lives in Vancouver and is at work on more fiction to do with hell.

SHEILA HETI is the author of the story collection *The Middle Stories* and the novel *Ticknor*. She is also the creator of the Trampoline Hall lecture series. She regularly conducts interviews for *The Believer* magazine. A slightly different version of "There Is No Time In Waterloo" was originally printed in *McSweeney's* #32.

ANOSH IRANI is the author of the acclaimed novels *The Song of Kahunsha*, a finalist for Canada Reads and the Ethel Wilson Fiction Prize in 2007, and *The Cripple and His Talismans*. His play

Bombay Black won four Dora Mavor Moore Awards in 2006 including Outstanding New Play, and he was nominated for the 2007 Governor General's Award for *The Bombay Plays: The Matka King and Bombay Black*. His new novel *Dahanu Road* will be published by Doubleday Canada in 2010.

MARK ANTHONY JARMAN is the author of 19 *Knives, New Orleans Is Sinking, Dancing Nightly in the Tavern*, the travel book *Ireland's Eye*, and *Salvage King Ya!*, which was chosen for Amazon.ca's list of 50 Essential Canadian Books. He is a graduate of The Iowa Writers' Workshop and has taught at the University of Victoria, the Banff Centre for the Arts, and the University of New Brunswick. His story collection, *My White Planet*, was published in 2008.

Variously employed as a meat room clean-up attendant, business school lecturer, and conceptual artist, OLIVER KELLHAMMER makes his home on Cortes Island where he spends his days whittling toothpicks and raising turtles. There will always be odd and interesting things at www.oliverk.org.

ANNABEL LYON is the author of *Oxygen* (stories), *The Best Thing for You* (novellas), *All-Season Edie* (a juvenile novel), and *The Golden Mean* (a novel), winner of the 2009 Rogers Writers' Trust Fiction Prize. She lives in New Westminster, B.C., with her husband and two children.

PASHA MALLA is the author of *The Withdrawal Method* (stories) and *All Our Grandfathers Are Ghosts* (poems, sort of).

STEPHEN MARCHE is the author of *Shining at the Bottom of the Sea* (2007) and *Raymond and Hannah* (2005).

YANN MARTEL's latest book is *What is Stephen Harper Reading?*, a collection of letters addressed to the prime minister about reading. His next novel will come out in 2010. He lives in Saskatoon.

HEATHER O'NEILL is the author of the best-selling novel *Lullabies for Little Criminals*. It won Canada Reads 2007 and the Hugh MacLennan Prize, and was also shortlisted for the Orange Prize for Fiction, the Governor General's Award, the Amazon.ca/Books in Canada First Novel Award, and the Grand Prix de Livre de Montreal. She lives in Montreal.

ADAM LEWIS SCHROEDER is the author of the short fiction collection *Kingdom of Monkeys* and the novels *Empress of Asia* and *In the Fabled East*. He lives in Penticton with his wife and kids, and he teaches writing at UBC Okanagan. In the near future he plans to open a chain of jet-pack maintenance shops up and down the West Coast. Lube, oil, strap adjustments. It's going to be big. Website: www.adamlewisschroeder.com

NEIL SMITH lives in Montreal. *Bang Crunch*, his story collection, has been published in Canada, America, Britain, France, Germany, and India. It was nominated for the Commonwealth Writers' Prize for Best First Book and the Hugh MacLennan Prize, and was chosen as a book of the year by the *Washington Post* and the *Globe and Mail*. The story in this collection is adapted from his novel in progress, *Heaven Is a Place Where Nothing Ever Happens*. Website: www.bangcrunch.com

TIMOTHY TAYLOR is the author of two novels, *Stanley Park* and *Story House*. His fiction has earned numerous accolades, including a Journey Prize, a National Magazine Award, and nominations for the Scotiabank Giller Prize and Rogers Writers' Trust Fiction Prize. His new novel, *The Blue Light Project*, will be published next year. He lives in Vancouver. Contact info and new writing can be found at www.timothytaylor.ca.

MATTHEW J. TRAFFORD's fiction has won the Far Horizons Award from *The Malahat Review*, been nominated for a National

Magazine Award, and twice been shortlisted for a CBC Literary Award. He lives in Toronto, where he works with deaf college students and performs long-form improv with his brother in their two-person troupe, The Bromos.

LAURA TRUNKEY's fiction and non-fiction have appeared in literary journals. Her first book, the children's novel *The Incredibly Ordinary Danny Chandelier*, was published in 2008. Currently, she is working on a collection of short fiction and another children's novel. She lives in Victoria, British Columbia.

DAVID WHITTON dedicates his story to his mother, Donna Whitton, a brave and noble Viking.

GRATITUDE

To D&M, for embracing *Darwin's Bastards*: the concept and the title and all the bastards themselves.

To Chris Labonté, for sharing the vision but giving free rein (and for the world's fastest email-response times).

To Peter Cocking, for "Clara," the grooviest cover ever.

To Melanie Little, for hawk-eyed and most companionable editing.

To Gudrun Will, editor of *Vancouver Review*, who lets me play in the sandbox and whose great magazine gave an early home to some of these stories.

To my grad students at UBC, past and present, for challenging me, with special thanks to Matthew J. Trafford and Laura Trunkey for the stories that were the inspiration for this book.

And especially to all the writers, for their boundless enthusiasm, their sense of derring-do, and their astounding stories.

And, as always, to Dexter, for rekindling my belief in other worlds.

Z.G.

THIS IS
THE END,
MY FRIEND